PASSIONATE PRAISE FOR THE NOVELS OF

REXANNE BECNEL

The Mistress of Rosecliffe

"THE MISTRESS OF ROSECLIFFE is a fitting and powerful end to the Rosecliffe Trilogy. The brilliant and golden threads of history, romance and magic are beautifully woven into a memorable tapestry. Ms. Becnel has brought the Middle Ages to life and breathes freshness and vitality into the genre."
—*Romantic Times*

The Knight of Rosecliffe

"Becnel brings the Middle Ages to life with an elaborate plot, daring adventures and satisfyingly complex characters."
—*Publishers Weekly*

"Rexanne Becnel is a marvelous storyteller who breathes life into characters . . . Sensual."
—*Romantic Times*

"Becnel's latest work features thoroughly enjoyable characters and is strongly plotted and quickly paced."
—*Booklist*

"The second novel in Rexanne Becnel's wonderful 'Rosecliffe' trilogy is an exciting, non-stop medieval romance. . . . The storyline is fast-paced and makes the middle of the twelfth century hum. The lead characters are intelligent and compassionate as they struggle between love and honor. THE KNIGHT OF ROSECLIFFE will leave readers anxiously awaiting the third tale from the magical Ms. Becnel."
—*Painted Rock Reviews*

TURN THE PAGE FOR MORE ACCLAIM . . .

The Bride of Rosecliffe

"Rexanne Becnel combines heartfelt emotions with a romance that touches readers with the magic and joy of falling in love!"
—*Romantic Times*

"Ms. Becnel creates the most intriguing characters and infuses them with fiery personalities and quick minds!"
—*The Literary Times*

"The pacing is quick, the passion is hot, the tone is intense, and the characters are larger than life. The plot contains enough twists, turns, and betrayals to keep the reader thoroughly engaged and looking forward to the planned sequel. Becnel's tale will please Woodiwiss admirers."
—*Booklist*

"[Becnel] paints a brilliant and romantic portrait of the medieval period."
—*Writer's Write*

Dangerous to Love

"Rexanne Becnel writes stories dripping with rich, passionate characters and a sensual wallop that will have you reeling!"
—*The Belles & Beaux of Romance*

The Maiden Bride

"A master medieval writer. Ms. Becnel writes emotional stories with a deft hand."
—*The Time Machine*

Heart of the Storm

"Great characters, a riveting plot and loads of sensuality . . . A fabulous book. I couldn't put it down!"
—Joan Johnston, author of *Maverick Heart*

Destined to be a bestseller from a star of the genre!"
—*Romantic Times*

"Well-written and enjoyable."
—*Publishers Weekly*

"Tempestuous and seductive, this winner from Rexanne Becnel will enthrall from the first page to the last."
—Deborah Martin, author of *Stormswept*

The Matchmaker

REXANNE BECNEL

St. Martin's Paperbacks

THE MATCHMAKER

ISBN: 0-312-97699-2

Printed in the United States of America

St. Martin's Paperbacks edition / February 2001

St. Martin's Paperbacks are published by St. Martin's Press, 175 Fifth Avenue, New York, N.Y. 10010.

10 9 8 7 6 5 4 3 2 1

For my other set of sisters
Denise, Karen, Carol, Lynette,
Carol Sue, Cheryl, and Catherine

The Matchmaker

CHAPTER

I

THERE was love in the air: delicate music, sweet perfumes, and the rustle of silks, all to be savored by the light of two hundred beeswax candles. Yes, all the trappings of love, at least, what passed for it in London society.

But for Olivia Byrde only one phrase resounded. *This will never do.*

She kept her smile firmly in place as she danced a German waltz with William DeLeary. She dipped and swayed and whirled, exasperated by Mr. DeLeary's besotted smile on her. From the perimeter of the ballroom she also sensed her mother's pleased one.

But all the while the phrase repeated itself in time to the sprightly melody. *This will never do. Never do. Never do.* To encourage dull Mr. DeLeary would be a grave mistake, for if he did not kill her with compliments, she would surely die from boredom. Consequently, when the set was finished she thanked him, then made a hasty retreat to the company of Clarissa, the nearest friend she could find in the crush.

"Surely they must lock the doors now to prevent anyone else crowding the place," Clarissa exclaimed, fanning herself in a desultory manner.

"We can only hope," Olivia replied as she surveyed the Burlingtons' splendid ballroom, filled to bursting with nearly seven hundred exquisitely tricked-out guests, every one of them there to see and be seen. It was the same at every ball and party and rout. The young ladies preened, hoping to entice particular young men. The young men postured, struggling to impress particular young ladies. Meanwhile the mamas fluttered around, determined to direct everything to their own satisfaction.

Olivia shook her head in amazement. Three years she'd been subject to this frivolity. Three seasons of just this sort of crush. If it weren't for her matchmaking projects, she would have long ago gone mad. As it was, she'd grown exceedingly weary of the entire rigmarole.

She consulted her dance card. Three dances still open. She'd already turned two men away, which her mother would not approve. Fortunately her mother, the lively and elegant Lady Dunmore, was presently engaged with one or another of her admirers.

"Did you hear?" Olivia said to Clarissa. "Prinny plans to make an appearance before the breakfast buffet is laid out. Lady Burlington is beside herself with pleasure. 'Tis a pity poor Anne may not be nearly so pleased with the progress of this evening as her mother."

"And why not?" Clarissa asked, waving to a friend. "Anne has danced every dance. That gold silk overdress she has from Madame Henri's is stunning, and the family sapphires complement it so well. She is quite the belle of the ball tonight. What could she possibly have to complain of?"

"Lord Dexler," Olivia answered, though quietly, so no one else would overhear. "Both she and her mother have fixed their attentions on him. Lady Burlington fancies a future earl for a son-in-law. As for Anne, well, I fear she may have also settled her personal affections upon him."

"But I thought he found her most agreeable. Has he developed a *tendre* for someone else? Oh, do tell, Olivia. You always know about such goings-on long before anyone else."

"It's nothing I've heard, but rather what I observe. The problem is, like his father, he is a legendary pinchpenny. How do you suppose he can feel about a woman who throws such lavish parties as this, and for no particular reason save that she wishes to?"

Clarissa grimaced. "Oh dear. You should have warned her."

"I did. But Anne is so easily swayed by her mother, and as you well know, Lady Burlington appreciates no one's opinion but her own."

Clarissa laughed. "Now, now. You can dispense advice, but you cannot force others to abide by it."

It was Olivia's turn to laugh, albeit ruefully. "I suppose my few matchmaking successes have gone to my head—and you and Robert are quite my greatest coup. Anne admires Lord Dexler so. But if she is as extravagant as her mother, then she and he will never suit."

"As you always say, better to learn that now than later. But tell me," Clarissa went on. "You keep notes on all the eligible men of the ton and offer sage advice to your friends. But when will you find a husband for yourself, Olivia? Despite all the men who beg for your attention, you seem to favor no particular one. Who's to make a match for you?"

Olivia gave her friend a wry smile but did not answer. She fingered the double strand of pearls at her throat. In truth, she did not object to marrying. But even after three seasons she'd yet to find the right match.

One by one her friends had paired off. Rosa and Merrill, Dorothy and Alfred, and now Clarissa and Robert. She prided herself that she'd helped them find marital bliss. But those successes made her feel more and more like someone's old maiden aunt. Though she had only recently celebrated her twenty-first birthday, sometimes she felt positively on the shelf.

What purpose did it serve that she wore the stunning aqua sheath her mother had insisted upon? What use was the sheer overdress ornamented with cream-colored bows at the hem and a deep froth of lace edging the low-cut bodice? She knew she looked especially well, but to what end save personal vanity? There was no one here she wanted to impress.

The trouble was, she saw all the same men at all the same parties. She knew which ones danced well, which ones would vanish to the gaming tables, and which ones became morose or silly or belligerent when they imbibed too much. She knew all that and more because she watched and she listened and she jotted everything down in her journal, the one her friends called her little matchmaker. She observed all the young men of the ton—and the young women as well—and in three seasons she'd become quite adept at matching up appropriate couples.

But she'd yet to meet the right man for herself.

"Well," Clarissa prodded her. "Is there anyone you favor this year?"

"No. Oh, look," she added, pointing her fan through the crowd. "Don't Judith and Mr. Morrison make a handsome couple? He's nearly as bashful as she, and yet they seem well able to converse between themselves." Olivia smiled in satisfaction, pleased with the young couple, the latest of the budding romances she'd prompted. Everyone else had thought a pair of shy mice such as they would have nothing whatever to say to one another. But she'd known that what they each needed was a quiet place with no other strident voices or opinions drowning them out. And sure enough, they'd each provided that quiet place for the other.

She sighed, reassured that there truly was a suitable partner for everyone, even her. It just took time to find them.

"Miss Byrde?" A hesitant male voice pulled her from her reverie.

She turned with a smile pasted firmly in place. "Lord Hendricks."

The beaming fellow bowed over her hand. "I believe this is the dance you promised to me."

"So it is," Olivia said, hiding any sign of resignation. At the moment Viscount Hendricks was her mother's favorite choice for a son-in-law, and she'd given Olivia strict orders to encourage his attentions.

"Have fun, you two," Clarissa said, giving Olivia a knowing look. Olivia rolled her eyes. But she took Lord Hendricks's arm and accompanied him to the floor. A true quadrille was her favorite dance and he was a fine dancer, not content to walk through the steps as some gentlemen were wont. Added to that he was well titled, with a more than adequate income, and he was smart. He'd taken a first at Cambridge, quite an accomplishment.

Even she had to agree they were a superb match, plus he made no secret of his admiration for her. But to her dismay, Olivia could muster no feelings for him beyond friendship.

It was truly baffling, for she was no silly girl searching for a grand passion. All that heart fluttering and breaths coming short was for novels, not for real life, as she well knew. She'd tried very hard to convince herself that she could be content with Lord Hendricks, but it had been no use. She wanted something more from a husband than he was ever likely to provide. What that was, however, remained an utter mystery.

The string quartet struck up the music, and as they began the elaborate figure of the dance, Olivia spied her mother nodding approval at her.

Olivia squared her shoulders. She would have to do something about this soon. She'd turned down three proposals her first season, five her second, and two already this year. She did not relish declining any other man's kind offer, for she'd rather spare both his feelings and her own. Her mother had sulked for weeks the last time.

Maybe a change of scenery was in order, she thought as they circled around. Her skirts belled out prettily and Lord Hendricks beamed down at her. She smiled back at him, but inside her mind churned. Yes, a change of scenery—if her mother could be convinced.

The next morning Olivia bent over her journal, rereading her latest entry.

> *Lord S: Dances well. Not known to gamble or drink except in moderation. Excessively devoted to his mother, though, and she is extraordinarily possessive of his time. But he is not a pinchpenny.*

She tapped her quill pen against her chin. In addition Lord Simington was as boring as a fence post, and not much better to look at. From her observation, he held no opinions of his own, only those of his autocratic parents. But he was neither a sot nor a womanizer, and that counted for quite a bit. She could think of three suitable young ladies for him, though Charlotte would no doubt quake beneath his mother's stern gaze.

Oh well, she'd known from the first that finding the right man for Charlotte Littleton would not be an easy task. "Mother," she called. "Is the Littletons' reception this Thursday or next?"

Augusta Lindford Byrde Palmer, Viscountess Dunmore, sat at her own desk prettily framed by two massive potted palms. As they had the previous two seasons, they'd taken up residence in Farley House, and they sat now in the morning room, Lady Augusta reviewing their invitations, Olivia making notations about last night's soirée, and twelve-year-old Sarah embroidering. Olivia's older brother, James Lindford, the young and eminently eligible Viscount Farley, had not yet arisen. No doubt another late night carousing with his dashing friends. He seemed in no hurry to marry.

Olivia flicked the feather quill back and forth beneath her chin. If only she had even a quarter of the freedom allowed him. "Mother," she prompted. "The Littletons?"

"Oh yes. The Littletons' reception." Lady Augusta shuffled through the invitations, a delicate frown on her still youthful brow. "I don't see the invitation on my desk, dear. Are you certain—"

" 'Tis Thursday next," the housekeeper, Mrs. McCaffery, stated as she carried in a salver of fresh calling cards. "And your mum's making other plans." The woman gave Olivia a meaningful glance but said no more.

Lady Augusta scowled at her longtime servant, a sure sign that something was up. But Mrs. McCaffery appeared supremely unconcerned. She'd been with Lady Augusta since her first marriage to the much older George Lindford, James's father, and had remained with her throughout the next two as well. She'd propped a devastated Augusta up through the funerals of all three of those husbands, and made no bones about the fact that she thought young Sarah's father the best of the lot, nor that she remained doubtful about Augusta's plans to capture husband number four.

Olivia blotted the page, then closed the cream-colored leather journal. "You're not going? I thought you and old lady Littleton were famous friends."

Augusta sent Olivia an aggrieved look. "There's no need to be rude, Olivia. Mildred Littleton is no more an old lady than am I. You young girls think anyone past five-and-twenty is an ancient drudge. Well, does your mother look like an ancient drudge to you?"

Olivia grinned. "You know you do not. But Mildred Littleton does."

A reluctant smile curved the corners of Augusta's lips. "Perhaps she does," she conceded. "But it is only that she neglects her figure and then—horrors!—allows that awful Madame LaNasa to dress her in puce and olive, colors that do nothing for her complexion."

"Or her disposition," young Sarah threw in.

"Don't you be rude either," Augusta admonished her youngest child.

"You still haven't explained why you will not be at the Littletons' next Thursday," Olivia pointed out.

Augusta glanced at Olivia, then away. "I'm thinking of taking a jaunt up to Yorkshire." She waved one perfectly manicured hand. "I do so need a change of atmosphere, and Penelope Cummings has invited me to stay a week or two with her. Mrs. Mac will remain in town with you and Sarah."

It was just the opportunity Olivia had been waiting for. "Actually, Mother, I too grow weary of London. How I would welcome a country sojourn, as I'm certain would Sarah." She pressed on. "I'm certain Penny would not object if we accompany you. But tell me, what is it about Yorkshire that interests you? I cannot believe it merely the country air."

" 'Tis Archie." Sarah stretched out the name and rolled her eyes.

Augusta stiffened and glared at her youngest child. "I'll thank you to be more respectful of your elders."

Sarah threw down her handiwork. "He may be my elder, but he's not yours, is he?"

Olivia grimaced. Could her mother have set her cap for Archibald Collins, the new Earl of Holdsworth, a man nearly ten years her junior?

Augusta rose from her seat quivering with fury. "You had better mind your tongue," she warned Sarah, "else I will send you packing back to Nottingham."

"I'd rather be there than here where I am forced to watch you make a fool of yourself!" With that Sarah stormed from the room, leaving an awful silence in her wake.

"Well," Augusta huffed, jerking angrily at the skirt of her sky-blue striped morning dress.

Even angry she was a pretty woman, and for a moment Olivia simply stared at her mother. Striking blue eyes; rich blond hair. If there was any gray it did not show. Her figure, too, was delicate and still youthful. Hard to believe she'd borne three children, one to each of her husbands.

But in the two years since Sarah's father had died, their mother had been terribly lonely. Even her children could not fill the void, for Augusta Lindford Byrde Palmer was a woman lost without a husband. It was an aspect of her mother's personality that Olivia did not understand. She'd wed an old man first, then a dashing wastrel, and finally a true gentleman. Wasn't that enough? Olivia could see no reason for Augusta ever to chain herself to a man again. She had an income in the vicinity of three thousand pounds a year, plus a country home near Nottingham, and James's town house. There was also the Byrde estate in Scotland, held in trust for Olivia from her father.

But though she had sufficient homes and sufficient children, Augusta still needed a man. Olivia and James did not oppose the idea of her remarrying. Young Sarah, unfortunately, could not bear the thought of anyone replacing her beloved Papa.

Olivia capped the bottle of ink, then sent a silent signal to Mrs. McCaffery to leave them. Once the housekeeper closed the door, she said, "Mother, surely you can understand Sarah's objections."

"He is only a very few years younger than I. A very few. Besides, no one can believe I am a day over thirty-five." She glanced at her reflection in the towering pier mirror, straightened her posture and lifted her chin. "And you needn't inform anyone to the contrary," she added with a stern look.

"It is not his age that has Sarah so upset."

Augusta made a circuit of the room, then halted in the open window and caught the billowing lace curtain in one hand. "My mourning period is long past."

"Yes. But that means nothing to Sarah. She loved her father dearly. We all did," Olivia added more softly. Humphrey Dunmore had been as good a father to Olivia and James as he had to Sarah, his only offspring.

Augusta bowed her head. "I do so miss him. But think, Olivia. James is Viscount Farley now and maintains his own household. Eventually he will wed, as will you. Then Sarah will have her come-out, and you know with her pretty face and considerable fortune she will go quickly. What am I to do then? Live alone or in my son's household? No." She looked up, shaking her head. "I simply could not bear that. So you see, I must remarry while I am still young enough to do so. 'Tis past time. Why can she not understand that?"

Olivia blew out a frustrated breath. Between her carefree brother, her childlike mother, and her moody sister, she often felt like the sole parent in their irregular sort of family. "It's hard for Sarah to understand that, Mother. You must give her time. And you must not get so upset by her outbursts. It will take a while for her to accept a new man in her mother's life. You forget that James and I have been through this before."

Augusta sent Olivia a fond smile. "You are such a good girl, Livvie. Such a wonderful daughter. You will make some lucky man a marvelous wife. And I shall miss you terribly."

Olivia laughed, then rose and, crossing to her mother, gave her a hug. "Then why do you press me so hard to marry and leave you?"

Augusta squeezed Olivia's arm. "You think me irresponsible, and perhaps in some matters I am—just a little. But I know my responsibility as a mother. I mean to see you properly wed, Livvie. This is your third season and you are already one-and-twenty. I'll not have it said that one of my girls is headed for the shelf. So tell me. You've turned down Mr. Prine already, and that other fellow—I always forget his name. But what of Lord Hendricks? I saw how you behaved last night. You practically ignored him, save for a dance or two. And you know the teeniest sign of encouragement would bring him swiftly up to scratch."

"I believe we were speaking of your prospects, Mother, not mine."

Augusta slipped her arm around Olivia's waist and gave her a grateful smile. "So you do not object to Archibald?"

"I didn't say that. I don't know him well enough to form an opinion."

"You mean you haven't made any notations about him in that shabby little journal you drag about?"

Olivia made a face at her. "He's only lately come on the scene. But I shall certainly pay attention to any remarks I hear of him in the future."

Augusta pulled away and patted her hair, checking for any imagined disarray in her perfect coiffure. "If you should hear anything about him—you know—anything that I should be aware of . . ."

"Such as his attentions to any other women?"

Augusta gave her a grateful smile. "Not only are you beautiful, but you're smart as well, and awfully kind to your poor mother." Then her demeanor grew solemn. "I know he is much younger than I, Olivia. And though he has heirs to spare from his first marriage, he would probably not object to more children—something I will never give him. But I do so like him. He is charming and amusing—and I've always wanted to be a countess. You do understand, don't you, dear?"

"Yes, Mama. I understand. But you must understand Sarah's feelings. She needs you now. She's lost one parent already. The last thing she needs is to believe she's losing the other one as well."

"Oh, pooh. How could she possibly believe such a thing of me?"

Again Olivia sighed. Although her mother did not have a mean bone in her body, her self-centeredness oftimes could be wounding. "Tell me about this sojourn to Yorkshire," she said. "I know why you are going. But why is Archie, Earl of Holdsworth, going? Aren't his estates in Suffolk?"

"Yes, but there is a horse race in Doncaster, Wednesday next, with a rather large purse, and a horse auction. All the sporting crowd attends, for it's quite the thing, and Lord Holdsworth is said to keep a very fine stable."

Olivia toyed with a stray curl as she considered. She, too, would love to get away from town, for she'd had quite enough of the season, and last night's ball had been absolutely the limit. But a week was not enough. She wanted to return to their country residence, only she knew her mother would never agree, especially if the Earl of Holdsworth remained in London.

Then from out of nowhere came inspiration. "Mother," she began. "Doesn't the shooting season for grouse begin in Scotland soon?"

"In Scotland? Yes, I believe so. Then after that there's the partridge season. Why do you ask—Oh!" Augusta looked at her, and Olivia fancied she could see the wheels turning in her pretty head. "The shooting season in Scotland," Augusta repeated. Then her fair face lit up. "Men do so love to shoot and tramp about in the woods. You're thinking about Byrde Manor, aren't you? We could host a country house party there. You've been wanting to go up to Byrde Manor these past several years anyway, haven't you?"

"And you've always found a reason to deter me."

"Oh, the countryside is so boring. Besides—well, never mind all that. Do you think Archie—Lord Holdsworth— would accept our invitation?"

"Unless he has a grousing club of his own, I don't see why not. We could get up a small party. I'm certain James would agree to play host. So what do you say, Mother? Shall we devise a guest list for a country house party? It would suit your purposes as well as mine."

"And what are your purposes?"

"I am weary of all this matchmaking you do on my behalf. A few months of country life would do me a world of good."

"But you have to find a husband, Olivia. You know you do."

"And I intend to. But I've met no one this year who interests me, nor am I likely to. Besides, if you want to spend time with your Archie and soften Sarah toward him, this is a perfect opportunity."

Olivia could see the tug of war in her mother's face. Though Augusta worried about her eldest daughter's marital status, it seemed she worried more about her own. Augusta pursed her lips. "I know precisely what you are doing, Olivia. You're trying to put off any decision on your own marriage." Then she laughed, as delighted and eager as a child. "Let's do it. Let's invite Archie and whomever else he likes. We can have picnics and long walks, and entertain ourselves with music and cards and charades in the evenings. And maybe we might even find a wild Scotsman for you, since English gentlemen do not seem to suit."

Olivia gave her mother an even stare. "Someone like my father?"

Augusta sobered at once and wove her fingers together. "Your father may have had his faults, Olivia. But he was not a bad man, no matter what tales Mrs. McCaffery tells you."

Olivia chose not to enter into that debate. "In truth, I hardly remember him." But what little she did remember supported everything Mrs. McCaffery had let slip. Still, although she took no comfort from remembering her father, memories of her childhood home always brought her a sense of peace. Just the thought of spending autumn in the wild Cheviot hills around Byrde Manor filled her now with a nameless longing.

She'd been back only once since her father's death. Five years ago her stepfather, dear Humphrey, had insisted over Augusta's objections, that Olivia reacquaint herself with the people of the country estate her father had left to her in trust. Since then she'd struck up a regular correspondence with the steward, old Mr. Hamilton. The estate produced little income, just enough to keep the house up and a few servants employed.

It would never be a grand place, but the grounds were glorious, and when she married, control of it would pass entirely to her. For practical purposes it already had.

She closed her eyes now and tried to remember it: a gray stone house, covered with centuries of moss and vines; wild hills, green valleys, and bright, rushing streams. Her father had been an avid sportsman, and according to Augusta their life in Scotland had been good. But Mrs. McCaffery's version was different. Drinking. Gambling. Womanizing. If it had seemed worse in London, it was only that he'd hidden it better in Scotland.

As a child Olivia had only seen that her mother was beautiful and her father dashing. But as time passed, she'd come to understand. Her father had not been a man suited for marriage. Perhaps that was why she analyzed the young men of the ton so carefully now. She did not wish to repeat her mother's mistake.

Despite her father, however, Byrde Manor was still the best part of her early childhood, and it had been left in trust to her. The thought of going there now filled Olivia with unexpected longing. How ironic if she found a husband among the Scottish half of her heritage. She suppressed a chuckle. Her socially aware mother had been jesting, but it would serve her right should it turn out that way.

She turned to face Augusta. "I believe for once that you and I are in complete agreement. Sarah is tired of town. I've been wanting to go to Byrde Manor, and you shall have your Archie all to yourself. Even James must approve this plan."

"Really, Olivia. You talk as if I can only interest Archie by getting him away from any other females. Nevertheless, I agree. A country house party is just the thing. You'll have to go ahead of the rest of us, however, to prepare the house."

"Yes, and I can take Sarah."

"You'll need to hire extra servants."

"Yes, I know."

"And air out the bedchambers. And wash and bleach the linens."

"I'm quite able to run a household, Mother."

Augusta patted Olivia's cheek and gave her a sweet smile. "So you are, darling. So you are. And I shall miss your competent handling of our domestic affairs when you finally marry. Some fine lord is going to be very lucky when you deign to bestow your hand upon him."

CHAPTER

2

NEVILLE Hawke jerked awake. His heart thudded with the sharp staccato of gunfire. His eyes darted around at the oppressive thunder of cannons.

But it was not cannon fire that besieged him, he realized as his head cleared. He heard three low echoing gongs. The tall case clock down the hall near the head of the stairs tolled the early morning hour.

He shuddered, then took a slow, shaky breath. All was as it had been. All was as it should be.

He pushed up from the deep leather chair and on unsteady feet headed for the liquor cabinet. The fire in the grated hearth had burned low, but the two oil lamps shone brightly still, and in his wood-paneled study they kept the dark at bay.

He ran a trembling hand through his unkempt hair. Thank God this accursed night neared its end. Thank God it was summer and the days were so long. Just two more hours or so and he would once more have defeated the unforgiving night.

He poured a short tumbler of whisky and tossed it back with quick efficiency. It burned his tongue and throat, and all the way down to his belly, and he shuddered anew at the harsh bite of the raw spirits. From the finest Scotch whisky, to the Duncan brothers' potent brew, to the locally made whisky distilled up the road in Fergus's shed, his choice in deadening agents had declined of late from smooth and subtle to strong and effective.

But nothing was effective enough to completely erase his memories or fight off these nightmares. No matter how hard he drove his body with work, or how heavily he sedated his brain with liquor, he could not escape these night terrors.

He reached for the crude pottery jug, so out of place among the empty crystal decanters arranged on the silver tray. His mother had purchased the set in Edinburgh, so long ago he could hardly remember. His father had always kept them filled with the best Scots, Irish, and English liquors, just as he'd kept the wine room stocked with the best French wines. But Neville had long ago emptied Woodford Court's stores of the good liquors.

He poured another shot of the raw stuff and downed it, then set the jug aside with a thud. One of the decanters tilted, teetering like a drunken man, then fell and shattered on the slate floor. He flinched at the sound, so abrupt in the quiet night, like the crash of buckshot through leaded glass windows. But it was not buckshot. It was only a frivolous decanter, splintered now across the floor of his father's study.

He stared at the other decanters and at the squat whisky jug with its double handles and thick corked mouth. How fitting it was to set the inelegant jug among its sparkling brethren, for he was much like that sturdy clay vessel. His family had been so noble and upright—and so fragile. One by one they'd shattered apart until now only he was left. The coward, crude and weak—and indestructible, he feared.

He swayed and pressed one hand over his eyes. He was so tired. All he wanted was to sleep. But sleep was a torture he was afraid to risk, not until the night was done. Not until the sun burned away the threat of his hideous dreams. He turned away from the whisky jug and scrubbed his face with both hands. He was pitiful. A craven drunkard by night who slept off his excesses by day.

For some inexplicable reason, his torturous dreams came only at night. If only he could hold out until daylight. Just two more hours and he would have his reprieve. But he was so tired, weary to the bone—to the depths of his soul.

He looked around, blinking back the insidious threat of sleep, and focused on one of the oil lamps. He crossed the room to it, staring all the time at the steady, glowing flame.

The glass chimney was hot and he spread his hands around it, holding his palms against the glass until he could not bear the pain. Then he held it longer still.

"Bloody hell!" he swore, jerking away from the pain at last. Breathing hard, he stared at his reddened palms. Damnation, that hurt! But the pain would keep him awake until the sun crept above the eastern horizon, and that was all he cared about. He could endure physical pain. But the memories, and the nightmares . . .

He yanked open the fringed burgundy draperies that covered the room's east-facing windows, ignoring the sting of the thick-piled velvet against his raw palms. Then he turned his chair to the window and threw himself into it with a groan.

Just two more hours, he told himself. Just two more hours. He slid his hands back and forth on the worn leather arms of the chair, reveling in the pain, for that pain would keep him awake. It would keep him safe.

But the hands of the tall case clock moved slowly. Too slowly. He heard the toll at four, and the chimes that marked the quarter hours that followed. The first hint of the dawn flirted with the horizon, a scene he had viewed every day since he'd returned from that damnable war.

But his lids grew heavy. His eyes closed, his head tilted to one side, and like the enemy it was, the stealthy dark of sleep crept up. Silently it settled over him like a heavy blanket, a smothering hand. Soft. Deceptive. Deadly.

Then the shooting began— the piercing pain of a bullet in his leg, the chilling screams of men attacking and men dying.

"No! No!" He lurched up from the chair, his heart pounding, his mind shrieking. "No!"

Neville knew it was only a dream, the same horrifying dream that refused to let him be. But that didn't matter. Now it was a dream. This night and every other, it was a dream.

But once it had been real.

He thrust his shaking hands through his hair, then ground his burned palms into the bristles of his beard. But that pain was minor compared to the intense tortures of his soul. He'd had enough. He could take no more. If even the liquor would not buy him peace, what was left for him to do?

He lurched over to his desk and yanked open the bottom drawer. There, among his medals and letters of commendation, lay his two pistols and a carved wooden box of ammunition. With trembling hands he grabbed the box and one of the weapons. He would end this torture once and for all.

He loaded the pistol, then stared about the brightly lit chamber. Not here. He could not do it here, in his father's study. It would insult the memory of his beloved parents, and they deserved better.

So he flung open the tall French doors and stepped out onto the east terrace. He clenched the weapon. His hand shook violently. Then he stared fixedly ahead and readied himself—until the pink edge of the dawn registered in his stricken eyes. Until the familiar silhouette of the long stable complex showed, and beyond it, the rooftops of the cottages at the home farm.

All around him the shapes of buildings and trees and fences—shapes he'd known all his life—came into focus. His home. His home that he should not abandon. Then he blinked as another realization struck him.

Morning had come.

The night was done.

With a sob he dropped to his knees, and the pistol fell harmlessly into a potted rhododendron. The night was done.

How long he stayed there, his head bowed, as dry sobs wracked his body, he did not know. When he finally dragged himself upright, the edge of the sun showed its hazy edge between the hills. The sunlight fell on his face, warm and reassuring. Now he could sleep. Now he could seek his bed and fall into the oblivion he craved.

He staggered back into the study, forgetting the pistol, forgetting the open window. He sloshed a generous glass full of the raw whisky, and banging open the door, headed blindly into the hall. Upstairs in his bedchamber he threw the window drapery wide and stared at the sun inching its slow way into the sky. A cock crowed. Soon the village would come to life. The weavers and dyers would be off to their daily tasks. The shepherds to their fields; the children to the village school—young Adrian among them.

He saw Otis, the stable master, shuffling up the gravel path to the stables. Forty years and more Otis had worked at Woodford, as had so many others.

Neville passed a shaking hand across his eyes.

He did not deserve their faithfulness. He did not deserve any of the loyalty and admiration and honor showered upon him. But the people around him chose not to see his wretchedness, his worthlessness. And he was too cowardly to confront them with it.

He shuddered and stared at the brilliant slice of the sun. Then he closed his eyes, finished off the contents of the glass, and once again shouldered his responsibilities. He needed to talk to Otis and his son Bart, the horse trainer, about the breeding mares and the horses they planned to run in the late season races. Later he must meet with the head carpenter about the lower sheep sheds. He also should approach old Hamilton again about leasing those fallow fields and meadows across the river.

But not now. Not now.

Now he needed to sleep. He'd had his moment of madness, and he'd once again survived. Now he could deaden his brain with whisky and finally disappear into the blackness of a sleep so deep that no dreams could ever find him.

Olivia tucked her journal into her portmanteau, then stepped back as one of the housemen hoisted it up. They'd spent two busy days in Nottingham preparing for their journey to Doncaster and then on to Scotland. Pulling on a pair of gray kidskin gloves, she glanced at her sister.

"I do wish you would reconsider, Sarah, and join Mother and me."

Sarah blew out a breath. "And watch Mother make a perfect goose of herself over that Archie person? Lord Holdsworth," she amended, imitating her mother. "Thank you, but no."

Olivia studied her younger sister. "I wonder. Is it Lord

Holdsworth you object to? Or would any man Mother liked rouse this antipathy in you?"

Sarah cocked her head and laid a finger against her chin. "Let's see," she began, her voice sharp with sarcasm. "Which answer should I make? That I think he's far too young for Mother—better that you set your cap for him than her? Or would you rather I tearfully confess that I don't want any new father at all? None." Her jaw jutted forward belligerently. She was the very picture of sullen disapproval.

But Olivia saw also the wounded look in her sister's eyes. She crossed her bedchamber and wrapped her arms around Sarah. At first the girl struggled against her. But finally she slumped against her in resignation.

Olivia rubbed her back. "Poor Sarah. I know how much you miss your father. I miss him too."

"But she doesn't miss him at all, does she? She can hardly wait to get married again. Then she'll forget all about Father, and all about me."

"No, Sarah, no. She would never do that. You forget that James and I have both been in identical circumstances as you. She didn't forget us when she married your father. Indeed, he made our lives ever so much better. He was that good to us."

"Yes, but James was too young to remember his father. And your father was a bounder. Everybody says so."

Olivia tugged one of Sarah's plaits. "It's not nice to speak ill of the dead." *Even if it is true.* "The point is, Mother is happiest when wed, and her children fare better with a father than without. If you will just give this fellow a chance you may find him quite agreeable."

Sarah slipped out of Olivia's hold. "He probably wants someone younger than her anyway."

"Perhaps. At any rate, this trip to Doncaster is our chance to observe him. Please say you'll come."

But Sarah only shook her head. "I'd rather stay here with James. You go on with Mother, Olivia, and I'll be along with Mrs. McCaffery next week to collect you in Doncaster. Then we'll have loads of time together on the ride up to Scotland."

Olivia stared at her sister, so young at twelve, and yet in

some ways so much older than her years. "Yes, we'll have a long ride and a long talk, and I'll bring you up to date on whatever I learn in Doncaster." She took Sarah by the hand. "We shall spend such a lovely time at Byrde Manor, so please, Sarah, try not to fret. Mother loves you, you know, and she wants you to be happy."

Sarah sighed and gave a lopsided grin. "I know. Just promise me you will not allow her to invite everyone she knows to join us. I'm so weary of being surrounded by people I don't know. Besides, Byrde Manor is your house, not hers."

"You needn't worry on that score. I plan to limit the guest list to a dozen, including the four of us. The house isn't that large."

A commotion in the hall ended their conversation. "Olivia! Come along, child." Augusta hurried down the hall, trailed by Mrs. McCaffery.

Sarah gave her mother a perfunctory kiss, but Augusta cocked a brow at her youngest child's bland expression. "Don't you dare get into any mischief while I'm gone, Sarah. I've given Mrs. McCaffery strict instructions. No riding without a groom in attendance. No fishing with the stable lads or gallivanting with the servants' children. You're getting too old for that. And lessons every day. Every day. Do you hear me? When we settle in at Byrde Manor I expect to be impressed by your skill on the pianoforte. Oh, that reminds me, Olivia," she said as they descended the front steps of the towering limestone house, and the coachman assisted her into the barouche. "As soon as you arrive at Byrde Manor, be sure to have the pianoforte in the second parlor tuned."

With a final hug Olivia bid her sister good-bye. Then they were off, with Augusta chattering about who would be attending the horse races, while Olivia daydreamed of a long quiet autumn in Scotland.

It was a two-day journey and they arrived at the Cummingses' sprawling residence a scant mile outside of Doncaster just as the sun settled over the allée of lime trees. A three-story red brick structure, the Cummings family seat had begun life as a fortified house. But in the ensuing centuries two wings and a central tower had been added, so that it now appeared an ungainly sprawl, vast, to be sure, but without a smidgen of grace.

Five days, Olivia told herself as the housekeeper ushered them upstairs to the adjoining chambers she and her mother would occupy. She had but five days to endure. Then it was on to Byrde Manor and the exhilaration of the Scottish countryside. She could hardly wait.

The casual summer supper had already been served to the other guests, so Olivia and her mother were served a tray in their rooms while a maid unpacked for them. Olivia would have preferred to turn in early with *Emma,* the new novel she'd brought with her, for she'd much enjoyed the author's previous books. But her mother was not of a mind to miss any opportunity. According to the maid, Lord Holdsworth was already in residence, along with several other of the Cummingses' guests.

"You never know whom you may meet," Augusta told Olivia as she donned a pair of gold earbobs with aqua stones that perfectly matched her eyes. "A horsewoman such as yourself should be quite at home here." She dabbed oil of roses behind her ears. "You've had more than your share of marriage offers. By rights you should be wed with one child in your arms and another on the way."

"Since when do you long to become a grandmother?"

Augusta ignored that. "Let us go down, shall we? The butler said they would be gathered in the rear drawing room by now."

The first thing Olivia noticed when they entered the Cummingses' drawing room was that there were no other female guests. Penny Cummings made the introductions, fluttering her hands and her eyelashes in the affected manner she sometimes displayed. Mr. Cummings was half asleep in his chair, but he managed a creditable greeting. The other three gentlemen rose at the entrance of two attractive women to their party. Mr. Clive Garret was up from Devon for the races and the Honorable Mr. Harry Harrington had come up from Bury St. Edmonds in Suffolk, here to replenish his own stables.

As for Lord Holdsworth, he was as charming as ever. But it was plain to Olivia that he was presently more interested in horses than he was in marriage. After greeting Augusta with no more intimacy than he greeted Olivia, he turned back to his host.

"Are you familiar with the bloodlines of the horses Hawke is planning to run?"

Mr. Cummings held up his glass for a servant to refill. "I only know the one. A tall Scottish animal, I'm told. Sired by that big black stallion of his, out of the same mare as begot Chieftain. Remember Chieftain? Now there was a horse. 'Bout five years ago. Took Ascot, as I recall."

"I hear he's also got a filly that can run," Mr. Harrington put in.

"So when is Hawke to arrive?" Holdsworth asked. "I'm eager to meet him and see his stock."

"Should've been here by now," Mr. Cummings replied. "Don't know what could be holding him up."

"Whom are they speaking of?" Augusta asked Penny.

"Neville Hawke. He's the last of our party."

"Hawke. That name sounds familiar," Augusta said.

Penny's hands fluttered again. "Perhaps you've heard of his exploits. He's a war hero, they say. Now he breeds racing stock—with some success, it would seem. I've yet to meet him myself, but the men all speak highly of him." She turned to her husband. "Mr. Cummings, is he bringing his wife?"

He gave a shrug. "Don't know as he has one."

Penny slanted a look at Olivia and leaned nearer. "Did you hear that?" she murmured. "Perhaps this will prove a worthwhile visit for both you and your mother."

Olivia only gave her a noncommittal smile.

Fortunately their party did not go on too late. The next morning would be an early one for the gentlemen as most of the racing animals had arrived in Doncaster, and they all wished to observe the training runs. Much money would be bet on the main race, as well as on the several lesser races and side matches that always popped up. Everyone expected their wagers to come out to the good, and so they all meant to watch and listen and augment their hunches with the best tips to be had.

So it was early to bed. Yet weary as her body was from their journey, Olivia's mind was not quite ready for sleep. She'd dozed off and on during their journey, and now her mind spun. But it was not the races and the society of Doncaster that had her in such a state, though she adored horses and prided herself on her firm seat in the saddle. It was thoughts of Byrde Manor. Riding a prescribed track on a very fast horse was all well and good. But a long ramble on a spirited animal through the stunning Cheviot Hills was much more to her liking.

When finally she fell asleep, it was to dream of crisp morning air and exhilarating countryside, of hawthorns and towering sycamores, and the haunting cries of terns and red kites and cormorants.

But sleep did not last long. Olivia awoke before dawn to the muted sound of horses' hooves and masculine voices. She rubbed her eyes and yawned. Even with all the racing excitement, she wouldn't have expected the men to be leaving quite this early.

Rising, she peered down from her window into the rear courtyard, but it was empty. Restless, she stared around her, then listened at the door between her room and her mother's. In the heavily curtained bed her mother slept on, her breathing slow and regular. Augusta believed in her beauty sleep, and it certainly seemed to work. She should try to do the same, Olivia told herself. But she knew she would not be able to doze off again.

Somewhere in the house a clock tolled the hour. Five o'clock. She stretched her arms high, then sighed. She was up, so she might as well dress herself. Perhaps she would take a turn in the little park she'd spied on the east side of the house. She hadn't been up before dawn since they'd gone down to London. Awaiting the sunrise would be a pleasant diversion.

She dressed in the dark in a simple muslin gown, pale green with cream-colored ruching at the neckline. A quick brush through her hair and hurried ablutions at the washstand completed her toilette. Then she slipped on her walking shoes and a light shawl, and at the last moment also snatched up her journal. Perhaps she'd enter her observations about Lord Holdsworth and the other two gentlemen she'd met last night.

Locating the stairs was easy, locating a door to the outdoors far less so. The sprawling house was even more confusing from within than from without. When she spied a light through a door standing partially ajar, she headed straight for it. Someone was up and about, probably a servant. Perhaps they would direct her.

The door, painted pretentiously enough in faux marble, opened on silent hinges to reveal a spacious library, and Olivia's eyes widened in delight. On a huge center table a host of books sprawled, mostly volumes on horses and racing, she saw. An empty tumbler sat beside a brace of candles that cast an amber glow across walls lined to the ceiling with leather-bound tomes. The window drapery was thrown open to the darkness beyond, but the room was empty. It must be as she'd supposed. The men had left for Doncaster after reviewing their research on the racehorses.

She moved farther into the room, forgetting about her walk. She'd not expected to discover such a large library here. In truth, she'd half-expected Penny Cummings to be illiterate. That was unkind, she scolded herself. And uncalled for.

She scanned the titles, trailing her fingers along the shelves. *A Journey to the Islands of Scotland,* by Samuel Johnson. *Account of Corsica,* by James Boswell. Voltaire's *Treatise on Religious Tolerance.* All serious, practical tomes. A High Street bookseller would be impressed with the choices.

"But no poetry," she mused aloud. She set her journal on a side table. "Hmm. Debrett's *Peerage of England, Scotland and Ireland.* No drama or plays either."

"Is there no drama among the peerage?"

Olivia whirled around at those startling words. From the sheltering embrace of a deep upholstered chair turned toward the window, a man leaned over the arm, staring at her. "It seems," he continued, "that the peerage is all about drama. Drama and little else."

For a moment Olivia remained too shocked to speak, for she'd believed herself to be alone. Nor did she recognize the man from the guests she'd previously met. His face was shadowed by the night as well as by the dark tint of his unshaven cheeks and jaw, as if he'd been sleeping in that chair before the window.

She swallowed hard and cleared her throat. Before she could find her voice, however, his eyes ran slowly over her, head to toe and everywhere in-between. It was out-and-out scrutiny, a bold perusal the like she'd never before suffered, and it unsettled her to the core. Then he spoke in a voice that was dark and low, and vibrating with warmth.

"If there was no poetry in this library before, there most certainly is now."

CHAPTER

3

NEVILLE could hardly believe his eyes, nor his immense good fortune. If this was a dream, it was a damn sight better than the visions that usually beset him. She was an angel, shining in the lamplight, with the most sumptuous auburn hair spilling around her shoulders. Her eyes glittered wide and amber-green; her lashes swept over them, a dark brown velvet. Her skin was pale and lustrous, and would be soft to the touch. Dressed in a simply adorned gown of flowing muslin, she clutched a flimsy shawl to her chest as she stared back at him.

Neville swallowed hard. She was the picture of grace and beauty, yet with a hint of wildness about her, like a startled doe, lovely yet tensed to bolt. But he did not want her to bolt. He wanted her to stay if only so he could continue staring at her.

He ran his eyes over her, admiring everything he saw and wanting to see more. The full breasts beneath the snug bodice, the long legs beneath the fluid gown. Was she a servant? Though she did not wear a uniform, she must be one of the staff, for who else would be up before dawn? A slow smile lifted one side of his mouth. Had he known Cummings kept such a lovely household staff, he would have arranged to arrive sooner in the evening and not wasted this long, torturous night in solitude.

He had planned deliberately to arrive late, for he'd been unready for the company of society folk. He needed to do business with Cummings and his friends, and so he'd had to come. But he'd timed his arrival for past midnight. By the time he'd settled the horses and dismissed his grooms, everyone else had been asleep, leaving him only a few hours to wait out the night. The library had suited his purpose, providing him with east-facing windows. And now it had provided him with this pretty young maid or governess or whoever she was.

He gave her an appreciative smile. "No ode to beauty has yet been written which does credit to the beauty I see before me now," he murmured, meaning every word. When she blushed in response his grin increased. He must be more drunk than he thought, he told himself, though he'd not delved very deeply into the bottle of brandy he'd found on a tray on a bow-fronted commode. He must be drunk or else damned lucky that such a delectable little baggage was up and about so early in the day.

"Tell me, what is your name?" he asked as he rose to his feet. He did not sway, and his head hardly spun—a good sign. For if he was not drunk enough to be having visions, then she must be real. And now that he thought of it, there could be but one reason a woman who looked like her would be tip-toeing about in a great hall like this at such an unlikely hour. It was too early even for servants to begin their daily tasks. But nighttime tasks . . .

He eyed her flushed cheeks and rosebud lips, and drew the only conclusion he could. Was it Cummings's bed she'd graced tonight, he wondered, or perhaps one of his other guests'?

His eyes ran over her again, and despite the effects of the brandy he felt the unfamiliar rise of desire. He hadn't been with a woman in weeks. He hadn't truly wanted one in months. But for some reason he wanted this one. There was a good hour yet until dawn. He would as happily spend it in bed with an eager young woman as with a bottle of whisky.

"Come, my little midnight muse. 'Tis plain it is not house cleaning you've been up to this night. So linger a while with me and inspire the poet in my soul," he coaxed, giving her a beckoning smile. "God knows I am in dire need of inspiration."

At his smile she frowned and clutched her white fringed

shawl tighter around her shoulders. "I fear you mistake me for someone else."

He shook his head. "That's not likely. Tell me," he repeated. "What is your name?"

Her eyes narrowed and he felt the full weight of her stare as she made a thorough canvass of his person. He straightened to his full height. Did she like what she saw? The front of his waistcoat was unfastened, and he was dirty with road dust and in sore need of a shave. But perhaps she would not mind. Some women liked their men rough around the edges.

"Your nighttime secrets are safe with me," he reassured her. "So come now. You need not be tongue-tied. A comely maid such as you has surely received her share of compliments."

"A few," she ventured in a voice as warm as a purr, despite her wariness. No giggles or sharp dialect from this one. Better and better.

He approached her slowly, holding her gaze with his own. "Eyes the color of autumn," he murmured. "Green and gold."

"The correct term is 'hazel.' "

He smiled at her curt reply, and felt the building of desire. "But hazel is not nearly poetic enough to describe them. And I believe you require poetry." He'd spout Shakespeare or Marlowe or Blake. Whoever it took to lure her to his bed.

As if she sensed the direction of his thoughts, she averted those striking eyes, sheltering them beneath the sweep of her velvet lashes. "I believe I had better depart now."

But Neville did not want her to go. When she turned he followed, and when she reached for the door, he held it closed with one hand flat against the panel.

She jerked around to face him, anger flashing in her eyes. "What do you think you're doing?"

"You haven't told me your name," he answered, leaning his weight against the door and deliberately blocking her departure.

"Nor am I likely to," she retorted, her husky voice vibrating with temper.

"Your eyes go green when you are riled," he said, smiling down into their mesmerizing depths. Then to his own surprise, he caught her by the chin and leaned forward until their faces were but inches apart. "Who are you, my lovely midnight maiden? And what must I do to coax you to share a glass of brandy with me?"

"A glass of brandy? 'Tis plain you've had too many glasses already." She batted his hand away, then ducked under his arm and backed toward the center of the room, past the chair where he'd been sitting. "Let me leave, else I shall scream down the house," she vowed.

He was behaving badly, Neville knew. Accosting his host's domestic staff was not his normal style. Then again, he'd not been a guest in anyone's home in so many years, who was to say what was normal for him anymore? Still, the fact that his numb emotions had reacted so immediately to this young woman was reason enough for him to continue his pursuit of her.

"There's no cause to do that, for I mean you no harm. Just your name," he said as she came up against the wall. "But I am remiss. Allow me to introduce myself. I am—"

"A rude and vulgar boor," she snapped. Then she reached for the latch on the adjacent French door, and before he could stop her, she fled into the night.

Olivia could scarcely believe the dilemma in which she found herself ensnared. Accosted in the library by some drunken lout. She paused to catch her breath behind a gnarled and twisted apple tree at the bottom of the narrow verandah. Her heart pounded still, though now with fury more than fear. Thank God he had decided not to pursue her. She wasn't sure what she would have done then.

She peered around the tree trunk toward the house. Botheration! He was still there, silhouetted in the open doorway by the well-lit library, his widespread arms braced on the door frame. Olivia's heart sped up once more. He was a big man, she saw, tall with wide shoulders and a reckless, dangerous air about him. Who was he?

Not a servant, she decided, now that distance gave her the opportunity to think. His waistcoat had been plainly adorned, but it had been a first-rate wool with a double row of carved silver buttons. Also, he spoke too well to be a servant. There were certain valets and butlers who spoke as well as their employers, but this man was no one's valet. Of that she was certain. Besides, there was something of the Eton clip to his speech. He must be a gentleman.

She laughed, albeit unpleasantly. No, he might have been raised a gentleman. What he'd turned out to be, however, was an ill-mannered ruffian, a man not above accosting innocent females. That he obviously thought her a housemaid excused nothing. She'd always considered men who harassed servants to be of the very lowest sort, taking advantage of their position in life.

Just then he stepped out onto the verandah, and she gasped and shrank back. Did he mean to pursue her after all?

But he only patted his pockets, then pulled out a small rolled cheroot. When he turned back to the library to light it at a candle, Olivia made her move. Stooping low and dodging from holly to box to rhododendron, she angled away from him, squinting into the darkness to avoid running headlong into a low wall or clipped shrub or poorly placed bit of garden statuary.

Her only consolation was that if she could not see, neither could he. She had almost reached the corner of the east wing and safety, when his voice disavowed her completely of that notion.

"Be careful, Hazel, lest your nighttime meanderings foster tales of a ghostly presence on these grounds."

Olivia halted, one hand on the brick corner. Ghostly presence? She frowned, then let out a little groan. Her pastel dress! Had he been able to see her all along?

"I apologize for frightening you," he went on, his voice as dark and warm as the late summer night. " 'Twas hardly my aim to do so. If you are a kindly ghost you will allow me a second chance to prove myself. If you will not join me in what remains of this night, then please, I beg you, come again on the morrow. I'll be here in the library until dawn."

Olivia pressed a trembling hand to her chest. The man was going to give her heart failure. As if any respectable young woman, servant or otherwise, would welcome such a coarse and insulting invitation. Outraged by his gall, she plunged into the darkness around the corner of the house, unmindful of the shrubbery she trampled in her haste. She would get to the bottom of this, she vowed, and the first thing she must do is determine just who he was. Then she would have quite a tale to tell about him in her journal.

She tripped to a halt. Her journal! She'd left her journal lying on the table in the library.

She spun around in a quandary, her fists knotted in frustration. She could not allow her journal and its often unflattering commentary to fall into the wrong hands, for it could be more than embarrassing. Her mother had often warned her about that possibility. But she'd always been so careful—until now. She stifled a very unladylike oath. How could she get it back before someone discovered it?

She knew at once that she could not return to the library, not while he was still there. That meant she would have to wait and retrieve it later. But what if he found it first? Olivia rubbed her temple where it had begun to throb. He would not notice it, she reassured herself. Why should he? In a room full of books one drunken lecher was not likely to notice another slim volume.

But what if he did?

Olivia gritted her teeth. If he did she would simply have to deal with the repercussions. How bad could they be?

Neville turned away from the verandah. The auburn-haired beauty was not going to return—and why should she? She'd looked like an angel, yet he'd approached her as if she were a wanton. He scrubbed his hands across his face, disgusted at his own depravity. Was he that far removed from common decency and good manners that he could behave so?

He stared at the decanter of brandy he'd set upon the mantel. It was the drink that made his behavior so reprehensible. *Then stop drinking.*

He clenched his eyes shut and pinched the bridge of his nose. "Bloody hell," he muttered, disgusted with himself. But then, he'd been disgusted with himself for years now. He couldn't blame his vile behavior on his drinking. Even drunk he knew when he was behaving abominably. Unfortunately, he'd long ago ceased to care what people thought of him, so long as he made it through the long, torturous nights. And he needed some sort of spirits to do that. Any sort.

The sad truth was that tonight's little episode was not all that bad when compared to some of the other wretched sins of his past.

He headed for the brandy, planning to finish what he'd begun, when a slim volume lying on the center table caught his eye. It was a small book, tattered and well used, much like the other books in the library. But it was bound in cream-colored leather with gold filigree. Cream-colored leather in a library dominated by burgundies and browns and blacks. It stood out like a beacon, and it drew him as inexorably as a light drew moths.

It hadn't been there before. He was sure of it.

He picked it up. Was it hers?

" 'Ex libris, Olivia B.' " He read the bookplate inside the cover. "Olivia," he repeated, liking the ring of it. A classic name for a classic beauty. He thumbed through the pages, noting the curious angle of her penmanship. Probably left-handed. And definitely a busybody. He'd expected poetry, but instead every page contained a series of notations about different people.

Lord N. Known to be very generous.

Lord D. A legendary pinchpenny.

Mr. G. A lecher of the first magnitude.

He frowned, examining the pages more closely. Each page appeared to pertain to a different man. Lord this; the Honorable that. All men with not one woman mentioned.

Why would a housemaid keep such notations? Did it pertain to visitors?

Then it hit him like a blow to the gut. She was no ordinary household servant. He should have seen that at once. He looked down at the slender, damning volume he held. Only one sort of woman was likely to keep notes on so many men this way, and that was a woman of suspicious virtue.

Shaking his head, he flipped through the book slowly, from beginning to end. All men. Though it seemed unlikely that a woman of her sort would be able to write so well, what else could she be but a very astute lady of the evening? And this little volume must be her personal listing of her clientele.

He stared unblinking at the open French doors, struggling with that unsettling thought. Somehow she seemed too young—and too genuinely affronted by him—to be that sort of woman. With her cultured voice and hasty exit he could better believe her a young woman of the ton than an accomplished harlot. Added to that, Cummings did not seem energetic enough to bring such a woman inside his very own home, especially while his wife was in residence.

Then again, did anyone ever reveal who they truly were? Neville let out a cynical laugh. He certainly did not. Why should he expect Cummings to do so—or the innocent-looking Olivia B.?

He tapped the book against his open palm. It seemed clear that this Olivia was here at the behest of Cummings or one of his other friends. Why else would she be creeping about the house at night? He looked back at the journal in his hand, seeing instead those autumn-colored eyes of hers. That she could appear so pure and lovely—and unsullied—after what must have been a long and energetic night in some lucky man's bed was astounding.

How he wished that bed had been his.

He let out a muffled curse at the return of a powerful desire. Whether she was whore or innocent, it didn't matter. He wanted her. With one thumb he ruffled the pages of her guilty little book, then grinned. He might not know precisely who she was, but he had something she would want back. He had only to wait for her to come to him.

Meanwhile he had another hour until dawn, and what looked like very interesting reading to help him pass the time.

CHAPTER

4

OLIVIA chewed her lip and stared out the bedroom window. Dawn had arrived at last, gray and moody. Below her Mr. Cummings and his guests ambled across the yard toward the stables. One and all they were dressed in riding gear. It appeared that despite the threatening weather, they meant to leave the carriage at home and instead take horses to Doncaster. Typical male behavior at a horse-racing weekend. Carriages that were considered a necessity in town were not manly enough here.

She let the lace panel fall back into place. So it had not been them in the yard before dawn. Had it been the man from the library? He was not among them now, she saw. So where was he?

Who was he?

After her narrow escape she'd returned to her chamber and lay fully clothed upon the narrow silk-upholstered settee, fuming over his vile behavior and his mysterious identity. The only guest not yet arrived was that fellow Hawke someone had mentioned last night. But if the cad was this Lord Hawke, wouldn't he be on his way to Doncaster with the others? Conversely, if her unsavory acquaintance was not a guest and wasn't on his way to Doncaster, that meant he could be anywhere—including the library where she had foolishly forgotten her journal. But who could he be? A relative perhaps? He'd certainly made himself comfortable in the library.

"Olivia?" her mother murmured from the next room. "Is that you? For heaven's sake, child, pull the drapes to or close the door. You may be an early riser, but I am not."

Olivia sighed and drew the ancient velvet drapes over the lace panel, then for good measure shut the door as well. Her mother would not rise until nearly noon, and if Penny Cummings were up, she was bound to be occupied with household matters. Olivia headed for the door. That meant she was left to her own devices for the next several hours. Normally that would suit her most agreeably. But with the possibility of that awful man roaming somewhere in the house, she was not certain what she should do.

In the hall she spied one of the upstairs maids. Though it was considered very bad form to quiz your hostess's help, Olivia could see no alternative—not if she wished to retrieve her journal.

"Excuse me. Could you tell me, has the Cummingses' last guest yet arrived?"

The mobcapped young woman bobbed a quick curtsey. "I cannot say, miss. We prepared his room yesterday but I haven't heard whether he has arrived. Shall I check for you?" She gave Olivia a frankly curious look.

"Oh no. That's not necessary, But I . . . ah . . . I do have an errand you might run for me. I forgot my book in the library last night. A little cream and gold book," she added. "Could you fetch it for me?"

"As you wish. Shall I leave it in your room?"

"No. Bring it to me in the breakfast room. I'm going down now. Is Mrs. Cummings up?" she added with forced nonchalance.

"Milady usually sleeps till mid-morning and the men are already departed. I fear, miss, that you are forced to dine alone."

"I am sure I shall not mind," Olivia replied. *So long as I truly am alone.* She turned for the stairs. Alone was much better than being beleaguered by an amorous drunk.

Neville stared into the small dressing mirror. Three hours of sleep would have to suffice. He normally slept till noon after his long restless nights. But he had business this morning. He had deals to make and horses to sell. Most of all, he had races to win. For winning horses meant a winning stable, and a plethora of contracts to stud. He would need every shilling of that stud money if he were to maintain Woodford Court as his parents always had.

Fortunately, the horse stables had always been kept in good repair. But despite six months of extensive repairs, the main house's elaborate slate roof still leaked in two places. The gutters needed releading too.

More important than the house, however, the sheep sheds, the shearing barns, and the shearers' cottages required immediate attention. A win at Doncaster would increase the value of all his horses, which would increase his income and allow him to continue his improvements and thereby keep more of the strapped folks of the Cheviot Hills employed.

He pulled on a pair of mahogany brown riding boots and grabbed his frock coat and his flat-brimmed hat. Time to move on with his plan. But he paused when he spied the delicate little book lying on the bedside table.

Miss Olivia B. was quite the enigma. He'd read a number of her entries with amusement. She'd been careful to reveal no names, though with a little investigation he was certain the identities of her numerous male acquaintances could be ferreted out. But more fascinating to him than the entries was the woman who had made them. Such a beautiful enigma.

She'd been quite thorough in some of her entries. And completely candid. Any woman considering a man's station in life and his acceptability as a protector would find her notations invaluable, though some of the men might find them insulting. To her credit, she'd not remarked on anyone's prowess or personal sexual proclivities; a smart move, he conceded.

Still his jaw clenched rhythmically as an unsavory thought assailed him. Was it possible that auburn-haired beauty, so angelic in demeanor, had partaken of carnal relations with every one of those men?

On the one hand that possibility should encourage him. For if she were indeed a lady-go-lightly she should be easy enough to entice to his bed. He was not so penurious that he could not afford her services. Nevertheless, Neville felt an edge of distaste. How had a woman who appeared so innocent and refined become embroiled in such a base profession?

"That's easy," he muttered to himself. He plucked the book up and slid it into his pocket, then turned for the door. How did anyone end up in the situations they found themselves? By accident or bad luck—or God's merciless humor. He grimaced. It didn't matter why this Olivia B. had become a harlot. It was enough that she had—and that he was in need of her expertise. He would not have to seek her out, though. For he had her book and she would surely be anxious to recover it. He could afford to wait for her to come to him.

He patted his pocket, feeling the well-used journal there as he strode down the stairs. First breakfast, then business, then with any luck, tonight he would not spend the dreaded hours after midnight alone.

Olivia muttered an extremely unladylike curse. "He took it, the bounder. He must have." The maid had intercepted her in the hall with the unhappy news that her journal was not to be found. But Olivia had to be sure. So she stood now just inside the library door, alert in case he should try once again to surprise her.

But the library was empty. The heavy burgundy draperies were drawn against the morning sun, and the wing chair he'd sat in had been turned around to face the room. The liquor tray was back in order, the decanters lined up, and the tumblers washed and neatly arranged. The only disorder was that of any library: more books than it could comfortably hold. Shelves jammed full, tables stacked high, and several large atlases lying in the corner on the floor. But not one sign of a cream and gold journal of no value to anyone but its owner. Why had he taken it?

Olivia scanned the room once more, her brow creased in aggravation. The housemaids had obviously been in. Perhaps one of them had already delivered it to the housekeeper. How embarrassing if the woman had read any of the entries.

Better the housekeeper, however, than that other nasty brute.

Completely out of sorts, she turned for the hall. The house-keeper was bound to look in on the breakfast table. Olivia would ask the woman then about her journal—and about the identity of her unpleasant companion of last night.

She found her way down the east wing hall, through the Cummingses' grand foyer, and into the central hall, which she thought led back to the small dining room where a breakfast was supposed to be laid out.

This house was far too big ever to be comfortable, she decided as she headed down another endless hallway. Not at all like Byrde Manor with its large pair of drawing rooms and cozy surrounding rooms. She vaguely remembered the family taking breakfast in the kitchen there when she was a small child. Could that be right? Somehow she could not picture her mother consenting to dine in any kitchen, not even the huge one in Windsor Castle.

But the faded image of the fragrant kitchen at Byrde Manor would not go away. Soon enough she would determine how accurate her memories were.

She turned left into a small sitting room—not what she was looking for. Was everything going to go badly during this visit?

The unhappy answer appeared to be yes. For when Olivia backed out of the room and turned around, it was to find him, her nighttime nemesis, in the hall just behind her.

She sucked in a startled breath, then exhaled in a hiss. The shock of his presence was horrid enough. But he was staring at her now with the same insolent amusement as before. It was simply too much to be borne.

"Who do you think you are?" she snapped, though her heart thudded with fear. She placed her hands on her hips. "I suggest you cease this hooliganism, or I will summon Mr. Cummings to deal with you."

"Mr. Cummings." He grinned, then crossed his arms and leaned negligently against the wall. Somehow he seemed even bigger and more dangerous than he had last night. "So it is old Cummings you turn to for protection. I had wondered."

"Who else?" she retorted. "And who are you to speak of him in such tones?"

"We are business acquaintances."

"You are a guest here?"

He smirked at her. "Of course."

Olivia's heart sank even as her anger increased. Did Mr. Cummings know what sort of ruffian he had loosed upon his household? "I assume then that you must be Mr. Hawke."

He straightened, smiling with satisfaction. "So he has mentioned me to you."

"He did. You are purported to be something of a horseman." Olivia jutted out her chin with more belligerence than she felt, and studied him closely. At least the man appeared sober this morning, though that affected neither her anger nor her caution. He was again well dressed in buckskin breeches and a tawny colored frock coat, and their fine cut set off his tall, manly figure. Broad shoulders, trim hips. He was younger than she would initially have guessed.

But his eyes were old, she realized, as if they'd seen more than a man needed to see.

Still, that was neither here nor there.

She crossed her arms and narrowed her gaze. "Have you taken my journal from the library, Mr. Hawke?"

"It's Lord Hawke," he said. "But you may call me Neville. And yes, I do have your journal in my possession. Olivia."

At once the alarm bells in her head which had sounded only a muffled din began wildly to clang. "It is Miss Byrde to you," she stated, her voice cold and haughty. She stuck out her hand. "I'll have it from you now."

He stepped nearer; she snatched her arm back.

"I'd like to speak to you about that very topic." He pushed open the door to the sitting room. "Shall we?"

Olivia took two hasty steps backward. "I don't think so. All I want from you is my book, Lord Hawke. Nothing more. Just give it to me now and I will try to forget your appalling behavior last night—and your rudeness this morning."

He grinned, a wicked half-grin that showed strong white teeth against his sun-browned face. She saw now the details she'd had no time to see last night: the crooked scar along his jawline, the thick black hair and slashing brows, and the moody blue eyes. A Gypsy horse trader in gentleman's attire, that's what he looked like. Dark and dangerous with nothing of the true gentleman beneath his handsome exterior.

"I'm afraid I shall never be able to forget last night," he said in a husky, intimate whisper. "I'd hoped you felt the same."

"I'm sure I shall never forget it," she snapped right back at him. "It was a figure of speech, as you well know. I meant only that I would not mention it to our hosts and thereby ruin what Mr. and Mrs. Cummings mean to be a pleasant holiday for their guests."

"I don't see why—" He broke off and stared intently at her, his head cocked slightly to one side. Slowly his smug expression faded. "Our hosts? You are acquainted with Mrs. Cummings—or rather, she is acquainted with you?"

"Of course. Like you, I am her guest in the company of my mother, Lady Dunmore. What did you think—"

"You are a guest here?"

Olivia frowned. Something was more than strange about this conversation. "I said that I was. Why else would I be here—"

"What were you doing wandering around before dawn?" he interrupted her, his tone hard and accusing.

"I could not sleep, not that it is any concern of yours. Why were you up? No. No, you needn't answer. 'Tis clear enough why you were up: to make a drunken fool of yourself."

It was a sharp set-down—deserved, to be sure. Nonetheless, Olivia was not accustomed to flinging insults at anyone. She'd never had the need. But this Mr. Hawke—Lord Hawke—seemed hardly to hear her curt remark.

"Bloody hell," he swore under his breath. "You are a lady."

"What else did you think?" She stared harder at him, then suddenly let out a sarcastic laugh. "Oh yes, you thought I was a servant, didn't you? You thought I was a servant and therefore amenable to the attentions of a peer, no matter how repugnant those attentions might be. You were hoping to compromise an innocent housemaid." She laughed at his discomfiture, though with little true mirth.

A muscle began to tick in his jaw. It was plain she'd figured him out, and plain also that he did not relish being made a fool of. Served him right, the cad.

"Actually," he said, his eyes dark and piercing upon her. "What I thought was that you were Cummings's paramour, come fresh from his bed."

Olivia gasped. "What?"

"Then I read your journal," he continued, scowling at her as if she had somehow done him wrong. "Endless entries and every one of them concerning a different man. Their habits, good and bad. Their financial situations. If you are as proper as this morning you profess to be, then what do all those entries signify?"

"You read my private journal!" Olivia had been angry before but that puny emotion paled beside the full-blown rage that gripped her now. "You read my journal. How dare you!"

"I read it," he admitted, clearly unrepentant. "And what I read casts grave suspicion on its writer's activities—" The crack of her hand across his face stopped him cold.

In the aftermath they glared at one another. A part of Olivia was horrified by what she'd just done. But she was more horrified by what he'd done—and what he'd implied. The list of his crimes was unforgivable. Were she a man she would call him out. By contrast, a slap was little enough punishment.

She drew herself up—she was trembling with emotion—and extended her hand palm up. "I'll have my journal back. Now," she added through gritted teeth.

She wasn't sure what to expect of so graceless a creature and so was hugely relieved when he reached inside his coat and pulled out the volume in dispute. But when she reached for it, he raised it just beyond her grasp.

"I am taking you at your word, Miss Byrde, that you are indeed a guest of the Cummingses."

"You have the gall to doubt it? Give me my book."

"On one condition."

"And what is that? God help you if it is anything vulgar."

"God help *me*?" He chuckled. "A true lady would be concerned more about her reputation than mine."

"Believe me, your reputation matters naught to me."

"But it does matter to me," he stated, serious once more. "You may have your book on the condition that this incident—this misunderstanding, shall we say—remains strictly between us."

"Why, you disgusting—"

"I have business to pursue with Cummings and his guests, and I would prefer this incident not impede it. I apologize for my mistake," he added. "And for any insult I may have cast upon you."

Olivia shut her open mouth with a snap. Finally, an apology. She stared at him. She supposed a true lady would accept it with chilly grace, then make her exit with her head high and her moral victory firmly in place. But Olivia was still furious. After all his insults she was supposed to let him off on the strength of that brief apology? She wanted him to beg. She wanted to see him grovel.

"Give me my journal."

"What of my condition?" One of his brows quirked upward. He appeared far less apologetic than before. She could swear he was more amused by the incident than concerned for his reputation, no matter what he said. Still, what she wanted was her journal. Having him plead for her forgiveness was something she instinctively knew this man would never do.

At least it had not fallen into the hands of someone familiar with the London scene. She'd neither seen nor heard of a Lord Hawke during the past three seasons. If he was unfamiliar with London society, he would not be able to figure out the identities of the various men referred to. That would be humiliating in the extreme.

"Regarding your condition, I assure you," she said in her coldest, haughtiest tone, "that I will not relish speaking of this unpleasant encounter with anyone of my acquaintance."

"Not even your mother?"

"Especially not her," she retorted, then wished at once she'd not been so forthright, for his other brow arched in interest. "If you will please hand it over," she demanded, fore-stalling any further inquiries from him.

With an insolent shrug of his wide shoulders he did so. But Olivia's relief upon reclaiming her journal was tempered by one unsettling fact. During the transfer his fingers met with hers. It was only for the merest part of a second, just a fleeting graze of his fingers along the side of hers. The impact, nevertheless, was stunning.

She averted her eyes and clutched the journal at once to her chest, praying he did not detect the sudden panic that assailed her. But she detected it—racing pulse, damp palms, a giddy turmoil in her stomach. Why had she not worn her gloves?

She turned wordlessly to depart, intent only on escape. But his next words stopped her. "I meant my apology most sincerely, Miss Byrde. I can only beg the ill effects of too much spirits for my appalling behavior last night."

Olivia looked up at him, somewhat mollified by his words though she did not wish to be. It was safer to be angry with him than to feel these strange stammering emotions that made no sense. She nodded. "Good day, Lord Hawke."

"One more thing before you go. Something I don't understand," he continued. "You have not explained the meaning of those entries in your journal. Why do you write of so many men?"

Anger rushed in to save her. "That is none of your concern."

"Perhaps not. But I've a curious nature and I find myself often beguiled by matters not entirely of my concern." He was grinning now, a cynical, one-sided smile that made a mockery of his apology.

"Well, that is simply your misfortune." She stared at him with frosty eyes. "I expect you to honor me with the same discretion you demanded."

"Of course." Then he added, "I wish it had been otherwise."

She gave him a smug, utterly false smile. "If you refer to our initial meeting, I'm afraid it's much too late to undo what has already transpired."

Rather than chastening him, however, her contemptuous tone seemed to challenge him instead, for those moody blue eyes of his swept over her, head to toe, darkening as they went. "I'm afraid you mistake my meaning. What I wish to be otherwise is you, Miss Byrde. Were you the sort of woman I initially believed," he continued, "I'd be a far happier fellow than I presently find myself."

For a moment Olivia did not precisely understand him. Then his meaning—his lewd and insulting meaning—dawned on her, and color flooded her face. To make matters worse, the outrageous rogue had the effrontery to wink at her and grin. "Good day," he said without the least show of remorse for his unforgivable behavior.

Then he strode nonchalantly away, and Olivia could only gape at him—insulted, appalled, and perversely enough, flattered.

CHAPTER

5

NEVILLE ran his hands down the filly's flank. She was ready. He had worried about her, but Otis had assured him that the trip from Woodford Court would only strengthen her leg. He smoothed his palm down her rump and along the muscle she'd injured two months previously. Yes, she was ready.

"All right, Kitti. Let's show them what you've got beneath that pretty little exterior of yours."

As if she understood, the filly whickered, then butted him with her head. She was as fine an animal as had ever come out of the Woodford stables. Even his father's mare, Valentine, had not been so perfect as young Kittiwake.

Bart Tillotson, his trainer, leaned over the stall door. "She'll take the ladies' race," he said, then spat into the corner for emphasis.

"But can she race two days afterward against the gents? Can she hold her own against Fleming's horse or that deep-chested animal of Wagner's?"

Bart nodded. "If the leg holds tomorrow, she'll be good when the three-year-olds run." He came into the stall and knelt beside the leg in question. "She's a brave one, our Kittiwake." He patted the horse with true affection. "She won't back down against those bad boys. She'll show 'em her pretty rump and lead 'em a merry chase."

That she would, Neville agreed as he moved on to check Kestrel, the acknowledged star of his stables. But as he crooned a nameless tune to the rambunctious animal and slipped him a dried apple from his pocket, Bart's words echoed in his head. *She won't back down from those bad boys.*

She'll lead 'em a merry chase. Only it was not the thorough-bred Kitti he was thinking of. It was the thoroughbred Miss Olivia Byrde.

With just a few discreet inquiries he'd determined that she was precisely who she said she was: the daughter of the wid-owed Lady Dunmore and the late Cameron Byrde. Of more interest, however, was the fact that her family owned the estate that lay south and across the Tweed River from his own. For years now that land had lain fallow, its fertile fields and grassy valleys unavailable for farming or grazing. The steward there was old and crusty, and had refused Neville's several offers to lease the land.

He should have made the connection between her and that estate the moment she'd revealed her name, but he hadn't. Perhaps he'd been too distracted by the woman and his phys-ical reaction to her. But now that he knew who she was he needed to keep that reaction under control.

Neville scratched down the arc of Kestrel's powerful neck. This was his chance to approach Lady Dunmore about the lease. It would be a great boon toward his efforts to revitalize the district if he could return that land to good use. First, however, he would have to improve Lady Dunmore's starchy daughter's opinion of him.

For a moment he let himself recall Olivia's outraged ex-pression when he'd left her standing in the hall. Even furious, with her eyes shooting daggers at him, she was magnificent. Did she know that he was her Scottish neighbor? he wondered.

Did she know he lusted after her?

He snorted at that. How could she not? He'd made it clear enough. She would be a long time forgetting or forgiving his insulting manner.

Stewing over that, Neville checked Kestrel's water bucket, then let himself out of the stall. Though he had been crude and boorish in his behavior toward her, he was not entirely to blame for his mistaken assumption about Miss Olivia Byrde. What else was a man to think of a woman possessed of so lush a body, so fiery a temperament, and so husky and com-pelling a voice? Add to that rich auburn hair, flashing green

eyes—no, hazel, he amended, grinning as he recalled her
words—and a tendency to wander around in the dark hours
before dawn. It was no wonder he'd been mistaken about her.

Then there was that curious journal she valued so highly.

He paused in the stable door and surveyed the yard without
really seeing anything. He'd been wondering all morning what
those entries meant, and he'd come to the only conclusion left.
It was not the men's values and shortcomings as customers
she had noted. Rather, it was their value as husbands. Like
every other woman of her age and class, Miss Olivia Byrde
was searching for a husband.

He chuckled out loud. What a mercenary little thing she
was, weighing the positive and negative aspects of every man
she met. How well they danced; their personal habits; their
gambling and drinking and devotion to their mothers.

Neville laughed again. He supposed to a young woman
those might appear important aspects of a potential husband's
temperament. But there had been thirty-eight entries in her
book. He knew because he'd counted them. Did that mean
she'd considered and rejected all of them? Or were some of
the men still under consideration?

Was she even now entering her opinion about him?

That sobered him at once. For if she wrote anything about
him in that book it was certain to be unflattering. What would
she say? A drunken boor. A lecherous cad, crude and insulting. And unrepentant.

Though she might conceal the circumstances of their first
meeting, as they'd agreed, that did not mean she wouldn't
discourage her mother from entering into a lease agreement
with him.

"Damnation," he swore. Once again he'd let this unholy
thirst of his make a fool of him. Only this time it was no
milkmaid or tavern wench he'd revealed his baser nature to.
Olivia Byrde was a gentlewoman, a peer's daughter, and a
virgin, protected from men like him. With her striking looks
and bold manner she'd no doubt slapped several faces before
his.

He rubbed his cheek, remembering her furious expression

and the fire in her eyes more than the pain of her blow. He also remembered the lust she'd roused in him, a lust he'd not felt in many a year.

He'd not been celibate since his return from the war. There had been women enough willing to pleasure the young heir to Woodford, and he'd been willing to use them. But that lust had been much like his drinking: he'd take whatever was available to slake his thirst.

What he felt for Olivia Byrde was somehow different. He wanted the same thing from her that he'd wanted from all the others: her pale body naked and eager for his. But he wanted her in particular. Not just any available woman, but her.

A breeze blew warm and fragrant in his face. Perhaps he wanted her because she'd made it clear just how much she disliked him. He'd never before had to work to gain a woman's interest. Maybe that was the attraction she held, a challenge to be met and overcome. She was a smart, opinionated beauty, the like he'd never known. Yes, she'd roused a mighty lust in him. He felt it still.

He had to keep his wits about him, though. He had to remember his reason for coming to Doncaster in the first place, and that reason was the primary source of his problem. Like him Miss Olivia Byrde was a guest of the Cummingses. It followed that they were bound to be thrown in one another's paths. If he behaved civilly, he had every reason to hope she would do the same. He'd come to Doncaster to sell horses and run races, and hopefully that purpose would not be subverted.

But he had another purpose now as well. He needed to ingratiate himself with her mother, and to do that he must somehow make amends with the daughter. Though he'd enjoyed the stunned look on her face after his parting words to her this morning, they'd been impulsive—and unwise. That she'd roused his ire with her contemptuous dismissal of him was no excuse. In the future he would have to restrain himself better. That was unfortunate, considering that the last thing he felt toward Miss Olivia Byrde was restraint.

Frustrated by this new complication, Neville shoved his hands in his pockets and scowled down at his boots. He was no good at moving about in proper society anymore. He should have stayed at Woodford Court, far from the social circles he'd abandoned four years ago. There he could drink himself into oblivion every night and not care whom he insulted with his crude manner.

But Woodford Court was in dire straits and its people relied on him to improve their lives. It was the one thing that kept him going. He'd failed everyone else in his life, but the people of Kelso still needed him, and he was terrified of failing them too. That's why he'd ventured down to the races at Doncaster with its large purses and so many wealthy nabobs in attendance. Success with the stables was the fastest way to accumulate the funds he needed to increase the productivity of his people. And putting the fallow fields of Byrde Manor to good use was the surest way to *keep* them productive.

"I've saddled Robin for you," Bart said, coming up behind him. "I'll bring Kitti around shortly."

Neville turned to his trainer and took the reins of the spirited bay gelding. "Good. Good," he repeated. "Today the trial runs. Tomorrow the first of the races."

But tonight . . . tonight would be his trial run, his first test. For Miss Byrde and her mother were certain to attend the reception and ball the Cummingses had planned to kick off the week of festivities at Doncaster. He could either continue to act like the crude oaf he was, or he could call on the manners his own mother had so long ago drummed into him and behave as he knew he should. For that, however, he might have to swear off drinking, and the very thought chilled him.

"Business first," he muttered. "You can drink yourself blind once you return home."

"What's that?" Bart said, coming out of the stables leading the racehorse.

"Nothing. Just . . . Just a prayer. For success," he added, knowing his devout trainer would approve.

"Aye, a prayer for success for our noble Kitti," Bart said, smoothing the mare's forelock.

But Neville felt no compulsion to pray for Kitti. She was a natural racer and her success was ensured. It was his own that worried him. And though it should not, Miss Olivia Byrde's unsettling entrance into his life had somehow made it seem much more difficult.

Olivia spent the morning seething. She'd barricaded herself in the library, even going so far as to lock the door. But Neville Hawke had not followed her this time. He'd been every bit as crude and insulting as before, but at least he'd not followed her.

How was she possibly to keep these two incidents to herself? It wouldn't be so bad if she weren't going to be cast in his path again. But they were guests in the same household, come to Doncaster for the same purpose, and bound to encounter one another at all the same social and sporting events.

Her stomach let out an unbecoming growl and she halted her pacing. She hadn't gone in to breakfast for fear of finding him there. The fact that she'd spied him and another man riding out with several horses a half hour ago hadn't been sufficient to draw her to the dining room either. For her mother and Penny Cummings must be up by now, and she had no particular desire to face them. She was that angry and unsettled by the awful Lord Hawke.

Her stomach growled again and she flung herself into a chair. She flipped her journal open and ruffled through the pages. How could he have thought her that sort of woman? What in her writing could possibly suggest that sort of lewd behavior?

"He needs no such excuses," she muttered. "A coarse mind such as his could create filth in anything." Still she searched. *Keeps a fine stable.* She turned a page. *Rather an earthy sort. Generous natured.* She flipped to still another entry. *Excessively attached to his mother.*

What was there to misunderstand in any of that? Then she turned to a blank page and reached for the pen and inkwell she'd located in a desk drawer.

"Lord H.," she began, saying the words out loud as she wrote. "Drinks too much. Ill-mannered and altogether too bold." She tapped the feather end of the quill against her chin.

"Though rough-edged, he is tall and reasonably handsome," she continued, pursing her lips in disapproval. "But he proves the rule that looks can be deceiving."

Ill-suited for marriage, she added, underlining it twice.

She would write more about him later, she decided. It would be interesting to see whether he tried to correct her initial reaction to him. As for herself, she meant to stay aloof and distant from him. Very distant. Under no circumstances would she allow herself to be caught alone with that man again. But she should not appear so rude as to arouse her mother's suspicions. That would never do. Fortunately Lord Holdsworth would capture most of Augusta's attention.

Olivia blotted her entry with a bit of felt then closed her book. Only four more days, then she would be gone from here, never to deal with the awful Lord Hawke again.

God grant her the strength to endure it.

Neville was elated—and he wanted a drink to celebrate. He wanted it in the worst way. But he had set himself a test and he was bound to pass it. No drinking until tonight's ball, and then only watered wine.

"She's a mover," Holdsworth admitted, clapping him on the back. "How many years will you run her before breeding her?"

"A season or two on the courses is all I expect of her."

"I want her first foal—colt or filly, it matters naught. I want her first foal, Hawke, unless you will change your mind and sell her to me now. The offer I made earlier still stands, and I'll match any other offers you might receive."

Neville nodded and winked at Bart. Kitti had placed first in the trials today, outshining several very good animals. As such she would have the coveted inside position for tomorrow's race. His blood roared, pumping exhilaration throughout his body. Bringing the horses to Doncaster had been a good decision. Though he'd dreaded it, perhaps all would work out as he'd hoped.

"I'll keep your offer in mind," he said. "There's still tomorrow's race to be run."

"When will we see your other animal put through his paces? He's a fine-looking one." Just then Holdsworth was jostled from behind and the tumbler he held sloshed whisky over the side.

Neville inhaled the sweet pungent scent of it. "Soon. Soon enough," he said, staring hungrily at the amber liquid.

Cummings had invited his houseguests plus a few locals for an end-of-the-day drink at the Eel and Elbow, Doncaster's finest public house. So far Neville had avoided spirits, only a mug of ale to assuage his thirst. But he could feel the siren call of the stronger stuffs.

Bart nudged him. "D'ye want to check Kitti's leg before I take 'er back to the stables, milord?"

Neville glanced at him, relieved at the interruption. Did Bart see how hard temptation rode him? He grimaced, but without rancor. Bart and Otis knew him better than any other men. They'd seen him roaring drunk one night, and deathly ill the next morn. They knew he sat up at night and slept until early afternoon. If they disapproved of the choices he sometimes made, they did not say. The common link they shared was the stables at Woodford, and the horses.

"I'll see the rest of you this evening," Neville said to his other companions. "I've horses to tend."

"Hold on a minute! Here's a toast to the fillies," Cummings said, raising his glass.

"And to the fillies we shall encounter at the ball," Holdsworth added, hoisting his glass high and grinning. "We shall need our dancing shoes tonight, lads."

Neville raised his empty glass with the rest of the happy crowd. Then with Bart behind him, made his escape from the tavern.

They rode the one mile out of town in silence. It had been a good day, a good beginning, and he breathed deep of the warm afternoon air. The smell of drying hay and warm horseflesh added to his contentment, as did the sun lingering late in the clear August sky. Soon enough the cool winds would arrive, and behind them the winter. By then he would be back among his people, hunkered down for the season with only his chores and the breeding mares to tend.

But if it was difficult to abstain from drinking now, it would be more so then. He rubbed one knuckle along the scar on his jaw. He knew from experience that he did his heaviest drinking during the long dark months of winter. It would be nearly impossible to fight his night demons without the numbing effects of whisky. He wasn't certain he could succeed. The whisky deadened his nerves, keeping the awful memories at bay, memories of a night spent in hell, a night thick with screams and death, and swimming with blood.

He swallowed hard. *A night he could have prevented if he'd just stayed awake.*

He shuddered, suddenly overwhelmed by the need for a drink. What did it matter if he drank himself sick? a resigned voice in his head whispered. After all, he had no one to impress with his sobriety—or lack thereof.

Then an image of Olivia Byrde flashed unexpectedly through his mind and he clung to it in relief. She would be there tonight, tempting him almost as fiercely as would Cummings's fine stock of brandies. He ran a hand through his hair. No doubt she would work very hard to avoid him. But so long as he remained sober, he could think of no good reason to let her succeed.

"No drinking," he said out loud.

"Very good, milord," Bart agreed.

Neville gave him a sidelong glance. He'd nearly forgotten the man's presence. "No drinking," he repeated, shifting in the saddle. "But I will see if I can remember how to dance."

Augusta adjusted the curl that lay against Olivia's cheek. "You will break hearts tonight, my dear. Why, just look at you. Normally I would not care for that particular shade of coral. Too much orange for my delicate complexion. However, I must say Madame Henri was correct, for it suits you so very well. You look absolutely stunning. Even your eyes seem to sparkle with more color than is their wont."

"Do you think so?" Olivia stared doubtfully at herself in the mirror. To be sure, her new gown was lovely, and such a pleasant change from the pastels her mother insisted she wear in town. Also, her hair was being most cooperative this evening. That new lavender rinse must be the reason it looked so soft and shiny.

But what accounted for the flush of color in her cheeks, and the glints of emerald and gold in her eyes? She wrinkled her nose at her reflection. She hated to think that nervous anticipation about encountering the awful Lord Hawke might actually enhance her appearance.

"It must be the country air," she said, turning away from the looking glass. "I told you I was weary of the crush in town."

"I feel obliged to warn you, then, that there should be quite a crush tonight. According to Penny, her ball is one of the biggest events of the year in Doncaster. There will be all sorts of new gentlemen here, not just the town society which you seem uninterested in of late, but at least one viscount, and several very wealthy squires."

Augusta removed her pearl earbobs and screwed on her favorite opals instead. She twisted her head from side to side, admiring the way they dangled and swayed. "By the by," she continued. "Did you hear? That Hawke fellow that we've yet to meet, he is actually Lord Hawke, Baron Hawke of Woodford Court. You won't remember, but Woodford Court is just a mile or so from Byrde Manor."

At that bit of startling news Olivia spun around, one of her gloves tugged but halfway up her arm. "Are you certain?" she asked, her voice high-pitched and strained.

"Oh yes," Augusta blithely continued. "We didn't know them well, for they were abroad quite often while your father and I were in Scotland. But I did meet them once or twice. Lovely family. He was just a lad then, twelve or so, I'd say. Away at school most of the time. I'm told that the rest of his family is dead now. His parents and his brother."

Augusta paused. "Did I mention that he's unmarried?" she added, her voice rousing from its somber musing. "Baron Neville Hawke of Woodford Court, never wed and nearly thirty. Tsk, tsk. Well, here's your opportunity, Olivia. You've been complaining about the gentlemen of the ton. Unless Lord Hawke is one of those awful Scottish bumpkins, bearded and too robust for proper manners, you may find him quite to your tastes."

Olivia listened to her mother with growing dread. That man was her neighbor? An odd shiver marked its way up her back. God help her if her mother took a liking to Lord Hawke as a son-in-law. "Are you so eager to marry me off that you would consign me to the wilds of Scotland, you who have ever found excuses to avoid visiting Byrde Manor?"

"I have nothing against Scotland, Olivia. Nor against Byrde Manor. In truth, the years I spent there were the best part of my marriage to your father. It was only in town—" She broke off and waved her hand. "Never mind all that. I enjoy country life and town life. It's only that Byrde Manor is a little too remote for me. However, your tastes differ from mine. I believe we both can agree on that. Come now," she added, tugging the scooped neckline of her bodice down another half inch. " 'Tis time for the two of us to make our entrance."

Entrance indeed, Olivia fretted, tugging her own bodice up. She did not want to see Lord Hawke, her neighbor. She stifled a muttered oath. If that man ruined her visit to Byrde Manor with his maddeningly arrogant manner—if he so much as raised one of his arrogant brows at her or smirked a mocking smirk—

She jerked the door open and started out. She didn't know exactly what she would do. But she knew she would not let him get away with it.

Neville had positioned himself in the entry hall with a clear view of the stairs. He'd finally introduced himself to his hostess earlier in the day and resolved to be on his best behavior tonight. It had not been difficult to charm Penelope Cummings, and when she spied him now, she hurried toward him smiling.

"Lord Hawke. How fortuitous that you are downstairs. I thought that you, Lord Holdsworth, and Lady Dunmore, as our ranking guests, might agree to stand in the receiving line with Mr. Cummings and myself."

He gave her an admiring glance, then bent low with a gallant flourish. Were it not for her annoying voice and nervous, fluttering manner, he might consider her a handsome woman. "I would be honored."

"Very good." She coyly patted his arm with her fan. "I don't believe you've met Lady Dunmore yet, nor her daughter, Miss Olivia Byrde. Ah, here they are now."

Neville straightened at once and stared up at the dual curving stair that led from the warren of rooms that made up the upper levels of the Cummingses' manse. Two women paused at the head of the rosewood stairway, two women equally lovely, but without the least similarity between them, he saw. Lady Dunmore was exquisite. Small and fair, she looked hardly old enough to parent the young woman at her side. Then he turned his gaze intently to the daughter.

Olivia Byrde was taller and more curvaceous then her mother, and her coloring was that of a Scotswoman, tempered only marginally by her English heritage. Auburn hair instead of red; hazel eyes instead of green. She had patrician features, yet colored with an earthy palette. He'd berated himself for mistaking her for a harlot, but he could understand now why he'd done so. Any number of women could be termed beautiful. But this particular one possessed also an innate sensuality. She was the sort of woman any man would desire. He most certainly did.

The two began their descent, the mother clearly conscious of the entrance she made. Olivia, however, appeared less self-assured. Was it on account of him?

One corner of his mouth turned up. He certainly hoped so.

". . . my particular friend," Mrs. Cummings nattered on as the women reached them. But Neville only had eyes for Olivia. And she, to his great pleasure, stared fixedly at him.

Did the glint in those lovely eyes bode good or ill for him? Whichever it was, he meant to turn it to his advantage. He would charm Miss Olivia Byrde and her mother, and gain those land leases no matter what it took. And perhaps, if he was lucky, he would take a little pleasure in the process as well.

CHAPTER

6

"MAY I have this dance?"

Olivia steeled herself against the beguiling darkness in Neville Hawke's voice. She'd been anticipating this moment all evening, ever since he'd bent so gallantly over her hand at their introduction. Since then he'd played at being a perfect gentleman. She knew because for the past two and a half hours she'd surreptitiously watched him.

He'd stood in the receiving line, so incredibly handsome and well mannered she could hardly credit that he was the same man with whom she'd already had two unfortunate run-ins. Then he'd circulated, speaking amiably with the men and dancing with his hostess, as well as several other women. It seemed now that she was next.

"Thank you," she answered, her voice cool, her expression bland. "But I am not keen on dancing."

He gave her a half-smile that was wholly masculine—and wholly dangerous. "You've accepted invitations from three other men. If you turn me down, you will hurt my feelings."

"How that shall worry me," she quipped. "I doubt you have any feelings," she added, though not so loud that anyone else might overhear.

"You will hurt my feelings," he repeated. "And you will rouse your mother's curiosity."

Olivia glanced swiftly to the circle around her mother. Sure enough, Augusta was staring at her and Lord Hawke. When Augusta smiled and waved, Olivia gave her an answering nod, then looked away. She raised her chin a notch and glared at him, all the while tapping her fan against her palm. "I thought we had an agreement."

"Yes. An agreement to be civil. And I, for one, think it would be grossly uncivil of me not to invite the most beautiful woman in the room to dance."

Olivia averted her eyes. She was accustomed to effusive compliments from gentlemen, and she was adept at separating the sincere from the perfunctory and from the out-and-out false. Still, she had to force herself not to gape at his words.

"The most beautiful woman in the room," she echoed, flicking her fan open and closed. "I should expect a more original piece of flattery from a rogue such as you. But save your breath," she added before he could respond. "You are correct about my mother. Sad to say, but it is easier if I dance with you than explain to her why I refuse to do so."

Haughty as a queen, Olivia reluctantly extended one hand to him. But instead of leading her onto the floor to line up for the cotillion, Lord Hawke simply stood still, holding her gloved hand in his and studying her intently. Though only a moment, it seemed to stretch out forever and it completely unsettled her—she, whom no man ever affected. Just like before, his touch unnerved her and left her positively breathless.

"I wish to apologize again for my boorish behavior," he said, so softly that no one but she could hear. "And I will continue to apologize to you until I am convinced you have forgiven me."

Olivia firmly ignored the little knot that tightened in her stomach. "I told you. It is forgotten."

"Forgotten. But forgiven?"

Thankfully the musicians struck up the call for the dancers and he had to escort her to their position. That provided a little time for Olivia to compose herself. The fact that she needed the time to do so was vexing in the extreme. But between the warm intimacy of his hand and the low intimacy of his voice, she found herself almost dizzy.

She tried to concentrate as the caller explained the figure, but all the time she fumed at the man beside her. He had deliberately picked a cotillion because it was such a lengthy dance and she would have to remain long in his presence. Well, he would not upset her, she vowed. He might think to continue his fun at her expense, but he would not succeed.

"So, Lord Hawke," she said at the first pause in the dancing. "Are you satisfied with the first day of the horse racing?"

"I am. Tell me, do you have an interest in horses?"

Olivia hesitated. She adored horses and riding, whether a long ramble, a rousing steeplechase, or an impromptu race. However, she did not wish to provide the two of them with any common ground. "I suppose I appreciate them as much as the next person."

They met and circled. His hand was warm.

"Do you keep your own saddle horse?"

"Yes," she admitted. "But she is too old for more than a sedate ride these days."

They bowed and parted and faced one another across the aisle of dancers. Again her stomach knotted and twisted as he studied her. Which was worse? she wondered. When their hands touched, or when they stood apart and he observed her with those dark hooded eyes?

The second change of the dance brought them back together. "Perhaps you might like to try one of my animals," he offered.

"Perhaps. I'm afraid, however, that my stay here may be too brief to arrange it."

"How about tomorrow afternoon?" His hand on her waist guided her in the promenade. Though his touch was light, Olivia felt it very clearly.

"I should think you will be occupied in Doncaster with your horses."

"Won't you be there also? After all, why else have you come to Doncaster except to see the races?"

"I haven't consulted with my mother yet, so I cannot say what our plans are for the morrow." She mentally crossed her fingers at that lie. Where Lord Holdsworth was, her mother would surely be, and Olivia knew that meant the racecourse.

"I would like it very much if you were there, Miss Byrde.

My filly, Kittiwake, is running. Having you there is bound to bring her luck."

Olivia rudely rolled her eyes. "Another cliché. I'm sure your Kittiwake will be quite oblivious to my presence."

He grinned. "You do not consider it more than coincidence that a pretty bird has fallen into the path of a Lord Hawke, who is running Kittiwake and Kestrel in the races? And you, my long-absent neighbor? Clearly it is fate which has cast us together, Miss Byrde."

Olivia tossed her head. "I acknowledge the play on bird names and the coincidence. But as for fate, no. I will attend the races, and perhaps I shall even wager on your horses. If they are as fast as their master, they should outdistance all the rest," she finished in scathing tones.

He grinned once more, a sinfully handsome grin that sent an unwonted quiver through her. When he spun her in the next figure, his touch was more forceful than before.

"Fast, you say." He released her as the ladies did their *centre moulinet,* and her heart was thumping by the time she returned to his side. There was a glimmer of devilment in his eyes, and she felt a perverse surge of anticipation. A scoundrel he might be, rude and dangerous one moment, and nothing but charming the next. But he could never be said to be boring.

"Too fast for the likes of me," she replied before he could make another leading remark. "I will, however, be certain to wager on your horses."

Better that you wager on me, Neville thought as he guided the stimulating Olivia Byrde through the cotillion's next change. It was truly amazing the effect a chance encounter with this woman had wrought in his attitude. Or was it Kitti's good showing today? Either way, he was actually enjoying himself. He'd not done that in years. He stared at his partner, trying to understand why she affected him so. One thing he knew. Olivia Byrde might disapprove of him, but she did not shy away from confrontation.

He smiled down at her, vitally aware of everything about her. Her eyes sparkled with life; her cheeks were flush with it. And her hair . . . The rich auburn mass was tamed into a sedate topknot tonight. But two curls framed her face, two warm, springy coils of vibrant color. How he ached to see the full length of her hair released to cascade gloriously over her alabaster skin—

"Ah! Excuse me," he muttered when he misstepped and nearly trod upon her toe. "Unlike your Lord S., it seems I am out of practice with dancing." *And with wooing.* If he were not careful, his wayward thoughts would prove most embarrassing to him. As it was, they certainly astounded him.

They danced the next two changes in silence, though her expressive eyes spoke volumes. She was still angry with him, and wary of his intentions. That was plain. But she had just enough wildness in her nature to be intrigued. It was to that little wildness he instinctively addressed himself.

"Why are you yet unmarried?" he asked after the gentlemen made their centre and circinate.

"What a rude question! Are you also out of practice with the good manners of polite society? Too much time in the stables, I'll warrant."

He grinned at her pursed expression, and it occurred to him that she'd drawn more smiles from him in two days than anyone else had in four years. "Perhaps you are too strong-willed to suit the milksops that populate society's upper crust," he replied, ignoring her barbs. "Certainly you are beautiful enough to have gone in your first season."

She gave him a withering look. "If I wished to wed just anyone, I could have done so years ago."

"Years ago. Oho, she speaks as if she were an ancient. Years ago. You could be a grandmother by now, I suppose."

That drew a tiny smile from her, one that left Neville wanting to see more. "You are an unrepentant rogue," she said.

His hand tightened against her waist, slender without the aid of heavy undergarments, and it was with regret he released her for the final figure. "Is that what you wrote of me in that little volume you keep? That I am an unrepentant rogue?"

Her eyes flashed green and gold in the lamplight. "You assume quite a lot, my lord. What makes you think I bother to write of you at all?"

They came together with arms crossed and hands held. "Because I understand you, Olivia," he whispered. "You are not a woman to do things by halves. No doubt you have already scribbled a page full of invective directed at me. My hope is that this night, as you sit in your dressing gown with your hair loose about your shoulders, you will write kinder words about me."

Then they parted, each to their respective position, and made their proper curtsey and bow. The music ended with a triple crescendo and the dance was done. There was nothing left but for him to return her to her friends or her mother. But damn, he did not want to do so. He wanted to dance her out that open ballroom door and sweep her into his arms—

He bowed stiffly again, aware of the pooling warmth in his loins. Surely he could control himself better than this! "I hope you will afford me another dance before the evening is done, Miss Byrde."

She stared up at him with troubled eyes, beautiful hazel eyes, green and brown with liveliness and worry. "I don't think that would be wise," she said, very quietly. Then she turned and fled his presence.

An hour later the supper room opened, and Olivia advanced in to dine on the arm of a Mr. Thompson, eldest son of the Cummingses' solicitor. If she could have begged off and retired upstairs to her bedchamber with a headache, she would happily have done so. But her mother would have wondered at that—and so would Lord Hawke.

What was wrong with her to be acting like such a ninny? First he frightened her, then he insulted her. Now he charmed her despite her personal knowledge of his untrustworthy ways. He was just like her father.

And she was just like her mother.

That dreadful thought made her stumble.

"Watch yourself, Miss Byrde," Mr. Thompson said. "The room is so crowded it's a wonder any of us can make our way through."

"Thank you," she murmured. Yet her thoughts remained fixed upon that uneasy revelation. Not that she disapproved of her mother. She loved her very much. But Augusta felt incomplete without a man at her side, and Olivia had always prided herself on being nothing like that. Yet here she was, fascinated by a man—for there was no other way to term it—fascinated by a man sure to bring her nothing but woe.

What a dangerous dilemma to find herself in.

But she was wiser than her mother, she told herself. And she knew enough of Lord Hawke's true personality to be amply forewarned. His final words to her—far too intimate for their casual acquaintance—was proof enough that he was a well-practiced seducer. In less than twenty-four hours he had shown himself to be a drunkard, a womanizer, and a determined flirt. In short, he was a rake. That he was handsome and charming only made him more dangerous to any young woman of good breeding. She, however, had no reason to fear, for she had only to remember her father and the heartache he had visited on her mother.

Fortunately, she had only four more days to endure Lord Hawke's proximity.

What of Scotland?

She stared blankly at the heavily laden buffet table. In Scotland they would be neighbors. But she would have her guests—and her brother as protection. She might be forced to see Lord Hawke once or twice, but otherwise she would keep well away from the man. Well away from him, she vowed.

Her appetite restored, she filled her plate and endured the obligatory small talk with the eager Mr. Thompson. Yes, how fortunate that the weather was so fine for the races. No, she did not mean to return right away to London. Yes, the musicians were very good for a country ensemble.

She ate and she nodded and she was immensely relieved when her mother approached. "Darling, are you enjoying yourself? Mr. Thompson," she continued, turning to favor the young man with her brightest smile, "would you be so good as to fetch me a glass of punch?"

He was no sooner away to his task than Augusta rounded on Olivia. "Well, my dear, I see you are quite enjoying yourself."

"As, I note, are you. How is dear Archie?" she asked, hoping to divert Augusta from the subject she suspected had drawn her here.

"He is delightful. A true gentleman. We danced twice before he was drawn away by that horse-mad crowd. But speaking of horse-mad," she said, her eyes shrewd. "Tell me about Lord Hawke. Will he have a favorable review in that little matchmaker of yours?"

Olivia dabbed her mouth with her napkin. "Really, Mother. One dance is hardly sufficient to determine anything about anyone."

"I don't know that I agree with that. He and I did not dance, but we did converse and I have already formed a most congenial opinion of the man."

"That's because he is a man, and a handsome, charming one at that. But if I considered handsome and charming sufficient attributes to commend a man, I would have wed Edward Marshton my first season out."

Augusta pursed her lips. "And how terrible would that have been? Oh, never mind all that. The point is, Lord Hawke is more than presentable. For heaven's sake, he is an avid horseman. I should think that sufficient on its own merit to commend him to you. Plus," she added, leaning forward, her eyes flashing dramatically. "Plus, he likes you."

Olivia ignored the ridiculous flutter in her chest. "And I suppose he told you that?"

Augusta flitted her hand impatiently. "No, no. Not in words, of course. But I saw his eyes, Olivia. They followed you when you danced with Mr. Lowell and with that skinny old man, what's his name."

"Lord Edgerton," Olivia automatically supplied.

"Even when he was dancing with Mrs. Gregory his eyes sought you out."

Olivia frowned. That silly tripping of her heart was not triumph, she told herself. Only a fool would believe a womanizer like him serious on the basis of such flimsy evidence.

"Really, Mother. You prattle like a girl fresh from the schoolroom. Believe me when I say Lord Hawke has no more interest in me than I have in him. He is a good dancer, and he is an interesting conversationalist. Beyond that we have nothing in common."

Augusta's face took on a mulish expression. "What of his horses? You know you adore horses. And then there's the added benefit that your lands run together." She tilted her head to the side and eyed Olivia closely. "He was very interested when I told him Byrde Manor is not mine but, rather, held in trust for you."

"I'm sure he was," Olivia answered through gritted teeth. "I'll thank you, Mother, not to tout my assets as if I am some mare on the auction block. I am not interested in Lord Hawke, so let it be."

"But Olivia—"

"Let it be, Mother."

Olivia spent the remainder of the evening in determined gaiety. She laughed and danced and never allowed herself to be without a partner. Even the obnoxious Lord Hawke could not be so rude as to break in on her when she was partnering another gentleman. Her only bad moment came when he escorted her mother onto the floor for a galop. The audacity of the man!

Augusta was at her best tonight. But then, elegant parties and handsome men always complemented her. As Lord Hawke whirled her around the floor, Olivia conceded that her mother looked much the same age as he did, and he could not be past thirty. Olivia stared over the shoulder of her own dance partner, the portly Sir Minturn, and watched as Augusta laughed at something Lord Hawke said. He smiled down at her and the tiniest spark of jealousy flickered to life in her chest.

Stifling a groan, Olivia tore her gaze away from them. She would not be jealous of her own mother!

Standing among a trio of gentlemen, Lord Holdsworth also watched Augusta and Lord Hawke. Now that was jealousy, Olivia decided when she spied him. Whatever she'd felt had been but a little nick of wounded pride. In truth, she felt much better to have been proven correct about Lord Hawke: he was quite the ladies' man. But one woman was much the same as another to that sort of man, and it behooved her to remember it.

So she finished the galop, then sat down to a game of whist as the final cotillion was formed up. She did not care whom her mother danced with, nor upon whom Lord Hawke bestowed his dubious charm. She *did* care that she lost a half-crown at the card tables. But that was better than losing her dignity or her self-esteem, she decided once the final dance ended and the guests began to depart. She could suffer the financial setback far better than the emotional one.

"Good night, darling," Augusta said to her. "You needn't wait up for me, for several of us plan to sit down to breakfast in the garden. Penny has several tables arranged with torches all around. Isn't it just the perfect ending for such a lovely evening?"

"Will your Archie be there?" Olivia asked, her brows raised.

Augusta smiled. "Yes. And Penny and Mr. Cummings and the Thompsons, both father and son. I'd ask you to join us, but Penny tells me Lord Hawke may be there—though I still cannot understand your disinterest in the man."

Olivia ignored that remark. "I'm afraid I am far too weary to do anything but seek my pillow," she said. "And far too weary to fend off your foolish matchmaking schemes," she added under her breath.

When Olivia turned for the stairs she did not scan the ballroom before she left, searching for a tall man with dark hair and a wickedly seductive grin. Nor did she glance down the hall that led to the library where they'd had their first unpleasant encounter. She only trudged up the stairs, determined to put him out of her mind. She would sink into the mattress and the oblivion of sleep. She would rise late, then attend the afternoon races. Tomorrow evening a fireworks display was scheduled in the town square, weather permitting, to be followed by an open-air dance.

It was really too bad Sarah had declined to come. She would have enjoyed the fireworks immensely.

When Olivia stopped before the door to her room, however,

her gaze was arrested by a curious sight: a bit of coral-colored lace tied upon the latch with a small rosette attached to it. Was it from her dress? She bent down to examine her skirt hem and sure enough discovered a torn section along one side.

Why had the maid not laid it upon the dresser?

She untied the lace scrap and started to enter when she heard a footfall behind her.

"It's yours, isn't it?"

Olivia spun around, her heart unaccountably in her throat. Lord Hawke stood but three paces away with his legs spread apart and his hands clasped solemnly behind his back. He was unbearably handsome. That was the idiotic thought that surfaced first in her temporarily stupefied brain. Despite that scar, despite the ruffian he hid behind his polished manner tonight, despite everything she knew about him, he remained unbearably handsome. She swallowed hard.

"I wasn't aware the rosette had come loose. I must have caught it on something," she muttered.

"I could have kept it, you know."

Like a panicked creature's, Olivia's heart began madly to pound. "Why should you wish to do that?"

He smiled and rocked a little on his heels. But he did not approach her and she thanked a merciful God for that. "Because it is yours," he said. "I seem to be making a habit of returning your misplaced possessions. First your entertaining journal and tonight this—"

"I thought we agreed that you would forget about the contents of my journal if I did not mention your drunken misbehavior toward me." Her hands knotted around the innocent rosette. "Is it your intention to continue to plague my every movement? Good night, Lord Hawke." She turned to enter her room.

"Now who's being rude?"

"Did I forget to thank you for this?" She shook the bit of lace at him, knowing she was being far more nasty than circumstances required. But she could not help herself. He seemed to bring out the absolute worst in her. "Thank you for my torn lace. And I'll thank you also not to linger outside my door where anyone might see you and draw the worst sort of conclusion."

Then she jerked open the door, slammed it behind her, and locked it with a decisive click.

In the aftermath she stood just inside the room with the blood roaring in her ears and her knees threatening to buckle. That she should feel so only increased her agitation. Why did she allow this ruffian to unsettle her? This ruffian in gentleman's attire. She blinked and cocked her head warily. Was he still outside her door?

Three ominous footsteps gave her the answer. She fell back from the door, then immediately rushed forward to make certain the lock had caught. Surely he would not force his way into her room. Even he could not be so lost to propriety as that!

His soft knock sounded like the bells of doom.

"Go away," she ordered, finally dredging up the remnants of her courage. "Begone from my door, Lord Hawke. Our earlier agreement does not include your continued poor conduct."

"It is not my wish to frighten you, Miss Byrde. I am aware that my presence here is not strictly proper."

"Then go away."

There was a short silence.

"Would you like to go riding with me tomorrow?"

Olivia shook her head, only belatedly realizing he could not see her. "No. I . . . I told you, tomorrow is not a good day."

"Then perhaps the next."

"I don't believe that would be wise."

She heard him shift positions. "Because you will be busy searching for a husband?"

"No! Besides, that's hardly your concern."

"What did you write about me in your little book?"

"Nothing at all," she swore, crossing her fingers. "Why should I?"

He chuckled. "Liar. We both know you've written a full page at least of unpleasant observations about my character.

Isn't that so? I'd wager a sovereign that you termed me a poor choice for a husband."

She felt a twinge of guilt. If he only knew. Still, what she wrote was her affair. "Whatever I might write—if I write anything at all—you would deserve every bit of it. Good night!" She turned away, determined to ignore him. But his soft, persistent knock was more demanding than if he threatened to beat down the door.

"Go away before someone comes along and my reputation is destroyed."

"Do you play chess?"

Olivia stared at the door. She could picture him so clearly standing there. Too clearly. She frowned. "Yes. But not with untrustworthy men such as you."

"Untrustworthy? I never cheat, Olivia. Not at anything. You can trust me."

"Do not call me that. I've not given you leave to address me so familiarly. Go away!"

"Very well. But should you have a change of heart, I will be in the library with the chessboard at the ready. I think we shall make the best sort of opponents. Hazel," he added.

Taken aback by his use of that name for her, Olivia was slow to reply. "You mean the worst sort." But there was no answer this time, and after several long moments, she leaned cautiously nearer and placed her ear against the door.

He was gone. Thank God for that. But still she stood there tensed and waiting. Her hand crept to the key. Did she dare unlock the door and check the hall?

No, she decided, turning away from temptation. Determined to drive the aggravating Lord Hawke out of her mind, she swiftly disrobed. Once she had donned her nightgown she clambered into the high bed with her hairbrush, her journal, and her novel. She wanted to reread the page she'd started about Lord Hawke and consider what else she might add. Then she would settle in with *Emma* and immerse herself in that young woman's entanglements and thereby forget her own.

But when Olivia opened the journal, a folded piece of foolscap fell out. Puzzled, she set the book aside and opened the note. Where had it come from? She was certain she'd not inserted anything in her journal.

Her heart plummeted when she spied the slashing, masculine script.

My dear Hazel,
I cannot like the words you have written about me. They are, however, your opinions, based upon your initial impressions of me, and therefore not to be disputed. That I have behaved badly I cannot argue. That my behavior continues to be outrageous, I will also not deny. But in you I detect a boldness that is intrigued by the outrageous, though you may deny it. I can only hope that time will improve your opinion of me.

Until tomorrow, N. H.

Olivia stared at the small white square in her hand, completely dumbfounded. That he would write so boldly to her *was* outrageous. That he'd invaded her private chamber, and slipped the missive within the pages of her private journal—and on the very page where she'd written of him—why, that was beyond belief!

She threw the note and the journal to the foot of the bed and snatched up her brush. With a ferocity that should have been painful, she thrust the brush through her hair, fuming with every stroke. She would have to do something, she decided. Something that would stop him in his tracks. She would tell her mother and consult with Penny Cummings.

No. She scratched that notion at once. Penny Cummings would find such goings-on much too juicy to keep to herself. Plus, the woman would never be able to hold her tongue about the existence of Olivia's little book.

She threw down the brush and snatched up the note once more. As she reread it, her outrage hardened to resolve. Lord Hawke had insulted her and he had invaded her privacy. He continued to provoke her and, furthermore, showed no signs of ending his unwanted attentions. Hadn't he just invited her to play chess in the library? As if an unmarried woman could safely spend time alone with such a rogue in the middle of the night. But if he thought he could best her, he was sadly mistaken.

She crumpled the note in one fist, then lay back on the big bed and pulled the yellow counterpane up to her chin. Her mind churned. He was not the only one who could be annoying and he was not the only one who could play this game. It remained only for her to discover his weakness and exploit it. No doubt he had more than one, but she could start with the one she'd already had experience with. He had been careful not to drink very heavily tonight, but tomorrow . . .

Tomorrow, if she could restrain her temper, she would ply him with drink. He'd already admitted how important his business was with Mr. Cummings and the other guests. If he drank too much and made a fool of himself, Mr. Cummings would have to reprimand him and perhaps he'd send him packing. Fitting justice, Olivia decided. He would be exposed for the ruffian he truly was, and denied access to the society he sought.

And he would be sorry for the day he first crossed paths with Olivia Byrde.

CHAPTER

7

"I won! I won!" Augusta jumped up and down, for once forgetting her dignity. She grabbed Lord Holdsworth by the arm. "I won!"

He threw an arm around her with equal enthusiasm, for he, too, had wagered on the filly, Kittiwake. Beside them Penny Cummings and Mr. Garret joined in the victory toast. Of their entire party, only Olivia did not celebrate Lord Hawke's victory.

Like the others, she'd bet on his handsome filly. By her reckoning, she'd won close to ten pounds, no small sum, and for that she was grateful. But Lord Hawke had won far more than that, and she was not presently of a mind to wish him success.

"Oh, let us go down to the winner's circle," Augusta said, and in a moment the others all surged forward. But Olivia hung back.

She'd spent a restless night, tossing and turning and plagued by angry dreams. As before she'd risen early, though after dawn this time. On her way to breakfast she had impulsively peered into the library. She'd not known why. But when she spied the curtains open, the big chair turned to the window, and the chess set sitting at the table beside it, her fury at Lord Hawke had modified to a more confusing emotion.

She did not understand the man at all. Added to that, he seemed never to sleep. Frowning, she searched the crowd for him. She ought to go down and join the others. She was being petulant, yet she could not help it. For all her plotting in the night against the arrogant Lord Neville, following through was another matter altogether.

So she sat alone in the pavilion that Mr. Cummings had erected for the duration of the races, she and the two menservants tending to the small party.

Below she saw the excited filly prance up to the winner's circle. The jockey grinned and waved, then angled the animal toward Lord Hawke, who enthusiastically clapped the fellow on the back. Even when the throng closed in around them, Olivia could not mistake Neville Hawke. It was not just his height, or his night-dark hair, gleaming in the afternoon sunlight. There was something about him, some presence, some sense of authority and command.

Then she recalled what Sally had said. He had been a military man, a war hero.

She stared harder at him, oblivious to the dust swirling in little eddies, or the constant hum and flow of people around the oval racetrack. Somewhere a dog yapped. A horse whinnied and the smell of stables and fried pies wafted over all. But Olivia focused solely on Neville Hawke.

The man sat up all night. He flaunted all the rules of society. And he did not behave at all like the other war veterans she'd met who were wont to go on and on about their wartime exploits. Not Neville Hawke. Despite his arrogant manners and supreme self-confidence—despite the fact that he was said to be a hero of the battle at Ligny—he did not boast of his war accomplishments. To her knowledge he hadn't made mention of his military career once since he'd arrived in Doncaster.

No doubt he'd had some horrifying experiences during those years. How could he not have? But some instinct told her there was more to it than that, something specific he did not like to recall. Perhaps she should make some inquiries. It was no more than she would do regarding any new man come on the scene, she told herself. Research for her little matchmaker. Besides, he had no qualms about tormenting her. Why should she hesitate to return the favor?

As she watched the jubilant crush below, she saw her mother make her way to Lord Hawke's side. He greeted her warmly and the others also, accepting their congratulations. He was quite the center of attention and appeared to play the part most graciously. Then he lifted his head and stared up at the pavilion, directly into Olivia's eyes.

The impact was stunning, and for a moment Olivia hesitated. She did not really wish to continue this conflict with him. What good could possibly come of it, save to mollify her insulted feelings?

Then he winked at her—winked at her!—and any inclination she had to relent vanished. The unmitigated gall of the man!

And when her mother, following the direction of his gaze, spied Olivia and smiled, Olivia's resolve became as fixed as that of a bull taunted by a waving red flag. He wanted to torment her? Well, she would teach him the meaning of the word.

So she smiled back and saw the faint arch of his dark brows. Then lifting her betting receipt in salute, she started toward him.

The crowd had begun to thin by the time she reached the jubilant circle around Lord Hawke and Kittiwake. Another race had been called and the betting queues soon would close.

Lord Hawke and Augusta were the only ones who took note of Olivia's arrival, and it was clear they both were pleased. His eyes glittered with mocking anticipation, her mother's with gleeful scheming.

"Olivia also bet upon your pretty filly," Augusta said, lightly tapping Lord Hawke's sleeve.

"Come, my dear," Lord Holdsworth said, steering Augusta away. "I'll show you where we collect our winnings. Remember," he added to Lord Hawke. "I made the first offer on this animal. I'm holding you to your promise not to sell her to anyone else—nor her first foal."

"I won't forget. You have my word as a gentleman."

It took all Olivia's will not to glare at him. His word as a gentleman? Hah!

As if he heard her very thoughts he smiled at her. Fortunately for Olivia, her mother interceded.

"Come. Give me your ticket, Olivia, and I'll collect your winnings for you. You'll keep her company while we're gone?" This last she directed to Lord Hawke.

"It will be my pleasure."

Olivia only gritted her teeth and smiled. She needed to have a heart-to-heart talk with her mother. Meanwhile, however, she must deal with Lord Hawke.

After Augusta and Lord Holdsworth and the others departed, the jockey slid down Kittiwake's rump and Lord Hawke turned to him.

"It was just like you said, milord. I pushed Dorsey—just sat with Kitti's nose at his animal's flank—and he panicked and went too early to the whip. Then in the end our girl came through with that kick of hers—" He broke off, shaking his head and grinning. "She's better than ever, milord. I could swear she was faster today e'en than yesterday."

Hawke took out his watch. "A second and a half faster than the trials." Then he clapped the tiny fellow on the back. "Go ahead and celebrate. Bart's holding a pint for you. I'll walk Kitti myself."

"Are you sure?" The jockey's eyes slanted toward Olivia.

Lord Hawke grinned. "Miss Byrde is mad for horses, or so her mother tells me." Then he asked her, "Will you walk Kitti with me?"

His voice sounded sincere, but his eyes, oh, how they mocked her. Olivia, however, was more than up for the challenge. Indeed, sparring with Neville Hawke and prying into his personal life might be the only thing to make the next three days interesting.

"Do not take my mother entirely at her word," Olivia replied. "For she is wont sometimes to exaggerate. To answer your question, however, yes, I will walk Kittiwake with you." She turned to the animal and rubbed the white streak of her forelock, amazed that she could sound so calm while her emotions churned. "Kitti is quite a remarkable girl. Will you run her again? I do believe she can best all the three-year-olds, not simply the fillies."

"Remind me to introduce you to my trainer," Lord Hawke

said as he took the reins from his rider. They turned away from the racecourse. "You and he are in complete agreement on that score."

"Why then, I'd say he sounds like an enlightened man, not underestimating the value of the female of the species."

He laughed. "There is no need to be subtle with me, Miss Byrde. I assume you refer to women now, not horses." That familiar one-sided smile curved his well-formed lips. "Be assured that I never underestimate women."

"No?" She allowed herself the same sort of smug smile. "And I never underestimate men."

"That is probably wise."

"It occurs to me," she continued, "that were I to know more of you, I might find attributes to cast you in a better light than our brief encounters have yet done. Certainly the past two nights' unpleasantries do not encourage me to either like you or trust you."

"But they did intrigue you, didn't they? 'Lord H. Tall and reasonably handsome. Proves the rule that looks can be deceiving,' " he quoted from her journal. When she sent a dagger-sharp glare his way, he laughed. "All right, then. I am encouraged that you wish to know me better."

Olivia did not respond to that. They had progressed far enough from the racecourse to be relatively alone now. Behind them the horn blew to call the next set of horses. Ahead of them the temporary horse stalls were only partially occupied. Kitti nickered and Olivia instinctively stroked her neck. As much as she mistrusted the man, there was a dark sort of pleasure to be had in this cat-and-mouse game they played. "I hope, Lord Hawke, that you will not lend some coarse interpretation to my simple request."

"Why not? Will that send you running away? It seems that my coarseness toward you is the only reason you are here now. Have you considered that?" He halted and turned to face her.

"Do not flatter yourself," she stated with a frankness unusual even for her. "It is merely a measure of my boredom." She met his bold gaze with a determined boldness of her own. Inside, however, she was quivering. Heavenly day, but he

could be incredibly beguiling when he set his mind to it. She
had better tread very carefully else he might actually suck her
in.

She gave a wave of her hand, and recklessly forged on.
"You are more entertaining than some men I have met. Unfortunately, you are also far more irritating."

"And yet you are here with me."

"So I am. As I said, I am bored."

"Then let me entertain you." That last was said in a husky
tone, low and most unsettling.

Olivia snapped open her fan and began briskly to ply it.
Oh, but he was beyond the limit! "I hardly know you," she
retorted. "And what little I do know does nothing to encourage
a continuation of our acquaintance. You drink too much; you
are not above seducing your host's household staff. You leap
to wild conclusions about completely innocent persons, and
you do not scruple to hold a person's private belongings hos-
tage. Oh, and lest I forget," she added with increasing asperity.
"You think it a prank to enter a person's private chambers and
pry among her personal possessions."

He had the good grace not to deny a word of her accusa-
tions, but not enough to appear in the least embarrassed. In
fact, he had the gall to grin at her. He spread his arms wide
in a gesture of innocence. "What can I do to redeem myself
in your estimation?"

"I doubt anything you do can alter my negative opinion of
you now."

"Then why are you here?" He smiled directly into her eyes.

Olivia swallowed hard and had to remind herself that it was
to put him in his place and no other reason. His seductive
manner meant nothing to her. Nor did his compelling eyes or
the charm he seemed able to turn on and off at will. She
snapped her fan shut. "As I said, I am bored here. Entertain
me with tales of your wastrel youth. Perhaps if I knew more
about you, I could build a case for empathy."

She turned and began again to walk, for her nerves were
stretched quite to the breaking point. He matched her pace and
the filly ambled between them.

"All I know of your past," she went on, "is that you have a great appreciation of horses and that you have come to Doncaster from lowland Scotland. Oh," she added, turning to watch his reaction. "And that you are a hero of the war on the Continent."

A shadow seemed to come over his face at that, and he stared straight ahead. But his voice, when he spoke, betrayed no emotion. "Say only that I fought in the war, not that I was a hero. The men who died are the heroes, not those of us who survived."

The words were bitter to hear, and like bile, must have been even more bitter to speak. Olivia felt an immediate stab of the empathy she'd jested of. "Does it pain you to speak of it?" she asked, her voice softening.

"Not particularly."

Liar. She studied him more closely. The erect carriage, the straight nose, the strong jawline with its curving scar. Despite his appearance of barely civilized masculinity, it struck her unexpectedly that there was something tragic about him. "Does that mean if I write in my journal that you bear the scars of war, both on your skin and in your heart, that you will not care?"

A muscle ticked just beneath that scar. "To what purpose do you keep notes on so many men in that book of yours? Do you plan to select your husband from among them? To weigh their merits and flaws and choose the best of the lot?"

When he glanced at her he looked angry, and it was her turn to look away.

"It is simply a hobby of mine, nothing more. I help the young women of my acquaintance weed out their suitors—and sometimes I steer them toward gentlemen they might otherwise overlook."

"Men like me?"

She met his mocking expression with a solemn mien. "At the moment I could not in good conscience steer any woman in your direction."

Their eyes held a long, disturbing moment. "Perhaps none

of the women of your acquaintance is the sort of woman I seek."

She dipped her head in acknowledgment of that possibility. "Does that mean you are seeking a wife? I assume you are unmarried."

He smiled. "You truly do think the worst of me, don't you? But yes, I am as yet unwed."

Olivia felt a perverse satisfaction which she firmly ignored. "And are you seeking to alter that state?"

"No."

"I see. And what of an heir? I should think your family eager for you to settle that issue."

"Are you prying, Miss Byrde?" Again he smiled, but there was a guarded look in his eyes.

She gave him a guileless smile in return. So, he did not like it when she inquired into his personal affairs. There was nothing that could have made her more tenacious. "But of course I am prying. How else am I to learn anything about you?"

He halted and studied her a moment. "Very well, then. My family history is no secret. My parents are deceased, as is my only brother. As for my heirs, why should I care who accedes to the Hawke barony? At that point I will not be around to judge them."

"I'm sorry about your family," she said, embarrassed now by her flippant questions. "I had heard something to that effect."

He shrugged. "They've been gone several years now. Besides, everyone dies someday."

He said it without any discernible emotion, and yet Olivia sensed a deep sorrow in him.

They had reached a line of trees that separated the town proper from a silvery stream of ice-cold water. But Lord Hawke continued on, following a narrow path into the shady bower. The docile filly, sensing water, pricked her ears forward, eager for the refreshment.

Olivia paused. They were completely alone and would be even more so beyond the trees. The fact that he had shown himself to be completely untrustworthy in such situations should have been sufficient to turn her right around. But the sun was shining, the stream beckoned, and she'd had quite enough of crowds. She glanced back toward the racecourse and the haze of dust that hung above it. By contrast, a bird somewhere ahead trilled an ode to life, and a pair of butterflies, one yellow, one orange and black, danced along the line between sunshine and shade.

The racecourse and all the people there were not so very far away, she reassured herself. Besides he was sober now, and she did not think him fool enough to risk losing the goodwill his horses had won him. At the moment he seemed willing to talk and she did not want to miss this chance.

So she hiked her skirt up a few inches and forged through the knee-high grasses. Once in the damp shade the grass gave way to arching ferns and, going deeper, to soft moss banks. He glanced over at her once, but it was too brief for her to read his expression.

Go back, the voice of reason warned her.

But curiosity urged her on. How had his parents and brother died, and why did he shy from marriage when it would be the perfect antidote to his loneliness? For one thing Olivia felt certain of: Neville Hawke was lonely. That was why he sat up at night and drank too much. Perhaps with her aid he could find the right woman to fill that void. Whoever she was, she would have to be a woman of considerable mettle and quite outside the bounds of normal society.

Olivia rolled her eyes at her own perversity. His tragic tale must be affecting her, for finding a wife for Lord Hawke had hardly been her intention when she set out to approach him today.

Then he ducked under a low-hanging oak branch, and in so doing, sent her that wicked one-sided grin of his. At once Olivia's foolish maunderings collided abruptly with reality. Neville Hawke needed no help finding a woman, and only an idiot would think otherwise. She should turn around at once— but if she were not going to do that, then she should at the least keep her purpose firmly before her. He had no reason to torment her, yet he chose to do so. It behooved her on behalf of decent women everywhere—be they maid or peeress or anything in between—to put him sharply in his place.

Her head was high as she came out into the clearing along the narrow streambed, and her purpose was firm. Just let him try anything with her and see how swiftly he was set down.

Kittiwake stood up to her hocks in the bright water as she took great draughts of its refreshing coolness. Olivia stared longingly at the handsome animal. How she wished she could wade barefoot through the stream, then leap onto Kitti for an exhilarating ride.

"Easy, girl. Not too fast," Lord Hawke said to the filly, tugging her away from the stream. The horse tossed her head and reached down for more, but he held her back, distracting her with a handful of grass. "Slow, Kitti. Let's cool you down slowly."

"It seems she has a mind of her own," Olivia said.

"Most interesting women do."

Was that steady gaze meant to imply that she was among that number? Olivia supposed she should appear taken in by his ploy. So she smiled, but her words remained focused on her goal. "Was your mother just such an interesting woman?"

After a moment he answered. "That's hard to say. Can a child ever see his parents clearly? Do you see yours clearly?"

"Perhaps. Perhaps not. You can form your own opinion about my mother. However, I can form no opinion of yours save, it seems, through you. You haven't answered my question, Lord Hawke."

"Why don't you call me Neville?"

"We are not sufficiently acquainted to warrant such familiarity."

"That can be arranged."

With those brief words and one potent look he made her stomach clench in a knot. She pulled a triplet leaf from an elder bush and twiddled it in her hand. "Are you trying to divert me from my question?"

One of his hands slid up and down Kitti's side. "It is you

who constantly diverts me, Olivia." He grinned. "Miss Byrde," he amended before she could correct him.

"Was your mother an interesting woman?" she repeated with some frustration.

He met her determined look, then finally shrugged. "My mother was a quiet person, concerned with family, propriety, and religion, in that order. She possessed all the skills a gentlewoman should and was a good wife and a good mother."

"But was she interesting?"

"My father thought so. The only cruelty he ever delivered her was that of dying before she could."

"Oh." Once again Olivia felt small and mean-spirited.

"He caught a cough he could not recover from. When he died she went into an immediate decline so that within months they were both gone."

"Were you still away at war?"

"No. I had returned." He averted his face.

Olivia bit her lower lip. He seemed deeply affected. "They must have been so proud of you," she offered. "At least you gave them that."

"Yes. I gave them that," he echoed, but there was a bitter cast to his words. "Shortly after their demise my older brother took a bad spill. He lingered two weeks, then died without ever regaining his senses. So you see, Miss Byrde." He raised his head and stared directly at her. "There is no one to care whether or not I marry, whether or not I produce an heir, and whether or not I behave as I ought."

He paused, then with unexpected candor added, "You should not be out here alone with me."

Olivia smiled with more confidence than she felt. "I suppose you are right. Since you have already accosted me twice, however, I suppose I grow jaded. Even you can only go so far in your efforts to shock me, so I feel relatively safe."

"Then again," he went on, a puzzled crease across his brow. "There is something curious about you. You are not like other young women of your set. You keep that perverse journal of yours. You wander about strange houses at night. Then you throw yourself in my path—with your mother's full encouragement, it seems. What is a man to think of all this? And now you quiz me about my family and my attitude toward marrying. That's more the behavior of an eager mother than a demure young lady. Are you so desperate to wed as all that, Olivia?" He came around Kitti so that they were but an arm's length apart. "Is there some secret you are keeping from me?"

For a moment she was baffled by his words. What secret could she have? If she was that eager to wed she would have done so long ago.

Then his gaze fell to her stomach and his meaning struck with painful clarity. She sucked in a horrified gasp. He thought she *needed* to wed? He thought she hid a secret that required a husband, and fast?

"Are you trying to trap me by compromising me?" he added, his eyes glittering with amusement.

It was that amusement at her expense which provided her some handhold on her temper. She crossed her arms and lifted her chin to a haughty angle. "You know you don't believe that, Lord Hawke. Your only purpose for making such ridiculous implications is to goad my temper."

He grinned. "Have I succeeded?"

"No." She shook her head. "You have not."

"I see. Well, perhaps this might do the trick." All at once he drew her against him, trapping her folded arms between them. "Are you angry yet?" He stared down into her eyes from a distance of mere inches.

"I'm getting there," Olivia muttered. She tried without success to pull away. Though his hold was not cruel, it was nonetheless implacable. "Let me go."

"Not yet." His face lowered. "You're not angry enough."

"Yes I am!" But Olivia's heart was racing more with fear and anticipation than with anger. "I am furious. Now let me go at once!"

"You need a little more goading, I think. Perhaps this—" Without warning his lips came down upon hers. Or perhaps there had been a warning, for she'd been warned away from him from their very first meeting, and every time thereafter. Nevertheless, she still was not prepared. She struggled, but only faintly, and only for a few brief moments.

When his lips moved and slanted for a closer fit, she forgot her anger. And when his arm wrapped around her shoulders, pulling her fully against him, she forgot to be afraid. When he nibbled her lower lip and teased her mouth open, then slid his tongue between her lips, Olivia felt a heated leap in her stomach and a frightening, compelling anticipation.

What would he do next?

What would she let him do?

CHAPTER

8

NEVILLE knew he was behaving badly. An innocent young woman of the ton was not the sort of woman a man was supposed to dally with. But Olivia Byrde's mouth was incredibly warm and incredibly soft, and it was plain she needed kissing. If her enthusiasm was any indication, she'd been hungry for just such a kiss a very long time.

So he kissed her, taking his time and doing a completely thorough job of it. She would not forget this kiss, he vowed as he tilted her backward in his arms. And she would have to write something very nice about him in that cursed journal she kept.

He slanted his mouth against hers, nibbling and probing. He felt the moment her lips parted, and felt no shame for delving deeper. She tasted like honey, like sunshine. It was enough to make a man drunk with desire, and he was not one to deny himself.

So he took full possession of her mouth, thrusting deeper and more insistently than he should. The fact that she curled her fingers around his lapels did nothing to discourage him. Boldly he stroked in and out, the intimate kiss of lovers.

Only when his arousal demanded the same sort of rhythm from his lower parts did he regain some portion of his senses. With a groan he reined in his rampaging emotions, raised his head, and stared down into her dazed eyes. "Is that what you wanted from me, Olivia? Is that why you have followed me here to this private place?"

As he looked down at her flushed face and the fullness of her delicious mouth, he had to stifle an oath. One kiss was not enough. But as he lowered his head for another sweet taste of her, she seemed finally to come to her senses.

"No!" She twisted her head to avoid his lips, then pushed away and stumbled back nearly to the water's edge, managing somehow to look properly insulted and temptingly disheveled, all at the same time.

"No," she repeated, raising one hand tentatively to her mouth. Her voice was low and shaky. "I think you've taken sufficient advantage of me for one day."

"I took advantage of you?" He laughed, determined to make her accept some portion of responsibility for their current situation. "Haven't you got that turned around?"

"Me?"

Neville was fascinated by the play of emotions on her expressive face. From fledgling arousal to humiliation to fury, her feelings tumbled pell-mell, darkening her eyes, pinkening her cheeks, and flustering her completely. She took a deep breath, then another, and he could not help admiring how well she filled out the cream-colored muslin of her bodice.

"You think I have taken advantage of you?" she sputtered. "I have taken advantage of *you*?"

"Haven't you?" He crossed his arms across his chest, enjoying himself as he had not done in years. "You followed me here of your own accord. Indeed, it would almost seem you have a hidden purpose. If it is not to trap a husband, then my second guess is that you hope to gain a paramour."

"Oh!" She stamped her foot. "You are absolutely the limit!"

"Not that either? Hmm." He frowned. "That leaves me with but one conclusion. I'm merely research for that little journal you keep, aren't I? What will you write this time? Lord H. Aggravating, but he kisses so well."

Was that a flash of guilt in her eyes? She averted her gaze too swiftly for him to be certain.

"I have no intention of listening to any more of this." She lifted her skirts and clambered up the sloping green bank, angling carefully around him. "Do not invite me to dance this evening, Lord Hawke, lest you are prepared to be rebuffed. I do not wish to continue my acquaintance with you."

"How shall you avoid it, I wonder?"

"I shall manage."

"What of your sojourn in Scotland?"

She whirled around and glared at him. "What of it? I can imagine no occasion when I will invite you to Byrde Manor, nor any reason to call upon you in your abode. So you see, we are done."

But Olivia's determined avowal only increased Neville's grin. He watched her storm away, head high and long, angry strides. She looked just as good from the back as she did from the front. No, they were not done, he and the redoubtable Miss Byrde, though he knew he trod on dangerous ground. If it was land leases he wanted from her, he was not pursuing them in a very logical manner. Yet he seemed unable to prevent himself from baiting her. Or from kissing her.

It was not lost on him that he took greater pleasure from this woman's rejection than he had from any other woman's welcome. But he'd long ago ceased to wonder at the paradox that was his life. Hailed a hero, yet in truth a traitor. Widely admired, yet consumed with self-hatred.

It was fitting that he be enamored of the first woman who despised him. But Olivia was as much a paradox as he, sometimes the proper Miss Byrde, other times his earthy Hazel. She was not like the other women of her set—like her mother or Penny Cummings or a hundred others of that ilk. Pretty baubles, the most of them, with no thought beyond the next party and what they would wear to it.

But Olivia was more opinionated, more spirited. And like him, she seemed to view society with a jaundiced eye.

His gaze tracked her departure until the trees hid her beautiful, prickly image from view. He should honor her request and simply avoid her.

But Neville knew he would not do that. He would pursue her and torment her and convince her to kiss him again. Eventually she would give him that lease. As for the future beyond that, he could not say. His life unfolded as it would, hideous nights, bearable days, and occasionally, like today, a flash of true brightness.

How could he turn his back on another chance to bask in that light?

Olivia thrashed through a bed of ferns and stomped up the narrow woodland path, jerking her skirts when they caught on a tuft of grass or a holly branch. He was without a doubt the most unpleasant, debauched clod she'd ever had the displeasure to know!

But he kisses very well.

She stumbled over a projecting oak root and only prevented herself falling by grabbing on to the tree. In the process, however, her glove ripped and she swore as no proper lady should. She stared at her new kidskin glove and the irreparable tear in the palm. Another crime to lay at Lord Hawke's door.

He still kisses very well, the mocking voice of her conscience said.

"I am *not* writing that in my matchmaker!"

A gray squirrel scolded her from the safety of the spreading oak, and a pair of sparrows darted away as if annoyed by her blundering into their heretofore peaceful home.

"I despise him," she threw defiantly at the disapproving birds. The fact that he knew his boldly taken kiss had melted every ounce of her resistance only made her dislike him more. A man was not born knowing how to kiss like that. He learned through extensive practice, and that meant loose women, lusty barmaids, overfriendly housemaids, and the like.

She started forward again, only glancing briefly backward to assure herself he did not follow. Truly, he was the most odious man alive—even if his kisses did curl her toes.

By the time she approached the racecourse, Olivia had regained a moderate control of her temper. Unfortunately, the other emotions her anger had suppressed rose promptly to the surface. Like a shadow she could not outrun, the memory of his every touch clung to her. It prickled in the places his strong hands had held her. It burned where the two of them had pressed together, knees to belly to chest. She'd felt his arousal against her stomach, and just remembering it set her nerves all ajangle.

Then there was that kiss.

Olivia came to a halt just beyond the tented pavilion and pressed the back of one hand against her lips, feeling the heightened sensitivity there. She'd never been kissed like that. Never. Raphael St. Julian had forced his tongue into her mouth once. But though she'd been curious about the much-discussed French manner of kissing, her primary reaction had been revulsion.

Neville Hawke's kiss, however, had not repulsed her. It should have, but it had not.

She licked her lips, then groaned at the unbidden thrill that swept like wildfire through her. She was behaving like a wanton, like the lowest sort of woman, and she was heartily ashamed of herself.

But she was made of sterner stuff than that, she told herself. She tucked a stray curl behind the ribbon that held her straw bonnet in place. Lord Hawke may have won this round in the absurd battle of wills they fought, but he would not win the war. Like every other well-bred young woman, she knew how to freeze a man, and she was not above giving him the cut direct.

"Oh, there you are!"

Olivia's head jerked up at the abrupt sound of her mother's voice. Of all times to run into her. Worse, she was arm in arm with Penny Cummings.

"Where is Lord Hawke?" Penny asked, her eyes sly upon Olivia.

"I believe he is still walking his horse. How much did you win?" she asked, deliberately turning her attention to her mother.

"Seven pounds. And Penny won the same. But you, my dear, won more than anyone. Ten pounds. Here you go." She handed Olivia a little sack of coins tied up in one of her lace handkerchiefs. "How wise of you to stake so much of your quarterly allowance on Lord Hawke."

Penny's knowing expression and her mother's eagerly raised brows were the only things that prevented a sharp retort. As it was, Olivia could not take that broad hint without some sort of reply. "It was the horse, not the man, that I committed my funds to. I have always felt a partiality to strong-willed females, no matter the species."

Augusta's bright blue eyes searched Olivia's face. She gave a pleased smile. "Go on without me, Penny. I would have a private word with my daughter."

Olivia frowned. Penny laughed. "You should be glad of your dear mother's concerns," she said. "She merely hopes to gain you an advantageous marriage without ruining your reputation in the process." Then she looked past them. "Oh, and here comes Lord Hawke."

As Penny minced away in the man's direction, Olivia sent a baleful glare at the woman's back. "Look to your own reputation," she muttered.

"Now, now. That is rather ungrateful of you, Olivia. As our hostess—and Lord Hawke's—it becomes dear Penny's responsibility to ensure the complete propriety of all within her household."

"How fortunate I am," Olivia tartly replied, "to have two matrons overseeing my every move."

"I'll thank you not to use that word in reference to me." Augusta raised her chin and rearranged the lacy shawl that lay across her shoulders. "It sounds so old and, well, matronly."

"And you most certainly are not that, right, Mother?" Olivia glanced past her to where Penny now strolled alongside Neville Hawke and his lovely racehorse. "Honestly, I do not understand why you are so anxious to remarry. Dealing with men can be so unbearable."

Following her daughter's gaze, Augusta smiled, then hooked her arm through Olivia's. "Do I detect a partiality toward Lord Hawke? He is a rather compelling young man."

Olivia wanted to be sharp and cutting in her rejection of the man, but her mother's warm concern was her undoing. She gave a great sigh as they started for the pavilion. "He can be compelling. I will grant you that. But he is also arrogant and aggravating, and extremely high-handed."

"Has he tried to kiss you?"

"Mother!" Olivia tried to sound appalled at the very idea.

But the color that flamed in her cheeks gave her away. "Oh, Mother." She sighed again. "It doesn't matter if he did or did not. He is not the sort of man I can be interested in."

"You say that about every man you meet."

"Very well, then. Will you believe me when I say he is the antithesis of everything I require in a husband?"

Augusta patted her arm. "My, my. Such strength of feeling he rouses in you."

Olivia turned to her mother. "I hate it when you deliberately misconstrue my words."

Augusta gave an elegant shrug that conceded nothing. "It is only that you and he seem so well suited in age and fortune and rank. Even your lands run together. Added to that, you look very well together. Everyone commented on it when the two of you danced together last night."

Olivia shook her head. She did not want to hear such things. "Yes, he dances well. He is also handsome enough, in a dark and brooding sort of way, and he loves horses and the outdoors. You're right. On the surface we appear very well suited. But he also drinks too much and is far too knowledgeable about women. In short, he is a rake of the worst sort and not to be trusted."

After that heated dialogue Augusta regarded her a long, pensive moment. "It seems you have made quite a study of Lord Hawke. You must admit, however, that he sounds quite unlike all the other suitors you have rejected." She smiled in a satisfied manner.

"And what do you imply from that? No, never mind. You just don't understand." Angry, Olivia pursed her lips and did not pause to consider her next words. "Perhaps this will make it clearer to you. Lord Hawke is just like my father. Dashing, dangerous, and not the sort of man a wise woman would marry—if, indeed, he even has marriage in mind."

Olivia did not linger to hear Augusta's response to that. The shocked expression on her mother's face was sufficient to know she'd made her point. They did not often discuss her father, for Augusta tended to ignore the man's faults, and that generally caused Olivia to magnify them.

She strode determinedly toward the little market that had sprung up in Doncaster's town green, determined to avoid Penny, her mother, and the impossible Neville Hawke. Untying her bonnet, she let it fall and dangle at her back—a rather unladylike gesture. But she did not care. At least now her mother would drop the subject of Lord Hawke, for above all things, her mother disliked arguing about Cameron Byrde.

The strings of Olivia's reticule cut into her wrist as she walked, and it swung in rhythmic thumps against her thigh. It was heavy with the weight of her winnings. She had Lord Hawke with his fast hands and bold ways to thank for her fattened purse, and it galled her to no end.

She would spend it, she decided on the spot. She would spend every last shilling and purchase frivolous things that he could not possibly approve of.

That was stupid, she immediately decided. Frivolity was all he understood. Drinking and loose women and wagering large sums of money on horse races. No, she amended. Better to spend her winnings sensibly, on items that enlightened the mind.

She scanned the festive arc of market stalls and the regular shops beyond them. Ribbons of every hue fluttered, creating a rainbow. The scent of roses and lavender and honeysuckle alerted her to the perfumers' corner. A young boy shouted the benefits of Dr. Smythe's Universal Antidote, while a woman exhorted a man to purchase a posy for his sweetheart. There were pastries and fried pies and ale and punch and wine. She spied Irish linens and Scottish wools, and garments beaded in the far-off Orient.

There was every sort of vendor in town for the races and Olivia's eyes ran restlessly over their booths, seeing everything and rejecting all. Then her gaze landed on a table laden with books and she headed straightaway for it. Her ten pounds in winnings could purchase more books than she could ever carry. Perfect.

By the time Olivia had made her purchases the sun had begun its descent to the horizon, the next two races had been run, and the bookseller was giddy with delight. "I'll send a boy with your purchases directly, miss."

"I'm staying with the Cummingses," she said. She'd spent eight pounds ten, and she held out her hand for the change.

When he glanced at her torn glove he bobbed his head. "Begging your pardon, miss, but my wife's brother has a leather goods stall around t'other side."

Olivia folded her fingers in a fist around the tear, for it reminded her of her flight from Lord Hawke and their kiss. She pressed her lips together and trembled at the disturbing memory. She did not want to remember that, or anything else having to do with that man. Unfortunately, everything seemed to remind her of him.

"Thank you," she said, as she turned away from the bookseller. She sighed, then bolstered her spirits with spite. Perhaps she should purchase something for Lord Hawke to remember her by—the one woman who was not taken in by his dashing manner. She allowed herself to indulge in that fantasy. A gift that would transmit her utter disdain to him. What could it be?

A bottle of cheap wine.

She grimaced. Though that was perfect, it would only make her look as low as him. Better to ignore him, she decided, and to brace herself for his ill behavior tonight. Despite her warning that she would not dance with him again, she did not put it past him to try to force the issue.

The change jingled in Olivia's reticule as she returned to the pavilion, irritating her. She would give it to the poor box in the village church, she decided. Then she spied a fine gray gelding being led by its trainer and she had a better idea. She would bet it on Lord Hawke's opponents and deposit all those winnings in the poor box.

And if the blasted man did not lose?

Olivia opened her hand and stared at the torn palm of her glove. He could not win every race. His horses could not all be that fast.

Kittiwake was, though. Olivia climbed the three steps up into the raised pavilion. That filly was as fine an animal as she'd ever seen. There was no way she could lay a wager against Kitti. In truth, she wouldn't mind owning the spirited animal herself.

But that was out of the question. She would no more do business with Neville Hawke than she would dance with him again.

Or kiss him.

CHAPTER

9

NEVILLE groomed Kestrel with a vengeance, paying close attention to the big animal's mane and tail, until the horse snorted and stamped in impatience.

"Easy, lad," Neville murmured, then shifted just before the horse struck out with its near back leg. "Easy, lad. I'm going. I'm going."

"He's more than ready to run," Bart commented, leaning over the stall wall and hanging a bucket of oats on a recessed hook.

"Tomorrow he'll have his chance." Neville slipped out of the stall, then hooked his arms over the gate and stood as Bart did, staring at the magnificent stallion.

"How are you managing?" Bart asked after a while.

"Well enough. And you?"

"Never better, though I'll be pleased to return home."

"You miss Maisie?" Bart was ten years married to Woodford's cook.

"Aye. And the little ones." When Neville did not say anything, Bart cleared his throat. "Have you never thought of marrying, milord?" He ducked his head when Neville shot him a sharp look.

"I've thought about it."

Another long silence ensued and Bart shifted. He was nervous, Neville realized. As well he should be. While their relationship was much closer than lord and hired man, there were some boundaries they'd never crossed. But today for some reason the man seemed determined to push those boundaries and broach the subject of marriage.

"Meself, I've never been so content," the horse trainer forged on. "What with a woman welcoming me home with a good meal, and the children all eager for their father's attention." He spat into the straw. "That kind of homecoming, well, it makes even a poor man feel like a king."

Neville turned and faced his trainer. "Out with it, Bart. What bush are you beating around?"

Bart stared at him without blinking. "If you wed, you might be able to sleep in the night. If you had a woman to lose yourself in—a good woman, not merely a convenient one— you might sate yourself with her instead of whisky. You might find peace that way, lad."

Neville had stiffened at the first mention of his night miseries. The reference to his drinking only riled him more. But this was Bart, a good and loyal employee. With an effort Neville tempered his response. "Your concern is noted."

When he turned to leave, however, Bart continued. "It's not only me as is concerned."

Slowly Neville pivoted, his jaw clenched. "Am I to understand that my personal habits are discussed among the people I employ at Woodford?"

Neville had faced down many a man with just such a dark glare and dangerously soft words. But Bart did not back down. His face blanched and his throat convulsed in a swallow, but he did not back down. "Your habits, as you say, are sometimes discussed by those who work for you—but only by those who care for you beyond their quarter day wages."

Simple words, and Neville could not in good faith doubt their sincerity. He exhaled slowly and rubbed the back of his neck. He would not be angry at the man's well-meant interference. "I thank you for your concern, Bart. But I'm not sure a woman is the answer to my problems."

"What of Miss Byrde, her being your neighbor after a fashion?"

Neville shook his head in amazement. "Have you been spying on me?"

Bart smiled faintly. "A blind man could see the attraction between the two of you. And I ain't blind."

Again Neville rubbed the back of his neck. "I don't think she holds a charitable opinion about me."

"You didn't insult the girl, did you? She's a lady—"

"She can take care of herself."

Bart's gaze narrowed. "If you want a woman to like you, you can't begin by treatin' her like some casual bit of—"

"I'm not looking for a wife!"

"Well, you should be."

"That's enough, damn you!" Neville caught a shuddering breath. "That's enough on that subject." They faced one another across the shadowed center aisle of the Cummingses' ancient stable. "Tend to the horses. I've other matters to occupy my mind."

When Bart did not answer back, Neville gave a curt nod and strode away. But the horse trainer seemed determined to have the last word. For when Neville reached the archway that led to the paddock he heard the man call out.

"Waltz with her. They act scandalized but all the women love waltzing. Waltz her, lad."

Neville fortified himself with a glass of brandy, but just one. He'd made a point to limit his drinking after his first night at Doncaster. Ever since his earlier conversation with Bart, however, he'd been consumed with a restless sort of energy. The sun neared the horizon. Already the common folk drifted toward the town square where the public dance was to be held. It was rare, a dance attended by peer and drudge alike. Silks would mingle with fustian. Embroidered slippers would dance to the same music as freshly cleaned work boots.

Had the queenly Miss Byrde ever joined in so lusty a celebration as this annual dance was purported to be? Though there was more than one area designated for dancing, and like tended to gather with like, Cummings had made it clear to his male guests that this was a rougher sort of dance than the ladies would be accustomed to. But that was its appeal, it seemed, and it was always well attended. It fell to the men of their party to ensure that no woman was ever left alone.

Neville combed his hair and retied his stock. He would

make certain that Miss Byrde was adequately chaperoned. Let her fume and stamp her foot and flash her amber-green eyes at him. He would not care. In fact, he anticipated the release of her temper with great eagerness. There was a mighty passion held in check beneath her properly sophisticated demeanor, and he seemed driven to see it released.

He paused and bent to stare at himself in the looking glass. Why was he doing this? Why had he fixed his attentions on her, when no other woman had compelled him this way since he was a green lad? It was more than the land lease, otherwise he would never have acted so recklessly toward her. If all he wanted was the lease of her properties, he would not have left that note in her journal, nor would he have kissed her so thoroughly by the stream.

Just to remember that kiss and her artless response to it caused his blood to warm.

No. It was not merely the lease. He wanted the woman too, fool that he was. And she wanted him. Bart had said a blind man could see the attraction between him and Olivia.

He pondered that a moment, then allowed himself to consider the rest of what Bart had said: that a wife might ease his nightmares; that a woman in his bed each night might give him the relief he sought. The distraction. The satisfaction.

Neville stared at himself, seeing the face so like his father's—and the scar on his jaw, a constant reminder of that fateful night in Ligny. He turned away and spying his tumbler, lifted it once more.

If he were a gentleman he would stay away from Miss Olivia Byrde. Then he laughed. If he were a true gentleman, there would be no reason to stay away. He would be perfectly acceptable to her and her mother.

But he was no gentleman. Once he might have been, but he was that man no longer. And he was not in the market for a wife.

He finished the brandy slowly, savoring its heat and bite, and anticipating the easing of his tension that would shortly follow.

He set the tumbler down. Bart had overstepped his bounds

this afternoon, but he'd been right about one thing. Women loved the waltz. He'd learned the dance in France, and though he'd not danced it recently, as with last night's cotillion, the steps would come back to him.

He would waltz with Olivia tonight, he vowed, bolstered by the brandy that surged through his bloodstream. She would avoid him, he would pursue her, but in the end she would be in his arms, sweet and yielding, as she'd been today beside the stream. Just the thought roused an unseemly lust in him.

But they would not end up in bed together, he reminded himself. That was out of the question. She was, after all, a lady. Unfortunately. Added to that, ruining her would ruin any hope he had of leasing her fallow fields and pastures.

Still, if he could tempt her, just a little, he would consider the night a success. He would expose her passions to her so that she would have to admit their existence. She might tell herself now that she despised him, but soon enough she would have to admit to her desire.

Even Bart knew that.

"You are coming, and that is my final word on the subject," Augusta declared. "You have no call to slight the Cummingses that way when they have been nothing but hospitable."

Olivia glared at her mother, hating that she was right.

"Besides," Augusta went on. "Penny tells me this public dance verges on the scandalous, what with it being open to everyone in the entire countryside. I should think it quite your cup of tea."

This time Olivia turned away. Again her mother was right. She would be quite ecstatic over this evening's entertainment if it were not for Lord Neville Hawke. And the worst of it was, that though she would be mortified to face him again, a part of her—the wickedest part of her—wanted to see him.

She pressed her fingers against her eyes, willing herself to a calm she'd been unable to attain all evening, ever since he'd kissed her.

Why on earth had she followed him to that private spot beside the river? Why had she let herself be alone with him, knowing the perverse attraction she felt for the man?

Because she'd thought reason well able to combat the primitive passion he roused in her.

She let out a sigh. She was not a stupid woman, nor a frivolous one, so there was no excuse for such infantile behavior. Goodness, she'd had three seasons. If nothing else, she'd learned how to handle unwelcome suitors. Not that he was acting remotely like a suitor. Rather, he was behaving like a boor. A wretch. One of those vile men with no good intentions, only bad ones.

But he was so very good at kissing.

"Olivia! I am speaking to you."

Olivia shuddered back to reality. Her mother would not give up until Olivia either went along with her plans or else explained precisely why she would not. And even if Olivia did try to explain about Lord Hawke, Augusta would probably advise her to encourage the man. If it was Augusta who kept a notebook on eligible men, she would consider Neville Hawke perfect: handsome and dashing, with both title and property.

Olivia picked up her hairbrush. "I heard you, Mother. I just didn't like what you said."

"When have you learned to be so willful toward your mother?"

"I'm sorry." Olivia sighed again. "You are right. I have no reason to avoid tonight's festivities. But promise me one thing, Mother. Please? Promise me you will not push any men at me tonight."

Augusta paused in the act of fastening a bracelet over her glove. She cocked her head and studied her daughter. "If you refer to Lord Hawke, as I think you must, I doubt I need push him at you. He seems interested enough without encouragement from me." At Olivia's stubborn expression, her eyes narrowed. "I cannot understand how you can possibly find him unacceptable!"

Olivia could have groaned. She did not want to have this conversation. "As always you jump to conclusions," she said peevishly. "I was not referring specifically to him. It's just that

I left London because the marriage mart has become so tedious. I certainly do not wish it to follow me here."

Augusta returned her attention to her bracelet. "Very well, then. I will refrain from introducing you to any unmarried gentlemen. Is that what you want? Only you must indulge me by answering one question. Just one. Agreed?"

Olivia gritted her teeth. What a choice. But one question was easier than an evening dodging her mother's machinations. "Just one."

"Very well. Here it is." She lifted her head and fixed Olivia with a wounded gaze. "Do you intend never to wed? Have you set your standards so impossibly high that no man can ever hope to meet them?" She pressed her clasped hands to her chest. "Have I wasted the past three years in futile hope? For I assure you, I do not wish to waste another three."

That was hardly what she had expected, and for a moment Olivia was nonplussed. "That's more than one question," she replied in lieu of answering.

"Perhaps, but they are essentially the same. Tell me the truth, Olivia, for I grow weary of this game you play."

Olivia bowed her head. How to answer? "Yes. I do wish to marry someday. But when I wed it will be to a man I love."

Augusta drew back. "That sounds like an accusation. Do you think I did not marry for love?"

Olivia could have groaned. As usual her mother turned everything around to focus upon herself. "That's not what I meant, Mother."

Augusta sniffed. "Yes. Well, you should nevertheless know that I loved all my husbands, though perhaps each of them in a different way." She stared into the distance. "George was much older, but he was a dear and very good to me. Your father, well, he was wild. I'll admit that. But I loved him passionately. As for Humphrey, surely you cannot doubt my love for him."

"No, of course not. It's just . . ." Olivia wrung her hands. "I just don't want to make a mistake. I want to be sure."

"What you want, my darling, is the perfect man. Unfortunately, the perfect man does not exist. But I suppose you must determine that for yourself." She came up to Olivia and softly patted her cheek. "Come along now. Finish dressing your hair. And do not wear your best slippers, for there will be dirt and mud."

Olivia nodded and focused on dressing for the evening's activities. Their conversation had not been as difficult as she'd feared, yet it nonetheless left her dispirited. Was she seeking the impossible? Was it too much to expect a man to be steady and kind and well read? Surely not. It was just that she'd been searching in the wrong places. And since when had love become a requirement of marriage for her?

With a heavy sigh she stuck a pair of glittering combs in her hair. She would have a pleasant time tonight and not worry about it, she resolved. Nor would she worry about Lord Hawke, she told herself.

At least she would try.

The three women rode in the carriage with Mr. Cummings. Mr. Garret, Mr. Harrington, Lord Holdsworth, and Lord Hawke all rode attendance on horses beside them on the short trip into town. Even so, Olivia was relieved not to have to face Lord Hawke yet. Instead she concentrated her thoughts on the other men, trying to drum up some enthusiasm for them, to no avail.

Once in town there was much to distract her. The entire square was lit with torches, and in the center of all was a raised platform for the musicians. Around the perimeter refreshments were placed, punch in one area, wine and brandy elsewhere, and at one corner, the ale carts.

"You ladies should confine your activities to this area between the musicians and the punch tables," Mr. Cummings instructed them. "None of the rowdies will be allowed in here."

"I should like to make a tour of the other areas, to see the maids and stablemen dancing. And the vicar," Olivia added with a faint grin.

"And we shall do so," Penny said. "That's all a part of the fun. But only as a group," she cautioned. "Do not go off alone, Olivia. You must promise me that."

"I assure you, I am no more eager to expose myself to the unwelcome attention of a shop clerk than to that of a peer."

Penny's brows lifted at that remark, but Olivia just turned away and took a deep breath. She was glad now that she had come. The evening air was redolent of torch smoke and summer dust, of earthy horses and forbidden French perfumes. From all directions people streamed into the square, every one of them dressed in their best.

A trio of young women strolled arm in arm. Probably merchants' daughters or housemaids, but Olivia stared after them, envious. They were laughing and shooting flirtatious looks at a stand of eager young men, most of whom appeared uncomfortable in starched collars and freshly slicked-back hair. But one sharp fellow hooted and called, "Say, Annie, will you save a dance for me?"

That sent the girls into gales of laughter. But the center girl, Annie, Olivia presumed, gave a nod, which started all the fellows cackling and punching one another in the arms as they laughed.

Olivia reluctantly turned away. Oh, to be that free, to choose a man based on nothing more than her sincere interest in him.

Penny clucked her disapproval at the casualness of the young people's exchange. But Augusta laughed with enjoyment. In her mother's eyes Olivia spied the sparkle that drew men so eagerly to her side. It struck her suddenly that her mother truly adored men. She saw the good in them first, whereas Olivia, always focused first upon their flaws.

Across the way the musicians had begun to warm up, but Olivia was too caught up in her sudden revelation to notice. If she meant what she told her mother about hoping someday to marry, then perhaps she must begin to follow her mother's lead. She must strive to see the good in the men she met and not simply catalogue their flaws.

Someone jostled her from behind and she stumbled to the side—only to be caught by a strong hand on her arm. The heat of that grasp should have warned her. Nevertheless it was a shock to stare up into Neville Hawke's darkly handsome face.

"Will you dance with me, Olivia? Despite your anger with me and your hasty words, I still would like to dance with you. And I believe you wish the same from me."

She did. It was humiliating—it was unimaginable. But Olivia did want to dance with him. Or at least her body did, traitorous creature that it was. She stared up into his fathomless blue eyes, almost black tonight, and felt every fiber of her being strain to fall into his arms. Only her pride and the remnants of good sense prevented her from doing just that.

"I believe . . . I believe I have already made my feelings clear on the subject. Anyway," she added, remembering only belatedly to extricate her arm from his firm hold, "I wish to stroll around first. And besides, the musicians have not yet begun."

He smiled, making it impossible for her to tear her gaze away from his. She was aware of her mother very near, watching them, and of Penny whispering something to her husband. But Olivia was trapped in Neville Hawke's intent gaze.

"I ask only for one dance, Miss Byrde. Surely you are not so heartless as to deny me that humble request."

Olivia's heart thundered; her mouth had become dry and thick. Like an idiot she could neither reason nor speak. Then someone nudged her—her mother?—and her senses began once more to function. After their candid conversation, was her mother already pushing her at a man Olivia could not want? She was so close to him now that she could smell the soap he'd used, and the brandy he'd drunk. Brandy. He was drinking again. It was just the fuel her flagging resolve needed.

"But I am heartless," she said. "Anyone in London could tell you that. I'm surprised you have not already determined as much. If you will excuse me?" And just that rudely she turned her back on him.

There was a little gasp. Olivia did not know from whom. But it was not from Neville Hawke. From him came only silence.

Olivia wanted to slink away, she was that ashamed of her

rudeness. But he deserved it. She tugged at her trailing satin-edged shawl. She'd warned him not to ask her to dance but he'd been too arrogant to believe her. He deserved the set-down she'd just given him, she told herself. He did.

But as the evening's gaieties began in earnest, Olivia could take no comfort in the rightness of her behavior. The music began, lively, raucous tunes, and it seemed that everyone participated in the dancing. Her mother and Penny never sat down. They scarcely had a chance to finish a glass of punch between sets. All the men of their group danced with them, and several other gentlemen they knew—everyone, that is, except Lord Hawke.

As Olivia circulated, morose in her chats with varying acquaintances, she tried not to search for him. But she could not help it. He was nowhere to be seen. Surely her slight had not wounded him so deeply as all that.

It didn't matter, she told herself as her gaze swept restlessly across the mass of gentlemen and ladies queuing up for a country line dance. Even if he were wounded, he would take consolation with his brandy or whisky, or even ale. She had no reason to think twice about him.

But try as she might, Olivia could muster no enthusiasm. She danced once, with Mr. Garret. But she was not a good partner and decided to spare any others the ignominy of her company. Perhaps another glass of punch.

As a galop began she backed up and circled around the dancers who were becoming more energetic as the evening wore on. The line of onlookers was thin between the group of gentlemen and ladies she was a part of, and the merchants and shopkeepers dancing in their own circle behind her. She bumped into someone and turned around to apologize, then stood watching this less finely dressed circle of dancers.

There was the girl she'd seen before, dancing with that same eager fellow. The girl's hair had come loose and her wheat-colored locks flew prettily around her shoulders. Her eyes sparkled and her cheeks glowed warm from the dancing. As for the fellow, he gazed down upon her with a look halfway between possessive man and smitten boy. There was no mistaking the attraction between them and Olivia could not help but follow their progress through the dance.

Was that what her mother had seen when she'd watched Olivia dance with Lord Hawke? Olivia's own cheeks grew warm. Surely not!

She stood there watching until the galop ended. But before the dancers could depart the dance area, another song struck up. This time a waltz. As Olivia watched, the young man spun the pretty girl into his arms—

And just as swiftly, someone did the same to her. Lord Hawke! One of his arms circled her waist; his free hand enveloped hers, and within a few mad moments they were a part of the swirling mass of dancers.

This could not be happening!

Yet Olivia could find no words to protest. The music was too insistent. Her mood was too mercurial. Or perhaps she knew the relentless Lord Hawke would not release her no matter what she said or did. At any rate, Olivia found herself clasped in Lord Hawke's implacable embrace, whirling to the frankly seductive music amidst an amorous crowd of complete strangers, and all the while staring up into the darkest, most compelling eyes she had ever beheld.

"If Miss Byrde will not dance with me," he murmured, "I'm glad to seek out sweet Hazel among the common folk."

With an effort Olivia averted her eyes from his and instead stared at his jaw and the scars that ran alongside it. Bad enough that she'd allowed him this liberty. She refused to appear a tongue-tied idiot. With an effort she marshaled her wits. "I've heard it said that the element of surprise is a key tool in military strategy." She watched in fascination as his mouth curved into a half-smile.

"It is."

"And you have much experience in the military."

"You might say that." His voice sounded more careful.

She raised her gaze to his. "I hear also that one battle does not constitute a war."

One of his dark brows arched. "We are speaking of you and me now, I presume."

She shrugged.

"Be forewarned, Hazel, that one battle can turn the tide."

Before she could respond he spun her around and in the process pulled her close so that their thighs bumped and his chest grazed her breasts. At once every nerve in her body went on alert. She was hot and breathless and she did not know if it was the dancing or the man.

"You take liberties you should not."

"Isn't that what you've come to expect of me?" His voice lowered. "Isn't that what attracts you to me?"

"If I am attracted to you, Lord Hawke, it is in the same manner that I am attracted to any tragedy: a house on fire; a carriage mishap."

He laughed at that. "A house on fire?"

But she only continued more heatedly. "Yes, or a carriage mishap. One cannot help but stare and hope never to experience such misfortune oneself."

"Too late, Hazel." He spun her out of the dance circle, his hand firm on her waist. Before she knew it, they were in a darkened alley between a cobbler's shop and an empty wagon. "Too late, Hazel, I'm afraid misfortune has found you after all."

CHAPTER

10

"IF you kiss me again I shall . . . I shall scream," Olivia blustered.

"I'm willing to take that chance."

Olivia's heart, already racing from the dance, increased to a painful rate. "You are worse than I thought. No gentleman at all."

"Perhaps not, for I am not normally attracted to young ladies of so-called good breeding. Then again, you are not like other ladies of that ilk."

"That's not so!"

"But it is." He smiled faintly and his eyes ran over her face. "By day you may be Olivia Byrde, proper young miss, planning coldheartedly how to snare the perfect gentleman of society so you can go on to live the perfect life of a society matron. But by night . . ." His hand at the small of her back pressed her closer until their bodies touched and sizzled with awareness. "By night you become Hazel, my lovely, willful Hazel."

Olivia could not move. She was too mesmerized by his words; too exhilarated by his touch. There was a terrible truth to what he said, and a certain relief. This Hazel he liked to invoke, was undeniably curious and a little wanton.

But she was not really Hazel, she reminded herself, and so she must fight her pull—and his. "I am afraid you delude yourself, Lord Hawke." She was breathless. "This Hazel is a figment of your imagination—"

He squelched her argument with a kiss. In the dark, against a slat-sided cart that smelled of sheep's wool and tallow can-

dles, with a hundred people not a shout away, he kissed her—
slowly, thoroughly—and in the process drew Hazel up to the
surface.

Somehow her arms came free and circled his neck. Somehow she tilted her head up to him, and he was quick to take
advantage. He was tall and well muscled, lean but hard, and
she felt the heretofore mysterious outline of the male form
against hers. Beyond them the music picked up tempo, and
the ebb and flow of genial conversation blurred to a hum. Male
voices, female voices, all entwined, thrumming together in a
way she'd never before noticed.

But in the dark quiet of their hideaway, Lord Hawke kissed
Olivia.

Neville kissed Hazel.

"How old are you?" he asked between kisses.

She was almost too breathless to answer. "One-and-
twenty."

"You're very good at this." His breath fanned her ear with
heat and she arched instinctively in response. "Very good," he
said, recapturing her lips with more force than before.

Insane as it was, Olivia was absurdly pleased by his words.
No man had ever kissed her with such complete authority,
such prowess and absolute conviction. His lips teased hers
apart. His tongue probed and caressed and stroked within her
mouth in the same blood-poundingly erotic manner he'd done
beside the river—

Dear God, what was she thinking?

She pulled back abruptly and twisted her head to the side.
He still held her, though, imprisoning her between his powerful body and the solid cart. "Have you kissed all the men
you list in that little book of yours?"

"No!" She stared indignantly at him. "You can let go of
me now."

"For if your research did include kissing those men," he
continued, ignoring her words, "I owe them my sincere thanks,
all thirty-eight of them."

"I told you before, I did not kiss all of those men! Now,
let go of me." She shoved against his chest—his solid hard-

as-a-rock chest—acutely aware of the contradictory emotions that wrestled within her: fury at his insulting assumption; satisfaction at his sensual approval; and humiliation at her easy capitulation.

She needed to get back to her area of the dance, away from Neville Hawke and his dangerous appeal. Despite everything, she could not deny that he was dangerously appealing. Disastrously appealing. Fatally appealing.

But he was not of a mind to let her go. He made that very clear. "How many did you kiss?"

Four, at most. "Not nearly as many as you have—kissed women, that is."

A distant torch limned his face with gold, just enough for her to see an arrogant male smile curve his lips. "Is that a compliment to my talent?"

"Only you would think so. It's an insult to your morals, of which you clearly possess none."

"To the contrary. I consider it my moral duty to please any woman who decides to kiss me."

"I did not decide to kiss you. *You* decided to kiss *me!*"

"I was reading your mind," he countered. "I'm doing it again," he added, lowering his head.

Though she was somewhat better prepared this time, the impact of his lips on hers was every bit as powerful. Perhaps even more so. Olivia had kissed four men in her life, only two of whom had ventured the intimate invasion that this man had so boldly taken. Only one had progressed beyond the barrier of her tightly clenched teeth, however, and she certainly hadn't enjoyed it. That Neville Hawke succeeded with so little effort was a wonder to her. That he so thoroughly delighted her in the process was truly amazing. She should make him stop and recoil from him in disgust. But she simply could not.

He kissed her and, fool that she was, she kissed him back. The music in the distance was the only other thing that registered in her pitifully besotted brain.

One of his hands cupped the back of her head, slanting her mouth better against his. His fingers tangled in her hair, almost as intimate an invasion as his tongue. Their bodies fit together despite the considerable difference in their height, and the profound difference in their anatomy. Hard chest to soft breasts. Muscular thighs to slender ones. And against her flat belly the growing evidence of his true interest in her.

This time when she pulled away from him, he let her go. As she gasped for breath, pressing one shaking hand to her lips and the other to her stomach, he leaned heavily on the cart, his hands clenched on the slats, his arms straight and rigid. "You," he said, nearly as breathless as she. "You should be kept under lock and key."

"Me?" Her chest hurt, her heart beat so rapidly. "This is your doing, not mine!"

"As I recall, we did it together—and very well, I might add."

Ruthlessly she suppressed the perverse pleasure that coursed through her. "Well, we shan't be doing it again."

"I'd wager a very large sum that we do."

"Then you'd lose." She turned to go, intent on stalking away and determined to abide by her avowal to avoid him. But his next words stopped her.

"Your hair is all mussed, Hazel. And your lips look distinctly well kissed. Whoever sees you will know at once what you've been up to. And probably with whom."

"Don't call me that!" Unfortunately, a quick hand to her hair confirmed the worst. Her neat coiffure was now a tousled mess with pins lost and curls dangling about her neck. "Botheration!" she muttered, turning her back to him as she attempted to repair the damage. For her lips, however, she had no remedy. She licked them once. Was it really so obvious?

She stole a peek at him, for she did not put it past him to lie to her. He had turned and leaned now with his back against the cart and his hands shoved into his pockets. Not a very lordly pose, and yet he looked more appealing than any man she'd ever seen.

More physically appealing, she amended as she jabbed the last hairpin in place. The passion he roused in her—for she could not deny he did rouse her to passion—that passion was the same sort of disastrous emotion that had drawn her mother to her vastly appealing father. Even she could remember how her father charmed every female in sight, from her mother to her to the housekeeper and serving girls and village women. She suspected that there had been other women as well, for there were at least three women of the ton to whom her mother refused to speak, though she would never say why.

Mostly, however, Olivia remembered the many tears her mother had shed over Cameron Byrde, and not just after he'd died.

She slid her knuckles across her sensitive lips. This had to stop, she told herself. This fascination she had for him must end at once.

She raised her chin and faced him with more courage than she felt. "My father was a man like you. Handsome and charming. Outrageous. He broke my mother's heart. Though I was young, I still remember how unhappy he made her." She stared up into his dark eyes, which showed no flicker of emotion. "I have no intention of making the same mistake she did."

She turned to go, unwilling to hear any response he might make, unwilling also to discover how weak her resolve might be. But before she could return to the crowd of revelers, he caught her by the arm. He did not stay her progress, but he tucked her hand firmly in his arm and matched her stride for stride.

At her bitter glare he remarked, "I'm certain even your blackguard of a father delivered his dance partners back to the safety of their family and friends."

"Don't forget to their husbands," she snapped, tugging futilely to free herself.

"Unless you are wed and have not so informed me, you cannot accuse me of that."

They were on the edge of the dancers once more and with a quick glance Olivia ascertained her whereabouts, then started toward the safety of the rest of their party. But even then Neville would not release her arm.

"I'll see you all the way back. I cannot risk being termed less than perfectly charming." They threaded through the crowd milling between the two areas of dancing, her arm firmly clamped against his. Once restored to the circle of silks and muslins and worsted wools, Olivia scanned the area for her mother. She found her dancing with a man Olivia did not know. Archie, Lord Holdsworth, danced near to her, with Penny Cummings as his partner.

"Your chaperones are occupied," Neville noted. "Shall I wait with you—"

"No. You need not wait here with me. You need not dance with me, either, and you need not dog my footsteps one moment longer."

"Do I not dance well enough for you?"

"That has nothing to do with it."

"Don't I kiss well enough?" His eyes ran over her face. "I could swear you enjoyed it, Olivia."

Olivia sucked in a painful breath. "That . . . that has nothing to do with it either," she croaked out most unconvincingly. Then she rallied. "In truth, were you less expert at kissing, I might more easily approve of you."

She was saved his response when the music ended and the dancers parted to much applause. *At last,* her flustered mind thought when Penny spied her and headed her way.

The woman's keen gaze skimmed Olivia head to toe. "Where have you two been?" she asked, a knowing glint in her eyes.

Olivia swallowed hard. Could Penny tell what they'd been doing? Was it as obvious as Lord Hawke had said? For a moment she was at a loss for how to respond. Then thankfully her wits rejoined her and she arrogantly raised her head. "Why, dancing, of course. And you?" She stared brazenly at Penny, daring her to imply anything, anything at all.

"Me? Oh, me." Penny giggled, then turned to Lord Holdsworth. "Why, Archie has been teaching me how they waltz in Spain. So energetically. And what of you, Lord Hawke? Is it your energetic dancing that has put roses in our Olivia's pretty cheeks?"

" 'Tis *my* energetic dancing that brings color to *his* cheeks," Olivia retorted before he could. Then she added, "Where is my mother?"

The rest of the evening was excruciating. To depart early was to invite all sorts of inquiry, and there was always the chance that Lord Hawke might follow her. The last thing she wanted was to be alone in that monstrous house with him.

So she spent the remainder of the evening as she had the previous one: avoiding Neville Hawke, pretending to be supremely unaware of him while in actuality she made note of his every move. Whom he spoke with, which women he danced with, and how often he filled his cup. This so-called pleasant diversion from town life was turning out even worse than she'd anticipated. And all on account of that horrible, troublesome man!

She danced with Mr. Garret and Mr. Cummings and a red-faced squire's son Penny introduced her to. She was aware of Neville's eyes upon her as she danced with that young man, and so redoubled her efforts to appear exuberant and gay. But it was terribly difficult and completely exhausting. At midnight when the fireworks were set off, her jaw hurt from clenching her teeth, and she had a raging headache.

It didn't help that she spied the girl she'd seen earlier go off arm in arm with her eager beau. If only her own life were so easy and uncomplicated.

"You are very quiet," her mother noted on the carriage ride home. "Did you not enjoy yourself?"

"I believe she and Lord Hawke have had a tiff," Penny put in, giggling behind her hand. In the darkened carriage Olivia's glare was quite lost on her tipsy hostess.

"I'm afraid Olivia is not impressed by handsome men possessed of great charm and wit," Augusta remarked.

"That's right, Mother. Find me an ugly, uncouth half-wit and I vow I shall drag him straightaway to the altar." She flung open the window curtain and stared moodily into the dark passing countryside.

Penny collapsed in another fit of giggling.

Augusta at least had the good grace not to. "Now, now, darling. We're only teasing you. It's just that it is hard for us to understand your resistance to Lord Hawke's clear interest in you."

"Please, Mother. Enough."

Augusta shrugged. "Very well. As you wish." She turned deliberately to Penny. "So. How shall we spend tomorrow?"

Once at the house, Olivia told Penny and her mother good night in the foyer before the men riding horseback could join them. She made her way directly to her chamber as her mother's laughter and Lord Holdsworth's rejoinder wafted up the stairwell to her. The fact that Augusta appeared to have succeeded in her conquest of Lord Holdsworth only increased Olivia's agitation. Like that pretty girl at the dance, her mother had an easy way with men. She drew them effortlessly to her, and kept them charmed and dancing eager attendance on her.

Olivia trudged into her room. What was she doing wrong? She attracted enough men, but there were none she wished to keep—save the worst one of all.

She rubbed her aching temple. Oh, how could she even think such insanity? She shut the door to her lonely chamber with unwarranted force. She could not take three more days of this, that was certain.

By the time she had undressed and made her evening ablutions, she had a new plan. There was no reason for her to continue at Doncaster that long. Sarah and Mrs. McCaffery were to arrive the day after tomorrow. Instead of resting for a day or two, Olivia decided that they would leave early for Scotland, the better to prepare the house. Portions of Byrde Manor had been closed up for fifteen years. Her task there was sure to be Herculean. The more reason to get an early start on it.

First thing the next morning Olivia informed her mother of the slight change in plans.

"Why such haste?" Augusta cried. "I do not understand you, child."

"You will not miss me at all, Mother, so do not pretend otherwise."

"Of course I shall miss you. So, I suspect, will someone else—who will remain nameless."

Olivia ignored that. She'd not seen Lord Hawke since yesterday and since she meant to avoid the races, she expected not to see him today. If Sarah and Mrs. McCaffery arrived tomorrow, as planned, that meant they could leave Friday morning and hopefully arrive at Byrde Manor by Sunday night.

It was early afternoon when Augusta and Penny left for the races. "Are you certain you won't reconsider and join us?" her mother asked.

"Thank you, but no."

"Would you like us to lay a wager for you?"

Remembering her winnings that yet remained from yesterday's wager, Olivia agreed. "One pound ten," she said, handing the coins to her mother.

"On Lord Hawke's Kestrel?"

"No. Any horse but."

Augusta shook her head. "You are being foolish, Olivia. Consider how well Kitti did."

"This is not Kitti." Though Olivia knew she was indeed behaving foolishly, she seemed unable to stop herself. She'd had all night to fret about Neville Hawke and his dangerous appeal, and to wonder if he was sitting up again in the library. That she could lose so much sleep over the man had brought her to a terrible conclusion. Though she had always thought herself completely unlike her mother, in truth they were exactly the same. They both harbored a weakness for rogues. The only difference was that up till now, Olivia had found it easy to resist those beguiling fellows who were all charm and style and no substance. She'd grown smug and confident, and had felt a little sorry for her more easily swayed mother. But she was smug no longer.

"Bet on the fastest horse opposing his," she told her mother. "Meanwhile, I shall have a quiet day to restore myself and prepare for the long journey north."

Augusta did not know what to think as the Cummingses' carriage carried her and Penny into Doncaster. While Penny chattered on, speculating about Olivia and the darkly handsome Lord Hawke, Augusta considered her daughter's odd behavior. That there was an attraction between them was unmistakable. But Olivia seemed determined to defeat it. She was not playing coy, Augusta knew, for that was not Olivia's way.

Was it as she'd said, that Neville Hawke was just like her father?

Olivia had been but six when her father had died. Could she still recall those difficult last years? Had they made such a lasting impression on her as a girl that she would now turn away from the first man who'd ever truly attracted her?

Augusta sighed and stared down at her perfectly manicured nails. It was more likely Mrs. McCaffery who was the cause of Olivia's attitude. The loyal housekeeper had never forgiven Cameron Byrde for making her mistress cry, and while back then it had been comforting for Augusta to turn to the woman, the repercussions yet lingered. Mrs. McCaffery hated Cameron Byrde, and through the years Olivia had absorbed much of that dislike—as well as an unfortunate distrust of most men.

But all was not lost, she decided as the carriage slowed. Lord Hawke was not a man easily ignored, nor easily deterred. He wanted Olivia, that was plain. Augusta smiled. Judging from Olivia's vehemence on the subject, Lord Hawke must have kissed her. He must have kissed her so thoroughly that her strong-minded daughter had yet to recover.

Augusta pressed one hand to her heart. She could still remember the first time Cameron had kissed her. She'd already been a widow with a little boy to raise, but her previous marriage had done nothing to prepare her for the likes of Cameron Byrde. Handsome as sin with laughing eyes and a sultry mouth. She'd fallen instantly in love with the dashing Scotsman, and the kiss he'd stolen that very same night had only sealed her fate.

Oh, but he'd been a wild one, passionate and too often careless with her feelings. She'd shed a thousand tears over him. A million. But in spite of all that—in spite of Mrs. McCaffery's opinion and Olivia's—she would not give up those seven years with him for anything in the world.

Once the carriage stopped in town, the coachman helped the two women alight. Augusta shaded her eyes with one hand as she glanced around the town square. Olivia had every right to be afraid of the likes of Neville Hawke. But her careful daughter also had the right to be happy, and Augusta had the strongest sense that Neville Hawke was the first man to come along who could do that.

"Let's go place our bets, shall we?" she said to Penny.

"After yesterday everyone will be betting on Hawke Stables. The odds will not be nearly so favorable," Penny complained.

"The odds in life never seem to be particularly favorable, do they? Yet we manage. We thrive."

"I, for one, should like my money to thrive just as well today as it did yesterday," Penny grumbled.

Augusta dug out the few coins Olivia had given her. What she wanted was for her daughter to thrive. And she was willing to bet everything that Neville Hawke was the man to help her do so.

CHAPTER

II

THE day was interminable. It took an army of servants to run the Cummingses' enormous household, but every time Olivia came upon one of them dusting or polishing or otherwise maintaining some aspect of that considerable establishment, they immediately disappeared.

As they should, she reminded herself. Good servants never labored in a room occupied by a guest. But Olivia was bored and she would have welcomed a chat even with the lowliest maid. She wandered from morning room to drawing room, from the gallery and outdoors to the verandah, until she found herself standing outside the library. The French doors were closed, but she could see them as she had that first night—was it only three days ago?—with Neville Hawke silhouetted in the opening.

She cupped her hands around her eyes and peered through the glass panes, spying the chair he'd been sitting in. Had he spent the entire night in it again? Did he spend every night in that chair instead of his bed? She squinted, seeing the table of books, the crowded shelves, and the commode with its decanters of brandy, whisky, and port. The real question, she told herself, was not whether he sat up every night drinking himself into a stupor but, rather, why he did it.

She tried the door but it was latched from within, so she turned away. It didn't matter why he did not sleep at night, nor would she ever learn the answer. Nor did she wish to. Better to contemplate her coming journey and the myriad tasks that awaited her at Byrde Manor.

But Olivia was too restless even for that. As she wandered

the gravel paths of the knot garden she heard the distant whinny of a horse, and for the first time that day she knew what she wanted to do. A quick trip to the stables to arrange for a mount, a dash back to the house to don her camel-colored riding habit, and within a half hour she was mounted. She guided the placid mare down a path through the rear gardens and toward the woodlands beyond, declining the stablemaster's offer of someone to accompany her.

"I mean to take no chances with your animal," she assured him. "No jumps, only a long slow ramble through the countryside."

She headed west now, away from Doncaster as the man had advised her, toward a tributary of the river Don and the ruins of some ancient castle. The sky was sharp and blue, streaked with the high clouds typical of August and promising no rain yet. But despite the heat of mid-afternoon, the forest was cool, and as she rode, Olivia began to relax. Scotland would be like this, only wilder and more exhilarating—and she would have her own saddle horse and have to answer to no one about when and where she might ride.

Down a hill they angled, the mare picking her way on sure feet, and came upon an open valley blanketed with rosebay willow herb. It grew so tall that the dark pink flowers brushed at her heels.

Olivia breathed deep of the fragrant air. On the way back she must gather an armful of the wild flowers and have a bouquet placed in her room. Too bad there would be no time to bring Sarah riding to this spot, for the girl would adore it. But there would be plenty of time for them to take long rides together at Byrde Manor.

So she headed on. The sun moved across the sky and she followed it. When the mare's ears flicked forward she knew the river could not be far, and sure enough, through a dense stand of alder and birch, the sparkle and rush of water beckoned.

"Ahh," Olivia sighed once she dismounted. She removed her boots and stockings and her bonnet and gloves. Then hiking her skirts up, she climbed onto a flattish rock along the river's edge, and sat, dangling her feet into the water.

She sighed again as the icy water lapped up her calves. A capricious breeze lifted her hair and toyed with the hems of her twill skirt and linen petticoats. Somewhere nearby a woodpecker drummed steadily. A pair of red birds darted about an ancient birch on the opposite bank. All around her the forest thrummed with the business of life: bees and butterflies, squirrels and woodmice. Insects hovered near the surface of the stream and in its shadowy depths fish moved about. Even in the shallows pollywogs and minnows and fingerlings pursued their daily routine. They ate and lived and reproduced.

Olivia stared down into the stream. It was not so very complicated, nor should her own life be. So why was she complicating it? Why did she not simply marry some acceptable fellow and just get on with it—or else put the whole subject of marriage completely out of her mind?

She leaned back on her elbows, closed her eyes, and lifted her face to the sun. What if she decided not to return to London at all? What if she liked Byrde Manor so well she decided to winter in Scotland? She would wear heavy wool stockings and a plaid shawl, and spend most of the day in the warm kitchen or the cozy parlor. She could pass her time knitting and reading; she could organize the library and work in the stables.

She laughed to even think of it. Her mother and most of her friends would be scandalized. A single woman living alone on her own estate in the wilds of Scotland. But she would not truly be alone. There were the servants, the villagers, and her neighbors—

But not *that* neighbor.

Olivia straightened up at the thought of Neville Hawke and pulled her feet out of the water. She'd so looked forward to Scotland, but now there was this blight upon it. Lord Hawke would undoubtedly ruin everything, he and this perverse attraction she held for him.

If only she could find another man who affected her so. Maybe she wasn't trying hard enough. Maybe another man's kisses would affect her just as powerfully—if she would let another man kiss her. It was an intriguing thought, and as she reclined back on the stone again, she resolved to think about it most seriously. But not right now. Right now she was tired and relaxed. She would just rest a little while longer before heading back.

As he rode in the direction the stablemaster had given him, Neville's thoughts were not so very different from Olivia's. He should not be here, trailing after a woman who was plainly avoiding him, especially now that Kestrel had upset the better-known animals at today's race. He should be at the Eel and Elbow, buying drinks and making deals, and laying wagers for Kitti's match tomorrow against a full field of three-year-olds. And if not that, he should be catching a brief nap, for he'd had little enough sleep this morning.

Instead he was riding through the woods, pursuing a woman who did not want to be found, least of all by him.

At least he had her mother's approval. Lady Dunmore had not been in the least subtle. She'd found him in the racing stable this afternoon, tapped him imperiously on the arm with her fan, then boldly asked him if he had anything to do with Olivia's black mood. Fortunately, she hadn't really wanted an answer, and he wasn't sure if he could have given her one. It was enough for the beautiful Lady Dunmore that he was interested in her daughter. For himself, he wasn't certain what he was doing, or why.

He scrubbed a hand across his face wearily. He wanted Olivia for the obvious physical reasons, and he wanted her lands for the obvious economic benefits to Woodford and its people. But he also wanted Olivia for no logical reason he could discern. He was the last man a woman of her sort should attach herself to, for he was unworthy of any proper young woman's attentions, and nothing good could come from such a union.

Yet how he wanted her! He wanted her will bent to his, her approval, her smiles—everything that was her. It was that idiotic nonsense that had sent him back to the Cummingses' household and now here into the forest, searching for a woman who did not want him to find her.

Or did she?

That was the bedeviling part of it. She enjoyed his kisses and yet she ran from him. Why was that? Because she was wise enough to recognize his complete unsuitability.

But not wise enough to bring a groom along with her on her ride.

Thus justifying his search, Neville continued on, only slowing when Robin's ears pricked forward. He could hear the river and through the trees he spotted a horse grazing in a narrow clearing along the riverbank. She was nearby.

Neville dismounted, then moved stealthily through the heavy summer undergrowth. He was acting like an insane man. There was no need to pursue her like this. He had several months to convince her to lease him her lands. Pursuing her when she obviously wished to be alone was illogical and sure to blacken his character even more in her esteem. But he seemed unable to do anything else. The thought of her out here without any protection made him crazy. If she intended to ride around the Cheviot Hills this way, careless of her safety, he would swiftly disabuse her of that notion.

He ducked beneath a low-hanging holly branch, then froze when a snatch of a melody drifted to him. His eyes narrowed, searching. Then a flash of fiery color drew his gaze to her. There, on a gray boulder with the late sun glinting copper and bronze off her unbound hair.

Her face was lifted to the sun as she half reclined upon the rock. Then she straightened and bent forward, shaking her hair down over the water so that the loose ends trailed nearly to the river's surface.

Neville sucked in a breath. Her feet were bare and her legs exposed up to her knees. Narrow ankles, shapely calves, smooth, pale skin. She appeared a woodland nymph, a Scottish faerie lost somehow in England, and his desire for her trebled. He must have this woman.

But there was only one way to have a woman like her, and that was through marriage.

He halted at that unsettling thought. But he did not shy away from it. It *would* take marriage to possess Olivia Byrde. Was he prepared to go that far?

He thought about Bart's admonition. Maybe the man was right. Maybe a woman was the answer. But not just any woman. There was only one woman he had ever wanted that fiercely.

He heard her soft voice, singing a familiar song, and his head and heart seemed to fill with it. God knew, he did not deserve a woman like her, and she certainly deserved better than the likes of him. But at the moment he did not care. He wanted her. He had to have her. And if the only way was through marriage, then so be it. He would propose marriage to Olivia.

And he would do whatever it took to convince her to say yes.

Struggling to quell the hot rush of blood to his loins, he began to hum, matching her melody. He started through the woods toward her. Once they were wed she would not behave so recklessly as this. But now was not a time to scold her. She would be angry enough with him for following her.

When she heard him, Olivia sprang to her feet, alarm on her face. But she was trapped on the boulder with her back to the river and no hope of escape. He could not resist a mild reprimand.

"You are safe, Olivia, though not due to any caution on your own part." He sauntered into the sunlight, satisfied by her frightened expression. That fright, however, swiftly gave way to suspicion.

"You followed me."

"Someone had to. That stableman ought to be sacked for allowing you go off without a groom."

"I insisted. Everyone was working at the races. Besides, I do not need a guardian—and don't you dare start any trouble for that poor fellow. I daresay, his greater error was in telling you where I went. But then, he could not know, as I do, how wicked a man you are."

"Wicked?" Neville laughed out loud. She didn't begin to

know the truth of it. If she even suspected the wicked direction of his thoughts—how her dishabille and their solitude both combined to arouse him—she would run panic-stricken in the opposite direction. As it was, he had to clench his hands behind his back to prevent himself reaching for her.

"I suppose that in the eyes of a cosseted society chit I do appear wicked and dark," he said.

She bristled. "Society chit? You have the nerve to denigrate me when I have done nothing?"

"You court disaster, Olivia. That is what you do. You wander strange houses at night. You walk out with men you should not. You ride alone then bare yourself for anyone to see." He gestured with one hand. "What else?"

"What I do is none of your concern!" she shouted, quivering with fury. "You are not my father nor my brother!"

"It would be damned inconvenient if I was," Neville muttered, his gaze locked upon hers.

There was no mistaking his meaning, and in the aftermath of that, the air fairly sizzled between them. He saw her swallow hard, and just that simple movement along her tender throat increased his inappropriate desire. He needed to get her on neutral territory—and fast—if he was to gain control of his unruly emotions. "I will see you back to the Cummingses' household," he said through gritted teeth.

A hunting bird let out a sharp cry and with a blink Olivia looked away from him. "I do not need your accompaniment," she stated, catching her loose hair in one hand. She twisted it into a knot and stabbed it deftly with a hairpin to hold it in place.

"Twilight is nearly upon us. You have to leave soon if you wish to get back before dark."

"But I don't have to go with you."

Neville crossed his arms and stared at her. "Very well. I'll keep my distance. But I *will* see you safely returned."

Olivia was so angry she could spit. How dare he order her around as if she were a child! It did not help matters at all that he was right about the fading daylight. The sun already dipped below the tops of the trees. Within an hour it would be dark.

But she did not need him to tell her that, nor to escort her back to the Cummingses' estate.

Unfortunately, there was no getting rid of him. Though she turned her back to him, her hands shook as she donned her stockings and shoes, then her bonnet and gloves. She tried very hard to project an icy hauteur, but ruined it by stomping past him on the way to retrieve her mare.

"Keep your distance," she warned him with a glare once she was mounted. Then with far more haste and far less calm, she urged Fanny up the riverbank and back the way she'd come.

That he kept his distance provided her with no comfort. She was acutely aware of him trailing her. She did not stop to collect any flowers. Nor did she say more than a curt word of thanks to the sheepish stableman when she handed Fanny over into his care. She strode for the house, straight up to her room. Then she snatched up her journal and turned to a page filled already with more notations than any other.

"He is an ogre. Contemptible. High-handed. He tries to corrupt me while all the while pretending to protect me from the untoward advances of others. Hah!"

She underlined every word, so heavy-handed with the pen that a thick ink blob marred the center of the page.

"Damn!" She threw the pen down on the desk, then rested her head in her trembling hands. Why did she let him upset her so? What had happened to her resolve to undermine him—or at the very least, ignore him? Why should she be forced to hide in her room, reduced to scribbling invective about him in her heretofore neat and analytical journal? Just because he'd kissed her?

She let out a choked laugh. Calling that last kiss merely a kiss was like calling the elegant Kitti a plowhorse. He hadn't simply kissed her, he'd rocked her off her feet, challenged her every notion of logic, and changed her entire perception of herself. That hadn't been a kiss, it had been a life-changing event. She knew she would always measure things as "before the kiss" and "after the kiss."

She stared down at the journal, at everything she'd written about him, all her high-minded ranting, then suddenly crumpled the page in her fist. She covered her eyes with her other hand and let out a heavy sigh. If she was going to be honest in what she wrote, she ought to begin with herself. She was the problem, not him. Her reaction to him was the problem. But what made him so different from all the other men she'd met and written about in her little matchmaker?

Maybe nothing more than the two kisses they'd shared.

Olivia lifted her head and stared blankly at the crumpled page. Maybe her inexperience with kissing was the problem.

Unbidden, his words came back to her. He'd said she was very good at kissing. He'd also asked her if she'd kissed all the men listed in her journal—the rude cad.

The fact remained, however, that if she had kissed a few more of those men, she might not now be so affected by this particular man.

Very well, she decided on the moment. She would just have to kiss a few more men, starting tonight. She slammed her journal shut, then hastily cleaned up the mess she'd made. She would not cower here in her room, afraid to face him. She would cure herself of this perverse fascination with Neville Hawke so that when she arrived in Scotland, his presence so nearby would become an entirely insignificant matter to her.

CHAPTER

12

AFTER the previous two gala evenings, dinner that night seemed a rather subdued affair with just the Cummingses and their six guests at the dining room table. Olivia considered it a good sign when she successfully avoided speaking to Neville Hawke in the drawing room, and doubly good when she was able to seat herself beside Mr. Cummings, with Mr. Garret between her and Neville, and Mr. Harrington opposite her.

Everyone was in a festive mood, for Hawke stables had again won. Kestrel had taken the daily purse, and everyone at the table had made profitable wagers on the fleet-footed stallion. Olivia arranged the napkin upon her lap. Everyone had made profitable wagers, that is, except her.

But she didn't care about that. Truly, she didn't. The meal progressed amid much good cheer, lubricated by a half-dozen bottles of wine. After dinner came port for the men as they adjourned to the billiards room with their cigars.

Penny caught Mr. Garret before he could go. "Do stay and play a hand of whist with us, Mr. Garret. Augusta and Olivia and I shall make up the rest of the table."

Olivia started to protest, for she was not interested in cards tonight. When Mr. Garret glanced first at her, then smiled, however, she reconsidered. He was a pleasant enough fellow. A good dancer and well mannered, and though no one would ever call him a brilliant conversationalist, that was all right. He was good-looking in a slightly dandified sort of way, with one blond lock falling just so across his brow. Plus, he liked her, that was obvious. If she was serious about her kissing experiment, he was the perfect candidate.

So she smiled back at him and added her plea to Penny's. "Yes, do say you'll play, Mr. Garret. You and I can partner against Penny and my mother." And if Neville Hawke heard her or cared what was going on, Olivia didn't give a fig.

Unfortunately, Olivia did not play well—her concentration seemed off tonight—and they lost. She supposed she was too preoccupied with her little plot to concentrate properly upon her cards. It was hard work to smile and flirt and be vivacious when your heart was simply not in it. But she was determined, and by the time Penny slapped down her cards in triumph she knew she had succeeded, for the very competitive Mr. Garret did not appear to care in the least about their loss.

"May I get you ladies some refreshments?"

"Don't worry yourself," Penny said with a casual wave. "I can ring for a tray."

Olivia cleared her throat. This was it. "I think I shall step outside for a breath of fresh air. It's such a pleasant evening." She sent Mr. Garret a sidelong look.

He rose to his feet. "I'd be happy to escort you."

"Why, thank you."

Penny's brows arched; Augusta's lowered. "Don't wander too far, Olivia."

"Of course not, Mother. Just a turn in the knot garden to catch the evening breeze." She smiled at Mr. Garret when he pulled her chair out, then placed her hand on his proffered arm. His chest swelled with a deep breath.

This was good. This was very good, she told herself as they made their way outside through the morning room doors. The moon was out and the grounds looked especially pretty in the warm, silvery light. Olivia squelched her faint twinge of misgivings beneath her need for Mr. Garret's kiss to be just as thrilling as Lord Hawke's.

"Shall we stroll toward the gazebo?" His voice was not as low and rumbling as she would like, but she ignored that.

"Very well. Tell me about the west country and your home there," she said.

For several minutes he waxed very eloquent. The moors,

the bogs, and the amazing rock piles of Dartmoor. The granite-faced headlands and the limestone cliffs.

"How poetic you are, Mr. Garret. You convince me that I must someday visit that part of the country," she said when he paused for breath. "It sounds very wild and beautiful."

"But not so beautiful as you, Miss Byrde." He stopped next to the gazebo and swung around to face her.

He was going to kiss her. Olivia could see it in his eyes. She tried to relax and prepare herself, for she was stiff with tension.

"You are so very beautiful," he repeated. "Might I call you Olivia?"

"Well. I suppose so. But only in private," she amended. *Hurry up.*

"And you may call me Clive."

"Very well. Clive." *Will you please get on with it?*

Finally he bent forward and kissed her, a flat, closed-mouth kiss that startled her but did nothing more.

He was breathing hard when he raised his head from hers. "I believe I am falling in love with you, my darling Olivia."

Drat. How could she compare this brief peck on the lips to the deep and ardent kiss Lord Hawke had pressed upon her? Then she realized what he had just said. "Love me? But you hardly know me well enough to think that." She forced herself to lean closer and lifted her face to his. "And I shall be leaving in just a day or two."

"Oh, but you torture my soul with such talk." He caught her by the shoulders. "Say you will stay."

"I cannot." *If you wish to kiss me, do it now.*

"But you must stay." Then abruptly, he kissed her again. And this time he stuck his tongue in her mouth.

She nearly gagged.

"Mr. Garret!"

"Clive," he said, trying again to kiss her. "Call me Clive, my darling girl." Somehow his hands were everywhere, and when he could not recapture her lips, he instead pressed his open mouth to her ear and neck and throat.

It was horrible.

"Stop that," she muttered. Then one of his hands fastened upon her left breast and she let out a yelp of outrage. "Stop that!"

A menacing voice added its threat to hers. "Do as she says."

Olivia wanted to cry with relief. Neville was here! Then immediately she wanted to groan. The last thing she needed was for him to witness this disaster!

In an instant Mr. Garret was jerked away from her, and she stumbled backward. She gasped anew, however, when she spied the stranglehold Lord Hawke had put on Mr. Garret. With his arm thrust straight out, Lord Hawke clenched the hapless Clive Garret around the throat. The poor fellow flailed like a fish on a gaffhook, making awful choking noises. Even in the dark Olivia could see that his face was turning purple.

"What are you doing?" She grabbed Lord Hawke's arm but it was like grabbing an iron rod. Though it was warm and quivered with strength, it remained completely inflexible.

Mr. Garret's spluttering changed to a distinctly less healthy sound. Good God, he was going to kill the man!

"Stop this. Stop it!" she cried, throwing her entire weight onto Lord Hawke's arm. "Please, Lord Hawke. Neville!"

"Did he hurt you?" His voice was harsh and frightening for its coldness.

"No. No, I am fine."

He abruptly released the man and Mr. Garret collapsed in a boneless heap, gasping for breath. Olivia would have collapsed as well, though with a different sort of relief, only Neville had exchanged his death grip on the pitiful Mr. Garret's neck for an equally relentless grip on her two arms. He glared into her shocked eyes. "You have a dangerous habit of going off with men you hardly know."

Any thought of thanking him fled in the rush of her quick fury. "You are not my keeper!" she snapped right back at him.

"So you keep saying. But it's plain you need one. Your mother is certainly unable to guard you from your unwise impulses."

"My impulses are not unwise!"

"Did you want him slobbering over you? Did you want his hands pawing at your chest?"

How Olivia wanted to say yes. She shook with the need to shout yes at his angry face and silence him once and for all. But her battered pride was not proof against the revulsion that filled her at the thought of Mr. Garret's crude grip upon her breast. She shuddered and looked away from Lord Hawke's thunderous expression. Only then did his tight grasp ease.

Behind them Mr. Garret scuttled away, leaving them alone in the garden. The air was redolent of roses and mint and lemon balm. Crickets chirruped down one dark path; the cool trickle of water beckoned from another. A romantic spot, to be sure. But Olivia's romantic experiment had failed miserably. And though she might flatter herself that Lord Hawke had followed her because he was jealous of her attention to Clive Garret, it was not romantic emotions that gripped him now.

She raised her face and met his angry glare. "I could have handled him myself."

"Like you handled me?" His voice was flat and hard.

Her chin jutted out. "No harm has come to me from you—"

He silenced her with a kiss, hard—almost brutal. He took violent possession of her mouth, allowing her no time to protest, and no breath with which to do it. Beneath the demanding onslaught she had no defense. He forced her mouth open and plundered it, an invasion that both scared and thrilled her.

Then just as suddenly as the kiss began, it ended. He shoved her away, though he did not release his hold on her. "If no harm has come to you, it's only because I am more trustworthy than Garret."

"I . . . I . . ." Olivia was far too flustered to get her mind in working order. Far too overwhelmed by the tumultuous emotions he'd roused in her. She burned. That was all she knew. His kiss made her burn deep down inside, while Mr. Garret's . . .

She shook her head, suddenly afraid of her own wicked emotions. "I could have handled him," she finally managed to say, though in a faltering voice. *It's you I cannot handle.*

But she could never admit that now. "I could have handled

him," she repeated, for that, at least, was true. "And if you had not interfered, I would have done so. Now you have embarrassed us all."

"I'm not embarrassed. But if Garret is here come the dawn, he'll be a damned sight more than embarrassed."

She stared at him frustrated, furious, and utterly confused. She had to get away from him, to think and reason out what was wrong with her. With no other idea how to get away, she struck out at him with words. "This is not your affair! I am not your concern!"

"Would you have preferred I not save you from his slobbering attentions?"

She shook her head. "This is not the war. You need not be a hero and save me at all."

His fingers tightened, a nearly imperceptible twitch. Then he released her and took a step back.

She'd hurt him. She wasn't sure how or why, but she knew at once that her words had struck him a painful blow.

"I see. Very well." He gave a curt nod. "I stand corrected. Be assured, Miss Byrde, that I will step aside and let the next fool you throw yourself at do whatever he will with you. Or should I say, whatever *you* will."

Then he turned and stalked away, leaving Olivia standing there in the dark staring after him. She let out a faint groan, disgusted with herself. *It was not what you think,* she wanted to shout after him. But of course she could not do that, for then she would have to explain why she had wanted to kiss Mr. Garret, and that must naturally lead to an explanation that her experiment had failed and that no other man's kisses had ever affected her like his own had done.

She dropped her head into her hands and let out another groan. She'd bungled this horribly. Now not only must she avoid Neville Hawke, there would be Mr. Garret to deal with.

She took a deep breath and squared her shoulders. There was no help for it. She must go back inside and rejoin the company, and pretend that nothing was wrong. She must shut out the memory of what she'd just done—and the stirring memory of how Neville's kiss had shaken her. Then, after a few minutes, she could escape undetected to her bedchamber.

She wrapped her arms around herself, aware that she was shivering. But it was not from the cold.

She took a shaky breath. Perhaps tomorrow she could complain to her mother of her monthly malady and stay abed all day—or at least until everyone else had departed for the races in town.

Anything to avoid again facing Neville Hawke and that awful, accusing tone in his voice.

Sarah and Mrs. McCaffery arrived the next afternoon. Olivia could not recall ever having been so happy to see her little sister, for she'd spent the morning miserably alone. Even though she could not confide in either Sarah or their housekeeper, they were far better company than the guilt and confusion which beset her. Even eviscerating Mr. Garret in her matchmaker journal had been no comfort, for she'd been forced to acknowledge her own guilty part in last night's disaster.

She'd been so stupid to encourage the man, and Lord Hawke had been absolutely right to come to her defense. She should have thanked him instead of venting her temper on him. But then, he should *never* have kissed her so brutally. And she should never have succumbed so wantonly to him. She'd been such a fool and had come awfully close to ruining her reputation entirely. She'd certainly ruined her own opinion of herself.

But Sarah was here now and soon they would escape this place—and Lord Neville. What a pity she could not outrun her unhappy thoughts as easily.

Augusta and their hostess returned from the races in Doncaster early. "Such a lovely child," Penny gushed, pinching Sarah's cheek. "Such pretty blue eyes; such a pretty pink complexion."

Olivia grabbed Sarah's hand and gave it a warning squeeze, for she saw the irritated glint in her precocious sister's "pretty blue eyes." Even Augusta must have sensed Sarah's impatience with Penny's prattle, for she wrapped one arm around the child's shoulders.

"If you'll excuse us, Penny dear. Since my girls are leaving in the morning, I need to give them a few final instructions."

"She pinched my cheek," Sarah muttered as they went up the stairs together. She sent a glare over her shoulder at their frivolous hostess. "You'd think I was still in leading strings the way she went on."

"Tut, tut." Augusta clucked her tongue. "Penny means well. But having never been blessed with children of her own, she hasn't the faintest idea how to deal with them."

Sarah looked over at Olivia and rolled her eyes. But at least she kept quiet. It was plain to Olivia that Sarah had missed them and that she'd had time to think about her mother's situation. Even when Augusta mentioned Archie Holdsworth, the girl's lips tightened but she made no sarcastic response.

Olivia was proud of her, and when Augusta brought up Lord Hawke's name, she struggled to be just as tactful as Sarah, though it cost her dearly.

". . . the most wonderful horses," Augusta said. "We've all won quite a bit of money—twenty pounds today. Did I tell you that, Olivia?"

Olivia smoothed a wrinkle in a shawl lying in her partially packed trunk. "My, my. Lord Hawke must be the most popular fellow in Doncaster these days."

"Indeed he is, I confess, I feel somewhat guilty to be the one taking him away from it all."

Olivia glanced sidelong at her mother, but refused to rise to her obvious bait. Sarah, however, was not so astute. "What does that mean?" the girl asked.

"Only that he is cutting short his stay in Doncaster."

A sudden suspicion threw a shadow over Olivia and her heart began to beat a little faster. When her mother smiled at her and shrugged, it began to thunder. "I only said that you were leaving on the morrow," Augusta continued. "It was his idea to accompany your carriage."

"Mother, no!" Olivia cried. She stared at her aghast, then threw the shawl back into the open trunk. For good measure she slammed the lid down as well. "No. I will not have it."

Augusta raised her hands in a gesture of complete innocence. "I don't understand why you should object. Besides, he offered. I would be a poor parent, indeed, to turn down the added security his presence will provide to my children during such a long journey."

Olivia stared panic-stricken at her mother. She was conscious of Sarah's wide interested eyes upon her, but it was her interfering mother she focused her ire upon.

"You knew I would object to such a plan. You needn't pretend otherwise."

"Who is this Lord Hawke?" Sarah asked.

Augusta smiled at the child. "A very nice man—"

"An arrogant, annoying . . . arrogant, annoying man—" Who could melt her with merely one kiss. She sputtered to a halt, then shook her head and shot her mother an accusing look. "You did this on purpose. Do not bother to deny it," she added when Augusta opened her mouth. "You did it on purpose but it will do no good. He and I could never suit, Mother. Never."

Then she spun on her heel and stalked from the room.

In the wake of her departure, Sarah turned a curious look on her mother. "What was that about? Who *is* this Lord Hawke?"

Augusta drummed her fingers together beneath her chin, still staring at the door Olivia had slammed behind her. "He is our neighbor in Scotland," she answered. "And I believe he is the only man who has ever roused such emotion in your sister."

Sarah made a rude noise. "I don't think she likes him very much."

"So she would like to believe." Augusta drummed her fingers together again and laughed. "So she would like to believe. Come." She turned and took Sarah by the shoulders. "I see those freckles. You've been spending far too much time out of doors, child. But a little vinegar and salt will bleach them out."

"But I've been wearing my bonnet," Sarah protested as they

left the room. Then she added, "It seems you approve of this Lord Hawke person."

"Indeed I do. And so will you. I would not be surprised if you did not fall in love with him too."

"Too? Who else is in love with him?"

"Why, Olivia, of course." Augusta gave Sarah a kiss upon her freckled nose. "She just doesn't want to admit it."

CHAPTER

13

THEY departed the next morning, a scant hour after dawn. Mrs. McCaffery, Sarah, and Olivia rode in the traveling coach with the trunks strapped behind and a guard in the front box with John, their driver. Lord Hawke, his trainer, and his jockey rode alongside, leading Kitti, Kestrel, and one other horse. They'd sold all their other animals.

In the forecourt Olivia had greeted Lord Hawke curtly, rattled to the core by the very sight of him. She climbed straightaway into the coach while Sarah and Mrs. McCaffery lingered with Augusta, who introduced them to Lord Hawke.

The conniving snake, Olivia fumed. He knew she did not want him to accompany them, not after that kiss. Every time she thought about that kiss she wanted to die, and seeing him . . . Seeing him even as briefly as she did unnerved her completely.

She perched on the forward seat and tried to compose herself. Neville Hawke *was* a snake and he should never have taken her mother's obvious bait. But that was precisely why he'd made the offer to Augusta to accompany the carriage. He was a snake and a rake, and he knew how profoundly that kiss had affected her.

Olivia threw her bonnet on the seat opposite her. He'd made the offer because he'd known Augusta would accept, and that Olivia would object.

Now as they pulled out of the long gravel drive and turned onto the York highway headed north, Olivia struggled to maintain her calm. It was a good day for traveling, she told herself. Cloudy and hopefully not so hot as it had been of late. The traces jingled in the quiet morning air. The horses' regular hoofbeats and the rhythmic swaying of the well-sprung coach should have added to her contentment, for this was a journey she'd longed for these several years and more.

Yet try as she might, Olivia could not work up the anticipation she should have felt. They would be three long days getting to Byrde Manor. Three days in Neville Hawke's constant proximity. She wasn't certain she could endure it.

Mrs. McCaffery dozed off and on all morning. Sarah read the novel Olivia had brought for herself, laughing out loud at Emma's matchmaking antics. "You should have read this before you tried to match up Lillian and Mr. Chelton," she remarked. She laid the book down and yawned, then eyed her older sister. "I bet you could write stories like this, Livvie. Perhaps we could write one together."

Olivia only gave her a halfhearted smile, then turned back to the window. If she were inclined to write anything at all, it would be a book of advice and instruction to warn unsuspecting women of the terrible attraction of handsome rogues—and the terrible, terrible danger.

Sarah fell asleep against Mrs. McCaffery's ample bosom. The carriage rumbled on through the pretty Yorkshire countryside and Olivia stewed glumly over her unhappy circumstances. That she did not once lay eyes on Neville Hawke was both a relief and an irritant. He and his entourage rode ahead of them to avoid the dust the heavy carriage raised. By the time they stopped outside of Selby to water the horses and refresh themselves, Olivia had worked herself up into quite a state. Just let Neville Hawke say one provoking word. Just one.

As they alighted he and his men were releasing their horses in a small corral. Sarah, impulsive as ever, made a beeline for their side, and Olivia could have cried. She did not want to deal with Neville Hawke. Not now, not ever. But there was no way to avoid it. So gritting her teeth and stiffening her resolve—and ignoring the violent thudding of her heart—she marched in her sister's wake. "Come along, Sarah. We have little enough time as it is. You must not waste it hanging about the stables."

But Sarah's attention was firmly fixed upon Neville. "I'm a very good rider. Just ask Olivia. She says I have a natural seat."

After a brief glance at Olivia, he turned to the child. "Have you started to jump yet?"

"Oh, yes—"

"When?" Olivia interrupted. She had a sneaking suspicion where this was heading. "When have you begun jumping?"

Sarah slanted a look and a smile at her sister. "James started me this spring, when you and Mother were preoccupied. Remember?" Her eyes sparked with mischief. "You had turned down Harold Prine's proposal and Mother was so disappointed she took to her sickbed and demanded you tend her."

"Poor Mr. Prine," Lord Hawke remarked, arching one brow at Olivia. "Did he also take to his sickbed in disappointment?"

Olivia glared at him but did not bother to answer. Sarah, however, laughed out loud. "Probably. He's just the sort that would." Then spying Olivia's angry countenance, she added, "Don't worry, Livvie. I'm relieved you didn't marry old Harry. He kept a terrible stable. Nothing like Lord Hawke's handsome animals."

"You think you've succeeded in changing the subject, Sarah, but you have not. You know how Mother feels about you jumping too early. And our ne'er-do-well of a brother knows it too."

"You can hardly call it jumping," Sarah protested. "Only one bar. Not even knee high, Livvie."

"Do you jump?" Lord Hawke directed his question at Olivia, and also his unnerving gaze.

She met it, determined not to let him know how profoundly unsettled he made her. "Yes, I jump. But I did not begin until I was nearly fourteen."

"But you wanted to jump sooner," Sarah threw in. "You told me that once."

Olivia resisted the urge to sigh, for Sarah made a very good point. Their mother was an indifferent rider and tended to be excessively cautious about her daughters' interest in horses. That made it very hard for Olivia to argue Augusta's position, for she did not entirely agree with it. "Yes, I did chafe at Mother's restrictions," she finally admitted. "But I was subject to her wishes then, as you are now. Come." She caught Sarah by the hand. "Let us get our dinner so we can continue on."

"Easy for you to say," Sarah grumbled, reluctantly giving in to Olivia's demand. "I spent the last two days in that carriage, and now today. I'm tired of being cooped up like that."

"Would you like to ride with me?"

Olivia and Sarah both looked up at Lord Hawke's offer. Though the invitation was clearly meant for Sarah, it was at Olivia he stared. "I'll take very good care of her," he added. "Absolutely no jumping."

"Oh, please, Livvie. Please?" Sarah bounced up and down, clinging tightly to Olivia's hand. "Please let me ride. I'll be very good. I promise. Please?"

Olivia gritted her teeth. She was trapped, just as she'd feared she would be. Though only twelve, Sarah was turning out to be every bit as manipulative as their mother. No doubt this was precisely what the girl had been angling for from the moment she'd stepped down from the coach. And unfortunately, Neville Hawke had once again taken the bait.

Now *she* was caught in the position of either being an ogre to her sister or else opening herself to the exact sort of camaraderie between herself and Lord Hawke which she had meant assiduously to avoid.

She tightened her hands on the strings of her reticule, determined not to be swayed by Sarah's pleading. But it was oh, so hard. How clearly she could remember her mother's strict rules—and her stepfather's many welcome interventions.

"Perhaps you would like to ride with us as well?"

At Lord Hawke's offer Olivia stiffened and shook her head. "No, thank you."

"But I can go?"

Sarah's voice was simply too hopeful to deny. With a sharp exhalation, Olivia conceded the fight—not the complete battle, just this one particular little skirmish. "All right. If Lord

Hawke is willing to have you as his companion, you may ride a while with him. But not all afternoon. Just an hour or so."

The last of her words was drowned out by Sarah's whoops of joy.

"Really, Sarah. Such behavior in so public a place would shock our mother."

"But not you, Livvie." With an effort the girl schooled her features into a more sedate expression. But her sparkling eyes could not hide her excitement. It struck Olivia that she had not seen that sort of brightness in her sister's eyes in the two years since the child's father had died. As quickly as that any lingering objections about Sarah's ride fled. What real harm was there if the child rode with the man?

Still, Olivia did not want Neville Hawke to assume anything from her capitulation. He'd already presumed far too much with her. "Now, then." She folded her hands primly. "If that is settled, may we adjourn to our dinner?"

Olivia kept Mrs. McCaffery close in the private dining room they took. Somehow the older woman's presence kept their small party from feeling too intimate. Sarah's enthusiasm for horses found a ready match in Neville Hawke, freeing Olivia to consume her chicken pie and creamed potatoes and observe him—while all the while pretending to ignore him.

Unfortunately she found the afternoon portion of their journey even more trying than the morning portion.

Though she had more space in the carriage and more privacy—for once again Mrs. McCaffery slept—Olivia was more restless than ever. Neither her novel, nor a knitting project she'd brought along, nor even the beauty of the passing countryside could hold her interest. What matter the brilliant purple of the heather just coming into flower, or the quaint streets of York? At another time her face would have been pasted to the window, savoring every sight, noting crumbling Roman walls, grand country estates, and towering church spires. This was a part of England she did not know well, but certainly wished to. Only she was too distracted—and she knew why.

But that just annoyed her all the more.

Across from her Mrs. McCaffery stirred, then blinked and

pushed herself upright. "Ach. 'Tis still midday," she complained.

Olivia smiled at the older woman's fuzzy expression. Mrs. Mac, as they called her, could have remained in town, queen of her domain. But where Augusta and her children went, so did she, albeit grumbling as she did. Despite the inconvenience of Augusta's gadding about this summer, Mrs. McCaffery had been determined to brave the lengthy journey north.

"Is your lumbago acting up?" Olivia asked as she handed her a pillow to prop herself up with.

The housekeeper twisted a bit, trying to get the pillow in just the right spot. She winced when the carriage jounced over a rocky patch of roadway. "Me bum is numb. And I don't aim to be entertaining you with me rhyme."

Olivia suppressed a grin. "If it makes you feel any better, we should come upon Eisingwold very soon. John Coachman tells me that Thirsk is less than three hours beyond there."

"Humph." Mrs. McCaffery shifted again, fitting the pillow at the small of her back. "And is Sarah still riding with Lord Hawke?"

Olivia kept her expression determinedly noncommittal. "She is."

The housekeeper peered past the open window. "That little hoyden is going to be sorry tomorrow, for she's not accustomed to spending so much time riding. Why haven't you called her back to the carriage?"

"And listen to her constant complaints?" Olivia rearranged her skirts, then took up her fan and began forcefully to ply it. "I certainly hope it's cooler in Scotland than it is here."

Mrs. McCaffery eyed her shrewdly. "D'you wish to explain your animosity toward Lord Hawke, child?"

Olivia forced a smile. "I should think it immediately obvious, especially to you."

The housekeeper's nearly nonexistent brows rose, furrowing her forehead. "Has he behaved too boldly with you? Is that it?"

"No." There was no reason for such a lie, but Olivia could not bring herself to discuss with anyone the unsettling effect

Neville Hawke's kisses had on her. "Don't you notice a re-semblance between him and someone else?" she said, to steer the conversation elsewhere.

The older woman's broad face creased in concentration. "Someone else? Who? One of the other suitors you dismissed?"

"No, no." Olivia heaved a sigh and clenched her jaw. "My father. He's just like my father."

"Pish. He looks nothing like your father. Cameron Byrde had hair the color of fire and he was—"

"Not in looks. In manner."

When Mrs. McCaffery just blinked at her, Olivia shook her head. "He's too charming. He dances too well." She ticked his faults off on her fingertips. "And he has a propensity to over-imbibe in spirits."

The woman eyed her closely. "I hadn't heard that about him. Indeed, from what your mother tells me, it's more like he's too good to be true."

Olivia swayed with the coach, all the while praying for patience. "Yes, and we both know she hasn't got the best judgment when it comes to men. Certainly my father was not nearly so good for her as he appeared. All that charm hid the truth of his selfish nature."

"On the other hand, she chose to marry Humphrey Palmer," Mrs. McCaffery pointed out. "He never once raised a hand to her nor gave her any cause to weep—save dying in his sleep. A better man than him you could not find."

The woman laid a warm hand on Olivia's knee. "I fear you are too hard on your mother, child. As for your father, it's true he had a charming manner. But he also had a cruel temper. If he hadn't drowned himself in whisky, then fallen off that pleasure barge and drowned in the filthy Thames, I might have been forced to smother him in his sleep." She tugged at her high neckline in agitation. "He caused your poor mother considerable grief. Considerable. But there's many a man less handsome and less charming who has made just as bad a husband as him. More's the pity. My point is, you cannot assume this Lord Hawke is of a kind with Cameron Byrde simply on account of his charming manner. You must give him more time, child."

Olivia resisted the urge to squirm. "There are other reasons as well," she muttered.

"Oh?" When Olivia did not respond, the older woman folded her hands across her ample bosom, watching her carefully. "Your mother likes him."

"So?"

"Sarah likes him as well."

"He bribed her with his horses." Olivia stared resentfully at her. "And you? Do you like him? Has he charmed you too?"

Mrs. McCaffery only shrugged. "I don't know the lad well enough yet to say. I'm sure, however, that I'll have sufficient time to form an opinion of him in the weeks to come."

"Yes. Well, I doubt we'll be seeing much of Lord Hawke. Once we reach Byrde Manor we'll be much too busy refurbishing the house. Besides, he has his own estates to manage."

The other woman snorted. "Do you really think that your mother will not invite the nearest peer to come calling? Your brother, too, is likely to invite him to join his shooting parties."

Olivia closed her fan with a snap and glared suspiciously at the housekeeper. "Botheration! Has Mother instructed you to push him on me, Mrs. Mac? Has she? For I will not have it."

"Tsk, tsk, child. Surely you know me better than that. I love your mother dearly, like the daughter I never had, and you three my own grandchildren. But my mind is my own, and my opinions too. You need a husband, never try to deny it. And you've been picky, to my great satisfaction. If Neville Hawke is not the right one for you, so be it. All I'm saying is, don't be too quick to compare him to your father."

"Very well, then." Olivia jutted her chin out. "I'll compare him to Humphrey, Humphrey who was steady, reliable, and kind. It has long been my intention to marry someone just like him, and so until I find such a gentleman, I shall enjoy my life as it is and do everything I can to discourage any other men who come calling. Especially Neville Hawke."

To Olivia's relief, Mrs. McCaffery allowed her the final

word. Yet Olivia took little comfort in it. For despite her vow to ignore the man, she suspected that Neville Hawke was going to remain a thorn in her side.

As the carriage rocked on through the lovely vale of York, she could not escape an even harder truth which she could admit to no one else. Neville Hawke was going to be a problem, not because he persisted in pursuing and taunting her but because of her perverse reaction to him. Like a traitor her body betrayed her with him. Her mind rightly said no to his appealing manner, but her body quivered shamefully with anticipation every time he turned his dark gaze upon her.

She let out a muffled groan. Even now, just remembering the way he'd kissed her made her stomach tighten in the most wanton manner. She plied her fan more vigorously, trying to cool the flushed skin of her neck and face. The peace she sought in the cool Scottish hills seemed more elusive than ever. But she comforted herself with the reminder that at least she would have Byrde Manor to occupy herself. In just two days she would take physical possession of her childhood home. With so much to prepare prior to the arrival of their guests, she would not have time to even think about Neville Hawke, never mind exchange any words with him—or kisses.

She grimaced at that last perverse thought, then closed her eyes and leaned her head back against the squabs. Two more days, she told herself. Just two more days. Surely she could control her unruly emotions that long.

The Mill House Inn just beyond the market town of Thirsk was a neat, prosperous sort of place. But it was small, with only four private rooms to let. Olivia, Sarah, and Mrs. McCaffery had to share one bedchamber while John Coachman and the guard took beds in the common room in the attic.

Where Neville Hawke and his men slept Olivia did not know. Nor did she know where he dined, for she rather rudely took a small dining room for the exclusive use of the women. After a plain but substantial meal of roast beef, roasted potatoes, and roasted vegetables, they retired promptly to their second-floor chamber.

But as she followed Sarah and Mrs. McCaffery toward the

stairs, Olivia glanced into the big taproom in the front of the inn and spied him sitting companionably with his man Bart. Her lips pursed in disapproval. Drinking, of course. When a pretty blond serving girl leaned over to whisper in his ear, Olivia's expression grew even more dour. Drinking *and* wenching. But then, what else should she expect?

As if Lord Hawke sensed her disapproval, he looked up. Their gazes collided, then held. Olivia sucked in a sharp breath. At the same moment he set down his cup and shook his head when the blonde bent to refill it.

Olivia swallowed hard when he rose to his feet, still staring at her. He meant to approach her. Though she wished desperately to scurry up to her chamber and slam the door closed, pride prevented her doing so. She would not hurry away like a frightened child and thereby reveal to him how easily he unsettled her emotions. So she waited for him, mindful that Sarah and Mrs. McCaffery had already disappeared from view up the narrow stairhall.

He stopped before her, the top of his head nearly brushing the low, planked ceiling. "I trust your accommodations are acceptable, Miss Byrde."

She nodded. "They are." Beyond them the clink of glasses sounded. The jovial hum of voices and the other everyday sounds of life continued. But Olivia's heightened senses focused solely on Lord Hawke. He appeared more at ease here than he had in Doncaster. His posture was more relaxed and at his throat his cravat was loosened. Most shocking of all, at least to her sensibilities, was that he had shed his coat in favor of only his waistcoat and shirtsleeves. Quite sensible given the warmth of the evening. But as they stood in the dimly lit hall, his dishabille lent a heady intimacy to their conversation, an inappropriate familiarity that she should not like. He was too overwhelmingly masculine like this, too virile, and far too attractive for her overwrought nerves.

She took a step back from him, gnawing on her lower lip. "I . . . um . . ." She glanced away from him, then back. "I wanted to . . . to thank you."

"Thank me?"

"For coming to my assistance. The other night."

One of his brows arched up a fraction. "With Mr. Garret, you mean."

She nodded. "I should have thanked you then, but I . . . Well, I'm sorry it took so long."

When he didn't respond right away, but only kept looking at her, heated color began to rise in her cheeks. "Well, then. Good night." She turned to leave.

"Wait. Before you go, I . . . ah . . . I wondered if you might prefer riding tomorrow instead of remaining in the confinement of the carriage. Like your mother, your sister insists that you are quite the horsewoman." He paused and his dark eyes seemed to grow darker and more intense. "You may ride Kitti, if you like."

Relieved that her awkward apology was over with, Olivia hesitated. The chance to ride Kitti! How she wished to accept his offer, for Kittiwake was quite the finest mare she'd ever seen. Certainly she'd never ridden an animal of such magnificent bloodlines. The quick "Thank you, but no" she meant to say died upon her lips. Instead she stared up at him, tempted beyond words by his offer.

Then he stepped forward—just one step nearer her—and all the reasons she must *not* accept his offer flared to life. Three times now he'd kissed her. Three times. And each time with an increasing ardor that made her go weak-kneed just to recall. Even now, standing in a public hallway, he somehow created an intimacy between them that was far too dangerous. Unlike her mother, however, she was too wise to succumb to that sort of temptation—no matter how much she wished to.

Willing her heart to cease its sudden thundering, she shook her head. "Thank you, but no. I . . . I prefer the carriage." Then, "Good night," and this time she turned for the stairs and began her ascent.

She almost reached the second floor without further incident. Almost.

"You're lying, Olivia," his soft, taunting words wafted up to her. "We both know you'd rather ride with me."

Olivia did not pause at the second floor, but ducked around

the corner, refusing to respond to his baiting, nor to his use of her given name.

But those last words of his echoed in her mind through the long sleepless night that followed. The mattress was lumpy; Sarah sprawled over her; and Mrs. McCaffery snored. But it was Neville Hawke's taunting voice that interrupted her sleep, Neville Hawke's voice that haunted her dreams. And in those dreams it was Neville Hawke and his magnificent horses that carried them hard and fast, riding together through the misty hills of Scotland.

But who followed whom? Who was pursued and who the pursuer? That she could never quite tell.

CHAPTER

14

"WHERE is he?" Sarah wondered for at least the tenth time.

They'd been on the road since early morning, the carriage and the accompanying riders—*sans* Lord Hawke.

"Don't put your head outside the window," Mrs. McCaffery scolded the girl. "As for Lord Hawke, I'm sure he will be along in his own good time. Just as his man explained."

Olivia shifted on the leather seat which somehow felt even harder than it had yesterday. She was tired and in a bad mood, and Sarah's insistent fretting over Neville Hawke grated on her nerves.

"If he runs true to form he no doubt overimbibed in the taproom last night and was unable to rise from his bed." *Assuming there were no other even more perverted reasons for his lingering in that bed. No blond reasons.*

Mrs. McCaffery raised one disapproving brow. "Why, Olivia, what an ungenerous remark. I'm surprised at you."

Again Olivia shifted on the seat. "Perhaps it is, but I have been exposed to more of Lord Hawke's behavior than have you."

Sarah glared at her. "You don't know why he's late. And just because you don't like him doesn't mean you have to criticize him. I like him," the girl pronounced. "He knows everything there is to know about horses. Everything. And he told me I can come up to Woodford Court whenever I wish to go riding."

"That won't be necessary," Olivia retorted. "James is bringing Goldie and Sugar up with him in a few days, so you needn't pester Lord Hawke."

"I'm not pestering him! He's happy to have me ride with me. He said so."

"I'm sure he is," Mrs. McCaffery interjected. "However, a well-mannered young lady never overstays her welcome. His offer is kind, to be sure. But I'm certain Lord Hawke does not intend for you to ride every day with him, Sarah. Nor will I allow it. He will rejoin us in his own good time. Until then, child, sit still. Read that book or take up your knitting. Otherwise, I will be forced to have you recite the orders of ascendancy or French grammar or"—she paused for effect—"your mathematical tables."

With that threat hanging over her, Sarah flopped back into her seat, albeit with much grumbling and several dark scowls directed as much at Olivia as at Mrs. McCaffery. Once Sarah settled into her corner with Olivia's novel, Mrs. McCaffery again dozed off. Olivia could scarcely believe it. The woman must be sleeping fully twenty hours a day.

Olivia rubbed her irritated eyes. How she wished she could do the same.

Neville was tired. He'd slept but four hours and had been astride for two now, pushing both himself and his stalwart mount to catch up with Olivia and her party. This past week had been a hard one. Too little sleep. Too much excitement. The thrill of winning; the successful sale of his racing stock.

Then there was the particular excitement associated with Miss Olivia Byrde. The unexpected excitement.

And the unexpected complication.

There had been a knot in the pit of his stomach ever since the incident with Clive Garret. How could she have thrown herself at the man that way? Was it for that damned journal of hers, research for a page on Clive Garret?

One thing was plain. She hadn't wanted Neville's help. She hadn't wanted him to step in and save her, she'd said, and she hadn't wanted him to kiss her. But he'd been unable to stop himself. Anger. Jealousy. Passion. They'd all combined to push him past the point of reason. The fact that she'd succumbed to her own passions in his arms had only confirmed what he already knew. She wanted him as fiercely as he wanted her.

But she absolutely refused to admit it.

So he'd stormed away furiously, swearing to abide by her wishes, misguided though they were. In the future he would leave her to her own defenses. She could throw herself in the path of the worst blackguard and he would not make a move to help her.

Or so he'd vowed at the time.

All that night he'd stewed over it, convinced that she'd kissed every man in that damned journal. Forty now, including him and that spineless Garret. In a weak moment he'd bolstered his seething anger with a bottle of twelve-year-old brandy, and come the dawn he'd succumbed with an aching head and roiling gut to a fitful few hours of sleep. But later, at her mother's first barely veiled hint, he'd leapt at the chance to escort her to Scotland. Afterward he'd berated himself for a fool. But he'd held to the promise he made to Olivia's mother.

Now, as he approached Croft, he knew he must make some decision about Miss Olivia Byrde. Court her or ignore her. There was no middle ground.

It had been easier yesterday to be distracted by her little sister. Then last night outside the taproom, to his utter surprise she had thanked him, though it had been as much an apology as thanks. He'd dwelt on it all night. By the time he'd gone to bed at dawn, he'd known he could avoid this dilemma no longer. There was an attraction between them that frightened her. And why not? It frightened him. It scared the hell out of him.

But he needed to see it through, to see if she was that good woman Bart said might bring him ease. They were well matched in temperament and passion, and that was far more than most marriages could boast.

So he leaned over Robin's withers, urging him on, and just beyond Darlington, in the courtyard of the Snail and Rook, he spied the heavily-loaded Dunmore traveling coach. He was no sooner dismounted, however, and handing his horse over to the ostler, than Olivia and Sarah came down the three granite steps, followed by their housekeeper. Sarah spied him and at once dashed across the yard to his side.

Neville removed his hat and thrust one hand through his rumpled hair. How nice it would be if Olivia evinced even half the enthusiasm for him that her sister did. But Olivia's face had pulled together in a faint frown, and though his normal response to that would be to taunt her or bait her with a wink or a grin, at the moment he could not muster the energy. He felt like an old man, tired and aching. Defeated and depressed.

"Lord Hawke, you're here!" Sarah's pretty little face glowed with excitement.

Somehow he managed a smile. To be that young again, and filled with such a zest for life. "I am indeed here, and I warrant I can read your mind."

"I warrant you can," she agreed, hopping in her anticipation from one foot to the other.

Mrs. McCaffery trained a stern eye on her young charge. "Sarah Palmer, it is hardly the behavior of a well-mannered young lady to press her wishes upon a gentleman who has already—"

"It's all right," Neville interrupted. "If she wishes to ride one of my horses again, she is most welcome."

"That's very generous of you," Olivia put in, "But quite unnecessary."

Neville sent her a sharp look. "You are welcome to ride with her."

She lifted her chin but did not quite meet his gaze. "Thank you, but no."

Mrs. McCaffery cleared her throat and fidgeted a moment with the carpetbag she held. "Might I . . . ah . . . presume to ride in her stead?" she ventured.

Neville's brows arched in surprise. "Why, of course. Though I do not have a sidesaddle."

"Pish. I am a Scotswoman and I grew up riding astride."

"She jumps too," Sarah threw in. "James told me," she added when the woman stared at her in surprise. The girl clapped her hands with glee, then sent her sister a gloating look. "It appears you shall have to keep to your own gloomy company today, Livvie, while we shall have a glorious time."

Olivia ignored her sister and addressed herself to Mrs. McCaffery instead. "Are you certain you will be comfortable astride?"

"Humph. After two and a half days jouncing along in that coach? Anything would be more comfortable than that. I'll just take one of those light traveling blankets—for modesty," she added with a prim nod.

It was then that the idea occurred to Neville. He glanced at the carriage, then back at Olivia. "Perhaps, Miss Byrde, you would be so kind as to allow me to share your carriage this afternoon. I find myself in need of a nap," he added when she opened her mouth—to object, he imagined. "I would consider it a great personal favor. You will not even know I am there."

When everyone turned to stare at her, Olivia closed her mouth with a snap. But she nearly choked on the words she forced down. What a sneaky, conniving . . . conniving . . . She was too incensed by his high-handedness to even think straight. Yet they all waited for her response, Sarah's eyes sparking with amusement, Mrs. McCaffery's brows raised in speculation, and Lord Hawke's face . . .

Lord Hawke's face looked tired. He looked weary, exhausted even. As quickly as that, Olivia's objections faded. He did need a nap, or better yet, a good night's sleep. What was it that made him keep such long hours, that drove him to this point of utter exhaustion? Perhaps today she might have the chance to find out.

She clutched her reticule and composed her face. But her hands trembled. "You are welcome to ride in the carriage, Lord Hawke. Considering your generosity to my sister, how could I possibly turn you away?"

She saw the surprise register in his dark eyes. But he only gave her a short bow. "If you will allow me a word with Bart, I will make the necessary arrangements for the horses."

"I will have the innkeeper pack you a luncheon," Mrs. McCaffery said, and as quickly as that the details of their altered traveling status were adjusted. The older woman returned to the inn. Sarah trailed after Lord Hawke, and Olivia was left standing alone beside the carriage. The enclosed carriage she would very shortly share with Neville Hawke.

Good lord. What had she done?

She had less than ten minutes to compose herself before John and the guard climbed into the driver's box, and Lord Hawke stepped into the carriage. She was already inside, with her bonnet and gloves off, and her book open on her lap.

"You may use that pillow," she said when he sat opposite her. Then she turned her attention to the window and the two who'd abandoned her to this awkward situation. "Be careful, Sarah," she called from the window. And you too, Mrs. Mac." When they grinned and waved gaily to her, she gritted her teeth. "No jumping," she added, under her breath. Then she focused her eyes deliberately back upon her novel.

It was nearly impossible, however, for her to keep them there.

The carriage lurched forward, wheeling slowly through the posting house yard and out into the highway, turning north. The horses settled into a regular pace; the carriage creaked and rocked. The lanterns and window shades swayed, and a midday breeze laden with the scents of grass and horses and fecund earth gusted warm against Olivia's cheek. The morning journey had been no different from this, she told herself. Nor had yesterday's.

And yet everything was different.

Across from her, Neville Hawke had positioned the pillow against the side wall and leaned back upon it, his legs sprawled across the seat and into the empty aisle. They were long legs, she noted from beneath the veil of her lashes. Long legs snugly encased in dark gray twill breeches that displayed powerfully muscled thighs and well-shaped knees. His lower legs were covered in tall riding boots, well worn but of the finest quality. Probably his favorite riding boots, worn when there was no need to impress. That he felt no need to impress her left her somewhat unsettled.

He'd tucked his gloves into his pocket, and his bare hands lay folded across his stomach. Square palms and long square-tipped fingers. His hands were big, she noted, just like the rest of him.

She focused harder on page 71 of her book. They were too big, she decided, recalling how those hands had swallowed up hers when they'd danced. Indeed, no matter what the occasion, by his very presence he seemed always to swallow up everything: her hands when they'd waltzed; her will when they kissed.

She took a deep breath. He even seemed to swallow up the air when they were enclosed together as they were now.

"What are you reading?"

She jerked in alarm and the book slid right off her lap. He retrieved it, thenn thumbed idly through the pages. "*Emma*. I hope this is one of those sensational novels frowned upon by the clergy."

Olivia eyed him warily. "Why should you hope for that?"

"Because it would confirm my opinion of you." He smiled, a slow, lazy grin made even more lazy by his semirecumbent posture, and offered the book to her.

"No doubt you expect me to ask just what that opinion is," she retorted.

"I believe you already know."

Olivia wanted to shrug off his words, so full of meanings she did not entirely comprehend. If he intended to rattle her nerves, he was succeeding most admirably. All she could do, however, was to affect the same dismissive manner she used with other men she wished not to engage in prolonged conversation. "Enjoy your nap, Lord Hawke. I know I shall enjoy my reading."

She reached for the slim volume he held out. In the transfer, however, their hands touched—merely the graze of their fingers. Nothing more. But there were no gloves to dilute the impact, no supple leather to disguise the warmth of that momentary contact. Olivia sucked in a little breath and clutched the book in her hands, and this time she stared straight at him.

"I don't know what your game is, Lord Hawke, but I do not wish to play it."

He heaved a great sigh. "No game, Olivia—Miss Byrde. I

wish only the luxury of a nap." So saying, he shifted his great length into a more comfortable position, folded his arms across his chest, and closed his eyes.

For long minutes silence reigned in the warm confines of the carriage. It was Olivia who broke it. "I notice you do not sleep well at night."

After a short silence he answered. "No."

She cleared her throat, then plunged on. "Is that why you drink so much?"

He opened one eye. "Should I assume any answer I make will find its way into your journal?"

"I've no need to write anything further of you, Lord Hawke, for it is unlikely my opinion of you will change. You will make no woman a good husband, I think, and so will I say should any of my friends consult me in the matter—which is also unlikely. So, to respond to your question, no, your answer will not find its way into my journal."

Both of his eyes were open now and fixed upon her. "Then why do you ask it? Never say that it is because you are interested in me."

He was smiling now, and she felt the tug of an answering smile on her own lips. Their eyes held too long, though, and her smile faded. "Why do you sit up and drink so late every night?"

He looked away, staring up at the cream-colored tufted leather ceiling. "That should be obvious to a woman of your keen perceptions. I do not like the nighttime and so I drink to get me through the long hours of darkness."

Olivia traced one finger back and forth across the spine of her book. There was nothing obvious about it. "Wouldn't sleep be a better solution?" she asked in a softer voice.

"I have trouble at night sleeping unless I am completely exhausted—or completely drunk. It is that simple and that complicated."

Olivia considered him, the long muscular body, the strong profile—the lines of weariness that bracketed his mouth and fanned out from the corners of his eyes. "I hope you do not intend to drink here, in my presence."

She thought that might provoke a rise from him, and indeed, she would have welcomed a tart retort, for there was something unsettling about this conversation. There was a vulnerability about him now, a humanity she did not like being forced to acknowledge.

"Never fear, Miss Byrde. I'll try not to offend your sense of propriety." He glanced at her, then away, then closed those moody blue eyes once more. "If I snore, I hope you will not add that to my list of sins. Just kick me and I'll try to stop."

He remained silent after that. Whether he slept, she could not tell, for he did not snore. But his breathing came slow and even, and aside from grimacing once or twice when the road grew especially rough, he did not stir.

Olivia, however, was not nearly so fortunate. Her mind spun, incited by the nearness of this man who managed to rouse so many new emotions in her. She focused repeatedly on the erstwhile heroine of her book, but Emma's machinations paled beside the complications of her own situation. The most exasperating man she'd ever known slept not two feet from her. How could she not stare and wonder and let her imagination soar?

He had a series of scars along his jaw. From the war? He suffered from sleeplessness and probably had been drinking most of the night. Again. Was that also due to his experience on the Continent? Or could it be due to something else? The loss of his family, perhaps. Or the loss of a woman.

Olivia gnawed the side of her mouth as she mulled over that somewhat unwelcome thought. Yet as her eyes roamed over him, she could not shake the idea. He was a man that women would always seek out. She knew the type. He was not the pretty, dandified sort that was so often preferred in the drawing rooms in town. But in the bedrooms . . .

She felt hot color rise in her cheeks. Heavens! She should not think such vulgar thoughts. Yet they persisted. Neville Hawke was no doubt the sort of man who knew his way around a woman's boudoir. Certainly he knew how to kiss a woman—and very well. He knew how to seduce with only his taunting eyes and his challenging words, never mind those overwhelming kisses. That bespoke a considerable experience, something she did not wish to think about. Those strong arms, those wide shoulders. He would be able to handle himself in a fight as well as in a lady's bedroom, and it behooved her to remember it.

Still, watching him sleep softened all that knowledge. It cast his vices in a more generous light. She did not wish to see his vulnerabilities, yet she could not look away. He needed a haircut, she decided, and someone to ease the lines of worry in his brow.

But not her.

She forced herself to stare out the window, to locate Sarah and examine the passing countryside. But her thoughts remained stubbornly on Neville Hawke. She did not intend to write anything further about him on the crowded page she'd given him in her journal. She'd vented herself more than enough on his account. But if she *were* to write about him again, it would only be fair to say that the night was not his friend, and that he was kind to children.

She turned again to gaze at him.

And that he was beautiful in his own hard, masculine manner. Almost too beautiful for her to resist.

Almost.

CHAPTER

15

I⊤ rained the last two hours of their journey that day. Roused by the storm, Neville rejoined Bart and the horses, while Sarah and Mrs. McCaffery returned to the shelter of the carriage. As was her wont, the housekeeper swiftly dozed off, as did Sarah.

But Olivia did not sleep. She peered glumly past the tied-down curtain, out into the gray slashing rainstorm. As the team of horses labored down the uneven highway, and the rumble of the wheels sloshed accompaniment to the irregular rumble of thunder, she told herself that the poor animals and the drenched coachman and guard had more troubles than she, for there seemed no relief in sight from the storm's violent onslaught.

Sympathy for the others did nothing to dispel her own dreary thoughts. She was behaving like an idiot where Neville Hawke was concerned, but she could not manage to stop herself.

The lowering clouds brought an early dusk, and though the rain relented to only a miserable drizzle, they were late arriving at the Bull's Manger alongside the Tyne River in Prudhoe. It was a place similar to last night's accommodations, and as before, the three women dined in a small private room. When Sarah and Mrs. McCaffery went up to make their nightly ablutions, however, Olivia remained behind. She wished only to check on John Coachman. But it was another she sought, and as she approached the low-ceilinged taproom, she could not deny it.

They sat at a scarred plank table, five men with Neville Hawke at the head. When he spied her he pushed at once to his feet. The others, following the direction of his gaze, turned toward her. There were a few other women there, but Olivia nonetheless felt intensely out of place. John Coachman rose also and hurried to her side.

"Is everything a'right, miss?" Without a hat his bald pate gleamed in the smoky light.

"We are fine," she answered, focusing with an effort on him. "I simply wanted to reassure myself that you have not taken a chill or . . . or anything."

He beamed at her. "Not a'tall, miss. Not a'tall. We saw to the horses—gave 'em an extra portion just like you said. Then we shed our wet duds and had us a good hot dinner."

"Yes. Well." Olivia glanced past him to the table where Neville had reseated himself. But he still stared at her. She looked away. "Yes. Well, good night, then. We'll see you in the morning."

Once upstairs she prepared for bed and read a short while by candlelight, alone in one moss-filled mattress while Mrs. McCaffery and Sarah shared the other. She was tired. Exhausted. Yet sleep remained elusive. She lay in the dark staring up at the ceiling. Was this how Neville Hawke spent his nights, his body weary but his mind churning with thoughts he could not escape?

She repositioned the coarse bed linens across her chest, then folded one arm under her head. Was that why he drank, to deaden his mind? Certainly he did not overimbibe during the day, or any other time he was in mixed company.

Unlike her father.

In the quiet of the darkened room—and the relative safety of it—Olivia closed her eyes. Perhaps Neville Hawke was not as much like her father as she initially feared. Except for their first unfortunate meeting—and his misunderstanding of who she was—she would have found him a perfectly acceptable fellow.

Across the room Mrs. McCaffery let out a snort. Sarah mumbled something, but the two of them quickly subsided to the even breathing of deep sleep. Olivia sighed at her own perversity. The truth was, Neville Hawke could never be classified a perfectly acceptable fellow, for he was like no other man she might place in that unobjectionable category. Or at least she reacted differently to him than she did to any of those other men.

Should she examine more closely the reason for that?

Was she fighting an attraction to him that she ought instead to explore? Olivia blew out a frustrated breath. She grew more confused by the day.

Turning onto her side, she grimaced at the stiffness in her back. Two days on the road was getting to her, no matter how well-sprung the carriage. She should have accepted Lord Hawke's offer to ride one of his fine animals.

She thought of his face as he lay sleeping in the carriage today, so peaceful and yet still so ruggedly handsome. She sighed and wriggled into a more comfortable position. Maybe tomorrow she would be a little friendlier toward him. Yes, friendlier, she thought as she drifted off. There was no harm in being pleasant to the man, was there?

She awoke with a start, groggy and confused, unaware she'd gone to sleep at all. What time was it? Where was she?

A shout, then an angry voice, brought all her senses suddenly alert. But the brouhaha was far away, not in the hall nor even in the room adjacent to theirs.

At a cry of pure anguish and a crash, she jerked upright in the bed. What in God's name was going on?

Mrs. McCaffery grumbled in her sleep; Sarah did not react at all. But Olivia slid out of bed, thoroughly alarmed. Some altercation was taking place. A man shouted, words she could not make out. Another voice broke in, then another crash. Were they fighting?

She snatched up her wrapper and ran for the door, though what she could do about such an imbroglio escaped her. Still, something niggled in her mind. She hoped Neville was not involved in the melee.

When she slipped out into the hall, she realized with a sinking heart that he was.

"Jesus God!" The voice was unmistakably his—and unmistakably drunk.

"C'mon, lad," a lower, calmer voice urged.

"Get the hell away from me. Get away!"

Olivia shrank back from the rage and misery in Neville's voice, a voice too much like her father's had been that time he'd struck her mother. The other man said something she could not make out, but Neville's reply was clear enough. "Oh no. Oh no. I'm sorry, Bart. I'm sorry."

"C'mon lad. It's all right. You're just too tired. I'll help you up to your chamber abovestairs."

"I can't sleep," Neville replied, in a voice laced with agony. "Ah, damn! Leave me be. Leave me be!"

Olivia bit her lip in indecision. Foolish as it was, she wanted to go to him. He'd just proven to her that he was exactly what she did not want in a man, and yet she foolishly wanted to go to him and somehow ease his unhappiness.

"But you can't," she said out loud. Then startled by her own voice and the tread of heavy feet up on the stairs, she pressed back against the door to her room, her arms wrapped tightly around her.

"We'll see to the damage," she heard Neville's horse trainer say to someone belowstairs. "You needn't fret on that score." That he spoke with the authority of someone who'd dealt with such scenes in the past only depressed Olivia further.

The footsteps grew nearer. Olivia knew she should slip back inside her room before anyone saw her. But something urged her to stay put.

"D'ye need help, milord?" Bart called up the stairs.

"No." Neville's response was slow to come. "No." Then he trudged up the last few steps to the landing and into her view.

Clad only in his shirtsleeves, with his hair disheveled and his posture a little unsteady, he reminded her in that instant of the first night they'd met. But then he'd been all smiles and charm, despite the considerable amount of liquor he must have consumed. Now he appeared truly miserable, his face haggard, his shoulders drooping.

She rubbed her hands up and down her arms. It was all so tragic.

He hesitated at the top of the stairs, raked his rumpled hair back with both hands, and turned away from her shadowed crevice. But then he paused and swung around—and speared her with his eyes.

Even in the dim hall, lit only with one flickering wall lamp near the head of the stairs, he managed to spy her. She stiffened at once, and he, too, straightened.

"Ah, Hazel," he murmured. "Still creeping about at night, I see."

"I . . . Something—a noise—awakened me."

"A noise. A dream." His eyes seemed to focus somewhere between them. "A nightmare."

She swallowed, and despite her garb of nightrail and thin wrapper, she stepped out of the protective doorway. "Were you dreaming? Is that it? I thought I heard someone fighting."

"There was a fight." His voice was strange and distant, only slightly slurred. Then, as she advanced nearer still, his gaze refocused on hers. "You are here."

Olivia stopped. She was an arm's length from him. Far too close. Far too dangerous. Yet after watching his face this afternoon as he slept, she was hard-pressed to fear for her safety. And she needed to understand why he was so unhappy. "Neville," she began.

"Shh." He lifted one finger to his lips. "Shh. There's people sleepin'." His gaze sharpened and ran over her. "You should be sleepin' too—or at least in bed."

Then without warning, he caught her by one wrist and began to drag her down the hall, away from her room and toward his.

Olivia struggled to get away, digging in her heels and twisting her arm. "Neville. Stop this. Stop it!"

"Shh." He caught her by the other arm as well and pressed her against the wall. "Shh. Hazel. Olivia."

She knew where this was going. Every fiber in her body knew where it was going. She knew also that she ought to scream the house down and let him deal with the repercussions.

She knew all that, and yet she was unable to do it. Or unwilling.

"Lord Hawke," she began again, trying, despite the violent thundering of her heart, to strike a reasonable tone. "You've had too much to drink. Please don't do anything now that you will regret come the morning."

"Regret?" He shook his head slowly, keeping his dark blue eyes fastened upon her lips. "When there's so much else to regret, how can I possibly regret this?"

Olivia expected him to kiss her. In truth, a part of her wanted him to. But though he lowered his head nearer and nearer, he did not kiss her. Instead his thumb traced the shape of her lower lip, then stroked slowly down her chin and throat. But that lightness of touch was a deception, for the impact on her equanimity was profound.

Then he drew his hand further down her chest to the valley between her breasts.

Olivia sucked in a breath, but otherwise she could not move.

"For once, no regrets," he murmured. Then that thumb moved to stroke across the taut peak of her left breast. He stroked across it, then around it, then back and forth in the most sultry manner imaginable.

No. In the most sultry manner *unimaginable*. Olivia never could have imagined him touching her there, or that it would affect her so.

She should make him stop. She had to make him stop!

But Olivia was frozen in place, frozen in this moment as he explored parts of her body only a husband should explore. Then he cupped that breast, taking its full weight in his hand, and undulated his palm against the aching peak of her nipple.

"Oh my." She breathed the words, feeling for all the world as if she were melting beneath him. "Oh my."

Heat welled up from her belly, damp and sweet, and she could hardly stand upright. Then he caught her other breast, kneading them both, and she had to clasp his arms not to melt into a boneless puddle on the floor.

That was when he chose to kiss her, capturing her mouth with his lips and tongue and taking full possession of it.

How Olivia loved his kisses. Despite all her protests to the contrary, in her heart of hearts, she admitted that she loved his kisses. But this kiss, as deep, thorough, and mind-drugging as it was—this kiss was not right. It was all wrong.

Though she rose into the kiss and his bold, rousing caress, some part of her drew apart from him. Then she realized the problem.

Whisky! He tasted of sweet, pungent whisky.

Olivia twisted her head aside. How could she forget he was drunk? Like on that first night he was drunk and willing to kiss any woman he happened upon—and perhaps do far worse than merely kiss her.

"No." She shoved against his chest, but he might have been the wall itself for all the effect she had. "Stop it. Stop, or I'll scream!"

When one of his hands slipped around to cup her derriere, however, and pressed her belly against his loins, the sound she let out was more a gulp than a scream. Her breasts. Her bottom. Was there no part of her that his touch did not bring to hot, seething life?

"Oh help," she murmured, though it was more a prayer than a cry for aid. She was succumbing to him, when she knew full well she should not.

He seemed to sense it as well. "At last, my Hazel," he whispered hotly in her ear. "At last I have you."

But he did not have her, she vowed on a renewed spurt of resolve. "I am not your Hazel," she swore through clenched teeth. She ducked down under one of his arms and managed somehow to evade his off-balanced grasp. She scrambled away. "I'm not Hazel at all!"

Then she fled, not looking back, nor wanting to see whether he pursued her or whether he was content to let her go.

Once in her room, she shoved the door bolt home, then leaned heavily against the sturdy planks, her heart racing. With eyes closed, she bowed her forehead against the door. But in her mind's eye she could still see Neville, shed of his coat and waistcoat, so tall and strong, yet weak and swaying, brought low by the quantity of liquor he'd consumed.

Just like that first night.

Despite her growing desire to explain that incident as an aberration, to justify it and ignore the greater implications, she knew she could not. That night had been no fluke, nor was tonight. It was the sleeping man in the carriage, vulnerable and momentarily at peace, who had been the aberration.

She pressed her ear to the door, listening for any sound from him. But there was none. Slowly her heart's pace began to relent. Slowly her panic eased, to be replaced by a truth she did not want to acknowledge: for all his charm, for all his dangerous appeal, there was something tragic about Neville Hawke. He bore some scar on his soul so deep it seemed unable to heal. Sleep did not lend him reprieve, nor did whisky. Most certainly she could not heal it by succumbing to his sensual appeal.

He was not the right man for her, she acknowledged, nor for any other sensible woman. She'd known that instinctively, though she'd begun to forget. But she would not forget it again.

In the silence of the night, broken only by the dripping of rainwater from the eaves above the window, Olivia crawled woodenly into bed. She lay as before, with the bed linens pulled up to her chin, staring up at the blank ceiling. But it was not the same. She was not the same. Her body was different, touched as it had never been touched before. Touched in a way she was likely never to forget. Her thoughts were different too. Darker. Gloomier. And over all hung the ugly truth she must accept once and for all. Neville Hawke had managed somehow, despite all her efforts, to worm his way into her affections.

But she must break the hold he had taken on her foolish emotions. She must break it now before he ended up breaking her heart.

Neville awoke with a pounding head and a mouth that tasted like stall scrapings. The room was bright. Too bright. He did not dare open his eyes. But his ears, they functioned well enough for him to know he was not home at Woodford Court. Where was he?

Somewhere outside a man called out. A horse whinnied and the wheels of a carriage clattered noisily across cobblestone paving. He laid one hand across his eyes, then winced. His head felt ready to split open. Slowly he flexed his neck, gingerly tilting his head from side to side. He was not at home, for this was not his bed. Where in hell was he?

Then he remembered, and he let out a groan. An inn outside the town of Prudhoe in Northumbria. Another day's journey to Woodford Court—with Olivia Byrde and her entourage to escort to Byrde Manor.

He sat up, clenching his teeth against a violent wave of nausea. He'd been doing so well of late. What idiocy had pushed him to drink to the point of passing out last night? More importantly, however, had he done anything he should know about? Anything stupid or cruel or destructive?

With an effort he swung his legs around. He was still dressed, boots and all. What had happened?

He sat on the edge of the bed a long while, gathering his strength and gathering his thoughts. He'd been so tired last night, too tired to fight sleep away until dawn arrived. So he'd sought relief in drink, enough drink to deaden his mind and keep the nightmares at bay.

But it hadn't worked.

He shuddered as a vague memory crept through the cracks in his mind. Bart dozing in the taproom; everyone else departed. He'd been alone, him and a bottle of strong Scotch whisky. Then the others had arrived. Men dead four years now. Enemies attacking; friends dying, their last breath a scream of agony. He shuddered now at the horror of it all. It had been pitch-dark and blood-red, and he'd been afraid and in pain and fighting for his life. Again.

His stomach knotted and he lurched to his feet. Grabbing for a bowl, he retched up the contents of his stomach. He emptied his guts through a stream of tears until he was empty. Completely empty.

Only then, with his head sagging low between his shoulders, did he wipe his eyes and take a long steadying breath—several long steadying breaths. He had to get up, to get moving. To find out what damage, if any, he'd wrought to either people or furnishings. After that he had to climb onto a horse and ride the last fifty miles to Woodford Court. At the moment, he wasn't sure he could do it.

Then he thought of Olivia who'd so reluctantly shared her carriage with him yesterday, of her wariness around him and her cautious interest. She would wonder again at his absence this morning. He knew her well enough now to know she had not been appeased by his vague replies to her inquiries about his nocturnal habits.

With an effort he raised his head and stared through gritty eyes at his simple surroundings. A sound roof over his head, a decent mattress, and enough to eat. That should be sufficient for any man.

And a woman for warmth and comfort.

He blinked as he considered that last. He had all those things, save for the woman. Did he dare try that? Did he dare woo Olivia Byrde for more than the fallow fields in her valley? Did he dare hope that she might revitalize the fallow fields of his soul?

He sucked in a long breath, sour with old drink and new vomit. He was a disgusting excuse for a man. A coward and a drunk. But the world hailed him as a hero and he had a way with horses. If he could just maintain the façade a little longer. If he could just make sure she never saw him as he'd been last night—as he was now. If he could just hold on long enough to woo her and win her, maybe he could find a way out of this pit of despair that was his life.

He thrust a hand through his hair. He did not deserve a woman like her. He was a selfish bastard to deceive her, to work so hard to seduce her. In the end she would grow to hate him. But he wanted her anyway. He needed her. And if nothing else good came of their union, he would at least improve the lot of the two hundred souls at Woodford and in the nearby town of Kelso who depended on him for their survival.

It was mid-afternoon, a gray afternoon threatening weather as vile as the previous day's, before Lord Hawke caught up with their carriage. By that time Olivia had steeled herself for the unpleasant task of facing him again.

Though a part of her wished to expose his coarse behavior to public condemnation, another part of her—the practical part of her—hesitated. In exposing his behavior she risked being tarred by the same brush. What was she doing in the hallway of a public inn, clad only in her nightclothes? Why had she not revealed his scandalous behavior at once? Why had she not informed her mother of his too forward manner from the beginning?

No, Olivia knew she dared not condemn him publicly now. Unfortunately, he was her neighbor, and that meant she must maintain some level of civility toward him. But nothing more, she vowed, not after last night.

It had taken but an innocent-sounding inquiry to the pinch-faced morning maid to uncover the rest of last night's sordid details. Lord Hawke had smashed a fine bottle of Scotch, shattered a tray of the landlord's glasses, and broken two chairs and a side table. He'd swung at the landlord and nearly struck his own man. He'd been mad with the drink, the woman had whispered, rolling her eyes and shuddering. Mad with the drink.

All day long Olivia had mulled those words over. As they'd neared the border with Scotland, she'd hardly noticed the low stone remnants of Hadrian's wall marching across the land-scape, separating the north country from the south. Likewise she'd been blind to the beauty of the Cheviot Hills the carriage had started to climb. Everything she saw was colored by her dark and dismal thoughts of Neville Hawke. He'd been mad with drink last night, destructive with it. That he drank to assuage the pain of some private torture she did not doubt. But knowing that changed nothing. He had frightened her last night and more so this morning when she'd learned the full extent of his destructive rage. She should count it a blessing that she hadn't fallen further under his spell than this.

Now as the thunder of hoofbeats came up beside the carriage, as Sarah's eyes lit up with the excitement of seeing him again, Olivia braced herself to remain cool and aloof, and immune from whatever charming façade he adopted today.

"You're late!" Sarah exclaimed, ignoring Mrs. McCaffery's disapproving frown. Her hands gripped the window edge and the wind whipped her curls around her eager face. "Why are you so late?"

"Better late than never," he said, tipping his hat to the exuberant child. When he peered inside the open window, however, Olivia refused to meet his gaze. He had the gall to approach her after last night? Instead she stared at the fine leather saddle he rode, and the smoothly bunching muscles of his horse's sleek flank. Still, she saw enough of him to know he'd slept poorly. He was clean and well groomed for a man who'd been stinking drunk last night, then ridden thirty miles already today. His posture was erect and he sat his animal as easily as most men sat upon their dinner chairs. Somehow it only increased her ire.

But for all that, his eyes looked tired and his face weary.

Even Sarah appeared to notice, for instead of broadly hinting her desire to ride, which desire she probably guessed Olivia would deny, she took quite the opposite tack. "Would you like to ride in the carriage with us? There's room enough. Isn't there, Livvie?"

Three sets of eyes turned her way, and it was all Olivia could do not to slouch down in her seat. Sarah, outspoken brat that she was, beamed at her with an utterly false smile of innocence. Mrs. McCaffery raised her brows and stared as if Olivia's answer was of particular interest to her. As for Lord Hawke, Olivia did not even bother to look at him, for she knew what she'd see on his face: triumph.

He guided his mount to within arm's reach of her window, and when she did not immediately speak up, he did. "If it is not inconvenient, I would happily accept your sister's kind offer, Miss Byrde. Robin here would appreciate it too," he said, patting his horse's damp neck. "For I have ridden him hard and fast this morning."

She was trapped and he knew it. Olivia pinched her lips together. She should have confided in Mrs. Mac; she wouldn't be in this dilemma if the proper housekeeper knew the liberties

Lord Hawke had taken with her. But Olivia hadn't told her, and now she must respond. "Very well," she muttered with less grace than she ought. The look she sent her much-too-forward sister, however, was clearly disapproving.

Sarah's eyes widened at once, as if to say, "What have I done?" But she knew, the little brat.

Within a few moments the carriage stopped and Lord Hawke gave Robin into his trainer's keeping. When he climbed into the spacious traveling coach it immediately grew smaller and more confining. That it was more than his physical size which caused Olivia's sudden sense of overwhelming closeness only increased her annoyance. Botheration! but he was the epitome of a rake: handsome, charming, and too over-whelmingly virile for her maidenly sensibilities. And all the while a drunken lout.

She was an idiot to be so affected by him, for he was utterly wrong for her. And adding insult to injury, he had the gall to behave as if nothing whatsoever had occurred last night. How dare he!

He sat beside her, a good foot of empty seat between them, for she had crowded up against the window. Yet she could swear heat radiated directly from his body into hers. A blustery wind began to clear the skies and also kept the afternoon temperature down. Yet Olivia felt perilously close to perspiring.

For an hour they rode thus, Olivia railing silently at him while he and Mrs. McCaffery filled Sarah's head with Scottish lore. Only when they paused on the crest of a hill and gazed down the long slope into the Borders of lowland Scotland, did she have a brief reprieve. She was as much Scottish as English, and so felt a tiny thrill as she gazed over her other homeland.

"These are pleasant rolling hills compared to the rocky crags of the Highlands," Lord Hawke said to Sarah.

"Ach. My mother was a Highlander," Mrs. McCaffery said. "It's been an age since I've looked upon the snowy peaks of Ben Nevis and Ben Alder."

"As the road angles east we shall begin to descend a bit," he said. "The river Tweed runs through a lovely green valley on its long trek to the North Sea." He paused and shifted, and Olivia had the distinct impression he was peering at her. She kept her eyes determinedly focused beyond the window, but a bead of moisture began a tickling trickle down between her breasts.

"There are several boats at Woodford Court," he went on. "If you are amenable, one day we can make an outing of it, head upstream to fish, then allow the river to deliver us back home in the afternoon." He paused. "What do you say, Miss Byrde? Would you and your sister enjoy that?"

Olivia glanced at him, then away. "I would not dream of presuming on your time that way."

"It would be my pleasure."

Gritting her teeth, Olivia said the only thing she could think of to end this conversation. "Perhaps." Spying Sarah's curious look, she tried to arrange her own face into a pleasanter expression. "Perhaps."

But inside she knew better. She would not be drawn into Neville Hawke's sphere again, nor charmed by his appealing manner. She would keep her emotions firmly in check. For by day Neville Hawke seemed to be everything she could want in a man. But by night he was something else again, dark and dangerous, both to himself and anyone who came too near.

And soon it would again be night.

As the heavy coach moved on, Olivia stared out the window to where the edge of the forest hid the lowering sun. The sky had cleared to lavender, and the air was soft. The sun gave a last glint of gold through the dark shadows of a stand of sycamores, one last, regretful glint, then it disappeared behind the towering silhouettes of the trees.

Gazing after it, Olivia realized that she was a creature of the day, and longed for the sun. But Neville Hawke was a creature of the night. He needed the dark to protect the ugly side of his personality from public view. Light and dark. Day and night. Even without his drunken misbehavior, that was enough reason to keep them apart.

At that moment he turned and gave her a quick, heart-stopping smile.

Olivia swallowed, then averted her gaze. She just hoped she could remember how ill-suited they were during the several months to come.

CHAPTER

16

THE last hour of their journey was accompanied by a thousand stars. A million. But there was no moon and almost complete darkness. Lights here and there guided them, however: a cottage in a little dale, a public house at a crossing.

Lord Hawke had returned to horseback, as this was familiar territory for him, and John Coachman was happy to follow his lead.

Beyond her window the river Tweed glinted but faintly in the absence of light. Olivia heard the play of water along the near shore, the cry of night birds. She breathed deeply of the cool night air, redolent of spruce and damp and other scents she did not recognize. Her home, place of her birth. Despite her weariness she felt a mounting excitement. When Neville called out to John to halt, she leaned out the window, squinting to see.

"Bart will continue up this road to Woodford Court with the horses. I'll guide you across the river here. It's a shorter passage to Byrde Manor."

"That's really not necessary," Olivia began. "If you'll just give us directions."

"It's no trouble. We cross at the ford just ahead," he said to John. "I'll lead the way."

Olivia sat back. High-handed wretch!

Sarah immediately took her place at the window. "I wish I could ride," she complained. "I'm tired of being cooped up in this old coach."

"Patience, child," said Mrs. McCaffery. "We're very nearly there as I recall. A mile at most."

Down the shallow riverbank they went, holding on to their seats, rocking with the carriage as the weary team picked its way across the gravel ford. "Don't worry," Olivia said. "You will have ample opportunity to apply all that pent-up energy starting first thing in the morning."

"Shall we go riding then?" Sarah asked. "Or exploring? Oh, I know. We can ride up to Woodford Court to visit—"

"We·shall be sweeping and scrubbing. Airing out linens and closed-off chambers," Olivia corrected her.

"Cleanin' the stove," Mrs. McCaffery added. "Trimmin' the garden."

"If there is a garden," Olivia said.

"O'course there's a garden. Don't you remember the old knot garden with the herb beds? Your mother used to sit there of a fine afternoon. An' you would tuck fragrant sprigs of mint and lavender and rosemary in your hair and hers."·

Olivia·smiled into the darkness, assailed by the sudden remembered scent of rosemary. She did recall that garden. Her mother would laugh. Her father would tickle her and James, and tickle Augusta too. In her mind's eye she could see that long-ago scene. Her beautiful mother with her fine blond hair and her athletic father with his flashing brown eyes and russet-colored mane. How handsome they'd appeared. How perfect in a little girl's eyes.

"Careful now." Neville Hawke's warning to John broke into her reverie. "This bit of road needs some work. You're on your own lands now," he added to Olivia from somewhere up ahead.·

Her own lands. That meant the maintenance of this road was her responsibility, Olivia realized as they jounced over an uneven spot. "Welcome to Byrde Manor," she said to no one in particular.

"'Tis glad I am to be here," Mrs. McCaffery said. "My bottom could'na take another day of this."·

"Are you glad to be here, Livvie?" Sarah asked. She scooted across the narrow space between the facing seats and sat close to Olivia. "Are you glad to be home?"

Olivia wrapped an arm around her sister. "Yes," she said,

with more confidence than she felt. "I'm glad to be home."

Down a narrow road they wended, past a stand of sober trees that rustled in the wind. The river to her right, and open land to her left. It all felt so familiar. An owl hooted; in the distance a fox yipped and another answered. Then suddenly the yellow glow of a lantern pierced the darkness up ahead, a little pool of pale light in the vastness of the ebony countryside, and they had their first glimpse of Byrde Manor. They turned into a gravel drive and on into a sort of courtyard, and Olivia was home.

Sarah tumbled out one of the carriage doors; in her wake Mrs. McCaffery stepped painfully down. But Olivia only sat there, peering out at the house she hardly remembered and beset alternately by anxiety and joy. She was here as she'd often professed the desire to be. But she had the oddest compulsion to flee.

A dog lumbered around the corner of the stone house barking, and Sarah immediately called to it.

"Ach. Be careful," Mrs. McCaffery cried. "Get back from that ugly beast."

A horse immediately cut between Sarah and the stiff-legged cur. Neville's horse. For a moment she'd forgotten he was still here. Jolted to action, Olivia disembarked from the carriage, her emotions still in flux. "Where is everyone?" she demanded of no one in particular. "I sent word ahead."

Neville dismounted. "Old Hamilton is growing deaf."

"That shouldn't affect his ability to read my note. He knew we were arriving tonight."

"The lantern on the post would seem to confirm that he expects you. I suspect he dozed off while waiting. But I'll rouse him."

Olivia shook her head. "That's not necessary. If you would show John to the stables, I can manage matters here at the house."

He dipped his head in assent, stroking Robin's neck with one hand. "Hamilton may not have remembered to hire a girl to assist you."

"We can manage—if that dog will cease its infernal barking," Olivia added in irritation. She reached into the carriage and rummaged around, then, finding a piece of cheese, she marched over to the dog, guarding its domain just at the edge of the lantern's meager circle.

"Come along, enough of that," she cajoled, stooping down to look smaller and less threatening. She threw half the cheese at the mangy-looking creature. The animal jumped back in alarm, but within seconds it sniffed out the treat and gobbled it up. Another piece coaxed it nearer still, and the last portion the dog took from her outstretched palm.

"There," Olivia crooned. "You're noisy enough to keep the job, I suppose. But it's plain your loyalties are not to be trusted for very long." When she stood the animal wagged its tail and looked up to her for more.

"He's awfully skinny," Sarah said, sidling up to Olivia. "I think we should name him Bones."

"He probably has a name already." Olivia turned back to Mrs. McCaffery who supervised the removal of their several trunks and bags from the coach. "Well, shall we go in?"

"Aye. And just wait till I get my hands on that good-for-nothin' old man," the stout housekeeper vowed. "I remember him well enough. An old grouch in his prime. No doubt he's an ancient stick by now."

She started toward the house with John and the guard behind her, loaded down with luggage. Sarah squatted down in the gravel and began to pet the now docile mutt. Olivia lingered in the open courtyard, however, and peered curiously around her. She felt a little better already. She'd brought the dog to heel; she could do the same with the house and servants—if there were any servants. Last autumn's leaves still rotted in a corner near the door, she noticed, and a vine grew out of control across three of the downstairs windows and up the corner onto the slate roof. All tasks she could see to in time.

"Do you linger outside for a reason?" Neville Hawke's voice brought her back to the moment.

"Yes. But not the one you were thinking," she added, hoping her tart tone hid her sudden nervousness.

"And which reason is that?" He shifted to stand in front of her. With the lantern behind him he became a tall dark shadow, the silhouette of a man made more dangerous to her by the night, the solitude, and their proximity. The fact that he seemed different here, wilder and in his element, started her already overwrought nerves thrumming with alarm—and anticipation.

Not at all the reaction she wanted to have toward this particular man.

"I linger here because . . . because I am overcome by a surprising mix of memories," she said, deciding to be honest, or at least relatively so. "This was my home long ago, and now that I am here, I find myself beset by recollections I suppose have long been buried."

His eyes seemed to burn into hers. Then he blinked and looked around the barely lit forecourt. "Memories of your father? You know, I remember him too." He went on without waiting for her response. "I met him several times."

"You did?"

He raked a hand through his hair. "In Kelso once, and a time or two out tramping and shooting in the woods."

When he went silent, she pressed him further. "What was your impression of him?"

He shrugged. "A man's man. A hale and hearty fellow."

Olivia lifted her chin. "I suppose that means he was drunk."

Again he shrugged. "That was my impression."

Suddenly deflated, Olivia scraped the toe of her leather half-boots in the fine gravel. "Considering your crude behavior last night, it would behoove you to learn the lesson he could not, Lord Hawke. Were it not for his love for spirits, he would be here with us now." Then knowing she'd said far more than she'd intended, she hurried into the house.

Neville stood in the forecourt, Robin's reins in his hand, and watched Olivia disappear. He had no ready reply to her low-pitched words. So she'd heard about his vile behavior last night, behavior he did not even remember. He'd had to ask Bart, and he cringed now to think of the damage he'd inflicted during his drunken dream. Acting out battles fought four years ago.

Wearily he rubbed the back of his neck. That, at least, explained her coolness toward him today. Her father had been a drunk and she rightfully cast Neville in the same mode. Nor could he could blame her. Cameron Byrde had already been part of the barrier kept so high between them. What she'd heard about last night had only raised it higher. He would have to work even harder now to breach that barrier, and the only way to do that was to quit drinking for good. Not just in public, but for good.

As hard as that would be, as painful, it was the only way to prove that he was nothing like her profligate father. And that was the only way to win her.

He paused, staring up at the night sky. Why had it become so important to him to have Olivia? To marry her? This was all Bart's fault. Bart, with his suggestion that the love of a good woman might be the answer he needed. Bart, who even now was probably being welcomed with open arms by Maisie and their several children.

Neville let loose a heavy sigh. Whatever the reason, his initial fascination with Olivia had grown into a gnawing need. She was the woman he wanted. The only one. And after all, despite what Bart had said, it wasn't as if he needed her to actually fall in love with him. He didn't delude himself on that score. He was not worthy of her love, nor that of any other respectable woman. But lust . . . Lust would suffice, lust enough to compromise her and convince her that they ought to wed. If he kept her happy on that score, perhaps she would not care about the rest.

"Would you know whose dog this is?" Sarah's voice interrupted his somber thoughts. To his right in the yellow lamplight, the girl knelt beside the animal. It lay on its back now, tongue lolling with happiness as she rubbed its stomach. He squatted down beside the two of them.

"I believe he is the yard dog here. He announces any visitors, keeps other animals away, and cleans up any kitchen scraps."

"A yard dog." Her young face puckered in thought. "Since it's Livvie's yard, that would make him Livvie's dog, wouldn't it?"

He grinned. "It would seem so."

She grinned back. "Good. I'm going to ask her if I can keep him." Then her eyes narrowed. "You like her, don't you?"

Neville arched one brow. There was no doubt as to whom she referred. "Should I assume whatever answer I make will be delivered straightaway to her?"

The girl gave him an indignant look. "I can keep a secret as well as anyone." Then she brightened with an impudent smile that displayed her dimples. "You do like her, don't you?"

Neville rubbed the skinny dog belly between them. "The question should more rightly be, does she like me?"

Sarah's eyes sparkled with mischief. "Do you want me to find out?"

He laughed out loud. "No. Don't do that. She's suspicious enough of my motives. I don't need her thinking I've corrupted her younger sister."

The front door of the manor house opened and John and the guard trudged out, then toward the stable. Olivia remained in the doorway. "Sarah. Come inside now."

"Can I bring Bones?"

"No."

"But what if he leaves in the night?"

"He won't," Neville said.

"He won't," Olivia echoed. "Now come along. It's late and we're all very tired."

Sarah stood up and the dog did too, shaking himself vigorously, then circling her and beating his ropelike tail against her skirts. "Well, good night, Bones." She looked up at Neville. "Good night, Lord Hawke. And don't worry, your secret is safe with me." Then she scampered off with old Bones trotting beside her.

The door slammed in the animal's face, however, and it sat down on the broad flagstone step and stared back at Neville —

as if bewildered. Neville picked up the lantern and turned toward the barn with Robin and Olivia's two hired men trailing him. He felt just like that old dog. There were some doors that would always be closed to him, even if Olivia did agree to marry him.

Olivia did not seek her bed until well after midnight, and even then she lay awake a very long time. They'd found Mr. Hamilton asleep in the kitchen, rattling the rafters with his snoring as he sat at the table, his head resting on his folded arms. A pot of soup kept warm on the banked fire and dishes laid out on a serving tray gave testament to some efforts at a welcome. But otherwise they'd been left to their own devices.

Mrs. McCaffery had been in a fury, quite ready to knock the chair right out from under the hapless old fellow. But Olivia had sent her a stern look. "It appears he is all done in. We can certainly see to our own needs for one night."

Unfortunately, the entire upper story of the rambling stone house seemed not to have been touched in a decade or more. Cobwebs hung from the dark exposed ceiling beams, draping them with dreary gray. A thick layer of dust coated the wood plank floors and gathered in the corners like the filmy clouds of her memory, shrouding the rooms and everything that had ever happened in them. The furnishings, too, were shrouded in dust covers, very likely the same ones placed there when they'd moved to London fifteen years ago.

As she'd trudged down the long upper hallway, Olivia had hardly known where to start, and on one level, she'd been a little afraid. She would uncover more than mahogany tables and rosewood settees in the days to come. But wasn't this what she wanted?

Even the bed linens had been musty. But that, at least, had provided her a starting point. While Sarah had fetched water from the kitchen, Mrs. McCaffery had wielded an old straw broom with a vengeance, and Olivia had located a trunk of fresh linens—fresh if you considered fifteen years of cedar and rosemary scenting fresh.

It was two hours before they'd bedded down, Olivia in one

of the guest chambers and Sarah and Mrs. McCaffery in her old nursery, and they'd all been utterly fagged out. Yet still her eyes remained stubbornly open.

Tomorrow Mrs. McCaffery would see to the hiring of at least half a dozen house servants and begin a thorough top-to-bottom cleaning. Meanwhile she would play steward and check on the stables, the brew house, the animal pens, the fencing and well house . . .

She yawned. There was also that rutted section of roadway that needed repair. And was the roof sound? And the gutters? There was so much to learn, and so much that required her attention, and less than a week to get ready.

It started to rain, a gentle pelting against the leaded windowpanes. A familiar sound, from her childhood, she realized. When she snuggled into her pillow, her nose twitched at the decades-old scent of rosemary. The rain began a harder rhythm, a regular downpour that was nonetheless pleasant. Once more she yawned and felt the wonderful lassitude of sleep steal over her. She hoped Neville was not caught out in the rain . . .

Across the river, less than a mile away as the crow flew, Neville stood in the open window of his study, staring out into the rain. He held a pipe in his hand, though the bowl had gone cold. Still, the pleasant fragrance of tobacco smoke lingered in the air, a fragrance that would forever remind him of his father—and his mother. For it was she who had always brought the pipe and tobacco pouch to his father after dinner. An altogether unimportant detail of their lives until examined over the distance of too many years and too much loss. Would a woman ever perform such a simple loving task for him?

Would Olivia Byrde do it?

He stared out at the rain and let the steady tattoo of a thousand raindrops wash through his mind. It drowned out his fears and all his anxieties, and allowed him, for a few moments at least, the luxury of imagining a different sort of life for himself. Olivia greeting him with open arms and a warm kiss, as Maisie greeted Bart. Olivia dousing the evening lamps, then beckoning him up the stairs to the master's chamber. Olivia letting her magnificent hair down while he unfastened the buttons of her gown.

His fist trembled around the pipe as lust rose hot and hard to overtake him.

God, yes, he could envision such a future for himself, making love to Olivia, to his wife, until dawn, then falling asleep with her in his arms.

A crack of lightning lit the sky momentarily, then left the world even darker in its wake, and he frowned. Eventually he would fill his nights with Olivia. But for this night and the ones just ahead, nothing had changed. He must manage as he always had: hard work during the day; planning and reading at night; and now his father's pipe.

But no liquor. He'd made his decision and he meant to stick with it, no matter how difficult it proved to be. No ale or whisky or brandy or wine. Not anymore.

He took a deep breath, then slowly exhaled and leaned out past the window into the weather that grew steadily worse. He'd better relight his pipe and pull out the account books, for it looked like a long night ahead for him. A long and lonely night.

CHAPTER

17

COME the morning, with the air washed clean by the overnight storm, the magnitude of the work ahead of them showed more clearly than ever. More depressingly. On the way downstairs Olivia peeked into the several other bedchambers, the ones she must prepare for next week's houseguests. Even the master's chamber, which she meant her mother to use, looked completely untouched since her childhood. Billowing ropes of dust, the faded damask window and bed draperies, and the telltale trail of mouse tracks painted a picture of neglect and, unaccountably, of sorrow.

Olivia closed the door to the room that had been her parents' private domain, then leaned for a moment back against the door. When she'd suggested this journey to the estate left to her, she'd not anticipated this assault on her memories, nor upon her emotions.

She stared down the hall. One part of her mind ticked off a list of tasks and weighed which to tackle first, then second, and so on. But another part of her examined the strange state of mind she found herself in of late. She'd been fine en route to Doncaster. Once there, however, once accosted by the drunken Lord Hawke, everything had begun to unravel.

But that only proved what she already knew. He was a bad influence on her, and if she were wise, she would keep a healthy distance away from him. Not that she hadn't known that from their very first encounter. But in Doncaster she'd allowed herself the luxury of baiting him—and being baited by him. An error, she now saw, caused by ego and pride and no small amount of righteous anger. But she was wiser now—

notwithstanding those weak moments when she'd gazed upon him sleeping on the carriage seat opposite her.

She straightened, then repositioned the pins of her apron and patted her hair, tightly drawn back from her brow and twisted into a bun. She had too much to do to waste time considering her unwise attraction to Neville Hawke. If she stayed busy—and stayed well away from him—she would manage just fine.

A sharp voice and a sudden crash drew her head around. Mrs. McCaffery. Then another voice, an angry old man's. Olivia started for the stairs. It was going to be a very long day.

What she found was the grizzled Mr. Hamilton, awake now, with a pot raised in his hand, facing down a fiercely scowling Mrs. McCaffery. Two women cowered behind the old fellow while Sarah peeked wide-eyed past the irate housekeeper.

". . . such a shoddy household as I've never seen! It'll be you thrown out on your ear, you old goat!" Mrs. McCaffery shouted. "Get out of my way, and those pitiful charwomen behind you too!"

Mr. Hamilton only raised the cast-iron pot higher. "I'm warnin' you, Bertie McCaffery. Get away from here. You got no call to be givin' orders in this household!"

Bertie? Olivia's alarm eased a bit. Mr. Hamilton knew the starchy Mrs. McCaffery as Bertie?

"You're the one as hasn't got the right," the steely-eyed woman shot right back at him.

"Me? I've got ev'ry right!" he sputtered, turning red in the face. Then spying Olivia in the doorway, he drew himself up and with a smug smile at "Bertie" set the pot down with a clang. "Good mornin' to you, Miss Livvie. 'Tis glad I am t'see you safely arrived."

"You slept right through her arrival," Mrs. McCaffery said with a snort. "The bedrooms were a shambles. No water. Dust on everything."

"Please, Mrs. McCaffery." Olivia held up one hand. "We've much to do, and casting blame will neither lighten our task nor speed its solution."

The housekeeper hiked up her chin, crossed her arms, and shifted her glare to Olivia. "Never tell me you're going to ignore this shirker's vast failings and allow him to—"

"I'm no shirker, you old battle—"

"I am in charge here!"

Everyone drew back at Olivia's unladylike bellow. That she stamped her foot and planted her fists on her hips for emphasis seemed to impress the four servants.

From Sarah, however, it drew only a giggle, which she promptly smothered when Olivia fixed her with a sharp look. "You may begin your tasks by stripping the bed linens from all the beds, Sarah. All of them. Starting now," she added when Sarah opened her mouth to object. Then Olivia turned on the servants.

Mr. Hamilton made a hasty bow that looked painful in one so bent and gray. "Welcome back, Miss Livvie. 'Tis a bonnie lass you've become."

Olivia graced him with a curt nod. "We'll see about that. Who do we have behind you?"

Mrs. Wilkins was the cook, a beefy but meek-looking woman of indeterminate age who bobbed and nodded but kept her mouth wisely shut. Mr. Hamilton's sister-in-law, as it happened. The work-worn lass behind her was their niece, a girl of simple mind but willing disposition who gave Olivia a lopsided grin that revealed several large gaps where teeth ought to be. Milly's grin turned into a muted "Ouch," when Mrs. Wilkins gave her a pinch. When Olivia sent Milly to start the laundry fires, the girl scurried off, smiling her relief to escape the tension in the kitchen.

"Now," Olivia began. "Mrs. Wilkins, I'd like you to prepare a soup or stew or some other such this morning, something that will not require too much of your attention. For today we clean. All of us," she added, glancing pointedly at Mr. Hamilton.

And so they did. Every curtain and rug was hauled out of doors and draped over fences, clotheslines, and even sturdy shrubs. Mrs. Wilkins sent word to two of her sisters, and by noon a small army of women appeared, each of them eager to earn a coin or two in service at Byrde Manor. By mid-afternoon every window gaped open, spewing pillows and mattresses airing out. One team of women dusted and swept, while another group followed them wielding soap and mops and scrub buckets.

The previous night's storm had dissipated into a fair day, allowing the washing to dry without mishap. Olivia toiled alongside the other women, forgoing her desire to explore the grounds. Only when the sun inched down in the western sky and the hired women began the half-mile trek back to the village and their own households did Olivia pause.

"Three of the women are willing to do day work, but I'm still in need of two live-in girls," Mrs. McCaffery said, fanning herself as they perched wearily upon a bench outside the kitchen door. "And a couple of lads to see to these pitiful gardens." She fanned harder with the pleated kitchen fan. "If I were you, Olivia, I'd give serious consideration to finding a steward who attends a mite better to his duties than does Donnie Hamilton."

Donnie, was it? Olivia glanced curiously at Mrs. Mc-Caffery. "How long have you and Mr. Hamilton known one another?"

The woman's lips twitched, then pursed in disapproval. "Too long. I'd have thought the old coot dead by now. By rights he should've died in boyhood—he was that wild. A hooligan then, and a ne'er-do-well ever since."

Smiling, Olivia swept her palm across her damp neck, lifting several stray curls that stuck to it. "The fault lies less with him than with me."

Mrs. McCaffery made a huffing noise. "I'd hardly think—"

"Now, Mrs. Mac. How many times have you remarked on the need for a tight hand with underservants?"

"Yes, but he's no underservant."

"He's had no guidance to speak of from me or my mother or any of her solicitors. Other than the twice-yearly accounting of income and expenditures, we have left him entirely to his own devices."

Mrs. McCaffery snorted. "You're just makin' excuses for him, and don't think I don't know it."

"Perhaps. But I intend to give him the opportunity to redeem himself. If he does his duties well, then he will retain his position."

"And if he doesn't?"

Olivia smiled and patted the indignant woman on the knee. "Coming back to Byrde Manor has been unsettling for all of us. Mr. Hamilton. Me. Even you. And I suspect it will be especially so for Mother. But in time I believe we shall all be the better for it. This is my home," she added, startled by the sudden quiver of emotion in her voice. Still she went on. "My childhood home. I was happy here once upon a time. I want to be happy here again."

"Ach, child." Mrs. McCaffery covered Olivia's hand with her own red-knuckled one. "You will be. In time you will be."

The next three days passed in a blur of polished brass fittings and crystal lamps, of oiled wood floors and waxed furniture, of washed windows, and cleaned-out gutters, and scrubbed-out chimneys and flues. Mrs. McCaffery commanded the servants with a fervor that would have done a colonel in the Royal Guard proud.

As the house began to rise from its neglected condition, Olivia turned her interests to the estate it commanded. Of all the outbuildings, the stables were the best maintained, for when it came to horses, Mr. Hamilton's interest coincided precisely with her own, even though there were few animals housed there. The rest of the grounds, however, were completely overrun, practically a thicket surrounding the house, like the vining thorns around the castle in the childhood tale of the sleeping princess.

Under her watchful eye three lads labored long hours, slashing away at dead brush, aggressive weeds, and overgrown shrubbery. They rediscovered slate paths, repaired stone walls, and unearthed treasures Olivia barely remembered, but which Mrs. McCaffery clearly did.

"Come April these rhododendron will bloom again," the housekeeper assured Olivia.

"I hope so." Olivia scrutinized the manor's forecourt. The driveway was at least passable now. The holes and ruts in the carriage court were daily being filled. A few shrubs in the matching cast-iron planters beside the front steps and the place might actually be termed handsome, she decided—if not by town standards, at least by country ones.

The two women stood there a few moments in silence, while the hum of work proceeded around them. A wheelbarrow squeaked as a young man fetched a load of gravel across the yard. An ancient pony whinnied at the corral, calling to Mr. Hamilton for its afternoon treat.

Mrs. McCaffery's eyes narrowed as the old steward hobbled across her line of vision, heeding the animal's call. "He ought to be ashamed to show his face around here," she muttered.

"He's done everything I've asked of him," Olivia countered. "With good grace, I might add."

"Harumph," was the only answer she received.

Olivia flexed her back. She was tired and hot, and she needed a reprieve. "I think I shall take a walk down to the river. I won't be long."

"You should take someone with you." Mrs. McCaffery rose reluctantly from the wooden bench rediscovered in a rose garden grown amuck but newly sheared.

"You needn't accompany me. I know you're tired."

"I was thinkin' of Sarah. Where has that child got to? Sarah!" she cried in carrying tones.

In short order Olivia and her sister were trekking down the curving drive, accompanied by the old dog, Bones, who'd become as completely enamored of Sarah as she was of him.

"He's smart as can be," Sarah boasted. "Watch this." The girl patted Bones's head and waved a stick in front of his face. "Fetch, Bones. Fetch." Then she flung the stick as far ahead of them as she could.

Bones watched the stick tumble end over end, then land in the middle of the drive. But he did not evidence any indication of fetching it back.

"Smart as a whip," Olivia wryly echoed her sister.

"Just you watch," Sarah protested. "You'll see."

Sure enough, when they reached the stick, old Bones nosed it around, looked up at Sarah, and yelped once. "Fetch," she repeated, and he did.

Sarah took the stick from him amid much petting and hugging, and even planted a kiss on his graying forehead. The dog wriggled and wagged his doggy pleasure, whacking both Olivia and Sarah with his eager tail.

"A stupid dog would run like a fool, exhausting himself on the hottest day ever," Sarah said, as they resumed their walk. "But Bones knows how to pace himself. A lesson," she added pointedly, "that you've yet to learn."

"So you say. But you overlook the fact that I have infinitely more energy than this ancient mutt, not to mention a world of responsibility." Olivia scrutinized her sister, attired in an everyday dress protected by a sturdy apron. "For all your complaints, you don't look any the worse for wear."

As they approached the front gate Sarah picked up another stick and tossed it clean across the road. "If I never have to hang wet, tangling bedsheets and curtains out to dry for as long as I live, it will not be soon enough."

Olivia laughed at the girl's puckered expression. "Should I interpret that to mean you enjoy polishing silverware?"

"No! Nor brass knobs. Nor crystal. Do you know how many crystals hang upon that dining room chandelier? Do you? Well, I do. One hundred sixty-eight!" She heaved another stick. "This isn't even the sort of house that's supposed to have crystal chandeliers."

"Be glad there's only one," Olivia retorted. But she smiled fondly at her sister. Despite her complaints, Sarah had been a great help, for the hired women did not dare shirk their responsibilities when the entire family worked so hard beside them. Olivia tucked a stray curl into one of the girl's bedraggled plaits. "What do you say we take a dip in the river?"

At once Sarah's eyes lit up. "I say yes." They stared at each other a moment, then in the same instant, both of them made a mad dash across the road. With their skirts held high, their laughter unfettered, and poor Bones baying in their wake, they plunged into the shady grove that separated the road from the river beyond.

Olivia had an impression of sycamore trees and holly bushes. She heard irate squirrels and scolding wrens, and caught the fecund scent of damp growth and crushed ferns. She'd tramped these woods with her father years before, and like then, she felt an overwhelming sense of freedom in their green dappled shade. She was no sensible, responsible woman here, but rather a simple, happy child. Sarah's laughter drew out her own, freer than it had been in years. By the time they made the riverbank, Sarah a step ahead of her, they were winded, as much by their robust laughter as by their madcap chase.

"I win!" Sarah crowed. "Now you must do as I say."

"We had no bet."

"Coward. Come on, off with your shoes. You must test the water with your bare feet and let me know how cold it is."

Olivia needed no real convincing, for at that moment the constraints of social and familial responsibilities seemed as inconsequential as the feathery clouds above them. Besides, she meant to do more than simply dampen her feet today. They were sheltered from view from the road, and across from them lay more forests. With no fishermen in sight, they had the river to themselves, or at least this portion of it. Grinning at her sister, she tossed her shoes and stockings aside, then shed her apron. Sarah did the same.

Olivia unfastened the coil that restrained her hair and shook it free. Sarah's brows lifted in surprise, but she mimicked her sister's move. Then Olivia raised her skirts and wriggled out of her single petticoat.

With understanding dawning in her eyes, Sarah giggled and slid just as quickly out of her own. They stared at one another in perfect sisterly attunement.

"Chemises only?" Sarah's eyes glittered with excitement.

"Chemises only."

If it passed through Olivia's mind that she was far too old for such shenanigans, she buried the thought in her haste to remove her hot, sticky gown. What harm in an afternoon swim? Who was to see or to care that two sisters frolicked together as they had not done in years?

On the opposite bank of the meandering river Tweed, Neville heard feminine laughter and it stopped him in his tracks. The wind was capricious, rustling through the willows and sycamores that crowded the river banks. The forest creatures were alive with sound this afternoon, twittering, scurrying, chattering. Perhaps it was not laughter at all, but something else. Still, he cocked his head, listening past all the ordinary sounds for the extraordinary one he could not have imagined. It came again, a little shriek, a peal of laughter—and the certainty that it must be Olivia settled over him. It must be her, for he knew now that she had a penchant for riverbanks.

Though a true gentleman would not spy on her, Neville could not resist.

Dismounting, he led his horse through the cool shade, following the voices—there were at least two—upstream a short way. Then a flash of movement, a splash, and a shriek, accompanied by a child's unfettered laughter, drew him to the edge of the willow glade, and to a sight he could hardly credit. Sarah Palmer stood knee deep in the river wearing only her chemise, and laughing so hard she could barely keep her balance.

But it was Olivia who took his breath away.

Olivia rising soaking wet from the river. Olivia with her long autumn-colored hair clinging to her shoulders and arms. Olivia with her knee-length chemise painted wetly to her skin, displaying the curve of her derriere, the shape of her thighs, and—when she flung her hair over her shoulder and turned laughing to pursue her sister—the perfect shape of her perfect breasts.

"Damnation." The oath whistled past his lips without conscious thought. His eyes, however, remained very conscious of everything they saw. Her arms were pale and bare; her knees and calves as well. And beneath the wet, revealing lawn of her undergarment, the rest of her would be pale and shapely as well—save for the taut peaks of her breasts. Those would be darker. Dusky. Rose-hued.

He let out a muffled groan when she pivoted away from him, denying him a frontal view and a longer glimpse of those pebbled nipples shadowed behind her flimsy garb. When she bent to direct a spray of water at her sister, however, the view of her lovely posterior was just as delectable, and he felt the heat of desire pool low in his groin.

He'd deliberately avoided Olivia for the past few days, allowing her and him some distance from one another. He'd also needed to master the nausea and shakiness that the absence of liquor had visited upon him. But he was feeling better today, and so had decided to ride over to Byrde Manor to see how his new neighbors were faring and make an offer of assistance to them. In truth, however, he just wanted to see Olivia again. He'd been desperate to do so.

Well, he could see her now, more of her than he'd dared hope. More of her than was wise, it would seem.

His eyes followed her, how she sank shoulder-deep in the river, how her hair spread like a dark red·mantle around her. He watched her float, first on her back, then on her stomach. When she rose and beckoned to her sister to venture deeper with her, he shifted from one foot to the other. She was a nymph, a woodland goddess. Were she naked, she could not appear any more desirable, any more delicious than she did in that film of clinging, translucent linen.

". . . won't let you sink. You were close to swimming when we had your last lesson," she cajoled Sarah.

"I don't trust you. James said he would not let me sink either, but I very nearly drowned."

"Surely you cannot compare me to our lunatic of a brother. He thinks everything is a joke."

From his position beneath a cascading willow, Neville watched Sarah frown. "You promise not to let go of me? Not to let me sink or let my head go under?"

Olivia stretched her arms wide and once more her lovely bosom appeared in profile, and this time her nipples showed, darker and peaked. He groaned in true pain.

"We will not even be over your head," she said. "Look, Sarah. You can stand up whenever you like."

It seemed to take forever. Neville remained as still as stone in his leafy bower as Sarah slowly waded deeper. Olivia was reassuring but firm, and Sarah grew braver as the lesson progressed. She floated a while, then finally ducked her face and came up laughing. It reminded him of training horses, the same sort of patience. The same sort of affection.

When Olivia and her sister finally chased one another out of the river and disappeared behind a stand of lilies and arrowheads to don their clothes, however, it seemed that time had sped by too fast. He blinked, trying to clear his eyes and his head, then with one hand rubbed the back of his neck.

Once more he'd played the cad, observing Olivia in a private moment that a better man than him would have respected. A gentleman would have turned away and not stood there gawking. A gentleman would not have succumbed to the wave of desire that rose in him now.

". . . just strip off your wet chemise and put your dry petticoat and dress on," he heard Olivia tell her sister. "No one will see us. And even if someone should come along, they would never know."

Someone would, Neville decided, banishing the gentleman he ought to be. Olivia sans undergarments, her hair wet and clinging to her disheveled gown. He could no more miss this opportunity than he could cease dreaming about his sweet and starchy neighbor. His prim yet wanton Hazel.

So he mounted Robin and began to whistle, and after a moment guided the animal through the woods, onto a narrow cowpath, and out into plain view along the grassy riverbank. Nary a sound came from the dressing grove across the way, and he did not look in that direction. He just kept whistling the same pretty melody he and Olivia had danced to, and guided Robin hock-deep into the merrily tripping waters.

"Lord Neville—"

"Shh."

"Hello?" He looked up, feigning surprise at Sarah's call—and Olivia's vain attempt to silence her. "Sarah, is that you? Have you come to fish? You know, there are better spots just downstream."

The child burst through the thicket, wet and grinning, but fully dressed. "We weren't fishing at all. I was just having a swimming lesson. It's fortunate you did not arrive two minutes earlier for you would most certainly have been surprised to see me and Olivia—"

"Sarah!"

Belatedly, Olivia stumbled from behind their verdant dressing screen. Her hair was twisted into a heavy damp rope and lay across one of her shoulders dampening her bodice. Otherwise, she looked reasonably presentable. But Neville knew she wore no chemise. Why that should send a surge of heat rocketing through him he did not understand, for she nonetheless remained entirely covered, neck to wrists to ankles. But she had not been just minutes ago, and his new knowledge of what lay hidden beneath all that female frippery—or perhaps *because* it was hidden—made his heart thud with unnatural violence.

Damn, but he wanted her!

That her green and golden brown eyes were wary and tinged, perhaps with guilt, only strengthened that reckless desire. She feared he knew and that he'd seen them.

While Robin gulped greedy draughts of the cold water, Neville doffed his hat to the two women. Perhaps he should increase Olivia's doubts, not assuage them.

"I heard splashing." He grinned. "Never tell me you two were swimming. Anyone coming along the road might have interrupted you, as I very nearly did."

Olivia went pale, her eyes glued to his. Young Sarah blushed. "I told Olivia that might happen. Didn't I?" She swiveled an accusing stare on her older, more decorous sibling. "I told you we might get caught."

Neville nudged Robin to cross the river, circling around the deeper area where they'd frolicked. "It's fortunate I didn't arrive any sooner."

Olivia grimaced but raised her chin a notch. "I'm certain your whistling would have alerted us in sufficient time to preserve our dignity. Come, Sarah. No doubt supper is awaiting."

The girl hung back. "Perhaps Lord Hawke would like to have supper with us."

"As a matter of fact I was heading over to Byrde Manor to see how you were settling in." He dismounted, then handed the reins to Sarah. "Would you like to ride Robin? I'll keep your sister company on the walk back."

"Oh yes. Thank you."

"Now, Sarah," Olivia protested.

But Neville cut her off. "It's all right." He tucked Olivia's hand firmly beneath his arm. "She's an excellent rider and Robin's a sensible mount. Besides, this will give us a chance to talk."

"To talk?" Olivia echoed as Sarah leapt into the saddle with the grace of a natural-born equestrian. That her toes barely reached the stirrups was no impediment at all to the girl.

"Yes, talk," Neville replied as Sarah took off with a jaunty wave. "Unless there is something else you would rather we do."

Olivia sucked in a quick breath. From the moment Neville's whistling had drifted to them her pulse had set up a blistering pace. She was as aware of his presence as if he carried an aura about him, of his scent and the heat of him beneath the cloth of his coat sleeve. Even worse, she was excruciatingly conscious of her half-dressed state, her skin still damp—the trickle of a drop of water down the back of her left leg. It coursed down her thigh and over the sensitive skin behind her knee, as arousing as the stroke of a fingertip.

Of his fingertip.

This time her breath came out in a little groan.

"Well, Olivia?" he prompted, his voice low and warm and far too near her ear. "Did you have something in mind other than talking?"

Somehow she gathered her flustered wits and managed a disapproving expression. "Are you never to cease this useless baiting, Lord Hawke? We are neighbors. We shall never be anything more."

"And why not? I don't see why we couldn't come to an arrangement that would please us both."

Olivia tugged her hand from his hold and stared at him incredulously. "An arrangement? What do you mean? Surely you can't be—I hope this is not your idea of a marriage proposal."

One of his dark brows arched up in surprise. One side of his mouth crooked down in a sardonic half-smile. "A marriage proposal?" He shook his head. "You've made your position on my suitability for marriage very clear. No, my dear Olivia. It is not marriage I have in mind—unless, of course, you are so inclined. I was thinking, rather, of a very different sort of proposition for you."

"A proposition?" Olivia could feel her cheeks heat despite her best effort to remain cool and in control. The man was incorrigible, even sober! "I hope this is not some attempt to insult me," she continued, tight-lipped, "for that would bode very ill for our future as neighbors."

"Insult you?" He pressed one hand to his chest in feigned shock. One very tan, very long-fingered hand, she noticed to her own chagrin. It was not a soft hand. Indeed, it showed the calluses and strength of a man who worked hard. But it was a gentleman's hand nonetheless, elegant and neatly manicured. With an effort she forced her gaze back up to his face, only to find devilment lurking there, devilment and temptation—and a more virile sort of danger than she was wholly prepared to face.

She clenched her teeth and focused on the springy woodland ground before her, making determined strides for Byrde Manor and safety. *One step, two steps. Keep going forward no matter what outrageous remark he comes up with.*

Of course, with his long legs he kept easy pace with her. "It is a business proposition I have for you, Olivia, nothing more sinister than that. Certainly not what your wicked mind is conjuring."

She ignored the last part of his statement. "A business proposition?" She kept her eyes on the clearing ahead that signaled the road and her escape from these green, enclosing woodlands. But he caught her arm before they reached the road and her nervous momentum swung her around to face him. That his eyes glittered with amusement at her expense did nothing to improve her mood.

"What is it, then?" she demanded, trying fruitlessly to tug her arm from his hold. "And why can't it wait?"

"Wait for what? Until your mother or brother is here to handle it? I was given to understand that Byrde Manor is to be yours."

"It is." Olivia jutted out her jaw and tried to tamp down her unruly emotions. She must not let him intimidate her, nor work his rakish charms on her. "All right then. I am not going to bolt, so you may let go of my wrist and tell me whatever it is you have on your mind."

For a long moment their eyes held and she had the distinct feeling of being probed by his intent gaze, of being examined far deeper than merely the surface of eyes and cheeks, nose and lips. Disconcerting as that would be, this was even worse. At least those strong fingers of his had unwrapped from her wrist, letting her reclaim her hand. She stepped back and averted her gaze, but still she felt the imprint of his grip—and of him.

He folded his hands behind his back. "I have been aware for some time that your estate here has not been well managed. No doubt you have already discovered the status of the house. The grounds, however, fare no better. Roads rutted, stone walls in disrepair. The hedgerows require upkeep and the wood lot desperately needs a woodsman's eye for selective cutting and clearing to maximize its output."

He was right, of course, but still Olivia bristled. "I hope you do not blame Mr. Hamilton for everything. I am well aware that I have been remiss in my guidance to him in the past, but I intend to correct that situation."

He nodded solemnly. "Do you intend to put your fallow fields to use?"

Her fallow fields? Olivia chewed the inside corner of her mouth. He really had come to discuss business, and for a moment she was sorely miffed. But it was a brief moment, and she swiftly regained her composure—and her good sense.

"Are you saying you are interested in making use of those fields?"

He stared at her a long unsettling moment. "I am. If we can come to terms."

Olivia nodded, momentarily at a loss for words. "What . . . ah . . . Which particular fields are you interested in?"

"All of them. All that I can get," he answered, his moody blue eyes growing darker by the moment.

Were they still speaking of fallow fields?

Then Sarah called out to them to hurry, he looked up, and that moment of crackling intensity ended. Olivia sucked in a shaky breath, feeling as if she'd forgotten all about breathing these past few minutes with him.

With a proprietary move he took her elbow and guided her toward the road again. Once they caught up with Sarah, prancing Robin up and down the lane as if he were a show horse, he released Olivia's arm. "If you are available tomorrow morning," he said to her, "perhaps you will join me for a ride and we can survey the fields in question."

Again Olivia nodded, then caught herself. She seemed to be doing that a lot, nodding agreement with him and becoming tongue-tied and breathless, like a green girl who had never held a conversation with a single gentleman before. She would do better to emulate his businesslike demeanor. "Very well," she said with a lift of her chin. "Tomorrow, say, nine o'clock?"

"As you wish. I'll bring you a riding mare."

Sarah pulled Robin to a halt before them. "You're going riding tomorrow? May I go along too?"

"What a good idea—"

"No," Neville cut in before Olivia could complete her thought. "Not this time, Sarah. But I'll make it up to you next week and take you fishing. All right?" He reached up a hand to help the girl dismount.

Though Sarah gave a great, disappointed sigh, it swiftly turned into a sunny smile. "Oh, very well. But mark my words, I shall hold you to your promise."

Olivia was hard-pressed not to gape at Sarah, for she could

barely credit her sister's response. Had she been the one to deny the girl's request, Sarah would have pleaded and cajoled all evening, for the child did not like taking no for an answer. But not a word of argument did the scamp give Neville Hawke. It occurred to Olivia that the girl showed a real knack for dealing with men. In a few more years their mother was going to have a serious problem on her hands.

"Till tomorrow," Lord Hawke said, mounting the horse and tipping his beaver hat.

"Yes. Till tomorrow," Olivia replied in a subdued tone. She didn't realize she was staring after him until Sarah giggled.

"What?" She glanced peevishly at the damp-haired child.

"You needn't scowl that way, Livvie, for I've done nothing to earn such black looks from you. Didn't I just try to save you from being alone with him tomorrow?"

"Oh, really? Well, if that was your intent, why did you ride off just now and leave us alone in the wood lot?"

Bones had rejoined them now that they were away from the water, and Sarah bent to give him a hug. "Your bodice is all wet," she pointed out, staring at Olivia's chest and laughing. Then she ran off toward the house with the dog baying at her heels, leaving Olivia to contemplate with horror the wet streak her hair had left across her bosom. The wet streak that had the summer-weight muslin clinging in the most revealing manner to her left breast, outlining every curve, including the peaked silhouette of her taut nipple.

"Oh, my goodness," she muttered, jerking her gaze to Neville Hawke's distant figure. Her shoulders sagged with dismay and her mouth turned down in despair. Somehow she always came off the worse in her dealings with Neville Hawke. Somehow she always felt gauche or naïve or simply stupid.

With her fists knotted she started across the road and stalked down the uneven driveway. Well, he would not catch her unawares tomorrow, she vowed. She would be perfectly groomed, perfectly attired, and perfectly prepared for his perverse combination of charm and danger. She would listen to his proposal for the fields he had his eye on, but she would not be pushed into any hasty decisions.

Then it occurred to her that nine o'clock was awfully early in the day for Neville Hawke, considering his strange nocturnal habits. She stomped into the kitchen with her wet chemise balled in her hand. It would serve him right to rise so early, she decided. She didn't care if he was exhausted during their ride, with eyes burning from lack of sleep. She would be all business. And the first thing she must do to prepare was consult with Mr. Hamilton.

Neville made sure to arrive early, for he wanted to be invited in for breakfast. It was not that he wished a second morning meal. Rather he wanted to see Olivia in her role as lady of the house. But as if she had anticipated his actions, she was already outside in the forecourt, instructing old Taran McCade and his middle grandson about the layout for a wheelbarrow full of ivy cuttings they were to add to the barren flower beds flanking the manor's front entrance.

She was dressed in a proper riding habit, a teal-colored muslin simply adorned with brass buttons and decorative stitching along the collar and cuffs and down the front of the bodice. Around her throat she'd knotted a filmy scarf in a creamy color that somehow emphasized both the graceful length and slender delicacy of that portion of her anatomy. Her bountiful hair she'd caught up in an artful knot at the back of her head, though how that silken mass defied gravity was quite beyond his ken. As he sat his hunter, taking advantage of her ignorance of his presence, he was struck by the image of him freeing that delicious length of hair. Of him tumbling the warm, springy mass down her back and filling his hands with the gleaming strands. Of weaving his fingers through it and flinging aside pins and combs and that ridiculously cocky little hat perched over her brow.

So real was the image that his brow beaded with sweat. He shifted restlessly in his saddle, and it was at that moment she looked up and spotted him.

The impact on Neville was powerful enough that even his

animal felt it, for the horse skittered backward and half reared
before he could settle him down and proceed forward. Olivia
made some last remark to old McCade, then turned to face
Neville. She looked so cool and collected it only increased his
agitation. He would never make it through the morning if he
began it in such an inappropriate state of physical arousal.

"Good morning, Lord Hawke." Her smile was bland with
no hint of her thoughts showing. "Aren't you the prompt one."
She freed her riding gloves from her waistband and began
casually to don them. "I'm afraid when I suggested nine
o'clock that I'd forgotten your penchant for sleeping in. I do
hope my own early habits have not inconvenienced you too
badly."

Her thoughts weren't showing, but her claws plainly were.
Neville smiled, more sure of himself now, and he leaned forward. "Is it a truthful answer you want, Olivia, or would a
banal pleasantry suit you better?"

Her eyes narrowed, just a fraction. Then she seemed to grab
hold of her temper and tamp it down. Again she gave him that
utterly false smile. "Why, the banal pleasantry, of course." She
shifted her gaze to the mare he'd brought for her to ride.
"What a pretty animal. Tell me about her."

And so they began their morning tour of her fields, with
her obviously determined to keep their conversation remote
and focused entirely on the business at hand. Meanwhile, although Neville remained equally intent on the business of ob-
taining the leases he sought, he intended also to batter down
the walls of her reserve, for he knew they were not so strong
as she would like to pretend.

He didn't quite understand what drove him, or why she had
become such a challenge to him, one he apparently was unable
to resist. But as they followed a rutted cart path that ran beside
the vine-covered spring house, then past a half-dozen sadly
neglected beehives, he accepted the challenge as fact. If
there'd been any last lingering doubt in his mind, yesterday's
inspiring view of her as water nymph had banished it completely.

He meant to have Olivia Byrde to wife, and pursuing the

land leases gave him the best opportunity to court her. If she could see him in a better light, as a careful and responsible land owner, it might soften her view of him as a cad of her father's ilk.

"You have a very nice estate here, Olivia. Enough fertile fields to provide a good crop for the house and for your people. Pasture enough to run your own livestock or lease it out. Fishing rights to a substantial portion of the prettiest river in the Borders."

"Yes, it is very fine—or it could be. And don't forget the hunting park," she added.

"The hunting park," he echoed, grinning. "Perhaps down in the south of England they're called parks. But I'd better term it a forest, rugged and wild, as is everything in Scotland."

That drew a sidelong glance from her and for a moment their eyes locked together. But she swiftly looked away and returned to her interested perusal of everything they passed. "Where is the northernmost boundary of Byrde Manor? Do you know?"

Neville gestured with his left hand. "Up that long hill, then down to a narrow creek. Would you like to see it?"

She shook her head. "Perhaps another time. Do you know where the best grousing fields are?"

"Just beyond that last overgrown pasture."

"The field you want to run your flock on."

"The very one."

She was silent a moment. "I should think your sheep would not like shooters so nearby."

"Sheep are rotated, Olivia, from field to field. If you over-populate a field, the pasture gets cropped too low, down to the roots, and eventually the crop is depleted. With more fields to rotate my flock through, I can increase the number of sheep. During the hunting season I will keep them in fields sufficiently distant from the shooting. I wouldn't want some drunken fool mistaking my animals for a deer or boar," he added.

This time her gaze met with his and held, and he realized he'd given her just the opening she wanted. "And you, of course, are well acquainted with the proclivities of drunken fools."

He grinned. "Touché. But Olivia, I have overimbibed but once in your presence. Do you plan never to forgive me for that single transgression?"

She did not smile back. "One transgression?" Her russet brows arched.

Neville shrugged but maintained his good humor. "Are you speaking of our several kisses now? For if you are, I must confess that I will never be able to consider those three kisses as transgressions, not when—"

"Four," Olivia interrupted, her lips pursed in disapproval. "Not three, but four. And I do think of them as transgressions."

"But you participated so eagerly," he countered. "And there were only three. Near the stream in Doncaster; at the town dance; and in the Cummingses' garden."

Her frown deepened and anger flashed in her eyes. "What of that last night of our journey, at the Bull's Manger in Prudhoe? You forget to mention *that* kiss."

"What?" He stared at her. "What are you talking about?"

"Oho. So you *have* forgotten. No doubt you were too drunk to remember. But I remember it. Very well."

Neville's chest was suddenly tight, and the pounding of his heart seemed to reverberate through his entire body. Once before they'd discussed his behavior of that night. But she'd said nothing about him kissing her. Had he kissed her? He couldn't remember. Had he done anything more than merely kiss her? He was afraid to find out.

All he could remember of that night was that he'd been exhausted and plagued with dreams. And though he'd vowed to avoid strong spirits, that night he had weakened. The next morning he'd been appalled by the destruction he'd caused. But he did not recall kissing Olivia. He didn't remember seeing her at all that night.

Then again, he didn't remember smashing those chairs, or that table.

She must have seen the confusion on his face, for her expression grew colder still. "You *don't* remember. You were that drunk."

Neville beat back a sudden wave of panic. Once or twice before he'd had this total loss of memory after a night of drinking, and it was terrifying. Was he going mad?

The answer, though clear, was painful to face. If he was going mad, it was due to the vast quantities of alcohol he consumed. But if he stopped drinking, he could stop the madness.

If he could stop drinking for good.

He looked over at her, but she stared straight ahead, concentrating on her horse and the overgrown cart track. He cleared his throat. "I understand now why you have been so cool to me of late. If I offended you with my behavior in Prudhoe, then I beg your forgiveness. You are . . . You are right that I do not remember the details of what happened that night."

He swallowed the bitterness of that admission and went on. "But I promise you—I promise you, Olivia—that you see before you a reformed man. I have sworn off all drinking, all wines and ales and strong spirits. If I did not have sufficient reason before to stop, you have just given it to me."

But she would not look at him.

She urged her horse off the cart track and into an open pasture, heading toward an old Roman stone wall. "I don't believe you, Lord Hawke. Certainly your inability to rise before noon indicates a long-standing habit of drinking away the night—though perhaps you are too drunk to remember most of the time."

He caught up with her and edged his horse near enough that his knee bumped hers. "I am up before noon today. Besides, my sleep habits have nothing to do with drinking." Though their discussion had taken a turn into the treacherous territory of why he could not sleep at night, he forced himself to continue. "I have been an insomniac for several years. Whether I drink strong spirits or not, my nights remain sleepless."

Finally she turned toward him with eyes that were steady and very, very green. "Why?"

This was not the conversation Neville wanted to have with her. None of it. Unfortunately there was no way to avoid her question, not when her attention was turned so fixedly upon him.

Fortunately an old military rule rescued him: when retreat was impossible, the best policy was to attack. He would attack with the truth, or at least one version of it.

He looked away from her and stretched the silence to a breaking point before responding with somber words. "My experiences in the war haunt me." *My guilt tortures me.*

"I see." She considered that. "I wondered if it might be related to that."

They had halted the horses in a patch of heather and he shifted in the saddle, then met her eyes once more. There was less condemnation in her expression now and a little crease had formed between her brows.

"I don't like to speak of it," he continued. That much certainly was true. "I'm sure you understand."

She nodded, but her eyes searched his, and it struck him, oddly enough, as being a more intimate connection than any other interaction they'd had. Even their several kisses paled next to this personal, probing stare.

"Perhaps," she said in a voice devoid now of any artifice. "Perhaps you might find ease in speaking to others about these troubling memories of yours."

A faint sheen of sweat broke out across his brow. Speak of it? Of his failure and the subsequent death of so many of his comrades? The very idea of her ever learning the truth about him turned Neville's blood to ice.

"I think not." His response sounded too curt. It came too fast.

"Yes, but that could be why you drink so much—"

He jerked his horse around and started up the hill, effectively cutting her off. "If you want to see the rest of your estate before the clouds break over us, we'd better be going."

Olivia stared after Neville, a little stunned by his sudden

rudeness. Then again, she supposed she'd been rude to throw his poor behavior in his face. Could he truly not remember? Apparently so, for he seemed genuinely shocked to learn of it. And now she'd upset him further with her inquiries about his insomnia and his war experiences. No doubt he saw it as an admission of weakness. But she did not see it so. From what she'd heard of the campaign in Ligny, it had been a bloody mess. Too many men had not come back, or had done so crippled or blind or otherwise maimed.

Leaning forward, she urged her mare on, her eyes fixed upon the broad and rigid shoulders of the man ahead of her. A little jolt of guilt snaked through her. Perhaps she was being too hard on him. Perhaps she should be more understanding, given all he'd been through.

And though she should not, the truth was, she wanted to know more about the nightly tortures he suffered, the ones she tried to numb with excessive amounts of alcohol.

She picked her way up the twisting hill, her mind all the while spinning. If he would just talk about it, he would surely feel better. If he could just cry, though she knew he would scoff at the idea. But she understood, as did most women, how much relief could come from a good bout of tears.

At the crest of the hill he turned slightly, just enough to make sure she still trailed him. It was enough also for her to see that he had composed himself once more, that he had beat back all his painful emotions and covered them with the arrogant veneer he wore so well. In spite of all she knew about him, that touched something in her heart, something she instinctively knew was dangerous.

"Oh no," she groaned, swiping at a limp curl that clung to her damp brow. Bad enough she found him physically attractive, intellectually challenging, and dangerously intriguing. To see him vulnerable as well could nigh well be fatal to her feminine composure. No matter his reasons, she reminded herself, he was still a drunk. No matter his wounds, he was far too much like her father. Indeed, it was on account of those wounds that he played the role of rogue so well. Rogue, rake, man-about-town. He was not looking for marriage, and even if he were, it would certainly not be the comfortable sort of marriage she sought.

He was a heartbreaker, pure and simple. She'd seen his kind in action before and warned several of her friends away from them. Even her mother, married though she'd been, had suffered a broken heart long before her second husband had died. Olivia knew all that and so she had assumed herself immune to men like Neville Hawke. She'd never imagined herself in danger from his kind.

But she was definitely in danger now.

Ahead of her Neville had paused and sat his horse at the crest of the hill. He made such a picture silhouetted against the turbulent sky. But Olivia vowed not to be swayed by the manly vigor and masculine beauty he wore with such nonchalance, for beneath it lay too much tragedy. He was not the man for her. Everything sensible in her nature proclaimed it so. Her purpose today was to hear his proposal to lease her fallow fields, that was all. He needed the use of her property, she needed his money. That was why she'd come, that was why she remained, and empathy had nothing to do with it. Nor did desire.

This was about business, nothing more.

Neville's thoughts circled around the same subject as Olivia's although with a decidedly different attitude. He'd anticipated that she would try to keep this outing as businesslike as possible, and he'd not been entirely opposed to the idea. For a variety of reasons she saw him as unsuitable, and he meant to prove her wrong. He wanted her to see that he took seriously his responsibilities to his lands and the people who worked it—just as he would take seriously his responsibilities as a husband.

He'd not expected her to confront him about his drunken excesses in Prudhoe. Had he done more than kiss her? God, he could not remember! Then she'd again brought up the subject of his insomnia, and to his chagrin he'd not responded well.

But he was calmer now and in control once more.

He glanced back at her as she came up the hill. The woman

was too perceptive by half. Too forthright. Too opinionated.

But then that was part of her attraction. She viewed life—or at least society life—with the same jaundiced eye as did he, and he knew instinctively that she would be content in these Scottish hills.

He watched her guide her mount up the hill, a graceful equestrian despite the awkwardness of the sidesaddle required of proper ladies. In truth, she was everything a man could desire in a woman—save submissive. Yet even that might be possible, he decided, under the right circumstances.

Though it was unwise in the extreme, he had the sudden and compelling need to make her submit in some manner to his will. In one manner in particular.

He dismounted and, when she reached him, caught her horse's reins. "Let me help you down."

When he reached up to help her, her eyes flashed in quick alarm. "Why are we stopping here?"

"I want to show you something." He kept his raised arms steady.

"I'm sure that's not necessary—"

"Oh, but it is. You've been away from these parts a long time—you were but a child then. If you hope to steward this land wisely, it behooves you to get to know it again. Intimately." His eyes remained on hers, which were green today, he noted. Green with a compelling rusty cast like cypress trees in the fall. Her eyes always seemed greener when her emotions ran high.

So why were her emotions running high right now? He had a strong suspicion he knew. "You do want to steward your lands wisely?" he prodded, not changing his stance.

She grimaced, then forced a halfhearted smile. "Of course I do." Albeit reluctantly, she unhooked her knee from the high pommel horn, then leaned toward him. He'd won this round, he thought, holding back his smile. But when her fingers touched his shoulder, when his two hands wrapped around her narrow waist, Neville was struck painfully with a new truth. He had not won. He had not won any battle with her at all. Instead, he had just jumped into water way over his head, and he was sinking like a fifty-pound grit stone. And the only thing that could keep him afloat was her.

He wanted Olivia Byrde to be his. He needed her to be his. And he would do whatever it took to get her.

So he lifted her down, reveling in the firm weight of her. He did not release her when he should, however. And when the color rose in her cheeks—when she made a weak effort to remove her hands from his shoulders and move out of his grasp—he did what he'd wanted to do for days now, what he wanted to do every time he laid eyes on her.

He dipped his head, staring at the shocked little O she made with her perfectly luscious mouth. He dipped his head, and he kissed her.

CHAPTER

19

OLIVIA wanted Neville to kiss her. No use to deny it. She'd wanted it from the moment he appeared in the forecourt at Byrde Manor, so tall and virile in his buff-colored breeches and dark blue riding coat.

She hadn't *wanted* to want his kiss. But she'd wanted it all the same—that lovely warm tingling sensation like before, half fear, half joy. Even the panic he'd roused in her when he'd fondled her breasts that time had become a perverse sort of desire, a longing for something she should not want at all. But now as his head dipped toward hers, she let out a guilty little sigh. *At last,* that sigh said.

At last.

Except that the remembered thrill of their previous kisses was nothing close to the powerful reality of this kiss. The fire of then was lukewarm compared to the conflagration of now. His mouth, so firm upon hers, was not tentative. There was no request in this kiss, but rather a demand.

Everything in Olivia that was sensible bade her answer that demand with a proper and resounding no. But everything in her that was sensible fled, dissipated like smoke in the wind at the first touch of his lips to hers. And when one of his arms dragged her body flush against his, and his free hand cupped the back of her head and held her steady against the onslaught of his very thorough kiss, what little sense she had of right and wrong, of proper and improper, disappeared. He kissed her like a starving man, and she kissed him right back as if she wanted him to feast upon her.

Which was precisely what she did want—and precisely what he proceeded to do.

Behind her the mare whickered as if confused by whether to stand and wait, or browse and nose around for the nearest stream. But Olivia did not care what the mare did. Neville nipped her lower lip and slid his tongue along the seam of her mouth, and she opened to him eagerly. Gratefully. His tongue delved deep and met with hers. His mouth shifted and hers did also, fitting them better, closer.

Their bodies moved in a hot slithering shifting that, despite the layers of garments between them, roused every surface of her skin. Her nipples peaked, her stomach clutched, and deeper, in places she'd rather believe did not exist, heat welled up, damp and quivering.

She let out a helpless little moan and clutched his longish hair in her hand. As hard and firm as he was—his chest and thighs and arms—she found his hair to be soft as silk. And warm, like everything else about him.

"Let me show you," he repeated in a hoarse whisper. His lips moved in a hot trail against her mouth and cheek and down the side of her throat.

"Yes," she breathed, arching back shamelessly. Could this wanton creature really be her? She wanted him to touch her aching breasts. She wanted him to ease this mad need that rose up inside her.

"Over here." He walked her backward, his knee sliding between her thighs with every step, abrading skin that had never known more than her own nonchalant swipe as she bathed. That daily ablution had roused no sensation at all, save that of cleanliness. This, however—this rough caress, casual and yet intense, and entirely uncontrolled by her—this ignited an inferno in her belly.

Back they went, step by step, her head thrown back, his lips at the base of her throat. His right leg shoved rhythmically between her thighs, and Olivia could do nothing but surrender herself completely to the madness of it. To her shame she even opened her legs a little wider, granting his muscular leg easier and deeper access.

Then she came up against a tree, his lips found hers once more, and he pressed his full weight against her.

Her arms were already around his neck, but now she felt the most perverse urge to wrap her legs around him as well. She went so far as to raise one knee, allowing him to fit his lean hips completely to hers—and she felt the hard pressure of his manly arousal.

She gasped at the stunning impact of that intimacy. But with oxygen came the first glimmer of returning sense. "Oh, my God."

Neville felt Olivia stiffen, but he ignored any sign of her resistance. He wanted her; he had to have her. And since he meant to marry her . . . Since his intentions were ultimately honorable . . .

When she turned her head aside he nipped her earlobe, then circled his tongue inside her delicate shell of an ear. At once her resistance melted away, and he felt the heated pliancy of her delectable body. Like a goad it urged him on, enflaming him beyond the bounds of all reason.

Every torturous night, every exhausting day, every lonely moment of the past four years seemed to have brought him to this moment, to this woman. It was an illogical thought, a mad thought. Yet it filled Neville with a conviction he could not shake off.

"Olivia." He breathed the word against her neck and she turned her face up to his. For a moment only their gazes met and held, one long moment of utter truth, stripped down to its purest form. He wanted her and she wanted him too.

Then she murmured his name, "Neville," and their course was irrevocably set. He caught her lips in a kiss of no return, of no going back, only forward. There was no restraint left in him, only the most basic need. Chest, loins, and legs, they strained together. His lips forced hers apart, his tongue tasted deeply of her. But she was a willing receptacle to his lust. Her arms circled his neck and her leg came up again around his thigh.

He caught her knee, lifting her leg higher still and thrust convulsively against the vulnerable warmth of her. Every one of their encounters had led them to this. Every one had been but an exquisite form of foreplay, he now saw. Their anger. Their misunderstandings. The taunting and baiting between them. Their dancing—the restraint of the cotillion, the unabashed sensuality of the waltz. Even the long journey to get here and their enforced proximity had only heightened this raw need they shared.

But there was no restraint now and no turning away. He took complete possession of her mouth, delving deep, mirroring the thrust of his pelvis against hers, and she strained for more. One of his hands cupped her derriere and through her bunched skirts he stroked the cleft of her femininity. She gasped and whimpered, but it was a whimper of need.

Somewhere beyond them the heavens boomed approval, a long, rumbling accompaniment to his thunderous pulse and throbbing body. The wind whipped around them, tangling her loosened hair in his hands. The tree that supported them shook its leaves over them, and Neville felt like one with all the elements. For this was nothing if not elemental. The mating of man to woman. Of a man to his woman, the one woman in all the world meant to be his.

He loosened the front buttons of her riding habit, then slid his hand in to cup her breasts. Against his lips she let out a strangled cry—of protest? No. For between his finger and thumb her nipple hardened with need. Her breath came in shallow gasps, urging him on.

At once he laid her down on the springy grass, flinging the sides of her bodice wide. Though her camisole hid her from view, the soft mounds of her breasts enticed him all the same.

"Neville?" She stared up at him, the perfect picture of wanton woman and innocent lady, of desire and hesitance. He vowed to rid her of any doubt.

"You are so beautiful," he murmured. "So perfect." He kissed her again and covered her body with his own. As before she responded to the kiss, and when he began to knead her breast she shifted with restless desire.

He shifted too, for his arousal had become painful, and he

raised her skirts, sliding his palm up the side of her smooth thigh. Again she moved in restless longing.

He thrust his hips against her in response. He was about to burst! But she was an innocent, he reminded himself. He must be certain she was ready. So he slid his hand between them and found the moist center of her desire.

"Soon enough," he said, trailing the words and kisses across her cheek to her jawline, then down to her throat. And all the while he stroked that wet, warm place. "Soon enough, Olivia. My lovely Hazel . . ."

She moaned with his every stroke, urging him on. Her eyes were closed now, her mouth partly opened, and as he stroked the rising nub of her desire, she began to pant and quiver. Despite the urgent demand of his own arousal, he watched her, entranced.

"Do you like that, love?" He moved his finger back and forth a little faster, a little harder.

"Yes. Oh. Oh . . ."

"Ah, damn," he muttered, struggling to tamp down his own desire even as he worked to increase hers.

"Oh, oh . . ." she panted. Then with a little shriek she bucked up, and against his hand he felt the convulsions in her belly.

"Oh . . . Oh . . ."

Neville watched in rapt fascination as she shuddered with her release. Color flooded up her chest and neck, and she sucked in huge draughts of air. For a moment her eyes opened and fastened upon his— those beautiful hazel eyes, glazed now with sexual fulfillment. Then she blinked, the glaze began to clear, and at the same moment, with a roar of fiendish delight, the heavens opened up over them.

"Bloody hell!" Neville tried to shield Olivia with his body, but there was no way to avoid the fierce onslaught of the storm. She gasped and turned away from the blinding assault of raindrops. Neville rolled her to the side, facing him, but she shoved him back, trying at the same time to close her bodice, pull down her skirts, and rise to her feet.

She failed at all three.

Nonetheless her frantic movements managed to convince Neville that their interlude was done. He cursed his wretched luck even as he pushed to his feet. Then he caught her by the elbow and helped her up. "Come on. We can shelter beneath those willows."

"No." She stared at him, her eyes huge. Then she jerked her arm free, averted her eyes, and fumbled with her already drenched bodice. The pounding rain made her awkward, blinding her eyes and dragging the skirt of her riding habit close against her legs.

"Bloody hell," Neville muttered. But he turned away, giving her some privacy. Sheltering his eyes with his hand, he collected the two nervous horses and led them beneath the thick, overhanging willows, then looked back at Olivia. She was staring at him now, and even through the downpour he could tell she was appalled by what had just happened, and that she wanted desperately to escape his presence. That, more than anything, stiffened his resolve. He might yet be bursting with unfulfilled desire, with no hope of easing it now, but he would be damned before he allowed her to ignore what had just passed between them.

A jolt of thunder crashed over them and Neville's hands tightened around the reins when the horses jerked. Olivia also cringed, and with no other choice, she joined him beneath the willows.

"We'll wait here a while," he said. "The storm should pass soon." Then he extended an arm. "Come here, Olivia. Let me shelter you."

She wrapped her arms around herself but advanced no nearer him. "I don't think I . . . That . . ." She shook her head, the picture of abject misery. "That should never have . . . have happened."

Neville had no intention of letting her get away with such thinking. He looped the reins around a branch, then faced her in the dripping shelter of the trees. "What happened just now was inevitable, Olivia. It's been inevitable since our very first meeting. But for the rain we would have fully culminated this attraction between us."

"Is that why you lured me up here?" She stabbed him with her accusing gaze. "That was your plan all along, wasn't it? You do not want any land leases from me—"

"You're wrong. My intentions were honest on that score. And they remain honest. I want those land leases. But now . . ." He thrust a hand through his dripping hair. "I had not intended to address this matter so soon, but there seems to be no helping it." He took a breath and stared intently at her. "I believe we ought to be wed."

Just saying the words out loud was unnerving. Olivia's stunned silence did nothing to reassure him. She stared at him as if she had not heard him at all—or wished she had not.

"Well?" he demanded, as aroused as ever, for her garments clung to her like a second skin, covering all, yet revealing everything. "Have you no response to what I said?"

Olivia could hardly believe her ears. She was hard-pressed to believe anything that had happened in the last quarter hour: the liberties he'd taken with her person; the liberties she'd allowed and, indeed, encouraged. And then that . . . that earthquake inside her!

She quivered to even recall the power of her response, it was that unbelievable. And now he was proposing marriage.

"If . . . if it is the land leases you want," she stammered. "You can have them."

"It's not the leases I'm speaking of. It's marriage. After what has just passed between us—"

"No!" She shook her head and backed away. "No. You will not force me—" She broke off. God in heaven, what had she done? How could she allow him such unimagined liberties and yet refuse to marry him? It was unheard of!

"Oh, my God," she moaned. "I must get away from here." She started out into the rain, but he followed.

"Olivia, wait! You can't run away from this."

"I'm not running away!" She spun around so abruptly he had to catch her by the shoulders to prevent himself from colliding with her, but he let her go at once.

Damn him for being so completely reasonable when she was spinning quite out of control.

"I'm not running away," she repeated. "But unlike you, I cannot turn my emotions on and off."

He met her accusation with a pained expression. "I assure you, my emotions are not turned off."

Against her wishes her gaze fell to his wet breeches where the evidence of his unrelieved desire clearly showed.

"Don't flee," he added when she stepped involuntarily backward. He paused a moment, all the while staring intently at her. "I think, Olivia, that we have to marry, and quickly."

Overhead thunder again rocked the heavens, but the rain began to ease. She dashed one hand across her eyes. "I am not so foolish as to believe we must wed. What you did— What we did—" She shook her head, at a loss for words. "No child can come of this," she finally said in a strangled voice.

One side of Neville's mouth lifted in a faint grin. So much for that tack. Still, he had no intention of wasting the advantage he'd gained. Though this was not the subject he'd meant to broach this morning, nor the manner in which he meant to broach it, it was out in the open now and could not be retracted. Nor did he wish to retract it, not with the effects of their frustrating encounter still ricocheting through his body. Even the rain could not cool his ardor. "We must marry, Olivia. Even you must see that."

"But . . . I do not see it. We are not at all suited to one another. Not really."

"We are perfectly suited," he countered. "As this episode so aptly demonstrates. In truth, were your mother or brother to hear of this latest incident between us, they would be entirely right to insist I do the proper thing and marry you without delay."

"Don't you dare tell them!"

"Then don't force me to."

Where that threat came from Neville could not say. But once said, he knew he would stand by it.

Her eyes widened in horror, then narrowed in fury. "You planned this all along, didn't you? To compromise me so that I am forced to marry you. Well, it won't work. I'll . . . I'll deny anything you say."

"That was not my purpose," he said. *Not originally*. But that didn't matter anymore. "It will do no good to deny it," he added. "For no one will believe you."

"Why would you want to force the issue!"

"I don't want to force it, Olivia. I don't want to force you at all." He gestured with his arms spread wide. "I have put this badly, it seems. Why don't we start back for Byrde Manor? All I'm asking of you is that you consider my offer."

She shook her head, but Neville pressed on. "I'll speak to your mother—"

"No!"

"—and your brother as soon as they arrive."

"You had better not!"

"Why not?" Neville caught her by the arms and lowered his head so that they were face to face. All of a sudden her objections were no longer amusing. They were too vehement to be just maidenly protests, and the fact that she was serious drove him a little bit mad. "Tell me, Olivia. Do you have something against all men, or is it just me?"

"Don't be ridiculous."

"Ridiculous? You forget that I've read that little journal of yours, every single page, and among all those men, there was not one whom you heartily endorsed."

"How dare you!" She twisted and turned, trying to shrug free of his hold. But he would not release her.

"Not one of them appealed to you for yourself. Not one of them. I'm beginning to wonder if you just hate all men."

"Not all of them. Just you!"

He shook his head, too angry to be cautious. "I think not. I think the last few minutes prove you like me. A lot."

"No—"

He cut off her protest with a kiss, forceful. Brutal, even. But it squelched her denial, and it drowned out his anger, leaving instead only passion, hot, demanding, and volatile. It flared through him like a wildfire in a coal mine, so violent and all-consuming that he had but one aim: to quench the fire here and now, to lay her down and sink inside her, and give them both the release they so desperately needed.

That her struggling had turned to desire only fanned the fire higher. But Neville was no fool, and despite his raging arousal, he somehow forced himself to restraint. One last delving kiss. One last cupping of her rounded derriere, to press that soft belly to his groin. He tangled his fingers in the heavy wet silk of her hair, then reluctantly drew them out.

As he'd done before, he thrust her an arm's length away from him. "Go home," he growled. "Go home and think about what has happened between us, Olivia. Then decide how you wish to tell your family. I give you a week, no longer."

Then he turned on his heel and made himself stalk away from her. Though it pained him with every step, he strode away and snatched up the reins. She would find her way home, storm or no. She was on her own lands and the route was clear. Besides, she was an accomplished rider, as at ease on a horse as he.

All these things he told himself as he mounted his hunter, then urged the animal down into the valley. But the real reason he left her was that he could not trust himself with her one minute longer. Despite all the practical reasons he might have to wed her, the real reason was not practical at all. He wanted her. Desperately, it seemed. More than he'd ever wanted a woman before. Enough that he'd turned down a perfectly luscious offer of a bed partner both nights of their journey, and had avoided the several women in Kelso that he knew to be ready and willing.

He'd begun to worry that there was something wrong with him—to be in a state of nearly constant arousal because of her, yet unwilling to take relief when it was offered elsewhere.

But there was nothing wrong with him, he knew as he willed his painful condition to subside. Nothing that Olivia Byrde could not cure.

One week he'd give her to accept his offer of marriage. After that, he would do whatever it took to seal their union.

CHAPTER

20

THE day careened on from one disaster to the next. Not that her mother and brother's arrival at Byrde Manor should have been considered a disaster. But coming as it did just hours after that unbelievable incident with Neville Hawke, the arrival of their jovial party felt like a disaster to Olivia. The last thing she wanted to do was see anyone at all.

She'd barely returned to the house and changed when James arrived along with three boon companions, all of them mounted on spirited steeds, and none of them much the worse for the storm. Though she was not in the mood for any male hijinks, Olivia had no choice but to smile and act very pleased to see them—and indeed she was pleased to see her beloved older brother with his wide smile and exuberant manner. Just not this particular evening.

"Livvie!" he cried, leaping from his favorite hunter. He grabbed her in a hug and swept her right off her feet. "This is my sister," he said to the men who dismounted behind him. "Olivia, may I introduce Nicholas Curtis, Viscount Dicharry. Also, the Honorable Justin St. Clare."

She was dizzy and barely back on her feet before the two men were bowing over her hand. Viscount Dicharry was a hearty spaniel sort of a fellow. Mr. St. Clare was older and calmer, with very correct manners.

"I believe you already know Lord Holdsworth," James added, his blue eyes glinting.

"Of course." She greeted the man her mother was so enamored of. "You are all very welcome—"

"James!" Sarah barreled from around the house and straight

into her brother's outstretched arms, and the scene replayed itself.

"Hullo, squirt."

Then the traveling coach splashed down the driveway, followed by another, smaller carriage, and all at once pandemonium took over. Augusta alighted, along with her friends whom she quickly introduced: the Honorable Anthony Skylock and his wife, Joanna, as well as the recently widowed Henrietta Wilkinson and her daughter Victoria. The women all complained of exhaustion, the men vowed they were invigorated, horses and servants milled about, and Bones barked the alarm from a safe distance away. All in all, were it not for Mrs. McCaffery, Olivia would have turned around and fled, leaving them all to their own devices. She was that overcome by their noisy descent upon her already shaky situation.

But she stood her ground and only pressed her fingers against her temples. She desperately needed time alone to think what to do and sort out her shattered emotions. What had she been thinking to invite all these people for a month of shooting at poor, unsuspecting grouse?

Thank God for Mrs. McCaffery, who was more than up to the task at hand. She dispensed the three newly hired menservants to unload and disperse the luggage to the appropriate rooms. Her four new maids served refreshments to the dusty travelers, whisky in the parlor for the gentlemen, tea in their rooms for the ladies. Mr. Hamilton and his two stablemen took the animals on to the stable, and by the time the late dinner was served, all was peaceful again—as peaceful as a country house party could be expected to be.

Somehow Olivia also affected an air of calm—at least on the outside. Inside, however, she was a knot of roiling emotion. Solitude did not assuage it any more than did company. Neither the stables, the kitchen, nor her bedroom afforded her any peace. She'd engaged in the most shocking behavior of her life, with results she could never have imagined—and with a man she could not approve of. Kissing him was terrible enough. But the rest of it!

And worst of all, she'd liked it!

Now as she sat at one end of the dining table, she suppressed the wicked shiver that curled up from her belly. Just remembering her intimate encounter with Neville Hawke made her knees go weak. Truly she must be the most wanton woman in creation.

It would serve her right if she caught a cold from her drenching, then developed a fever and died. Certainly that could not feel worse than this terrible guilt and shame. Unfortunately, she felt as healthy and robust as ever. More was the pity.

She needed to speak to someone about what had happened, and about what she could do regarding the threat Lord Hawke had hung over her head. She only had a week.

But she could never confide this in her mother, she realized during a lull before the final dessert course. As if to prove that true, Augusta gave Olivia a measuring look and said, "So how is our dear neighbor?"

Her voice held an expectant note, and guilty heat quickly suffused Olivia's face. Before she could formulate an appropriately bland answer, however, Augusta turned to their guests and rattled on. "Neville Hawke, Baron Hawke of Woodford Court, is our nearest neighbor. He's the one Archie is pursuing in hopes of purchasing that fabulous mare."

"The one that outran every three-year-old at Doncaster," Archie threw in. "And who I believe is faster than any three-year-old—filly or stallion—in the whole of Great Britain."

"I'd certainly like to take a look at her," James said, signaling for more wine. "What say we take a ride over there tomorrow?" He glanced at Olivia. "You can introduce us. I understand from Mother that you and he became quite friendly," he added, watching her closely.

Beneath the table Olivia's knotted fists began to shake. With his fair hair and blue eyes, James appeared affable enough. But he had a core of steel and a strong sense of responsibility, especially toward the women in his family. If he ever found out just how friendly she'd become with their neighbor, he was liable to call the man out. Just as Neville threatened, James would demand that they marry. Olivia stifled a groan at the thought. Thank God James did not know anything—at least not yet.

She would have to do something to make sure he never did. But what?

"Yes, Olivia. That's an excellent idea," Augusta chimed in. "We should send a note round to Woodford Court tonight— it would be rude to show up on his doorstep unannounced. Will you see to it, dear?"

From disaster to disaster to further disaster. By the time Olivia was at last alone in her own bedchamber she was frantic, for she'd had swift word back from Neville Hawke that he would be pleased to entertain all of them with a tour of his properties and a picnic luncheon.

How on earth was she to deal with him?

How was she to avert the catastrophe bearing down upon her?

She turned down the lamp and pulled the sheets up to her chin. He'd given her a week to decide. That meant she had a week to figure a way out of this mess. A week to avert an utter fiasco.

But though Olivia's waking moments were consumed by fear and rage and frustration at Neville Hawke's high-handed threat, when she finally slept she dreamed of laughter and joy and peace. In her dreams she rode a beautiful mare, and beside her rode a beautiful man. A baby gurgled and cooed, birds sang, and the sun shone. When she awoke, for the first few moments of the day she simply lay in her bed, well rested, marveling at how utterly content she felt.

And why should she not be content? She was away from town, in her own home with the clean scent of lemon wax and fresh country air surrounding her. She'd been right to come back to Byrde Manor, she thought, stretching like a lazy, well-fed cat. Her family was here with her, everything was perfect.

Then she remembered her guests, and her neighbor—and what they'd done together—and she bolted upright. Everything was not perfect. In fact, matters could not be worse!

She stared at the window in alarm. It was just past dawn.

She had only a few hours to prepare herself for the dreaded jaunt to Woodford Court.

At the last minute she opted to play the coward.

As their extensive party filed out into the courtyard, the women climbing into the open phaeton, the men onto their horses, Olivia pleaded a headache. Despite her mother's cajoling and James's suspicious looks, she remained adamant. So they rode out without her, the men casually dressed in riding breeches and short frock coats, the women arrayed like colorful birds in the open carriage.

No sooner had they departed, however, than Olivia began to worry anew. What might Neville say to them? Would he be angry enough at her absence to blurt out everything? She was terrified to face him and just as terrified not to be there with the others. How had he managed to turn an outspoken, generally fearless woman into such a quivering little coward?

"Botheration," she muttered. "Damn the man," she added, deciding he deserved more forceful curse words. "Damn you for the most troublesome, high-handed, deceitful wretch I've ever had the misfortune to know," she swore, stamping her foot in agitation. Then she snatched up her riding ensemble from her armoire. If she didn't hurry he might paint a picture even more dreadful than what had actually passed between them. She wouldn't put it past him.

Once up on Goldie, her own mare that had been a gift from Humphrey upon her tenth birthday, Olivia felt a trifle more in control. After all, no one could actually force her to marry if she was truly opposed to the match. They couldn't march her down the aisle and drag the words out of her mouth. They might try, but they would not succeed.

She patted Goldie's neck and urged her into a slow, rocking canter. When her hat slid off and swung behind her back by its strings, she urged the mare on even faster. It felt so good to ride this swiftly, with the wind in her hair. She felt stronger and better able to face the coming confrontation. Even if Lord Hawke went so far as to cause a scandal, she decided she could survive it. She would simply remain here at Byrde Manor, away from all the malicious talk in London. She'd been thinking of remaining here anyway, so her plans need not change on that score. Besides, the gossip would die down in time. Soon enough a new scandal would come along to occupy all the twittering brains that made up most of society.

Her mother would be horrified, though, as would James. They would be publicly humiliated. As for Sarah, in six years the girl would have her own come-out. Would Sarah's prospects be damaged by her older sister's behavior now?

Olivia slumped in the saddle and Goldie responded by slowing her eager pace. What a turmoil!

Then a new thought crept into Olivia's head, an idea too foreign to consider. Yet once there, it would not go away. What if she consented to marry Neville Hawke?

What if she just agreed to his demand, as unfair as it was?

Her brow creased in earnest thought. Her mother would be thrilled, of course, as would Sarah. James would be satisfied. As everyone agreed, Neville Hawke matched her in rank and fortune, and their lands did run together.

Certainly they were well matched in the passions of the body.

Olivia groaned at that shameful thought. Oh, but this was an impossible situation.

Still, the idea of marrying Neville Hawke would not go away. As she approached the small village of Kelso she decided to at least consider the idea for a while, to weigh the matter unemotionally—if that were possible. If not for his drinking, she would probably have found him more than acceptable. But he did drink—far too much, as she'd sadly come to learn.

Then again, he had vowed to quit. Could she believe him? She just did not know. She sighed. She would just have to see how Lord Hawke behaved today. Then she would make her decision.

Once in the village, Olivia stared about with considerable interest, for no matter her decision, this place was soon to become her home. Though not excessively prosperous-looking, it was, at least, neat and well maintained. A slat-sided cart rumbled by on uneven wheels, carrying a load of produce in burlap sacks. Several boys and two old men fished off the bridge, while another fellow on a tall ladder trimmed thatch on a substantial-looking cottage. As she turned for the bridge, she saw a small town green in the opposite direction, and across it, an old Norman-styled church.

She hadn't yet called on the vicar, she realized. She would have to remedy that at once.

She turned Goldie to cross the bridge over the river Tweed. There she saw a few more cottages, small places set behind the stone wall that edged the north side of the road. Toward the rear of the tiny residences a woman hung clothes out to dry. In the common front yard three children played.

When they spied her they ran to the road and one of them, a little boy about five years old, swiftly clambered onto the wall and stood, balancing himself with outstretched arms. It put him nearly face to face with Olivia. But like the two little girls hanging on the wall, he did not speak but only stared at her through wide blue eyes.

She drew Goldie to a halt. "Hello," she began, smiling at his serious little face. "I believe I may be lost. I was wondering, do you think you might direct me to Woodford Court?"

"Woodford Court?" one of the two little blond girls said. "Why, that's easy enough to find. Just go down the road that-away." She pointed. "Why d'you want to go there?"

Olivia smiled at the child. She was old enough to have lost two teeth already and so had a funny, gap-toothed grin. "I'm going to meet with someone."

"Lord Hawke?" The boy finally spoke. Olivia shifted her smile to him, but he did not smile back. His eyes remained fixed on her, however, dark blue eyes, moody and suspicious.

"Yes. Lord Hawke, among others."

"We saw them other riders," the gap-toothed girl said. "How come you didn't go with them?"

For a moment Olivia did not answer, she just kept staring at the boy. Had she seen him somewhere before? He looked so familiar. "I . . . um . . . I overslept," she finally replied.

The third child, obviously unwilling to be left out of the

conversation, piped up with, "My mother says the quality always oversleeps."

Olivia's eyebrows arched. "Does she now?"

Just then the woman hurried over, abandoning her laundry. "Mary. What are you saying? And Margaret. The two of you get home to your mother this very minute." She snatched the boy down from his perch on the wall, then held him close, pressing him back against her legs while her hands crossed protectively over his chest. Her expression seemed resentful, but her words were polite enough. "Can I be helping you, miss?"

Olivia smiled at her, but received no more response from the woman than she had from her son. That it was her son, Olivia had no doubt, even though they looked nothing alike. Her eyes were brown, as was her hair. With the spattering of freckles across her cheeks, she was a soft, warm-looking woman, despite her cool expression. The boy, however, had raven hair to contrast with his striking blue eyes, and his summer tan emphasized his coloring.

In that regard he reminded her of Neville.

Neville!

She must have gasped, or in some other manner revealed the shocking turn of her thoughts, for the woman's hold on the child tightened. She whispered in the boy's ear, then gave him a little shove toward the cottage. With disbelieving eyes, Olivia watched him head over to his two playmates, only once turning to give her a last unsmiling look.

Could it be true? Was that little boy fathered by the lord of Woodford Court?

"I'll thank you not to single my boy out for your animosity."

Olivia's head jerked around at the woman's belligerent words. "Animosity? I assure you, I would never—"

"You're Miss Byrde, aren't you? The lady as has come to live at Byrde Manor."

"Well, yes, I am. But—"

"If I could've kept his parentage hidden I would've," she broke in again. "But I can't. He looks too much like his father to be deceiving anyone. But I'll not have him slighted for it. Not even by you high-and-mighty types. An' you needn't complain to Lord Neville about me oversteppin' my bounds." She sniffed and folded her arms across her chest. "He's made it clear he'll provide for me and my Adrian, no matter what."

Olivia had been taken aback by the sight of the child Adrian. No denying that. And the woman's unexpected confrontation had caught her completely off guard. But she bristled at the woman's assumption that she would do anything to slight an innocent child, and her temper flared at the woman's contemptuous tone.

Her tightened grasp upon the reins caused Goldie to snort and stamp. The animal was impatient to be off. For that matter, so was Olivia. But first she needed to conclude this awkward conversation. Her chin jutted forward. "I assure you, madam, that I would never blame a child for its parents' behavior. As for you, you have my complete sympathy. It's plain that your past associations with the gentry have soured your disposition. Understandably so. Rest assured that I shall keep your experience in mind in my future dealings with Lord Hawke."

Then she turned Goldie and urged her up the road. She heard the woman call out to her, but she ignored her. What she wanted was to gallop, to escape from her emotions in the dangers of a headlong dash up the narrow curving road. But she did not gallop. She rode as a lady ought: straight back and decorous pace, never revealing the emotions that seethed just beneath her composed exterior.

She should not be so disappointed in the man, Olivia told herself repeatedly on the short ride to Woodford Court. She should not be so angry with him. It was not unheard of for men of the peerage and landed gentry to get babes upon lesser folk. Servants; working women; the daughters of their tenants. For all she knew, her father might have gotten a child on some poor woman. But young ladies were not supposed to understand about such things.

At least Lord Hawke was supporting his child, she told herself. But she was angry and disappointed. And hurt.

At least he was single and not dallying behind his wife's

back, she rationalized. But would he cease such behavior once he wed?

Her mouth turned down. Not likely. Her father certainly hadn't. He'd continued to drink and he'd continued to dally where he ought not. Why should she expect any better of Neville Hawke? Olivia squared her shoulders against the disappointment she felt. To think she'd actually been considering marriage to the man!

But there was no way she could agree to an alliance with him now, she told herself as she reached the pair of massive pillars that marked the entry to Woodford Court. If she'd had the slightest doubt on the subject of marrying him, she had it no more. Whatever trials she might face in the weeks to come, they would surely be easier than marriage to a drunken philanderer.

But her relief at having escaped his clutches did nothing to assuage Olivia's anger at him. As his property revealed itself— the long shaded allée of spruce trees, the carefully tended wood lot that framed several picture-perfect vistas—even the pair of swans that glided across a lily-ringed pond increased her ire. His estate was magnificent, with the mature trees and moss-edged stone fences that bespoke centuries of loving care. Many a lord with considerably higher title did not possess nearly so lovely a home.

Then she came around a bend in the drive, the house appeared beyond another small lake, and she actually drew Goldie to a halt.

It was a castle, or more accurately a fortress. An old Scottish fortified house, built during an earlier, more tumultuous time. A tall stone tower punctuated the roof, providing a view over the surrounding lands. A stout wall formed a protected courtyard in front of the U-shaped house, giving the distinct feeling of a bailey. Today, however, instead of fending off invaders, the tall metal-strapped gates stood open to welcome the lord's guests.

As Olivia rode slowly between the two gate towers, she felt very like a poor medieval maiden might, being thrust into her enemy's stronghold—and everyone but she blind to the danger he presented.

A skinny young man ran out to greet her. "Good morning, miss. Are you come to see Lord Hawke?"

Despite her simmering rage she forced an appropriate smile. "Yes. I believe the rest of my family is already here."

In short order he took Goldie in hand, then directed her toward the small party touring the stables. She spied Neville at once. His back was to her as he strolled between Lord Holdsworth and James, the three of them deeply immersed in talk of horses and bloodlines and racing times. Sarah hung on a stall door, offering a dried apple to a pretty young blaze-faced animal. The others meandered behind them, Viscount Dicharry in the clutches of Mrs. Wilkinson and her aging daughter, the Skylocks behind them, and bringing up the rear, Augusta and the animated Mr. St. Clare.

For a moment Olivia held back and just observed the scene. Her mother looked particularly beautiful today, dressed in a shade of blue that never failed to flatter her, much that Archie seemed to care. But Augusta was not sulking. Instead she made the most of her present companion, while at the same time studying her environs with a calculating expression. It was the expression Olivia had come to think of as her "society mama in search of a son-in-law" expression. Augusta already approved of Lord Hawke as a man—more was the pity. It was plain to see that she approved equally well of his properties.

It was enough to make Olivia reconsider and retreat before anyone noticed her.

There was, unfortunately, no time for her to do that, for as Augusta scanned the long row of stalls filled with valuable horseflesh, her eyes fell upon Olivia. At once her face lit up with satisfaction.

"There you are!" She patted Mr. St. Clare on the arm, then disentangled herself from him and made her way over to Olivia. Her arms spread wide in greeting, but her eyes gleamed with speculation.

Olivia could have groaned. Of course Augusta would choose to believe the worst, that Olivia had been drawn to

Woodford Court despite the splitting headache she'd claimed, drawn here by the lure of Neville Hawke—which was on one level partially true.

When Augusta pressed her palm to Olivia's brow, Olivia ducked her head. "It was a headache, not a fever. And I'm much better."

Augusta pursed her lips knowingly. "I'm so pleased to hear you're better. It must be that wonderful tisane Mrs. McCaffery makes. I swear, that concoction cures nearly every ill known to mankind. But come. Come, my darling, and join us. Look, everyone!" She gestured to the others. "Olivia has come after all."

Olivia wanted to cringe. What had possessed her to come trailing after them? She must appear like some child afraid to miss out on the least amount of fun. As for what Neville Hawke thought . . .

She didn't care, she told herself. She didn't care at all, for she already thought the very worst of him.

Still, she did not want to reveal her feelings here in front of everyone, and so she was relieved when James made his way to her side. "That's more like the sister I know." He circled her shoulders with one arm and drew her over to where Neville and Lord Holdsworth stood. "There's not much that can keep our Livvie down."

"We're to have a picnic," Sarah announced, leaping down from the stall door. "But first Lord Hawke is going to show us this year's foals."

"How lovely," Olivia replied, assiduously avoiding Neville's avid gaze.

Fortunately Augusta stepped in and, hooking one arm in Neville's and the other in Lord Holdsworth's, she imperiously steered the two men down the stable's long central aisle. "Well I, for one, have worked up an appetite. All this outdoor air, you know. Let us continue on with the tour, Lord Hawke. You, Archie, and James may finish your debate about grain-fed cattle versus open range over tea and biscuits."

Olivia had to give her mother credit, for she had a way of taking people in hand, especially men, and then charmingly directing them precisely where she wished them to go. It was the same talent Sarah had begun to develop of late. Too bad *she* was not so adept at it, she fretted, as they wandered down the stables, then out toward a fenced field spotted with horses.

Woodford Court was a handsome and industrious estate, that was plain to see as the tour wended along. Neatly maintained. Humming with activity. People, horses, chickens — even the dogs and cats appeared healthy and well fed. Yet still Olivia glared daggers at its lord's back. Competent he might be in matters of property and money—much more so than she had been with Byrde Manor—but he was still a despoiler of women and sire to who knew how many children outside the bounds of wedlock.

As if he sensed her sharp glare, he turned his head and gave her a brief but intense smile—the wretch! When he turned back to his other guests, she was left with the unpleasant sensation of dangling on tenterhooks, breathless, nervous, and furious. Still, she had no alternative but to go along, at least for now, with this charade.

Honestly, she didn't know which was worse: confrontation or suspense!

So their party strolled in Augusta's wake. They viewed the several colts and fillies that had been born the previous spring, and watched as Bart, Woodford's trainer, introduced one leggy chestnut-colored animal to the long lead. They looked over the breeding mares grazing peaceably in the late summer sunshine, their swelling stomachs so handsome with the new lives inside them. A square table laden with dishes awaited them in an oak grove beside an oval lake where more swans and a small flock of ducks congregated. Truly it would have been a lovely day with every detail attended to, if not for the guillotine blade hovering over Olivia's head. Between avoiding his knowing gaze and expecting him at every turn to allude by word or expression to his threat or their encounter, she was twitching with nervousness.

By the end of the afternoon she almost wanted him to bring it up. But he did not, and as they packed for their return trip to Byrde Manor she found herself exhausted.

"Come, darling, ride in the phaeton with us," Augusta implored. "You're looking a little peaked. Has your headache returned?"

"No. I'm quite fine." This lie was quite the opposite of the morning's lie, for now her head really did ache.

"You've been working so hard to get the house in order. And you did a lovely job of it," Augusta added. "But tomorrow I want you to just relax. I'll see to everything. You won't have to lift a finger."

"And we'll be out of your hair," James said, mounting his spirited animal. "We've got up our first shooting party. Lord Hawke's going to show us all the best spots for grouse."

"It will be my pleasure," Neville said.

Now when had he sneaked up beside her?

"Do you hunt, Miss Byrde?" he asked. For the first time that day their eyes met and held.

"No." If it were possible to stumble over a monosyllabic word, at that moment Olivia surely would have done so. Her heart had begun to pound that violently.

He smiled. "May I give you a hand up?" Then without waiting for her reply, he caught her about the waist and set her squarely on Goldie's back. "Have you thought further on our conversation of yesterday?"

Olivia sucked in a breath. She'd let down her guard for only a moment and look what happened.

"What conversation?" Augusta asked.

"And when?" James frowned, only belatedly assuming his role as older brother and man of the family.

Olivia's mouth had gone too dry to speak. Besides, what was she to say, "His kisses thrill me, his touch makes my skin heat, he knows how to make my soul shatter apart—but he's just not good husband material"?

Perhaps Neville saw the panic in her eyes. Or perhaps he'd intended all along only to frighten her. In any event, he smiled at her, then over at her mother and brother. "Miss Byrde has consented to grant me a lease on several of her fallow fields, though we have yet to come to terms."

"Oh. What a good idea," Augusta said. But her voice

clearly revealed her disappointment that it was merely land they'd discussed.

James glanced at Olivia. "Why didn't you tell me about that? I'll be happy to handle the matter for you."

"It's my property and I can handle my own negotiations," she replied rather tartly, for it was safer to be angry with James than with Neville. "Besides, as he said, we haven't yet come to terms."

Suddenly she felt a hand on her ankle, a strong male hand. Completely hidden beneath the trailing ends of her long skirt, it curled in the most intimate manner around her ankle.

Aghast at his boldness—and her visceral reaction to it— Olivia stared down into Neville's piercing blue eyes. He smiled up at her, as straight-faced as if his thumb were not now sliding in hot little circles along her skin, creating the warmest, most shocking sort of friction. Very like he'd done yesterday.

"No, we have not yet come to terms," he said. "But I believe we will. I believe we soon will."

CHAPTER

21

In the morning the men went hunting. The women wandered independently down to breakfast, Olivia and Sarah first, later the Wilkinsons and Mrs. Skylock. Then one by one, they meandered off to entertain themselves as they preferred. Only then did Augusta descend to the dining room. At her behest, Mrs. McCaffery joined her.

"Here. Sit." Augusta patted the place next to her. "I know you've eaten, but have some chocolate or tea with me." Once her long-time housekeeper was settled, she went on. "So tell me. How fares the budding romance?"

"The budding romance?" Mrs. McCaffery's hand trembled a bit and hot water sloshed onto her saucer. But she recovered quickly. "The budding romance? Ooh. The budding romance. Olivia and Lord Hawke."

Augusta tilted her head and stared at her faithful servant. "Yes. Olivia and Lord Hawke. Who else would I mean?"

Mrs. McCaffery set down her cup and began vigorously to plunge the tea ball up and down in the water. "No one else. But I confess, I haven't given them much thought of late. I've been that busy around here. It was a mess, you know." She gestured with her chin. "To look at it now you canna tell, but this house was in terrible condition. Terrible."

Augusta stared around the dining room with its heavy furnishings and wall of windows. At the moment sunshine streamed in, warm and comfortable. "It looks very nice to me. Nothing has seemed to change at all, even after all these years."

"The grounds were a sight. And the sycamores are bigger. They've quite overgrown the house."

"Yes. And the double swing is gone." Augusta smiled and gazed beyond the multipaned windows. "Do you remember how Cameron used to push me so high? James and Olivia would sit together on one side of the swing and I would sit on the other."

Mrs. McCaffery stirred honey into her tea. "I remember that swing."

Augusta looked over at the other woman, and her smile faded. "I know you will always think the worst of Cameron. But we did have some lovely days. They did not stay lovely, but for a while . . . Ah, well. I cannot complain anymore. My Cameron was a bonny fellow, but a tragic one, as it turned out. Thank goodness Humphrey came along to fill the hole in my heart."

"And will Lord Holdsworth now fill the space dear Humphrey left?"

Augusta concentrated on her ham and scones. "Perhaps. I am not certain. But what about Olivia and Neville? Was their enforced proximity during the journey here sufficient to break down her foolish resistance to him? I swear, I simply do not understand that child."

"He was very good, very well behaved and charming to us all. He certainly won over Sarah."

"And you?" Augusta asked, dimpling. "You can pretend you are unaffected by a handsome man, Bertie McCaffery, but I know you better than that."

The older woman chuckled. "I'll admit he has winning ways. And despite all her protests, I'd swear Livvie thinks so too. Whenever he comes around she gets this look." The housekeeper shook her head. "I just don't know."

Augusta drummed her fingernails upon her glass. "I've noticed the very same thing. And yet she seems so determined to avoid him. That entire business yesterday, about her staying home—it just didn't ring true." She shook her head. "I just don't understand."

They sat in silence a few minutes, Augusta eating and Mrs.

McCaffery sipping her tea. Finally the housekeeper set down her cup. "They went out riding day before yesterday, just the two of them. To look over the fields he wants to lease from her."

"Do you think there was more to it than that?"

The housekeeper shook her graying head. "I don't know. I tried to figure it out, but I couldna. She came back alone, drenched by the storm. Then you arrived and I've had no chance to talk to her since. You know, Gussie," she added. "There's no accountin' for tastes. If she doesn't care for him in that way . . ."

Augusta thought for a moment. "Does he want her?"

Mrs. McCaffery nodded. "Oh, I believe he does. I've had it from Donnie—Mr. Hamilton, that is—who had it from the innkeeper who is brother to Woodford's housekeeper, that Lord Hawke is usually a solitary sort. Keeps to himself most o' the time. All work, hardly any socializing a'tall, save a jaunt now and again to the tavern. Yet he's been nothin' but neighborly and sociable since we arrived. And then there's the way he looks at her, like he could eat her up with his eyes alone." She cocked her head. "Yes. I'd say he wants our Livvie, and rather badly."

A slow smile crept over Augusta's face and she steepled her perfectly manicured fingers under her chin. "Perhaps we can assist their floundering romance."

The housekeeper leaned forward. "How d'you mean?"

"Well. What if they were caught in a compromising position?"

Mrs. McCaffery frowned. "That would be a dirty trick."

Augusta fixed her bright blue gaze upon the woman. "It's not as if anyone would be forcing them into that compromising position. I'm only suggesting that we pay close attention to their comings and goings, and catch them at it. You know what I mean. A kiss. An embrace. If they choose to behave so—and get caught—'tis their own misfortune. Or good fortune," she added, smirking at the thought. "Olivia simply does not know her own mind these days. She spends too much time analyzing the men she meets and jotting notes down in that silly book of hers, when she ought to spend her time more profitably by listening to her heart."

"And you mean to force her to listen to her heart?"

Again Augusta smiled. "What else is a loving mother to do?"

The hunters returned shortly before afternoon tea. Olivia had spent the day in determined activity. She didn't want to rest, for to rest was to think and she desperately did not want to think about what had happened between her and Neville. Nor of his threat. When she discussed the subject of the land leases with Mr. Hamilton he had not been at all opposed to the idea, especially when she told him the terms Lord Hawke had offered.

So why didn't you enter into such a lease years ago? she wanted to ask the steward. But she did not. She'd determined very quickly that Mr. Hamilton, though hardworking, was not a man of much imagination. Things were still managed at Byrde Manor "just as your da' would have it," he'd told her several times now. To the old man's mind that apparently meant the workers were not replaced as they retired or died. Nor was the stock.

Time had taken its toll on Byrde Manor, and on Mr. Hamilton. But though Olivia was up to the task of repairing and maintaining her property, she was not up to rebuilding the herds of cattle and flocks of sheep, nor of running the place as a profitable farming venture. It was enough that the leases would pay for the additional expenses of her setting up housekeeping at Byrde Manor—although she wondered now whether that was still wise.

But she was not going to think about that today. She was not going to let Neville Hawke and his threats dominate her life or alter her plans. Instead she applied herself to compiling a list of the particular fields he wanted, as well as access, water rights, time limitations, and payment schedule. When it was completed she needed only to review it with her brother, then send it to the local solicitor to draw up the copies. So when she heard male voices in the forecourt, she hurried from the downstairs study—*her* study now—and outside to speak to James. She wanted this matter settled before the *other* matter between her and Lord Hawke could be raised.

Unfortunately, Neville Hawke was still with the hunters.

When she spied him she skidded to a halt. As desperately as she wanted to ignore his presence, she could not. Her eyes were drawn to him, as if his tall, virile form were a magnet. Her entire being reacted that way. This was the man who made her heart thump. He made her body run hot, and he knew how to raise her to unheard of heights of physical pleasure. For the short while that she'd actually considered marrying him, she'd been quite idiotically happy.

But then his darker side had resurfaced in the form of that little boy. The child, his natural son, was living proof of the sort of man Neville Hawke actually was: one she would be an utter fool to wed.

Her mother had come out to greet the hunters, and she stood now beside Neville, smiling up at him. Olivia feared that boded ill for her.

She had no hope for retreat, however, for James had already seen her and was waving her over. "Come see, Livvie. We've had a jolly good day. Why didn't you suggest coming up here years ago?"

"I believe I did," she muttered. "But as I recall, no one paid any attention to me."

"I asked Mrs. Mac to bring tea into the parlor," Augusta put in. "It's the least we can offer Lord Hawke, considering how generous he's been with his time these past two days."

Neville smiled at Augusta, then at Olivia, as if he had no ulterior motive. The wretch! There was nothing for Olivia to do but force a smile in return.

So it was tea with him, then supper as well, followed by a rowdy game of charades and two tables of whist. And all the while Olivia's body waged war with her mind. Physical desire fought with good sense. The heated knot of remembered excitement that churned deep in her belly fought against intellect and logic.

The strain was enough to give her a splitting headache.

It didn't ease the pain in her temple that Neville was nothing but charming and pleasant the entire evening. Her face hurt from trying to maintain a cool, calm expression, when inside she was a bundle of nerves. Then there was the constant struggle to remain aloof when she felt each touch of his gaze like an actual caress on her bare skin.

Pretending not to notice him did not work. But she knew she must do something soon, for she could not continue much longer in this insane fashion.

Finally the evening ended. The farewells were made, and she nearly escaped to the privacy of her bedchamber. But her mother accosted her in the upper hall, and Olivia's heart sank at the avid look in her eyes.

"Come, Livvie. Sit with me a while. We've hardly had a chance to chat, we've been so busy. Here." Augusta indicated the settee positioned opposite her tall, curtained bed.

They sat down together. Augusta kicked off her shoes and wriggled her toes. "So. How do you find Byrde Manor? Is it as you remembered? After all, you were so very young when we left."

Olivia tried to relax. "Some things are as I remember. Others . . ." She shrugged.

"But you like it here?"

Olivia grimaced to herself. Might as well get right to it. She kicked off her shoes. "I like it very much. In fact, I believe I shall stay here even after you, James, and Sarah return south."

"You will? Oh, Olivia. That makes me so happy."

Of course it did, and Olivia knew why. But she played along with the game. "That's a relief. I had expected you to object."

Augusta twisted on the settee to face her. "Whyever would you think that? You know it is my fondest wish for you to wed."

Olivia merely smiled and raised her brows. "I said nothing about marriage, Mother."

"Yes. But if you are planning to stay it can only be—"

"In spite of Lord Hawke. Not *because* of his proximity, but in *spite* of it."

Augusta's face was a study in confusion. "But I don't understand. Why would you wish to stay here if not because of him?"

"There is nothing to understand—" Olivia broke off. She'd meant to remain calm but it was too hard. So agitated, she stood and began to pace. "I do not wish to return to town and get sucked back into the marriage mart."

"But you have always seemed to enjoy the parties and routs. What of that"—Augusta fluttered her hand—"that book you keep? The matchmaker, you and your friends call it."

Olivia folded her arms and stood her ground. "I am done with all of that."

"Done with it?" Augusta abruptly stood, and though she was a half head shorter than Olivia, at that moment she appeared as fierce as any Amazon. Certainly there was no mistaking the maternal authority on her face. "You are only one-and-twenty, Olivia. That you have not yet found the man who suits you is no reason to entirely abandon the idea of marriage. That is too ridiculous an idea to believe."

"That's not what I meant!"

"Then what *do* you mean?"

In truth, Olivia was not certain. Though her chest heaved with emotion and she had to work very hard not to shout, she did not know why. She took a heavy breath, then let her shoulders droop. "What it means is that for a year or so I should like not to think constantly about my future—a husband, children, whatever. I like it here." Her hand swept the air. "In less than two weeks Mrs. Mac, Sarah, and I have effected quite a change, and it . . . it makes me feel good. So . . . so I want to spend the winter here as well, to continue putting the estate to rights. Then come the spring, well, we'll see."

Augusta opened her mouth as if to speak. But when Olivia squared her shoulders and once again arched her brows, Augusta subsided. But the expression on her face was pained.

"I can see you are firmly set on this, so I suppose it does me no good to argue with you—even though I think you will become quite bored once all of us leave. You know," she added, "your brother is not going to be very happy about your decision."

"Then please allow me to tell him in my own good time, will you?"

"As you wish," Augusta said with an elegant shrug. "As you wish." But when Olivia bade her good-night and made her exit, Augusta's eyes narrowed. This was all very interesting. Something was afoot that Olivia was intent on hiding. But time would see it out. Augusta was certain that time would see it out.

Time was running out. Three more days passed with every semblance of an idyllic country holiday. Fishing jaunts, hunting parties. Picnics, horseback riding. Charades, card games, and quiet reading. Olivia worked very hard to maintain the illusion of a carefree existence. But with each day that passed her tension mounted.

The fact that Lord Hawke stayed busy on his own estates did not make matters any easier. Though his presence always unsettled her, so, it seemed, did his absence. She was sick to death of her fun-seeking companions, yet afraid to go off alone in case she should run into him.

So why did she want to continue on through the winter at Byrde Manor? Why not simply return to town with her family?

A hundred times she pondered that question. A thousand. The only answer she came up with was that Byrde Manor—without the outside pressures caused by people—was a truly wonderful place. The wild hills, the verdant valley, and the solid, reassuring old house. She found comfort in them all.

If only she could rid herself of the people with whom she must share them. That also was a source of new stress to her. In the past she'd always enjoyed the company of pleasant, sociable people. Now, however, she found everyone a trial.

But soon enough her guests would leave, she told herself. Neville Hawke, however, would not. Nor was his odious threat going away. Three days left to find a way to defuse the situation, and she was no nearer a solution than before.

Then on one morning a note came, addressed to her and carried by one of Woodford's menservants. Olivia's heart turned to lead.

Sitting across the breakfast table, Augusta spread jam on a scone. "Has Lord Hawke carved some time from his busy schedule to accept my invitation?"

Olivia looked up from the unopened envelope. Her hands were shaking. "You invited him here? For what occasion?"

Augusta smiled around the table at Sarah, James, and Mr. St. Clare. "My goodness, to hear her talk you'd think I'd invited the Prince Regent." She glanced slyly at Olivia. " 'Tis a general invitation I speak of, dear. Lord Hawke knows he is welcome here anytime. Heaven knows, we owe him the same sort of entertainments he has twice provided to us."

Just then Lord Holdsworth strode into the room. "What's this I hear? Lord Hawke is coming over?" He pulled out a chair and sat adjacent to Augusta. "Did he say whether he has made a decision about that filly of his?"

Olivia stared down at the brief message. "No. Nothing about that. He asks that I meet him this afternoon at his solicitor's office in Kelso." She raised her head and glanced at her mother. "It's to review the lease and sign it."

James nodded. "I shall have to accompany you, Livvie, for I am legally the head of the family."

Olivia looked at her fair-haired brother and frowned. "I don't see why that should matter. You are not in any way connected to my father or his properties."

"But I am your guardian until such time as you wed." He refilled his plate from a platter one of the serving women held, immune to Olivia's irritated glare.

"I hardly see the sense in that. You forget that I have reached my majority. Besides, in a month you will be gone from here and oblivious to anything that should occur at Byrde Manor."

"So will you," he retorted as he sprinkled salt onto his eggs.

Olivia could have groaned. She shot a nervous glance at her mother. Would she reveal all now? But Augusta had a determinedly innocent expression on her face. Too innocent, it turned out, for when neither Olivia nor Augusta responded to his remark, James looked up.

It took only a moment for his eyes, as blue as their mother's, to narrow in suspicion. "Is something going on that I should know about? Mother?" He focused on her. "What is it?"

"Well," Augusta began, looking over at Olivia helplessly and shrugging.

Olivia lurched to her feet. "I shall be happy to discuss this matter in the study," she bit out, glaring at James. "*My* study, not yours." Then forgetting eggs, ham, and scones, she marched from the room.

In the aftermath James turned his probing gaze back to his mother. "What was that all about?"

Once again Augusta shrugged. But Sarah was not so reticent. "Livvie wishes to handle her own affairs. What's so awful about that, I'd like to know?"

"And I suppose you will wish to do the same?" James replied.

"Indeed I do. What is the point in being a great heiress if you cannot do whatever you wish?"

Lord Holdsworth laughed. "And that, in a nutshell, is why women should never be allowed to inherit anything. Do whatever you wish!" he sarcastically mimicked, and again laughed.

Augusta frowned at that. Mr. St. Clare looked mildly embarrassed. James wisely caught Sarah by the elbow and gave her a cautionary squeeze. But it was a silent brother and sister who finished their breakfast while the others moved on to less controversial topics of conversation. And James made certain to bring Sarah with him when he left to search out Olivia.

"Is something upsetting Livvie?" he asked his little sister.

Sarah marched beside him. "She's in love with Lord Hawke. Ooh, I hate that Archibald person! If Mother marries him I shall run away from home."

"Wait. What? Olivia loves Neville Hawke? But they hardly know one another. Besides, beyond these leases she does not appear to want anything to do with him."

The look Sarah gave her brother mingled frustration and

condescension. "Are all men as dense as you? For if they are, I doubt I shall bother to marry one. And I do not intend to let you manage my properties."

James could only stare at her. "If I had the time I would give you a good switching, brat. Sadly, however, I fear it is too late to do any good."

Sarah stopped and, glaring at him, planted her fists on her hips. "Tell me this. As the 'head of the family,' can you prevent Mother from marrying that oaf, Lord Holdsworth?"

"He's not an oaf."

"You can't do anything about it, can you? Can you?" She did not wait for an answer but stalked away, leaving a bewildered James staring after her.

He rubbed one palm back and forth against the back of his neck. The day had begun so well. Clear skies. A hearty breakfast. He'd intended to spend the morning fishing, the afternoon riding, and the evening drinking at Kelso's finest pub. But now he had two angry sisters on his hands, and a mother whose innocent smile invariably covered some manipulation or another.

"God's bones," he muttered, starting toward the study. Some holiday this was turning out to be.

OLIVIA tried to compose herself as she waited for James. She pulled out her initial draft of the leasehold agreement. She set a chair in place for him near her desk while she, herself, sat at the desk. "Head of the family, indeed," she muttered as she straightened the desk pad and repositioned the pen holder and inkwell. Men and their insufferable attitude of universal superiority! They were all the same. James. Neville Hawke. Clive Garret, and before him, Mr. Prine and all the others whose offers she'd declined.

Then there was her father.

She blew out a rude breath. From lowly stable hand to Prince Regent, they were an aggravating, troublesome lot and there was no reason at all for women to put up with them.

But there was one reason, an irritating voice in her head whispered to her.

Olivia grimaced and her fingers began to drum an anxious tattoo on the polished mahogany desktop. Yes, there was that one, terrible, wonderful reason for men to exist, one she was hopelessly unable to forget.

But though she could not forget the exquisite pleasure she had found with Neville Hawke, Olivia refused to let it change anything. She could not let it change anything. So she suppressed the shiver of remembered passion that snaked up from her stomach. Except for performing their husbandly duty and siring children, men were, on the whole, a worthless lot. Like rutting stallions, they should all be kept separate from the mares.

That brooding thought still circled in her head when James

strode into the room. He was dressed like a country squire in tall tramping boots, snug-fitting breeches, and a comfortably tailored tweed frock coat. Most irritating, he wore the confident air of a man who believed he, not she, was the one in charge. She narrowed her eyes in warning. "Should you ever deign to wed, I assure you, brother, that it will not be to any woman I consider worth knowing."

"What does that mean?" he asked, but with an amused smirk.

She smirked right back. "Only that I will warn any woman I know well away from you and your medieval ways of reasoning."

He lowered his lanky frame into a chair, stretched out his legs, and folded his hands across his stomach. "Have I done something to offend you, Livvie? I cannot believe you are this angry with me solely because I wish to make certain Lord Hawke does not take advantage of you."

It was only an accident of words, a poor choice on his part. But knowing he referred to the land lease did not prevent Olivia's face from going scarlet. That he began to laugh and crowed, "So it is true. You do love him," only increased her humiliation.

She leapt to her feet. "I do not love him! I despise him!"

Another poor choice of words. For James sobered and leaned forward, resting his elbows on her desk. "Love him or hate him, he plainly rouses more emotion in you than any other man has done. So tell me why you hate this man you are leasing your lands to."

Just that fast did he take all the wind out of her sails. Olivia sat down with a little bump and stared at her brother whom she had always adored and trusted. How desperately she wished to confide in him!

She swallowed hard. "I don't know what to do about him," she admitted in a small, muffled voice.

He sighed. "I assume we are not speaking about these leases."

Olivia shook her head. In three days Neville would tell James everything. Though she dreaded the thought, she knew it would be better for James to hear the truth from her—or at least a modified version of it.

Once more she focused on the desk pad, aligning it with the edge of the desk. She cleared her throat. "The thing is, he wishes to marry me."

James nodded. "And?"

"And . . . I don't believe he and I suit one another."

"He seems like a good enough chap to me. A sporting man, but aware of his responsibilities. Even-tempered, too." James shrugged. "But if you are not inclined to accept his offer, Livvie, so be it. As he is your neighbor, you should try to let him down as easily as you can. But that shouldn't be a problem; you've sent any number of fellows packing in the past. Why do you fret over doing the same to this one?"

When she didn't answer he reached out and caught her hand in his. "Are you sure you two do not suit? Or is it that you are afraid to wed?"

She pulled her hand away. "I'm not afraid to marry," she vowed, though she was not entirely certain that was true.

"Then I confess, I do not understand what you mean when you say 'I don't know what to do about him.' "

Olivia pressed her lips together. *Just tell him and get it over with.* She took a deep breath. "Will you promise to listen to what I say and not interrupt until I am done? Nor get angry?"

His brows lowered in concern. "What is this all about?"

"Promise me, James."

"I'll promise not to interrupt. As for my anger, I can promise nothing about that until I've heard whatever it is you're apparently keeping from me."

After a moment Olivia sighed and said, "Very well." She folded her hands together on the desktop. "Lord Hawke wishes to marry me, I believe, for all the usual reasons. Our lands run together and there is a similarity in rank and fortune that makes a match between us quite sensible."

"Not to mention age and appearance and interests in common."

"You promised not to interrupt."

"Sorry."

Olivia tried to compose her flustered thoughts. "You are right in all you say. And to complicate matters, there is some . . . some attraction between us," she confessed, knowing her face had again gone red.

James laughed. "I may be your brother, Olivia, but I am not blind. No right-thinking man in Christendom would not be attracted to you." He peered intently at her. "Are you saying you find him attractive?"

After a moment she gave one curt nod. "I do. But," she hastened to add, "that does not mean I wish to marry him."

James stared at her with a baffled expression on his face. "Fine. Though it makes no sense, I suppose I can accept that. But that still does not explain what has you so bedeviled."

Olivia let out a little groan. She was handling this badly. "All right, then. Here is the problem. He has kissed me."

James grinned. "Has he?"

"More than once."

"Was it more than a chaste peck on the cheek?"

She pressed her lips together. "Yes."

His grin faded a little. "How much more?"

She met his frank stare as directly as she could. "I believe it is referred to as the French manner of—"

"More than once?" His grin fled. "He kissed you so . . . so . . . Like that more than once?"

"Yes. But it meant nothing, so you needn't glower at me. I knew you would get angry."

For a moment he was silent. When he spoke, the words seemed reluctant. "Did he do anything more?" His face began to redden. "You know. Did he touch you . . . any place he shouldn't?"

Olivia wanted to die. She wanted to lie and say that he'd done nothing beyond kiss her. That she'd done nothing beyond kiss him back. But she knew Neville meant to reveal all to James. So she needed to be honest.

"Yes," she admitted. "And now it is his intention to use our indiscretion as a way to force me to marry him."

James lurched to his feet and leaned on rigid arms over the

desk. "Your indiscretion? Could you be more specific?" Then, "No!" He raised both hands and backed away. "No. I don't want to know the details!"

Olivia stood as well. "Will you please calm down, James? We've done nothing to warrant—"

"Nothing!" His eyes bulged from his face. "Nothing, you say!" He began to pace, gesturing wildly with his hands. "Tell me this." He stopped and again leaned over the desk so that they were eye to eye. "Did he force you or were you a willing party to those—to that—" He broke off, breathing hard, but his gaze never wavered from hers. "Well?"

In the face of his brotherly outrage it took all of her courage to tell the truth. "He . . . He did not force me. I admit it—"

"Sit down!"

She obeyed, then immediately regretted it. "You needn't shout at me."

He looked ready to shout again. But somehow he restrained himself, and after a moment he too sat. Long seconds elapsed as he took several deep breaths.

"I want to understand, Olivia. But I do not. How can you be willing to share such intimacies with the man—whatever they were—and to do so more than once, and not be willing to marry him?"

"I . . . I did kiss him more than once. But . . . but the other . . . That was only once. Besides," she continued, rallying. "I think you *do* understand. Tell me, have you ever kissed a woman in the French manner?"

The look of consternation on his face was almost comical. "Well—What does that have to do with any of this?"

"You have. I know it and I'm certain you've done far more than merely that. Yet you're not wed to any of those women."

He folded his arms stiffly across his chest. "It's not the same thing."

"Perhaps not to you. But what about to those women?"

His jaw began to twitch. "You cannot compare those women to you. The situations are not the same."

"None of them? Are you saying that not one of those women was an innocent girl of a good family?" When he did not answer but only glared at her, she leaned forward. "I have admitted to an attraction to Neville Hawke. But it goes no further than that. He . . . He is too like my father. Too wild. Too volatile. When I marry it will be to a man like Humphrey. Sweet and steady. So you see, I shall not be forced into marrying Lord Hawke. Not by him and not by you either."

She stared at him and debated whether to tell him about Neville's child, born to that village woman. But her remark about her own father and their stepfather, Humphrey, seemed to have struck home, for the deep furrows in James's brow eased somewhat. His mouth, however, turned down in disapproval. "I suppose I can understand that. But I don't like it. And under the circumstances I don't think you should sign these leases. He will not be invited here again, and certainly you will not linger at Byrde Manor beyond the duration of our shooting party."

"But I need those leases. Byrde Manor has been neglected long enough. The money he will pay for use of my fields will finance the repairs that have already been delayed too long."

"I can advance you the funds you need."

"No. I don't want your money, not when I can raise the funds with this lease." She shook the papers at him. "This will guarantee a recurring income. That's far better than going into debt, even if it is to you."

He pursed his lips. "All right, then. We can sign the leases. But you cannot stay on here alone, Olivia. Yes, Mother told me of your plans. Then, I thought it merely foolish. Now I see it as dangerous in the extreme."

He was probably right. Still, Olivia did not want to admit it. In the two weeks she'd been back she'd fallen completely in love with her old home, and she did not want to leave. "Once he knows he cannot bully me into marriage, things will settle down. You'll see. I'm glad you're being so reasonable," she added.

He fixed her with a scowl. "Reasonable? If I had my way you'd be wed to him tomorrow. But as you say, I cannot force you. I cannot make you mouth the words 'I do,' more's the pity. Nevertheless, I shall be watching you, Olivia. You're to stay strictly away from that man. And whether you like it or not, you *will* return to town with us." He stood, towering over her. "As for meeting Hawke at the solicitor's office, I *will* accompany you there."

So saying, he left, and in the silent aftermath of their conversation, Olivia let out a relieved sigh. She'd defused Neville's threat—at least with her brother. She just hoped James did not explode when the two men met face to face today. As for her mother, well, she would just have to see how things proceeded.

In the shadows of the upper stairway, Augusta watched her eldest daughter leave the study, just as she'd watched James depart. Her son had stalked away, angry and frustrated. Olivia, however, looked smug, as if she'd pulled· the wool over her brother's eyes. But not for long, Augusta vowed. Not for long.

She bent forward, listening, then slowly descended the stairs. If Olivia thought this subject was done with, she was sorely mistaken. The girl obviously didn't understand that the attraction between her and Lord Hawke was too strong for her to long resist. Even Augusta, who understood about such things, was not immune. Hadn't she decided to surrender to her new love instead of holding out until after he proposed?

The little flutter in her stomach brought a smile to her lips. Ah, love. What a wondrous, troubling, overwhelming emotion it was. Once caught in its snare, no one could resist its lure. Neither the daughter nor the mother.

Neville was not stupid. When Olivia walked into his solicitor's office arm-in-arm with her brother, and a faint but smug smile on her face, he knew something was afoot. Once he cut his gaze to James's stormy expression, he knew exactly what it was. She'd somehow made James into her ally.

The question was, had she told him the whole truth—and would her version of it have a bearing on their lease agreement? Soon enough he would know.

"Good morning, Miss Byrde. Lord Farley."

James's cold stare precluded him extending his hand. "If

we can review the documents and get this over with, my sister and I have another engagement."

Neville met him stare for stare. "I had hoped to have a private word with you afterward."

James's jaw clenched and unclenched. He shot a glance at his sister before replying to Neville. "Today is inconvenient."

Neville was gratified to see that Olivia's faint smile had disappeared. Whatever she'd revealed to her brother about them, she was still not entirely sure of his support. He decided to bide his time.

Sensing the tension between the men, the solicitor laid out the papers and in short order the lease documents were signed and witnessed, one copy for each of the principals and one for the solicitor's files. When Olivia and her brother immediately turned to depart, Neville rubbed one knuckle along the scar on his jaw. It was time for action.

"Before the two of you go." He glanced at the solicitor. "May I borrow your office for five minutes?"

"Certainly, my lord."

"That won't be necessary," Olivia interrupted.

"No," James said. "I think I might like to hear what he has to say after all."

"James!"

Neville repressed a smile at her barely disguised panic. When the door closed behind the solicitor, however, his amusement faded. James Lindford, Viscount Farley, was not in a mellow mood.

"Well?" the younger man demanded, his stance belligerent.

Neville faced him. "I assume Olivia has informed you of my desire to marry her."

James crossed his arms. "She has. Though by her description it seems more a threat."

Neville's gaze shifted to Olivia, whose expression was a confusion of wariness and triumph. Somehow she'd convinced James that she'd not been entirely compromised. Had she told her brother the whole truth? Surely not. Neville also crossed his arms. "If it sounded like a threat, it is only because my feelings are so strong in this matter."

"Hers are equally strong," James bit back. "Given the situation I advise you to keep your distance from Olivia. Were it up to me, we would sever all relations with you. But Olivia insists on following through with this lease arrangement. As head of the family, however, I draw the line there. Best you content yourself with that, Hawke."

Neville watched as James took Olivia by the arm and guided her toward the door. Had he overplayed his hand? Had he misjudged Olivia and how far she could be pushed or should he push further? Should he make sure James knew all the facts of his involvement with Olivia?

For a long, agonizing moment he debated back and forth.

But then he considered. She'd given him the leases against her brother's wishes, it seemed. Why? Probably to fund the maintenance Byrde Manor so urgently needed. That could mean she intended to remain in residence.

As he watched them depart he saw Olivia shrug off her brother's proprietary hold. Neville shook his head. The minx had an independent streak sadly at odds with her role as a compliant, innocent young lady of the ton. She would be a handful whether under a brother's or a husband's rule. But then, that independence was what attracted him so—that and a few other things about her.

He caught a glimpse of her scowling at her brother as James held the door for her, and this time it was James who shook his head in frustration. He glanced back at Neville, and for a brief but unmistakable moment the two men shared a wry look.

As quickly as that Neville knew that all was not lost. Let Olivia believe she'd defeated him for now. The truth was, a young woman could not live alone on her own estate. He knew that, and apparently so did her brother.

It was just a matter of time before she would know it too.

CHAPTER

23

A week went by. A long, boring week. The deadline for Neville's threat passed without incident, though Olivia was a nervous goose that entire day. But it seemed her bluff with James at the solicitor's office had paid off.

After that, time passed even more slowly. Had it not been for Sarah, Olivia would have gone quite mad with boredom.

Not that there weren't an endless number of details that required her attention. Minor repairs to the house and grounds continued. There were also the daily decisions that went along with entertaining. In addition she fished and rode, played cards and also the pianoforte. In truth, she kept busy from dawn until long past dusk.

But she was nonetheless bored.

The days dragged by. James remained aloof. He was still angry with her because she had refused Neville Hawke's suit, and she hated the separation that caused. Added to that, several of their guests had begun to grate upon her nerves, chief among them, Archibald Collins, Lord Holdsworth.

Her mother's laugh drifted to her now from beyond the open doors of the back parlor, along with Archie's amused response. They sat just inside the doors playing cards with Mr. St. Clare, Viscount Dicharry, and the Wilkinson women. It had rained earlier, keeping everyone indoors. But at the first break in the weather, Olivia had headed outside, with Sarah fast upon her heels. They were going into town now, anything to escape the house.

"Do you think she's going to marry Lord Holdsworth?" Sarah complained once Olivia took the reins of the pony cart.

"I don't know. Probably," she added after a moment. "If she can bring him up to scratch."

"But I don't want her to. He's . . . He's . . . He's so selfish!" Sarah finally blurted out. "And he treats Mother just like he treats me, as if we're both children without an ounce of sense."

"In Mother's case that's probably appropriate," Olivia muttered. "But let's not speak of that any longer. Let's just enjoy a pleasant diversion. Mrs. Mac wants us to collect her order from the baker as well as two crates of wine."

"I'd like to go up to the saddlers and see about a nice leather collar for Bones. One of those spiked ones."

Olivia smiled. "Very well."

Her smile slipped a little when they reached Kelso and the turnoff that led to Woodford Court. But she clucked to the horse and angled it left toward the village center, forcing herself not to think of Neville Hawke. He had his life; she had hers.

Yet there was a part of her too honest to deny the truth. Her boredom and restlessness were not caused entirely by her guests. She hadn't laid eyes on Neville Hawke in a week, and had no reason to expect to do so anytime soon, and that irritated her.

Worse, she hated that she wanted to see him. But it was true and she did not know what to make of it. *Was* he the reason she wanted to stay at Byrde Manor?

Exasperated with herself, she snapped the reins. The two-wheeled pony cart rattled down the cobbled main street, splashing through puddles as it passed whitewashed houses, several shops with awnings stretched over the windows, the small village green, and the old common well. A few of the townsfolk nodded to her, and she acknowledged them with a polite smile.

Sarah was more exuberant, turning and craning her neck at the several young girls and boys she spied. "Is there a school here?" she asked.

"I believe Mr. Hamilton mentioned it. Look, there's the saddlers. Shall we go in there first?"

They were not long at their errands, but at the bakery they were detained by the baker's mother, a gray-haired ancient perched in a window seat that allowed her to survey both the shop and the street with her eagle-sharp eyes.

"We all been wonderin' when one of the Byrdes would return to their lands," she began, not waiting for an introduction. "I hope you're plannin' to take a Scotsman to your bed."

Olivia gaped at the woman in shock.

Choking in dismay, the baker hurried forward. "Have you no sense, old woman?" He turned to Olivia, nervously twisting the front of his apron in his hands. "She means no harm, miss. Only that she hopes you'll consider marrying a Scotsman someday."

Olivia knew what the old woman meant. Nevertheless her blunt words had taken her aback. "I . . . I have no immediate plans of that sort," she stammered.

The old woman's eyes swept over her. "An' why not? You're not so bad to look upon."

Olivia glanced from the forthright old woman to her horrified son, then clasped the basket of baked goods tighter against her chest. "If you'll excuse me."

She could hear the baker chastising his mother while she fled the shop, and Sarah's giggles as the girl trailed behind. "It's true, Livvie. You're not all that bad to look upon."

"You had better button your lip, Sarah. For I can make your life miserable if you don't."

"What did I say?" the girl asked, all innocence.

Refusing to be drawn, Olivia shoved the basket onto the floor of the pony cart. "Come on. Let's go."

But Sarah did not move. "Oh my. Look who it is. Lord Hawke." She waved and started across the street, calling out to him. "Lord Hawke!"

At once the most inappropriate thumping started in Olivia's chest, as if her heart meant to lurch into a new position. It did no good to chastise herself for her reaction to his presence, nor Sarah for hers, for the damage was done. Neville Hawke looked up at Sarah's cry and for Olivia the world seemed to tilt sideways.

Then from behind his tall, imposing form, another face peeped—a small boy with raven-black hair—and reality returned with an unpleasant jolt. It did not help that the boy's face darkened at the sight of Olivia.

Holding the boy by his hand, Neville crossed the street to them and doffed his hat. "Good morning, Miss Byrde. Sarah."

"Hello!" Sarah replied when Olivia did not. "We haven't seen you in the longest time," she added. "Have you been ill?"

"No. Just busy." For a moment his gaze held with Olivia's, melting her insides with their penetrating heat. Then, noticing Sarah's attention on the boy, he tousled the lad's hair. "Adrian, these are our new neighbors. Miss Byrde, Sarah, may I present my nephew, Adrian."

"Your nephew?" Olivia hadn't meant to blurt it out so rudely, nor with such incredulity in her voice.

At her words Neville's expression turned guarded. "My late brother's only child."

"Oh. Your brother's child," Olivia echoed, as understanding slowly dawned, understanding and relief. He was not Neville's natural son, but his brother's. That Neville was so forthright about their relationship was extremely generous, she realized, and most unusual.

But then Neville Hawke was a most unusual man. She stared at him, struck by that one, simple fact. He was a most unusual man.

Recovering, she smiled down at the little boy, who would be fatherless, it seemed, except for the attention of his uncle. Her smile, however, was met with a fierce scowl from the child.

"My father was a baron," he announced. "Just like my uncle."

Olivia nodded. Was it her imagination, or did the boy dislike her?

"My brother's a viscount," Sarah retorted, picking up on the boy's belligerence.

He turned his brilliant blue eyes on her. "Girls don't count."

"They do so—"

Olivia caught Sarah by the arm even as Neville's hand

came down on the boy's shoulder. "That's enough, Adrian," he said.

Meanwhile Olivia's warning grip on Sarah squelched any further retort from the girl. To Neville she said, "I hadn't realized you had any family left."

For once there was neither challenge nor taunt in his eyes. "There are many things you do not know about me, Olivia."

That quiet remark haunted Olivia all the way home.

Their conversation with Neville and his difficult nephew had been brief, and they'd quickly parted. But that one remark and the unnervingly direct stare that accompanied it remained centered in Olivia's mind. She let Sarah handle the cart, as much to preoccupy the girl as to free her own thoughts to wander. As they turned along the river road, she stared across the bridge down the lane that led to Woodford Court—and past the cottage where young Adrian lived.

Had the child's mother given the impression that he was Neville's son, or had Olivia made that assumption on her own? Given the child's ill-disguised animosity toward her, Olivia had to assume the former. The woman wanted Olivia to think the worst of Neville. But why?

The answer was ludicrously clear. Two unmarried peers living side by side? No doubt any number of the tenants and villagers speculated on a marriage between the two of them. What had the baker's mother said? "I hope you plan to take a Scotsman to your bed." Already she'd come perilously close to doing that.

It was plain that Adrian's mother feared Neville's interest in another woman. Whether the woman wanted Neville for herself or not, she could not like the idea of his marrying and siring children of his own, children who must become his heirs and usurp the place of his only other heir: her son, Adrian.

Olivia stared blindly at the passing scenery for the rest of their short journey, hardly aware of Sarah's gay chatter. Mr. Hamilton met them when they pulled into the stables. "I believe most everyone has gone fishing, miss," he said as he helped them down.

"Did Archie—I mean, Lord Holdsworth go too?" Sarah asked, not hiding her dislike for the man.

The steward shrugged. "I believe he must've. He ain't been around here."

"Then I'm not going to join them." The girl sent a sulky look at Olivia. "Let's go riding, shall we? We could have a good gallop over to Woodford."

"Not today," Olivia answered, already preoccupied with disturbing thoughts of Neville Hawke.

"But I'm bored!"

Olivia shook her head. "I'm afraid you'll just have to entertain yourself. Look. There's Bones. Play with him. I'll be in my room if anyone needs me." Then she excused herself and made for the house. She needed time alone. She needed time to think. For something momentous had happened today, something very simple. Yet it had altered everything.

In the quiet of her plainly furnished bedchamber Olivia went directly to her bureau and fished out her matchmaker journal. Climbing into the bed, she sat cross-legged and stared at the slender, battered tome. She hadn't written anything in it in weeks. Not since her last notation about Neville back in Doncaster.

She turned the book over in her hands but did not open it. She could have entered her thoughts about the self-centered Lord Holdsworth, or about James's friends, Justin St. Clare and Nicholas Curtis. But she hadn't. The thought hadn't even occurred to her until now.

She opened the book and began slowly to flip through the pages. How innocent her scribblings now read. How young and unworldly her words and observations. The pairing up of men and women was far more complex than she'd previously imagined.

To so many in the ton, wealth and family position were the major considerations. She'd always disdained those superficial qualities in favor of compatible personalities and interests, and had imagined her thinking quite superior. But there had been a serious flaw in her reasoning, she now saw. A huge gap in her understanding of men and women.

The power of physical attraction, the primitive urgings of desire, of lust—these could not be ignored. But could they make up for other differences, other practical reasons why a man and woman might be ill-suited?

No use to pretend her speculations were general in nature, for they were not. It was Neville Hawke on her mind. Neville Hawke and herself.

But despite her new knowledge of the man and his relationship to young Adrian, there remained the fact that he was not the steady, predictable sort she'd always imagined she would wed. That their attraction was powerful could not be denied, and it seemed he might not have fathered a child outside of wedlock. But he was still a man of strong passions. Too strong. Though he'd been careful since they reached Scotland not to drink in her presence, she feared his resolve could not last. The tragedies that drove him to the bottle had not disappeared. How could she ever be certain they would not drive him there again?

Closing her journal, Olivia plopped back on her pillows and just lay there. She could hear Sarah in the forecourt playing with Bones, and also the soft putterings of the several housemaids. Mrs. McCaffery's voice drifted to her, and from farther away, Mr. Hamilton's. She yawned. At least those two were tolerating one another now. They'd been at each other's throats that first day . . .

Some time later Olivia awoke with a start to the sound of shrieks and a slamming door. "I hate you!" Sarah's furious cry reverberated through the upstairs hallway.

Olivia sat up, her mind still muddled from her unplanned nap. What now? The girl's footsteps clattered down the uncarpeted stairwell, but in their wake other voices rose.

"Good God!" a man cursed.

"Oh dear," a woman cried. "Oh dear! Sarah? Sarah!"

Olivia swung her legs off the bed. That was her mother's voice. What on earth was going on?

She no sooner burst fuzzy-headed into the hall than the answer became clear. Much too clear.

The door to her mother's private chambers stood partially

ajar. Augusta stood in the hall in front of it, struggling to don a wrapper over her delicate, nearly transparent chemise. That was a little odd, but not particularly troubling, given that their male guests had all gone fishing.

Except that they had not *all* gone fishing. For behind Augusta in her bedchamber, hopping around on one foot as he tried to pull a boot onto the other, was Justin St. Clare. Not Archibald Collins, but the Honorable Justin St. Clare.

For a moment Olivia could only stand there, gaping at the two of them. Her mother and Mr. St. Clare?

Under Olivia's stunned stare Augusta actually blushed. "It's not what you . . ." Her hand fluttered at her throat. "I . . . I can explain," she stammered.

She tried nervously to rearrange her loosened hair but it was pointless. Then her paramour came up behind her and she gave up any pretense of explanation. She dropped her face into her hands and began to cry. Mr. St. Clare at once wrapped his arms around her and she turned gratefully in his embrace, to direct her tears to his shirtfront.

It was such an intimate display that Olivia could only gape like a dumbstruck fool. Her mother, clad in her clinging wrapper, was weeping upon the chest of a man dressed in just his shirtsleeves—and in the middle of the afternoon! Had the world gone completely mad?

"Mother," Olivia began with some difficulty. "What, precisely, did Sarah see?"

That made Augusta cry all the harder, forcing Mr. St. Clare to answer. "I accept complete responsibility," he earnestly vowed. "And of course I mean to do the proper thing by Augusta."

The proper thing. In a moment of complete absurdity Olivia wondered if Mr. St. Clare hadn't already done the proper thing and pleased Augusta as properly as Neville Hawke had pleased her.

"Oh no!" She shook her head at such a wicked thought.

"But I must!" Mr. St. Clare replied, misunderstanding her reaction. "I must wed her. It's only right!"

"What is all this hubbub?" James's voice rose questioning from the first floor.

"Good heavens!" Augusta shrieked. She dashed into her room. Mr. St. Clare stood there, plainly at a loss when Augusta slammed the door shut.

Olivia heard her brother's heavy footsteps mounting the stair. "Olivia? Mother? What's wrong with Sarah? She was crying and ran off—" James halted mid-sentence and mid-step when he spied the strange tableau in the upper hall. From Mr. St. Clare's obvious dishabille, James's gaze narrowed and swung to Olivia. His thick brows lowered in quick fury.

"What in God's name? Olivia! Are you mad? Justin—" His hands knotted into fists. "By damn, I'll kill you!"

"No. No!" Olivia leapt between them. "It's not what you think."

"Not what I think!" He tried to shove her aside but she clung to his jacket front. "First Hawke!" he exclaimed. "Now St. Clare!"

"It was Mother," she shouted. "Not me. Mother!"

"What?"

When he hesitated Olivia took quick advantage. "Sarah must have barged into Mother's bedroom without knocking and found . . . and found them. Together."

"Together? With Mother?" For a moment James was at a loss for words. Then his fury returned tenfold and he glared past her at the unfortunate Mr. St. Clare.

The man nervously cleared his throat. "I'm afraid so. But I mean to do right by her," he hurriedly went on. "You needn't fear on that score."

Caught still between fury and shock, James stood there, mired in utter confusion. Olivia understood precisely how he felt. Then Augusta ventured from her room hastily dressed, just as Lord Holdsworth and Viscount Dicharry came up the stairs. Alerted to the hubbub and not to be shortchanged, the Skylocks and the Wilkinson women followed behind.

Olivia wanted to chase them away, for she could just imagine what they were thinking. No sense missing any detail of what sounded like a shocking scandal unfolding in their midst.

As witnesses, they would be in demand at all the parties back in town. This was the most delicious scandal in ages, something to bandy about for months to come: the beautiful widow Dunmore discovered *in flagrante delicto* with the very wealthy Mr. St. Clare, a man several years her junior and a friend of her son's. And caught in the act by her three children!

Fortunately Mrs. McCaffery appeared just then to hustle Augusta back into her room. James stalked off to the study, followed by Mr. St. Clare, after he had retrieved the rest of his clothing. That left Olivia to deal with the rest of their guests, and her patience was worn so thin as to barely support civility.

"Well!" Henrietta Wilkinson huffed as Olivia herded everyone downstairs. "I can see this is not at all the environment for delicate young ladies." She placed an arm around her daughter as if to shelter her from whatever other evils lurked in the rafters and corners of the house.

Olivia gritted her teeth. "I understand completely. I will have the coach prepared at once. You can depart before suppertime."

"Before suppertime?" The woman stared at her as if she were more shocked by the possibility of missing a free meal than by anything else.

"I'll have the cook pack you a basket," Olivia retorted, refusing to back down. She wanted everyone except family out of her house, and the sooner the better. She swung her slitted gaze on the two lords. "Will you ride in the carriage with the Wilkinsons and Skylocks, or will you take your horses?"

Lord Dicharry cleared his throat. "I say, are you putting us out?"

"Who would want to stay?" Lord Holdsworth snapped. "With such goings-on, and in broad daylight, no decent person can wish to linger in this household. Indeed, Miss Byrde, it behooves you and your sister to depart with us. Your brother is the only one fit to deal with this unfortunate matter."

Olivia glared at him. "I am not a person to abandon my family when it is in need. The fact that you are says plainly that my mother has selected a better man in Mr. St. Clare. Good day, Lord Holdsworth. I'll send servants to help all of you pack. The coach will leave in two hours. Sharp."

Those two hours passed in a bitter blur. For as fiercely as Olivia defended her mother to their haughty guests, she nonetheless was shocked by what had occurred.

How could her mother have behaved so?

But she knew how. Passion was a beast of extraordinary might, with amazing powers of persuasion. Hadn't she learned that lesson herself? She grimaced at the thought.

Perhaps a better question was, how could her mother and Mr. St. Clare have been so careless?

But again, she knew the answer, for hadn't she been even more careless? At least Augusta and Mr. St. Clare had not fallen upon one another outside where anyone might have seen them.

Olivia pinched her lips together, willing away the throbbing ache that had begun behind her eyes. Thank God no one had seen her and Lord Hawke together that day. For that would have been the ultimate humiliation. Poor Mother.

Then she thought of her distraught sister, and she stiffened. Poor Sarah, to come upon her mother and Mr. St. Clare that way. Where had the child run off to?

Once the carriage rumbled away, with the two obnoxious young lords riding alongside, Olivia let out a long, frustrated sigh. Good riddance to them all. She hoped the gathering storm clouds caught them and thoroughly soaked them, and that they all caught their death of cold.

"Really, Olivia. Get a hold of yourself," she muttered as she turned back to the house. Rather than throw curses on their fair-weather friends, she needed to find Sarah. Then together they must go and speak with their mother.

Inside James stood in the study, his hands clasped behind his back as he stared out at the departing carriage.

"Well," Olivia asked. "Is everything settled?"

He looked tired when he turned to face her. Tired, but relieved. "It's all arranged. St. Clare is to purchase a special license. I've sent him to take a room in the posting house in

Kelso—for the time being." He let out a sigh. "Have you considered, Livvie? We shall have a new father within the week."

"A new father." Olivia shook her head, then sank into a chair. "No. I hadn't thought of it that way. But I suppose you are right."

"Damn me, but when I invited St. Clare to join us I was thinking more of a connection between him and you. Not him and Mother."

Olivia stared at him in mild reproof. "That should teach you not to meddle. Though I suppose I ought to feel slighted that he preferred her to me," she added. "Fortunately, he's not my type."

"No. But we both know who is." He fixed her with a stern gaze. "I've been thinking, Olivia, that Mother and St. Clare are behaving as they ought. I mean, once caught they have owned up to their responsibilities. Unlike you."

Olivia stiffened. "I know what you're going to say, but you waste your breath. I will not be coerced into marriage by you or anyone else. All you would succeed in doing is tarnishing my reputation, and by association, Sarah's. Mother's behavior is bad enough, but think, James. Who would wish to offer for the poor girl if both her mother *and* her sister have flirted with scandal?"

He frowned but, thankfully, did not argue.

"Speaking of Sarah, I suppose we'd better go have a look for her," he said. "She seemed awfully upset." He shoved his fists into his pockets. "Just how am I to explain all of this to her? She's only a little girl, and they—" He broke off, scowling.

Olivia heaved a sigh, then pushed to her feet. "I'll find her and I'll explain it all."

"Everything?" The expression of relief on his handsome face was almost comical. Then just as quickly it darkened. "Everything? How can you explain everything? You don't *know* everything. At least you'd better not."

Olivia pushed to her feet. "I know enough about what goes on between men and women to explain it to Sarah. I'm going out to find her," she added. "She's probably hiding somewhere up a tree or in the stable loft. I'll find her and we'll talk, and then I'll bring her home."

A roll of muffled thunder pierced the quiet of the room. "It's going to storm," James said. "That will bring her home. That and hunger."

"I know. But she'll feel better if she knows someone is concerned about her. Don't worry, she can't have gone far."

CHAPTER

24

THE storm pressed the air down over the land, hot and heavy with threat. Olivia paused and lifted a damp lock of hair from her neck. She'd been searching for Sarah more than an hour with no success. The stable, the overgrown orchard, the riverbanks. Now, on Goldie, she meant to search farther afield.

No, she amended as she guided the compliant mare into a ground-eating canter. She meant to go to the only other place she could think of that Sarah might run to.

She was heading to Woodford Court.

From the west lightning flashed dully behind the heavy clouds, and after a few seconds, thunder rolled over the land. It would be dark before long, yet Olivia was undeterred. Sarah liked Neville Hawke; they'd seen him in town just a few hours ago; and his was the only other household Sarah knew in the area. All quite logical. Yet this nervousness, this clutching in Olivia's stomach and the pounding of her heart as she approached Lord Hawke's estate was anything but logical. It was only her fear for Sarah's whereabouts that gave her the courage to go on, for she knew she could not avoid seeing him. If those brief moments in the village with him had shaken her to her bones, how was she to survive the coming interview?

Between the bridge and Woodford Court the wind began to rise. From warm and damp, she was swiftly cooled. By the time the handsome fortified house came into view, rain had begun to fall.

"Have you seen my sister?" she called to the stableman before he'd even taken hold of Goldie's bridle. It was Bart, she realized. Lord Hawke's trainer.

"Your sister, Miss Sarah? With the old dog?" The man nodded and smiled. "She's up t'the house, miss. With milord."

With milord. Olivia stared across the yard and through the rain to the house while the stableman led Goldie into the stable. She was already disheveled and damp, and though she tried to adjust her collar and cuffs, she knew it for a hopeless case. She must look a fright. By the time she reached the front door she would be completely soaked as well.

As if he sensed her dilemma, Bart pointed to another door nearer the stable. "That there is the kitchen door. Cook could get you dry, then bring you up to Lord Hawke. If you don't mind enterin' through the kitchen," he added.

On her dash across the yard with a feed bag over her head, it occurred to Olivia that her friends among the ton would be horrified at such a scenario as she was playing out. Certainly her own mother had never made so inelegant an entrance into a peer's home. But since she was not trying to impress this particular peer, Olivia did not care. It might even put Neville Hawke off to see her so.

"My gracious!" the cook exclaimed when Olivia burst out of the sharply angled rain and through the open half-door.

"I'm sorry, but the storm—" Olivia removed the feed bag, noticing too late the oat seeds that clung to her damp hair.

"Don't worry yourself over that, miss. I'm easily startled, that's all." She studied Olivia a moment, then handed her a clean cloth from a stack on the open shelf of a side dresser. "I'm Maisie Tillotson, at your service. I cook for Lord Neville. And you must be Miss Olivia Byrde, from Byrde Manor. You've come to fetch Miss Sarah home. Am I right?"

"Yes. Is she all right? Has she been any trouble?"

"No trouble at all, though the dogs raised quite a ruckus when they spied that bony pet of hers. As to how she is, himself has calmed her down." The woman's round face creased in a smile. "But then, he's always had a way with creatures that are wild or unsettled."

Olivia shook out her skirts, then patted her ruined coiffure. "Horses and little girls?"

"Big girls too. I was just preparin' a tray for them," the

woman continued, ducking her head to avoid the shocked stare her words garnered from Olivia. "Will you be wantin' tea?"

And so it was that Olivia trailed after Mrs. Tillotson. Through the private back passages of Woodford Court they went, beneath ancient arches and past centuries-old leaded-glass windows. The public hall was a grand, soaring space, and the back gallery provided a peek at the history of the family that had so long resided there. Blond women, plump-cheeked little children. But every one of the men was raven-haired and blue-eyed.

Olivia couldn't help staring,, it was such a fascinating glimpse into Neville's life.

When they arrived at his sitting room, however, Olivia's curiosity reverted to anxiety. Not only must she deal with Sarah's trauma, she must do so in Neville Hawke's presence.

Resolving not to reveal the true state of her nerves, Olivia knocked, then opened the door so that Mrs. Tillotson could enter with the tray.

She wasn't certain what she expected, but the scene that met her eyes was remarkable. Bones lay on the floor in front of an enormous Chesterfield sofa. When he spied them he thumped his bony tail. Neville and Sarah sat side by side upon the sofa with a large book spread open across their laps. Their two dark heads were bent together over it.

"Shall I just set the tray on your desk?" Mrs. Tillotson asked when the two did not look up from their studies.

"Yes. Thank you, Maisie— See? Here it is, Sarah. Your great great-great-grandfather on your father's maternal line."

Mrs. Tillotson smiled at Olivia, but she did not announce her to the intent pair. When the woman silently left, Olivia turned back to observe the sister she'd expected to find distraught, and the man she'd expected to find rattled by the presence of the temperamental little girl.

"My great-great-great-grandfather," Sarah repeated. "Why, he was born almost two hundred years ago. That's even before the Civil War."

"Very good," Neville said. "It seems you've been paying attention to your lessons."

Sarah looked up, beaming at his compliment, and it was then she spied her sister. "Livvie!" she cried. But her glad expression swiftly turned stormy, and she leaned back into the sofa. "If you've come to take me home, I'm not going."

As if he were not at all surprised to see her, Neville regarded Olivia with dark, observant eyes. Then he gestured toward the tea tray. "Would you mind pouring?"

Olivia nodded and without a word began that simple, domestic task. Only it did not feel at all simple, not when she was doing it in Neville Hawke's home.

She handed round the teacups, then set the plate of biscuits on a table near the sofa and seated herself carefully on the edge of a Hepplewhite armchair. Neville folded the big book away and for a moment they all sipped their tea in silence. Despite her fractured nerves at having Neville's eyes upon her, Olivia knew she must address her purpose in coming.

"You should never have run off like that, Sarah," she began. She glanced at Neville. Did he know precisely what had prompted her sister's flight? Probably. She took a deep breath. "I know you've had a shock. Nevertheless, frightening all of us out of our wits is hardly the proper way to deal with it."

"I hate them!" the child swore. Her face screwed up in a ferocious scowl. "I hate them and I'm not going to live with Mother anymore. I want to stay here," she finished, again pressing close to Neville's side.

"You can't possibly stay here. Lord Hawke has been very kind," Olivia conceded. "But you can't—"

"Not in his house. I mean in Scotland. With you. At Byrde Manor."

"So you're still planning to stay in Scotland?"

Olivia ignored Neville's question, for it somehow implied a connection with him, an intimacy she was not prepared to address. And anyway, how was she to respond? *Yes, I'm staying here—against every measure of good judgment I am staying near to a man from whom I ought to stay a hundred leagues away.*

She set her teacup down with only a little rattle and spoke to the petulant girl. "You needn't live with them if you feel that strongly about it, Sarah, dear. Besides, I suspect thcy will want to take a holiday after the wedding, if only to avoid any scandal which might slip out." She smiled sympathetically at her younger sister. "It will be all right, you know."

Sarah's chin trembled and she dashed her hands against her eyes. "It will never be all right again. Never." Then she began to cry in earnest.

At once Olivia moved to the sofa beside Sarah, and wrapped her arms around the child.

"I ha . . . hate her," Sarah sobbed into Olivia's already damp bodice. "How could she do . . . do that with *him*?"

Over the girl's head Olivia's gaze connected with Neville's and held. It was a curiously intimate moment, but not like before. This was an intimacy, not of the flesh, but of the mind. Or, more accurately, of the heart. They were united in the aid and comfort of a child, just as parents might be.

Olivia smoothed Sarah's tousled hair, but her gaze remained locked with Neville's. She'd so often thought his eyes turbulent and moody. But today, though dark, they were clear. If she stared long enough, she fancied she might see all the way down, to the secrets in his soul.

That she wanted to know those secrets was unsettling. But she was slowly coming to the realization that for all her doubts about him, there might be depths to him worth plumbing. Did she dare to take that chance?

It was almost painful to maintain such a personal connection to him, and nearly as painful to break it. But there was Sarah to deal with, and the child had worked herself into a terrible state.

"Sarah, Sarah. Hush now," Olivia crooned, stroking the child's back and kissing the crown of her head. "You make too much of this. I know you must have been shocked to come across them together . . ."

She sent a guilty glance at Neville, then away. "But when you are older . . ." Again she trailed off, unable to explain to Sarah what she hardly understood herself. Certainly no one could have explained about the attraction between men and women well enough for her to truly understand. It was something a woman had to experience.

Then Neville leaned forward and with one large, square-tipped finger traced a tear track down Sarah's cheek. "I remember how terrified I was when my father died, Sarah. I was a grown man, and yet losing him was like . . . like the ground being pulled from beneath my feet. First my fellow soldiers had died, my friends in the war. Then my father and, soon after, my mother too. And just as I had begun to recognize how very much I loved my parents, my brother slipped away as well."

He caught another of her tears. "I know how afraid you are now. So many changes in your life. But you have a family that loves you. You must never forget that, nor take it for granted." He smiled down at her. "Your father will always be with you, you know. It might help you to consider what he would want you to do."

Sarah lay very still in her arms, and Olivia could tell that the child was listening to his low, soothing words. "Is that what you do?"

His face sobered, and he was slow to answer. "My parents loved Woodford Court. It was the center of their world. So, yes, I suppose that is why I work so hard to improve it. But I would give it all away," he continued more quietly. "Everything I own to have my family back again."

The girl shifted. "You have that boy. Your nephew. You still have him."

Again Neville smiled, and as he did, he raised his gaze to Olivia's. "Yes. I have Adrian, and he is more special to me than I ever guessed a child could be. You've become special to me also."

Olivia pressed her lips together, for his careful tenderness had raised a lump in her throat. He'd bared a little bit of his soul, she realized. And though his words were meant to comfort Sarah, his eyes spoke volumes to her.

She could love this man.

That understanding struck Olivia with a strange sense of certainty. Hard and scarred and arrogant as he was, she could easily love Neville Hawke, if only for the vulnerability he now revealed to her heartbroken little sister.

Sarah sniffed. "So you think I shouldn't be angry with Mama." She turned in Olivia's arms so that she faced Neville. "But if you would just marry Livvie, then . . . then I could live here with the two of you."

Olivia tore her gaze from Neville's, embarrassed by the child's bluntness. "I don't think that's what Lord Hawke meant, Sarah. You know your father would want you to stay with Mother. She loves you very much."

Sarah wiped one fist across her eyes. "I know. But . . . but she's going to marry that awful Lord Holdsworth now."

"Lord Holdsworth? What has this to do with Lord Holdsworth—" Olivia broke off as she finally understood. She pulled a little back from Sarah. "It was not Lord Holdsworth you discovered with Mother."

Sarah blinked and looked over at her. "It wasn't?"

"It wasn't?" Neville echoed.

Olivia felt heated color creep up her neck and into her cheeks. She did not like to reveal anything unflattering about her mother, but it was plain Neville knew all the sordid details—or at least as much as Sarah did.

"It was not Lord Holdsworth in her chamber. In fact, he and all the others have already departed Byrde Manor. No doubt gone off to spread the gossip," she added bitterly. "I probably should not have run them off so fast, but rather, forced them to witness the marriage."

Sarah tugged at Olivia's collar. "Who, Livvie? Who was it?"

Olivia gave her a crooked half-smile. "It was Mr. St. Clare."

The girl sat up straighter. "Mr. St. Clare?"

"Yes. Justin St. Clare. And since it appears he is to become your stepfather within the week, it behooves you to put yourself on better terms with him."

Sarah digested that for a moment. "Mr. St. Clare." She glanced at Neville who raised one brow at her. In return the girl gave a sheepish grin. "Oh well. I suppose he's not such a bad sort." She dried her damp eyes on her sleeve. "Not like that awful Archie person."

"Justin St. Clare," Neville mused as the tension in the room began to ease. He chuckled. "I wouldn't have credited the man with—" He broke off when Sarah and Olivia both looked at him.

"Credited him with what?" Sarah inquired.

He cleared his throat. "Ah . . . I wouldn't have credited him with capturing the heart of a woman like Augusta," he said, then smiled. Though he sat back on the sofa, the three of them were still very close together, and when he stretched out his arm along the back of the seat, his hand lay just a finger's width from Olivia's shoulder.

"I understand St. Clare keeps a sailboat at his estate on the Isle of Wight," he continued. "You should pester him to take you sailing, Sarah."

The child perked up. "A sailboat? Huh. Maybe I will, for I've never been sailing. Anyway, that's the least he can do, given all the trouble he has caused." Then she yawned and snuggled back into Olivia's embrace. "I'm glad you came after me, Livvie. I'm sorry I ran away and gave you such a fright. But I'm glad you came to find me."

Over her head Neville's eyes caught with Olivia's and held. *I'm glad you came too*, those deep-set eyes seemed to say. And she was glad also.

For a long moment they sat that way, close upon the sofa while the rain beat a lulling tattoo upon the windowpanes. Sarah yawned again and Olivia felt the child's body begin to relax. It had been a long, exhausting day and they still must return home.

As if he sensed her thoughts, Neville said, "You cannot go home in this storm, Olivia."

She averted her gaze. "We cannot stay the night here." *Not when I am so fiercely drawn to you.*

"Maisie is nearby. And also the housekeeper. Besides, you have Sarah. You're perfectly safe at Woodford—as safe as you wish to be."

There was no mistaking the meaning in that last, and it

should have set her mind firmly against staying. But Olivia's mind was not working quite as it ought. It was still overwhelmed by the new truth of her feelings for Neville, and how terrifyingly deep they ran.

In her arms Sarah sighed and snuggled into a more comfortable position. Olivia smoothed a curl from the child's brow. Already she had dozed off, while the rain outside fell harder, as if in fierce determination to keep her there.

Perhaps she ought to stay.

When she did not object, Neville stood. "I'll alert the housekeeper to prepare a room and send a rider to Byrde Manor to let them know you're both here."

By the time he returned, Sarah was snoring peacefully, soundly sleeping in Olivia's arms. "I'll carry her," he said, and lifted the child with no effort. Then he led the way up one flight of wide wooden stairs, and down a dim, carpeted hallway to a circular room faced with rough stone walls. It was obviously part of the old tower.

Someone had already been there to light a lamp, and a small fire burned in the wall hearth. Neville laid Sarah gently upon the turned-down bed and removed the child's shoes. "I thought it better for Sarah that you share a room."

Olivia nodded agreement. But even with Sarah there, standing in the small bedchamber with Neville beside her set every one of Olivia's senses on alert. He was so tall and virile. Though casually dressed in the comfort of his own home, he remained every inch the imposing lord of the manor. Strong, yet able to be gentle, and more compelling than any man she'd ever known.

How could she not fall in love with him?

He shoved his hands into his pockets. "Can I send anything up for you? Something to eat or drink?"

"No. Thank you."

Silence stretched out between them. She trailed her hand along the edge of the bed. "I'll just tuck Sarah in."

He nodded, then cleared his throat. "If you don't mind, I would like to have a word with you after that. Outside." He gestured toward the door.

At once Olivia's awareness of him increased tenfold. To be alone with him in any way was dangerous, and more so now than ever. That a long, stormy night stretched before them only exacerbated the situation. She'd succumbed to him in far less likely circumstances, and that was when she hadn't even liked him. Heaven knew what she would do now that she'd discovered these new feelings for him.

But she did know. She knew exactly what would happen between them.

"I . . . I don't think that is wise," she said in little more than a whisper.

One side of his mouth curved up in a wry grin and he spread his arms wide. "I promise not to touch you, Olivia. Not to come within five feet of you, if that is your wish."

But it's not my wish. Quite the opposite.

Ruthlessly she squelched that thought. "Perhaps you ought to just say whatever it is you have to say here. Now."

He was slow to answer. He glanced first at the bed where Sarah lay, lost to sleep. The amber light from the lamp melded with the flickering glow from the fireplace to limn his face with gold. Olivia traced his profile with her eyes, marveling at the strong planes—the bold brow and straight nose, the curved lips and hooded eyes. He was beautiful in the harsh manner that was purely male. Beautiful and dangerous, and irresistible. Whatever he proposed, she knew she would be powerless to deny him.

She should be stronger than that. The morals of a lifetime should provide her the ability to turn away from him. But she knew better. A kiss. An embrace. The wonderful, terrifying tumult of their last encounter. And on top of everything, she knew now that she loved him.

Then he turned and fixed those moody blue eyes on her, and the breath caught in her throat.

"I think, Olivia, that your sister's suggestion is a wise one."

When she blinked, not understanding, he went on. "There is no sensible reason why we should not wed. I have held back on approaching your brother again, for despite your poor image of me, it is not my wish to harm you or humiliate you.

But I hope you will reconsider your earlier decision. You have already admitted that you mean to remain in Scotland, and we both know the attraction between us is strong. I've seen that notebook you keep, and I know you have turned down any number of acceptable suitors."

He took a step toward her, his eyes intent. "We are a well-matched pair, Livvie. Neither of us is suited to town life. You will be happy here. I'll do whatever it takes to make you happy. Just say you will marry me."

Olivia could hardly breathe. Marry him! That was hardly what she'd expected to hear after she'd turned him down so emphatically. She was prepared to be seduced. She should not be, but she was. In truth, she wanted to be seduced. But a proposal, as welcome as it was, nonetheless left her speechless. She'd been fighting the idea so many days now that it seemed astounding to actually consider agreeing to it.

He closed the space between them so that she had to tilt her head up to meet his mesmerizing gaze. He overwhelmed her with his nearness. But he still did not touch her. "Is the idea really so repugnant to you?" he asked when she did not respond. He reached out a hand and with one finger stroked slowly down her arm, from shoulder to elbow, and down along her bare forearm. "There is an attraction between us. I feel it. You feel it. You're feeling it right now, aren't you?"

"Yes." The word was a pitiful, strangled confession.

"Then marry me and we can explore the depths of that attraction. What you felt before was only the beginning, Livvie. Only the very beginning—"

Olivia silenced him with a kiss. To his amazement and her own, she caught the front of his waistcoat in her fists, then pressed up on her tiptoes, and proceeded to silence his words with a long-overdue kiss.

CHAPTER

25

NEVILLE exulted at Olivia's sudden capitulation. She was his!

He wrapped his arms around her. More than anything he wanted to crush her to him. But he was careful not to hurt her. She was his, the refrain echoed in his head as he kissed her back. With her kiss she gave him her answer. She would marry him, and he would keep her forever.

But first he would make love to her. He would make love to her and bind her to him through the power of her passionate nature.

So he accepted the offer of her seeking lips and straining body. She was sweet and soft, yet overbrimming with passion. And all of it for him. In return he gave her all the passion he held so tenuously in check. He feasted on her mouth, kissing her hard, forcing her lips apart, and delving deep with his tongue. Questing, claiming. With rhythmic thrusts he plundered her mouth while pressing her hips against his raging arousal.

At last he would find relief from this aching need she raised in him.

"Do you know how much I want you?" he whispered between kisses that bordered on the desperate. "Do you know how hard the wait has been?"

But the wait was over. Without giving her time to answer, he swung her up into his arms, as he'd done with her sister. His purpose now, however, could not be more different. He was through the door and half the way up the old tower stairs before she reacted.

"Wait. Neville . . ."

He paused at the first landing and feasted again on her warm, trembling lips until her caution was banished by desire. Then up the final flight of stairs he swept, up to his private chambers.

There was no lamp burning in this room, however, no fire crackling upon the hearth. For this was not a room he frequented during the night. He might sleep by day in this place, but never by night.

But then, it was not slumber he aspired to this night.

He set Olivia on the bed. Though loath to let her go, he wanted a light to see her by. With three sharp flicks of the flint the tinder caught and he lit a single candle. Then he looked down at her and felt the sharpest, most vivid pang of longing he'd ever known. In a lifetime of longing for things he could not have—saving his friends' lives, a little more time with his family, and peace, just one night of peace—in all that time he'd never known such a pure and pervasive longing as he knew now.

And he'd never been so close to getting what he longed for.

He stripped off his waistcoat, watching as Olivia took in his every move. His shirt was next, and he saw her beautiful eyes widen.

"Take off your bodice, Olivia. I want to watch you disrobe for me."

A little gasp escaped her lips, but she complied. God bless her, she complied.

He tugged off his boots and she removed her shoes. Then he stripped off his breeches and stood before her clad only in his undergarments, and she froze. Her hands stilled on her lap, knotted in her skirts as she sat awkwardly upon his bed, staring up at him.

"Neville," she began, ducking her head. "I . . . I don't know how . . ."

"I'll help you," he answered, and swiftly he untied the tapes and tugged her skirt from beneath her hips—her skirt, and her single petticoat. He tossed them aside, then turned back to her. Clad only in her chemise, with arms and legs bare to his view, she was the most perfect woman he'd ever known. And she was his now. She always would be.

"We'll marry within the week," he murmured reassuringly as he laid her back, then braced himself on his arms over her. The bed creaked as he knelt on the mattress. His muscles trembled from the effort it took not to fall upon her like a rutting stallion. "I'll speak to your brother and mother tomorrow."

"They will be much relieved," she replied.

He lowered his head and lightly kissed her. When the kiss was done she looked up at him trustingly. *Ah, but you should not trust me, sweet Olivia.* That's what he should tell her. Only he was so near to having what he wanted from her. What he needed. He should send her back to the safety of her family before she found out what sort of man she'd married.

But he could not. Instead he let his weight come to rest part of the way on her.

She let out a little shocked gasp at the intimacy of it, but she did not object. As he shifted his weight over her, using his body to stroke the entire length of her, their gazes remained locked. She was innocent of any man's touch but his, he knew. And yet she brought to that innocence a sensuality more potent than that of the most accomplished courtesan. She wanted him and also feared what he meant to do to her. Yet she did not flinch away.

He dragged his hot, burning body up along hers again, and this time her slender hands slid curiously along his arms. "Oh my," she whispered.

The breathy sound fanned the fire of his passion. Then she pressed a kiss against his chest, very near to his nipple, and Neville groaned out loud. He let his full weight down, pressing her into the mattress, then slid down, letting her feel the full heat and weight of his arousal. As he did, she kissed her way up along him, shoulder, throat, chin, and jaw, then caught his face between her hands and kissed him fully upon the mouth.

When her tongue stole between his lips, it destroyed the last remnants of his control. He kicked out of his undergarments and tore her chemise roughly over her head. In the scant second before he came down on her again, he had a glimpse

f pale smooth flesh, of sweet curves of light and shadow. Her
breasts, full and soft, were tipped with dusky nipples that he
meant to lavish his attention upon—but later. He covered her
with his body, his burning hot skin upon her cool, delicious
flesh, and caught her face between his hands. If he did not
make love to her now, he would die from the torture.

"It may hurt a bit," he said, his voice hoarse with passion.
"I'll try to be easy."

She smiled up at him then, and it was the most beautiful
smile he'd ever seen. It warmed him and soothed him and
filled him with a feeling he could not describe. "I know you
will," she whispered as he positioned his arousal in the warm
vee between her legs. "I love you, Neville. Oh—"

Her warm, throaty admission caught him by surprise, but
Neville covered his shock with the physical act of possessing
her. He thrust into her, then, when he met her virgin's barrier,
thrust deeper still.

Beneath him she lay very still, not even breathing, but only
trembling ever so slightly. He was trembling too, but not
merely from the power of a mighty passion held now on the
brink of release. She'd said she loved him. Did he mean it?
Did she understand what she'd just said? Did she have any
idea?

"Neville . . ." She took a quick breath that seemed to release
them both from this state of suspended passion.

"Are you all right?" he asked, his voice tight with strain.

Her eyes were so wide, so huge, that even in the dangerous
night shadows of his bedroom, all her emotions lay wide open
to his view. Wonder. Passion.

Love.

He closed his eyes and, without waiting for her reply, began
the slow rhythm that would bring him the relief he sought—
and her as well. But he did not want to stare into those warm,
loving eyes.

He could bring her physical completion, but he did not want
her to love him, not when he knew how undeserving he was
of that love. From the very first he'd set out to seduce her.
He'd convinced himself she could ease his pain and so had

ignored any qualm of conscience as he'd pursued her.

He was a selfish bastard, but knowing that changed nothing. He wanted her; he had to have her. But he knew he did not deserve her love. Nor could he ever return it. He'd lost that ability long ago. But give her pleasure? That much he could do for her.

So he bent himself to the task at hand, the welcome task he'd pursued since the first moment he'd laid eyes on her. He would rouse her and give her a pleasure beyond anything she'd ever imagined, and in the process he would find the release he so desperately needed.

As Neville began to move over her, Olivia felt the tightness begin to ease. She'd felt too full at first. Shocked by the intrusion, overwhelmed by the excruciating intimacy. But now with the slow pattern of withdraw and thrust, of heat and friction, her shock turned to wonder and then to eagerness. So this was the wonderful, mysterious, whispered-about secret of men and women together. Her entire body seemed to swell and throb and join with the rhythm he created.

Why had she resisted him for so long? To have him move over her, his powerful body focused so wholly upon her . . . There was nothing Olivia could compare it to.

Her hands moved restlessly over his back and shoulders, sliding upon the taut muscles with their sheen of dampness. At once his movements quickened from careful to demanding. "Oh, Neville," she moaned, unaware of her words. The feelings were so strong, increasing like a fire stoked and stoked, and stoked again, so that it burned ever hotter, ever higher.

"Neville, Neville," she panted with his every stroke. And with every chant of his name he responded until they were racing together, body to body. Olivia was on fire. She felt too full for her own skin, as if she were about to burst right out of it and emerge an altogether different creature than before. The astounding thing was, she wanted that to happen. She wanted him never to stop. Never.

"Neville, Neville. Oh, my love. Oh—"

She felt, more than heard, his answer. He strained over her, every muscle in his powerful body centered on her, then pushed her over the edge. Olivia let out a helpless cry of utter capitulation and felt the explosion take her. It filled her, burst out of her, and enveloped him also. For he stiffened and let out a huge cry, then plunged deep inside her with a prolonged shudder.

In the heated aftermath of that shattering moment, that glorious tumult, they lay together. Collapsed together. So this was making love, Olivia mused in the foggy recesses of her completely sated mind.

Sated mind. Sated body. The very concept was foreign, and yet it was also exactly right. She sighed, and so did Neville, sinking them both deeper into the thick mattress.

"I love you," she murmured, reveling in the intimate press of his hard, heavy body on hers. It was a huge admission and yet she knew it for the truth. "I love you, Neville."

Slowly he rose up and propped himself to the side. "Are you all right?"

Olivia smiled up at him. "Yes. Oh, yes." How could everything not be right after what they'd just shared?

But Neville did not smile back. Instead he rolled to his side and pulled her close, tucking her head beneath his chin. Though she could not see the expression on his face, she could feel the uneasiness in his body. She knew instinctively that this should be a moment of perfect peacefulness. But there was a tension between them, a tension emanating from Neville.

Had she done something wrong?

"Neville," she began.

"Shh. Listen to me, Olivia. Listen to me. We have to plan. Tomorrow you will inform your mother that we are to wed. I'll speak to James. He will be angry with me for what has passed between us, but in the main I believe he will be relieved."

"But Neville." She struggled to rise on one elbow. "You are right, but—" She broke off when she met his wary gaze. Why should he feel wary now?

But Olivia knew why. Ever since she'd confessed her feelings for him he'd been uneasy. From her very first admission of love.

The damp skin on her arms and shoulders prickled in the cool night air. She'd said she loved him, but he had made no similar reply. Could he wish to marry her and yet not love her?

Though Olivia knew that was the way of most marriages, after what they'd just shared, she did not want to believe it possible for them. No matter that she'd always been the pragmatist in matters of marriage, she could not be pragmatic now. She loved him and she needed him to love her in return.

"I love you," she stated, thrusting the words at him like a challenge. The words were out; the gauntlet was thrown; and in his eyes Olivia saw him retreat from her.

Like a cold wind, the truth of that retreat settled over her, and she shivered.

At once he pulled her closer and tried to cover her with the tangled bed linens. "You love me? After all the times I've made you angry you love me?" he said, adopting a teasing tone. He rolled her over so that he lay between her legs once more. "You love me? Or is it this you love?" Then he began to kiss her and caress her and rouse her as he had before.

His lips were so clever and his hands so adept that had she not understood his motives, Olivia would have succumbed to the drowning pleasure of it all. He meant to bring her back to that high peak of excitement, that culmination of desire and love and forever—except that he brought no love to it. She did but he did not, and so she struggled against the seductive pull of desire.

"Don't do that. Look at me." She caught his head between her hands and forced him to face her. "Listen to me."

"No." Neville thrust Olivia's hands aside, capturing them above her head. She'd caught him by surprise with her words of love, and for a moment he'd been overwhelmed by panic. But he'd recovered now. He'd recovered and he'd regained control. "No, Olivia. You listen to me. I know what you want from me. What you want me to say. But those are only words.

Meaningless words. What matters is that we are so well matched—in temperament, in interests, in attitudes. And we desire one another." He moved his body over hers in a long, voluptuous stroke. "We are well matched, you and I." And he proceeded to prove it to her.

It was not hard to rouse her to desire. She was a woman of strong passions, his Olivia. His Hazel. Careful and analytical, yet brave and bold of spirit.

She will need every bit of that bravery to deal with you.

That ugly truth raised beads of sweat on Neville's brow. But it only goaded him on. He plundered her mouth with his and felt her resistance slacken. He moved his lips and tongue to the attention of her breasts, lovely and soft with their dark tips peaked in perfect arousal.

He pulled one deep in his mouth and felt her groan of pleasure. She was alive with passion, quivering beneath him with it, and he quivered in response.

Couldn't she see that he'd never cared so much for any other woman's satisfaction? Couldn't she understand that her pleasure magnified his own? Just the knowledge that he could make her writhe beneath him made him instantly hard. The fact that he could make her pant and cry out, brought him nearly to completion. She made him feel like a green lad, randy and utterly consumed with her.

Couldn't that be enough for her?

He vowed to make it enough.

He might be unable to love her as she wanted to be loved. His emotions had been too scarred by the past for that. But he could love her body and provide for her and keep her safe.

So he bent himself to loving her body. He found every secret, erotic place. The inner corner of her elbow, the tender flesh beneath her ear. He counted each rib with kisses and marked every hollow and curve of her waist and belly and hips. Down the smooth, warm legs, skirting her thrusting hips, ignoring her frantic pleas for him to join with her.

He trained his horses with patience and care. How much more patience and care would he shower on this woman. With enough time and enough practice she would learn to find that ultimate satisfaction from only his kisses.

And that would be enough for her. She would not need those three overused words which meant less than the air used to expel them.

CHAPTER

26

OLIVIA awakened alone in Neville's bed. She was not confused by her strange surroundings. She knew at once where she was.

But where was Neville?

A cool breeze ruffled the partially drawn draperies. Summer was done. Fall was in the air. Though the solitary candle had long guttered out, a half-moon pierced the storm clouds and lent a silver glow to the room, enough to reveal a chamber simply furnished and with little indication of its owner's complex personality.

Olivia sat up and looked around, frowning. Perhaps the room's spareness told a story in itself—or a part of it. Though in some ways a man open and blunt, he nonetheless was a man of many secrets. He would share his life and his properties with her, but he could not share anything of his true self. Hadn't he just made love to her? Yet he'd not been able to say he loved her. Hadn't he brought her to his private chamber? Yet he'd not remained to sleep beside her.

Had he no emotions at all? Was he so devoid of any feelings, save those of physical desire?

Though she knew in her heart that was not entirely true, at the moment Olivia was hard-pressed to feel any charity for Neville. He'd made love to her—in truth, that last time he had seduced her. Then he'd abandoned her. From the moment she'd revealed her love for him he had seemed almost to panic. His lovemaking had become frantic, desperate, as if he must prove something to her. Or perhaps to himself.

A cloud moved across the moon, casting the room into

deeper shadow. She pushed her tangled hair away from her face. Where was he? She'd forgotten that he did not seem ever to sleep at night. So what did he do? Where did he go?

Suddenly, a host of powerful emotions rushed over her and hot tears rose unbidden in Olivia's eyes. Why could he not love her? What was so terrible about her that he could not feel as deeply for her as she had come to feel about him?

She shifted, and the rumpled bed linens gave off the lingering scent of their union, increasing Olivia's misery tenfold. It was not fair!

And if she could not bear his remoteness now, how could she bear a lifetime of loving him and not receiving his love in return? Could she be like her mother, loving a man she could never fully possess?

With a corner of the sheet Olivia dabbed away her tears. The truth was, she could not do it. No matter what had passed between them this night, for them to wed would guarantee her nothing but endless heartache. She had but to think of her mother and father to know that.

Moving with unaccustomed stiffness she slid off the bed. Her skirt and bodice lay in a pale heap on the floor; her petticoat draped like a ghost across a chair. She found her shoes and one of her stockings, and managed to dress herself. She was conscious, however, of the changes wrought in her body, the soreness, the new fullness.

But she had one thought only in her mind: she must find Neville and tell him they could not wed. Nor could she remain in his home any longer, for it was too painful.

She knew, though, that running away from him would not bring her any real relief. He had somehow become a part of her in a way no other man had ever done. They were connected on some plane that defied explanation. And they always would be.

She stood on shaky legs and smoothed her skirts around her. She loved him and she had made love with him. But now she must go.

And if she should find herself with child by him?

That gave her pause. But she recovered well enough, beating down any glimmer of joy at such a thought. She would face that problem when and if it presented itself. For now she must deal with a man unable—or unwilling—to love like a normal man.

After a silent, nape-tickling search of the somber old house, Olivia found Neville in his study. He'd built a fire in the hearth, a huge leaping blaze at odds with the pleasantly cool night. The logs popped and crackled, and the flames sent strange, mocking shadows across the room.

Neville sat in a heavy leather chair with its back to her, facing the open windows, much as he had sat on that first night they'd met. He was sprawled back, his legs stretched out and one hand dangling over the arm of the chair. A half-emptied decanter of some pale liquor perched on the table beside him. An empty tumbler sat alongside it.

Olivia pressed her fingers to her mouth. He was drinking again. Sitting up all night alone, getting drunk.

An ineffable sadness settled over her. Though she'd searched him out in order to sever their fledgling betrothal, she did not wish him ill. Certainly she would never wish for him all the miseries that went along with his drinking. Of late it seemed he'd been doing better on that score. So why had he reverted to his old ways tonight? Why had he left her alone in his bed to come down here and drink? Was it something about her? Or perhaps it was what she'd said about loving him.

Heartsore, she stared at him, not certain what she ought to do. Then he said something, mumbled words she did not understand, and her heart sank further still. He sounded completely drunk.

Angry, upset, and inexplicably sad, Olivia crept further into the room and around the chair until she saw him. His head was tilted to one side and his hair fell in rumpled disarray across his brow. But there was no odor of liquor about him, she realized.

She cocked her head, staring at him. Was he merely sleeping? Her heart began a hopeful rhythm as her gaze darted from him to the glass—the dry glass which held no remnants of liquor in it.

He was not drunk at all. He'd only fallen asleep in his chair.

His dark lashes shuttered his eyes and though he was every inch a virile man, in that moment there was an innocence about him, as endearing as it was unsettling. For a long moment Olivia simply studied him, recalling another time when she'd watched him sleep. He'd looked peaceful then, and so much younger. Not a man beset by demons of the night, but a man strong and vulnerable, all at one time. A man who had entranced her.

Was it on that day in the carriage that she'd first begun to love him?

In the silence of his study it took every bit of Olivia's resolve not to take him by the hand, kiss him awake, and lead him back to bed.

But that way would lead her only to heartbreak, for he did not love her. No matter how much she loved him, she couldn't force him to love her in return. Her mother's experience with Cameron Byrde was proof of that.

"But your heart is going to break anyway." She whispered the words out loud. "It's breaking right now."

As if he heard her, Neville frowned, then shifted in the chair. Olivia shrank away from him. She should leave now while she still had the strength. At least she should go to Sarah and wait out this long night with her.

She started for the door. But just as she reached for the handle Neville mumbled again, words she could hardly understand. At first.

". . . so tired. Don't . . . Be careful. Don't sleep. Don't fall 'sleep . . ."

Olivia turned, frowning, to look back at him. Was he dreaming?

"Watch out. No!" He jerked upright in the chair so violently that Olivia flinched back against the door leaf.

"Macklin! Look out!" he cried in a voice laced with unspeakable pain. "Simpson! Behind you! No. No!"

This time he lurched to his feet. Olivia could see his body

trembling, as if he were terrified. Then he suddenly was wracked by an even more violent shudder, one that must have shaken him awake. Even though he faced away from her, toward the window and its view of the night, she sensed he no longer slept. With an anguished groan he bowed his head and just stood there, the heels of his hands pressed tight against his eyes.

"Oh, God," he murmured, swaying slightly. "Oh, God. Make it stop."

At that heartrending utterance, tears sprang into Olivia's eyes. So this was why he feared to sleep. This was the nightmare that haunted him. His friends dying in a war while he survived. Did he blame himself?

She knew he did.

He stood silhouetted in the dark window, the very image of misery. She wanted to go to him and took the first step forward. But when he turned halfway around and, spying the decanter, reached for it, Olivia froze. He lifted the vessel up and slowly, slowly, removed the stopper.

Don't, Olivia wanted to cry. *Don't!* But it was not her place; somehow she knew that. She could not doubt the depths of his misery, but she understood instinctively that how he dealt with it was his decision. Only his. If Neville chose the stupefaction of drink, no one could stop him. Especially not her, a woman he would not—or could not—love.

But knowing that, Olivia still could not abandon the room. She watched as his swaying figure steadied. She watched as he raised the decanter to a level even with his face and stared at the amber liquor swirling behind its cut-crystal facade. The firelight glinted through the decanter, painting him with golden color. Like a sinister rainbow the gray shadows, the flickering firelight, and the golden allure of the liquor fell in bands across his unhappy face.

Olivia realized she was holding her breath. She pressed the knot of her fists against her mouth. *Please, Neville. You will never find happiness that way.* Hadn't her father been proof enough of that?

Then he shuddered and, with a sudden jerky movement, heaved the crystal decanter at the hearth.

Olivia leapt at the shattering sound, then gasped when the liquor burst into bright flame. Like a living creature it licked up the face of the mantel and across the slate floor toward Neville's booted feet.

Neville looked up at her gasp, belatedly discovering her presence. But he wasted no time. He snatched up a small carpet and threw it over the flames, then stomped on it until the fire was completely smothered.

In a matter of seconds it was over, all but the smoke and the reek of burnt alcohol and wool.

When he lifted his head, his face was so haggard Olivia wanted to weep. Was it the battle with the liquor or the nightmare? Or was it her?

"You saw it all, didn't you?" His voice was low and hoarse.

She nodded. He did not want her to see him at his weakest moment, and in truth, she would not have chosen to do so. But now that she had . . .

Olivia blinked her eyes. She could not explain it, but now that she had seen him afraid and vulnerable, it made her all the more confident of his strength. Though paradoxical, the truth shone through clear as sunlight. He was so much stronger than he knew.

She took a deep breath, shaking off her fear. "Neville—"

"No." He shook his head slowly. "You needn't say it. You will want to renege now on our marriage agreement, and I will not fight you. You said from the first that I would make no one a good husband, least of all you. And now you have the proof."

"But it's not true," she protested.

"Don't!" He held his hands up as if to fend off her approach. "You don't know me, Olivia. You don't know what a wretched excuse for a man I am. In an attempt to find some sort of peace, I have ruined you. I . . . I thought making you mine—making love to you, marrying you—I thought it might bring an end to these . . . these nightmares that haunt me."

His eyes closed and he gripped his head between his hands. "But it hasn't. It hasn't."

He opened his eyes, and the misery Olivia saw there nearly broke her heart. "I don't deserve you," he went on in a low, tortured voice. "I cannot undo the wrong I have done you, Olivia. But I see now that making you my wife would be an even greater wrong. For you to marry me would be the biggest mistake of your life. You deserve better."

It was awful to hear those words of his. Awful to hear them, but even worse to know that he believed them. She shivered and wrapped her arms around herself, but she did not turn away. For she knew with a bone-deep conviction that he needed her. He'd thought making love to her might cure him, and it plainly had not. But being loved by her, and loving her in return—that was where happiness lay. She was convinced of it. It was the only place either of them would ever find contentment.

But first he had to accept her love and trust her with the truth of his nightmares. To cleanse himself of whatever guilt he suffered.

"Nightmares or no," she began, "I intend for us to be wed, Neville. Nothing that has occurred tonight has changed my mind on that score."

He hunched his shoulders against her words, reminding her of a bear-baiting she had witnessed as a child. The great beast had understood its role and, though wounded by the first several dogs, had girded itself for more of the same. It had been a hideous spectacle and she had run away in tears.

But she would not run away this time. This time she would stay, for this was her wounded bear of a man, and she meant to help him patch the bleeding scars on both his heart and his soul.

"Do not try to warn me away," she said, starting purposefully toward him. "For I am quite determined to have you for a husband."

He stared at her through wary eyes. "I cannot let you do that. You don't know what you are letting yourself in for, Livvie."

"No. For the first time I do understand. In the beginning I thought you merely a charming ne'er-do-well. A man to whom I should feel no attraction but, unfortunately, did. But I have come to know you better, Neville. Slowly but steadily, and often against my will, I have come to know you."

She stopped less than an arm's length from him. *Please give me the right words to say,* she prayed. She took a deep breath. "First I discovered a superior horseman who maintains an impeccable stable. Then I discovered that you are a good landlord to your tenants and workers. Fair to them and just as hard-working as they. I will confess that at the time I did not want that to be the case. But now I am glad. You are a good man, Neville, and most important of all, you have proven yourself to be a caring uncle and, tonight, a man uncannily kind to a heartsore little girl."

His lips thinned in an unhappy half-smile. "How quickly you forget the man who insulted you and who tried repeatedly to seduce you."

Soberly Olivia shook her head. "No. I haven't forgotten that man, though I admit I do not understand him. Why, when you are so kind to everyone else, have you always been so troublesome with me? So challenging to everything I said or did?"

She caught a glimmer of light in his dark, troubled eyes. "Because you are such a worthy opponent."

A smile began on Olivia's lips. But it quickly faded when a distressing thought intruded. "A worthy opponent," she echoed. "But there are no more battles to fight, Neville. Not with me, nor with yourself. And most certainly not with the men who haunt your dreams."

At that remark the spark in his eyes snuffed out and he turned away. "Those men . . ." He hesitated and she knew he struggled with his words. "Those men will never leave me. They will haunt my life—my nights—forever. I thought I could be rid of them. But I cannot."

The defeat in his voice made Olivia's heart ache in her chest. Her mind spun, searching for the best way to address this blight upon his life. "Remember what you told Sarah this evening, that she has a family that loves her, and that she should never take that for granted? You also said that her father would always be a part of her and that she ought to think about what he would want her to do. That was such good advice, Neville, and it brought her so much comfort. But you should follow that advice too."

"I do. I keep up Woodford Court in their memory, though it sometimes—"

"I'm not speaking of what your parents would want you to do. I mean your friends. Those soldiers who haunt your dreams, the men who died alongside you."

His face had grown haggard with emotion, and the sight brought a huge lump to her throat. "I . . . I think, Neville, that they would want you to remember the lives they had, not agonize over the lives they might have had. I don't believe they would want you to feel such guilt for surviving when they did not. They would not want you to turn away from living the life given to you. If nothing else, live your life for them."

Neville stood there, hardly able to look at Olivia. She was being so kind, so incredibly careful of his feelings, when he deserved no such consideration. Most unbelievable of all, she still wanted to marry him. Despite having witnessed his grue-some nightmare, his weakness and fear, she still vowed to marry him. Him, a man who would never sleep a night at her side. A man small-minded enough to seduce her for his own selfish purposes.

All his plotting had paid off, and yet victory now tasted bitter upon his tongue. She deserved so much better than the likes of him. He'd done her a huge disservice when he'd se-duced her. A better man would let her go.

He'd never been as strong as he should be. He'd always fallen short. But not this time. For once he would truly be brave. He would finally reveal to someone—to her, the person he most cared about—exactly what he'd done, the whole truth of his shameful, craven nature.

As he lifted his head to face her, a terror as fierce as that of impending battle settled over him like a heavy, smothering blanket. "You don't know the whole of it. Nobody does."

Then he began. "At Ligny we faced a fierce enemy."

In the long pause that followed she said, "And the British forces prevailed."

"We prevailed." His throat was dry. It was painful to talk. "But . . . But too many died. I fell asleep," he blurted out.

At her quizzical look he rushed on. "I had the watch. Macklin and I. We'd been up for days. Everyone had. Snatching naps when we could. But it was quiet that night." He drew a shaky breath. "Macklin dozed off. I knew it, but I decided to let him sleep, at least for a little while. But then I—"

He broke off. His heart was racing, beating a hole in his chest as he recounted the horrors of that fateful night. "I fell asleep. Just for a moment— No," he amended. "That's not true. I don't know how long I slept. I'll never know. But it was long enough." He closed his eyes. "It was long enough that the French forces were able to surprise us."

He started shaking. He tried to control it, but he could not. "They surprised us, and the men—my men. My friends—" Again he broke off, unable to go on. Four years gone, yet the horror of it was as fresh and hideous as ever. And the guilt continued to grow.

"But Neville. Everyone says you were a hero at Ligny, that you saved so many of your men. If not for you . . ."

Her voice startled him, for in the midst of his misery he'd nearly forgotten her presence. How he wanted to turn to her, to reach out for her and hold on to her like a lifeline. But she could not save him from the truth of his past. No one could.

"Yes. They say I am a hero. That I fought like a man possessed." He laughed bitterly. "Well, I was a man possessed. Perhaps . . . perhaps I still am. Because for every man I am said to have saved, another—" Again he faltered. It hurt, like a physical pain, to admit such awful truths. But he bowed his head and forced himself on. "They say I am a hero, but that is only part of the truth. I saved a few. But I let those others down. I let all those other men down."

A silence filled the room, ugly and damning. Then Neville felt a touch upon his arm. She should be repulsed by his shameful admission, but instead she had moved even nearer and laid her hand upon his sleeve.

"It is hard for me to imagine you deliberately letting anyone down, Neville. I think that is one of the reasons I wish to marry you. Your every ambition seems to be for the benefit of others. Not for your pleasure or gain, but for someone else's. For your tenants. For your nephew. For me." Her hand slid up and down upon his wrist in a soothing fashion. "And for your fellow soldiers. You would have given your life for them, I suspect."

He shuddered, "It would have been better if I'd died along-side them. I wanted to die with them."

"But you didn't. You didn't die with them, or for them, so . . . so maybe instead you are meant to live for them. Please, Neville." Her voice softened to a whispered plea. "Choose to live. Choose to live!"

He looked down at her, at her serious face turned up to his in entreaty. "If you are afraid I might deliberately end my life, I promise you, Livvie, that I will not. I've thought about it, but coward that I am, I've never been able to follow through."

She shook her head. "That's not what I meant at all. I mean, choose to live for them, Neville. Live the life of good purpose that those men cannot now live. Live as they would want you to, and be the best man you can be as . . . as an honor to them."

He heard her words, and a part of him wanted to embrace them. It would be so simple and the very least he could do for them. But he was afraid. Afraid of the night and the dreams they held. And the overwhelming guilt they dredged up when he could not fight back.

As if she sensed his fear, Olivia moved in closer, circling his waist with her arms and resting her cheek against his shoulder. "You are a much better man than my father ever was. I am ashamed that I ever compared you to him."

He wrapped his arms around her, because at that moment he needed to hold her, to crush her to him with more force than he should. "It could be that Cameron Byrde was not nearly so bad as you believe."

"I'm afraid he was. But he doesn't matter to me. He's my

past. You're my future." She gazed up at him. "I love you, Neville. You don't want to hear that," she went on when he stiffened. "But I love you just the same. It's time to leave the past behind and get on with your future. Our future."

He stared down at her, down into the hazel-colored eyes that had captured him from the first. "How can you be certain about the future we'll have?"

She smiled then, a beautiful smile, so trusting that he felt it all the way into his heart. "I'm not. For so long I tried to be careful and to analyze everything. Everyone. I thought if I picked just the right man, I could keep my life calm and uncomplicated, and plan out my whole future. I suppose I thought I could control it. But then you came along and turned my life upside down. I'm not certain at all of the future, Neville. But I am certain that I love you and that I want to spend my future with you. You're the right man for me. The only man."

In her beautiful hazel eyes, the truth of her feelings shone, and it warmed Neville to the depths of his shriveled, tarnished soul. Like the rising sun always rescued him from the terrifying night, her love, given without regard to her own needs, was rescuing him from the dark night of his past.

Did he dare accept the love she offered him? Could he ever give to her as much as she'd already given him?

Then like the saving light of dawn touching him with infinite grace, he suddenly understood. To love her in return was all she wanted from him. Just to love her. And she was willing to wait for that love to come.

Only there was no reason to wait.

"Livvie . . ." He faltered, for powerful emotions filled his chest and clogged his throat. "I love you. God." He crushed her to him. "I love you. I love you."

Then he kissed her, really kissed her, with honesty and love and absolute truth. "God, how I love you."

"Oh, Neville."

Only when he felt the sweet dampness of tears upon her cheeks did he draw back. "If you will have me, Livvie, then I will marry you. I choose you. I choose life."

She laughed, the most beautiful sound he'd ever heard, then reached up on tiptoes to kiss him fully upon the mouth. "And I choose you. Come, let us go back to bed, Neville, for I wish to sleep in your arms, and have you sleep in mine." Before he could protest she added, "We shall conquer the past. You'll see."

He glanced beyond her, to where the shards of the decanter lay. He'd already chosen to fight the lure of drink and the false relief it gave. He'd done it because he knew he could not have her any other way. Now it was time to fight the rest of his demons. To choose to truly live again. If she was willing to fight that battle alongside him, then so must he be.

"Yes," he said, smiling down at this amazing woman who had saved him with the bright shining light of her love. "Yes. I want to lie down and sleep beside you, my Olivia. My wife."

Then he scooped her up and headed for the door. There were three hours until the dawn. Enough time to make love to her again, then time to sleep beside her and dream of a future he'd never thought to find.

EPILOGUE

OLIVIA came awake with a start.

The mewling cry came again, so faint and breathy that it should not have disturbed her sleep. But she had the heightened senses of a new mother now, and at little Catherine's first cry, Olivia's slumber had fled.

She pushed the bedclothes aside and slipped from the bed, careful not to disturb Neville. He'd been working long hours of late, what with the sheep shearing under way and the new weaving shed finally in full production. Add to that, his utter fascination with his dark-haired baby girl, and it was plain he needed his rest. Dawn would come soon enough to awaken him, she decided. Already the sky beyond the open window showed the first pale streaks of the approaching day.

"Come to Mama," she murmured as she scooped up the carefully swaddled child. With newly acquired skill she replaced her baby daughter's damp cloths, then settled with her in a large chair that faced the window. "My, but you're a hungry little thing," she whispered as little Catherine rooted instinctively for her mother's full breasts.

She opened the front of her gown, then with a pillow to prop her arm, settled back to nurse the child that had taken three years to come. If heaven could be found any place on earth, it was here, in this room with her husband and her child, and the sun rising over a peaceful countryside.

She sighed, a sound of happy contentment which Neville, awake now in their bed, completely understood. He'd slept well, a happenstance which, though commonplace these days, still managed sometimes to amaze him. It had been ages since he'd had his old nightmare.

He shifted to his side, just enough that he could see his wife and their new baby. But he did not alert Olivia that he was awake. For a few minutes he wished merely to look upon her, to gaze upon the woman and child who had become the center of his world. Though they were little more than shadows silhouetted against the paler gray of the window, he saw every detail that mattered. For love radiated from the woman sitting in his big old chair. Love, warm and nurturing and forgiving. Love that never ran dry, that expanded and grew until he finally had come to believe it would never disappear.

He listened to her soft humming as she held their child to her breasts. He'd thought he might feel jealous of the time she lavished on Catherine. But to his astonishment he felt more bound to her than ever. To both of them. That Olivia was a wonderful mother did not surprise him. She'd long ago turned Woodford back into a home, just as she'd turned him into a contented husband.

Most of all she'd healed him with the gentle power of her unwavering love.

She murmured some sweet nonsense to the baby, then shifted Catherine to her other breast. "I love you so much," she crooned. "So much."

"And I love you both."

She was smiling when she turned her face to him. The early dawn shed enough light now for him to see the slope of her cheek and the curve of her lips. "Did I wake you?"

"I reached for you and you were gone. Come back. Bring Catherine with you."

"All right, then. But only for a little while. We have a busy day ahead, for Sarah is to arrive this morning, and Mrs. Mac— I mean Mrs. Hamilton—has an elaborate luncheon planned."

"With Sarah here to entertain her new niece, maybe we can find a few more private moments for ourselves," he said, settling the coverlet over the three of them. He nuzzled the side of her neck, kissing the spot where he knew she was most sensitive.

"Mmm," Olivia giggled. "That would be nice."

"Indeed it would." He blew softly, suggestively in her ear. "And I bet, if I put a little effort into it, I could give you something very nice to write about in that journal of yours. 'Lord H. A man of remarkable talents and incredible stamina.'"

At that she laughed.

Neville laughed too, filled with such joy and peace he could hardly believe it. Even though it was not unusual for him to feel that way, he nonetheless luxuriated in the pure happiness of that moment.

As he lay there with his wife in his arms and their beloved child nestled between them, it occurred to him that his life could not be any better. He could deal with whatever trials and tribulations lay ahead, and be content no matter what happened, just so long as Olivia loved him. For the past three years had proven one thing to him. Olivia might not be the perfect matchmaker, but she was his perfect match.

In debt to a scoundrel . . .
Wed to a scoundrel . . .

SEDUCED BY A SCOUNDREL
Barbara Dawson Smith

Society shunned the handsome, base-born rogue, save
for many women who secretly dreamed of his touch.
No one expected Drake Wilder to force his way into
nobility—by coercing a very proper lady to the altar.
And though she despises the arrogant rakehell, Lady
Alicia Pemberton agrees to wed Drake in order to
save her family from ruin. But he has plans for his
lovely, high-born wife. First, he will use Alicia to
exact revenge on the father he never knew. Then he
will work his scoundrel's charm to seduce her into
his bed...

"Barbara Dawson Smith is wonderful!"
—*Affaire de Coeur*

"One of America's best-loved authors of
historical romance!"
—*RomEx Reviews*

AVAILABLE WHEREVER BOOKS ARE SOLD
FROM ST. MARTIN'S PAPERBACKS

SBAS 6/00